www.rbwm.gov.uk
Royal Borough of Windsor & Maidenhead

Windsor and Maidenhead
95800000208452

Grace

Also by Victoria Scott

Patience

Grace

Victoria Scott

An Aria Book

First published in the United Kingdom in 2022 by Head of Zeus Ltd,
part of Bloomsbury publishing Plc

9 7 5 3 1 2 4 6 8

A CIP catalogue record for this book is available from the British Library.

ISBN (HB): 9781800240926
ISBN (XTPB): 9781800240933
ISBN (E): 9781800240957

Typeset by Divaddict Publishing Solutions Ltd

Printed and bound in Great Britain by
CPI Group (UK) Ltd, Croydon CR0 4YY

Head of Zeus
First Floor East
5–8 Hardwick Street
London EC1R 4RG

WWW.HEADOFZEUS.COM

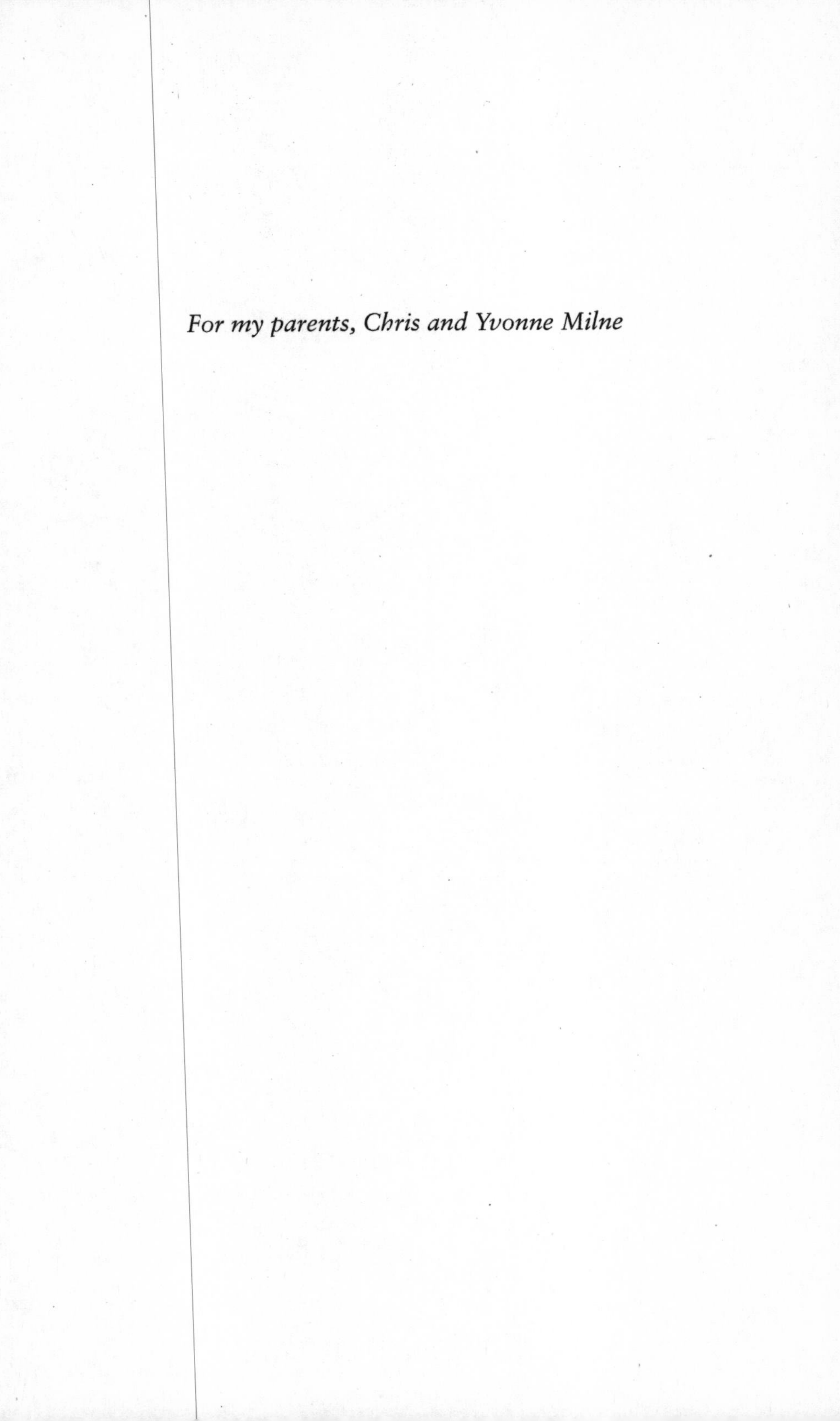

For my parents, Chris and Yvonne Milne

Prologue

October 8th

Michelle

'*Arrrrggggbhhh.*'

'Just breathe for me.'

'*Ahhhhhhhhhhh.*'

Michelle tried to suck in air, but the deep searing pain that radiated out from her cervix seemed to be blocking the way. Instead, she exhaled, producing a guttural grunt. She closed her eyes to block out the scene in front her – there were far too many people in the room, witnessing her undoing – and focused on the living being inside her instead.

She had named her when she had felt her first kick. She had sung to her at bedtime, had read to her in the early hours, and had whispered to her at dawn. They had grown to love each other. And now they were to be parted.

'Okay, good girl. Now pant, just pant.'

Michelle took a series of short breaths, keen to please the midwife, who had been nothing but kind to her since she'd arrived at the hospital almost ten hours ago. But in truth, part of her wanted to freeze time. If she could stop this, she would. And not just because of the pain.

'There's the head! You clever girl… And there's baby's shoulder. One more push, and she will be out.'

No, no, Michelle thought. *I am not clever.*

'Here she is! You have a beautiful baby girl.'

The atmosphere in the room had changed. Michelle opened her eyes and saw the figures in the corner of the room were now staring between her spreadeagled legs, at the wriggling, bloody infant who was just about to emit her first cry. The midwife rubbed her with a towel and then lifted her up, placing her on Michelle's naked chest.

'There you go, pet. Well done. You were a champ. Here's your reward.'

Michelle looked down at the face she had been imagining for months: at her two warm, soft cheeks, her deep blue eyes and quizzical expression, her swollen pink lips. She was astounding. As she took her daughter in, an involuntary cry escaped her mouth before she could stop it. Then that woman arrived beside their bed.

'Okay, Michelle. We know this is going to be difficult. But you've got a day or two with her before the hearing. I know it's hard, but try to make the most of it.'

Michelle looked at her. She was a new one, quite young, fresh out of training probably, not someone she'd even got to know. And she knew nothing, not about life, or this, or her. *Nothing.*

'Take her,' said Michelle.

'But you can…'

'I said, *take her*.' Michelle could not bear the pain for one minute longer. She wanted it over with, now.

'But Michelle lovely…'

'*Take her*. I need a kip…'

Michelle watched as the social worker glanced anxiously at her more senior colleague, who was lurking in the shadows, and saw the nod of agreement that passed between them. The woman then leaned over her and wrapped her hands around the baby, lifting her up like a prize. She watched as the midwife took her from them and swaddled her, before handing her back to them without a word.

'We'll put her in the nursery,' the social worker said, as they walked towards the door. 'She'll be there if you want to see her.'

Michelle did not reply. But just before the door closed, she called out after them.

'Her name is Grace, you hear me?' she shouted. '*Grace*.'

PART ONE

1

October 8th

Amelia

Amelia held the foil pack in her left hand and ripped its top off with her teeth. Then with practised ease, she pulled down both her brown cord trousers and white cotton pants with her right hand before parting her legs and squatting in slow motion, her quadriceps quivering with the effort. She pulled a white stick out of the pack, removing its plastic cap and placing it on top of the cistern, before twisting back around and positioning its exposed end between her legs.

Now.

She released a stream onto the stick for the prescribed five seconds. While she forced herself to count to five slowly – one potato, two potato, three – Amelia focused on the leaves of the oak tree outside, which were shadow dancing on the window blind, lit by a streetlamp. It was half past five and getting dark already.

When she reached five, she retrieved the cap and replaced it on the stick, saying a silent prayer as she did so. She needed to, didn't she? But she wasn't sure why she was bothering. After all, she never prayed when she was told to, during chapel. She sat there each week in that awe-inspiring building, her head bowed as required, but her mind was full of shopping lists and household chores, not heavenly wishes and words. Her tiny rebellion went entirely unnoticed, she was certain, but here, in the bathroom of the grace-and-favour flat that came with Piers' job, and to which absolutely nothing charming, beautiful or unique could ever be done, she *did* feel like talking to God. Odd.

Amelia placed the white stick back onto the cistern, making sure to keep it flat. The pack had said to leave it for three minutes, so she'd give it that, at least. She wiped herself, discarded the tissue in the bowl and stood up quickly. She pulled up her knickers and her trousers, fastened them and then checked her long, thick brown hair, which was pulled back into a ponytail, in the mirror above the sink. It was prone to frizz, and a quick glance revealed that it had returned to this favoured state, despite all efforts to the contrary. It was drizzling outside, and the merest whiff of damp made it disobedient. She smoothed it down on top as best she could and searched it for greys in the bald halogen light overhead. It was depressingly easy to find them now. She located one, a small wiry one near her parting, and plucked it out with her fingers.

Unfortunately, it wasn't so easy to rid herself of the other signs of ageing now that forty was on the horizon. She had developed crow's feet around her eyes in recent years and she could see furrows beginning to form on her forehead. Her daily application of Nivea, encouraged by her mother from childhood, had failed to live up to its promise of holding back the years. It seemed that genetics could not be beaten after all. It might be easier to give up now, she thought. Ageing was just another thing to fight.

She checked her battered brown leather watch. Three minutes had passed. Some of the women on the groups had seen a BFP – 'Big Fat Positive', such an optimistic acronym, she thought, so affirmative – after just a few seconds. Should she look now? No. Watching it reveal its secrets felt to her like tempting fate.

She preferred being kept in suspense. She preferred holding on to hope.

Amelia had adored those internet groups, right up until that horrific day when she'd said goodbye to Leila. After that, she'd preferred her own echo chamber. Those groups were full of women from all over the world all blathering on about the stuff they had in common, the stuff their real-life friends and partners had long since tired of hearing, but none of them seemed to understand her pain. Some had even offered meaningless platitudes, and she had acknowledged them politely before logging off for good. Those groups had been her best friend, hands down, during their hideous years of IVF, but now they were just an unwanted depository of depressing statistics about her remaining chances of getting pregnant again.

She hadn't told Piers that she was still testing every month. It was for his own good, she thought; it didn't do to get his hopes up. They had been through enough, where infertility was concerned – four cycles of IVF, the last of which had led to Leila. They had run out of money – and hope – after that.

It had taken them both a while to get themselves together afterwards and they had both chosen different pathways out of their pain. For Amelia, it was this monthly testing ritual. She knew her chances of conceiving naturally were infinitesimally small, of course. She wasn't an idiot. And yet she still tried, every month, refusing to accept reality, as all idiots do, she thought.

Piers, meanwhile, had focused on adoption as their pathway to parenthood, and despite her early misgivings, his enthusiasm for the idea had finally won her over. A year after they'd made the first enquiry, they had been placed on a waiting list for a child. It had been twelve months so far, and nothing. The process was horribly reminiscent of trying to conceive, she reckoned, riddled as it was with uncertainty, waiting and dashed hopes.

Piers, on the other hand, was absolutely convinced that social services departments up and down the land were quite literally desperate to give them a baby. After all, as he'd told her many times, who wouldn't want to give a child who'd had a rocky start to a well-off, stable, well-educated couple like them? His optimism was far too overt to be comfortable, she felt, given the horrors they'd experienced, but she was doing her best to accept it and run with it. She knew she was given to negativity, and after all, he was usually right.

Amelia stepped over to the toilet and picked up the ridiculously expensive plastic stick, her eyes darting towards its small grey window, which should, if the stars had aligned, show 'Pregnant' in unmistakeable, unarguable English.

Shit.

Amelia felt her throat tighten and a spasm grow in her abdomen.

Still, it might be too early.

Gillian, one of the women in the groups, had gone back to check a discarded test hours after she'd chucked it in the bin, and she'd got a positive result. She had a baby boy now, called Joseph.

The thing was, though, she knew, *absolutely knew*, that she wasn't too early. Nobody, even her old cheerleaders online, could spin this situation in a positive light. She *knew* that it was exactly fourteen days since she'd ovulated, because she'd been taking her basal temperature every morning.

She was suddenly possessed by a paroxysm of rage. She lobbed the pointless, taunting stick in the direction of their chrome bathroom waste bin, hearing it clatter down to the bottom as she ran out of the room and into their bedroom, where she threw herself onto the bed. She hammered her fists into the pillows and roared. It was a roar of failure and of frustration. And of self-hatred, most of all.

She drew herself up as quickly as she had thrown herself down, and began to tear off her clothes, flinging them away with wild abandon, so that they made a patchwork pattern on the carpet. Within minutes she had replaced them with black running tights and a white tank top, and had pulled on her trainers, which were always sitting beside her bed, waiting.

She grabbed her keys from the top of the dresser in the hall and plunged out into the night, taking a deep breath and inhaling the twin scents of wood smoke and rotting leaves which enveloped her. Then she began to run. She forged a path up the steep road outside their home, her trainers struggling to grip on the slippery leaves, her arms pumping relentlessly forwards. She looked up ahead of her and could just make out the looming presence of the Worcestershire Beacon. It was to be both her challenge and her salvation tonight.

Fifteen minutes later, the colour had risen in her cheeks, her calves were twinging in protest and her chest was beginning to burn. But she had begun to fly; her feet had taken on a rhythm of their own and her heart and lungs were working in emphatic harmony. As she passed the final Victorian streetlamp on the path and entered the inky darkness of the hill trail, her mind cleared. There was no time for melancholy or reflection when she was running. There was just the here and now.

On and on she ran, her footsteps flicking mud up her legs, her fingertips tingling with cold, her sweat making her eyes sore. But none of it mattered. The sky was clear, and she could see the summit of the hill above her, getting closer with every step.

She looked down for the last fifty metres, concentrating fiercely on the final flight of steps, determined not to fall now. One, two, three, four, five – each step, each impact of her foot was a moment of failure that she needed to extinguish. She took a deep breath and hit the ground harder, pounding into the earth, aware more than ever of the gravity which weighed her down.

Just five more steps.

Four.

Three.

Two.

One.

For the first time in forty-five minutes, Amelia's feet were still. Gasping for breath, she stretched her limbs, and raised her head.

The view that met her never failed to stun. Below her lay a patchwork quilt of rural towns and villages, ancient hedgerows and historic castles, cathedrals and churches. The bright lights of Birmingham, Worcester and Gloucester burned in the distance, and beneath her, nestled up against the hill, was Great Malvern.

Once a small village that had sprung up around an ancient monastery, the town had grown in the nineteenth century due to the Victorians' love of its natural mineral water. Its wide streets were now home to palatial villas constructed from granite gouged out from the very hills they looked upon. There were also several large private schools, housed in old hotel buildings that had now become surplus to requirements. Once a venue for recuperation and restoration, the town was now more focused on revision and results.

The tolling of a bell startled Amelia. It had come from Malvern Priory. Situated halfway down the hill, the ancient church's striking multi-coloured stone exterior was illuminated by bright floodlights. The bell chimed six more times.

'*Shit*,' she said out loud, the first word she'd spoken in almost an hour, before beginning to run back down the hill at speed. It was seven o'clock.

The planning meeting for parents' evening was due to begin at half past seven, and she had completely forgotten about it until now. School tradition dictated that the housemaster's spouse should be there – Langland College never missed an opportunity to harness unpaid labour – and she doubted whether Piers would think her running clothes were suitable attire for the occasion, either.

It was time once again to pull on her armour of presentable clothes and well-kept hair and defend her emotional inner world from all comers.

She would not let anyone know how devastated she felt about her empty womb. Because it was her secret. Her sorrow. Her shame.

2

October 10th

Michelle

'Miss Jenkins?' Michelle heard her name and looked up at the severe-looking old woman wearing the tight black high-necked dress, who was looming over her. 'Do you have anything you'd like to add?'

The lawyer she'd picked at random from a list thrust at her by social services when she was in the hospital – a skinny, shiny young woman called Sally who she'd met only an hour ago – had just said a whole load of stuff to the judge really quickly. It'd sounded like it was being said in Klingon. And now it looked like it was supposed to be her turn. But she was never going to say a word to anyone in here. *Never*.

Before they'd started the hearing, when they'd been sitting on the cold metal chairs outside, the lawyer and that other woman, the older one – the children's guardian, she'd said she was – they had both tried to get her to give in to a whole load of stuff, too. But she'd refused, hadn't she? She was always going to. It was the only way to keep Grace safe.

They'd said that if Michelle would *just* let social services take care of them both right now, away from *him*, then she could keep the baby. They'd also said that if she could prove she was a *sensible, capable parent*, they wouldn't take her away at all.

As if. Michelle was never going to let social services mess with her ever again. They lied, always, to get what they wanted. And she *wasn't* sensible, she knew that, and she definitely wasn't capable, so that was out. The sooner Grace was out of *their* hands forever, the better.

Michelle remained silent, playing idly with the hospital tag on her right hand. She felt them all staring at her, all of the suits. First, there was the toff in the pinstripe over to her far left, who was on the side of social services; then there was the knackered-looking woman with a lined face and overly-tight tweed to her right, the children's guardian; and next to her, her own lawyer, who she'd only chosen because her name fell exactly halfway down the alphabetical list. Those lawyers, and the social workers who were sitting behind her, seemed to her to be like a bunch of crows dancing around a half-eaten carcass.

She could just imagine what they were all thinking, because she looked a bloody state, didn't she? She was wearing the clothes she'd been wearing when she'd gone into labour. She hadn't brought anything else into the hospital with her, and they'd come straight here from the ward. Her black pregnancy leggings were now so loose that she'd had to fold them over her deflated belly twice, and her t-shirt, which she'd absolutely soaked with sweat during labour, was hanging off her. She looked down and noticed that two small damp patches were forming on her chest; her milk had come in that morning, and the nurses had said just to ignore it, if she wasn't going to feed the baby. She'd almost changed her mind when she'd woken up with swollen, aching boobs and had almost asked the nurse to bring Grace in to see her, to try to feed her, just once. But she had stopped herself, because she wasn't going to keep her. That was something she'd decided long before she'd entered this court. It made things simpler. She wasn't going to let history repeat itself, no way. This needed nipping in the bud, now. But…

'Miss Jenkins,' the judge tried again. 'I just wondered

whether you could explain why you haven't given consent for the adoption, when you have told social services that's what you want?'

Michelle cleared her throat, as if she was getting ready to speak, but enjoyed the silence when she didn't do so. She couldn't explain why she hadn't given them the go-ahead properly yet, because she didn't really know. She just didn't feel ready. Seeing Grace had given her a shock, if she was being honest with herself. She needed time to process everything. But what she *did* know was that adoption was *way* better than a lifetime of social services 'doing their best'. No, that would be like throwing her new-born daughter to the wolves. Yes, she'd give in eventually and sign her over to them, she knew that. But not today. She wanted to make them wait.

The judge sighed and turned to the woman in the tweed.

'Marion Stone, you're the court guardian for the child, appointed by Cafcass. Can I hear your thoughts on the case?'

Michelle looked across at the fluffy-haired woman, whose kind-looking face was bare and shiny, as if it had been buffed. She reminded her of one of her primary school teachers, a soft, gentle woman called Miss Matthews, who'd once taken her aside after school, aged five, and patiently combed out all of her nits, while entertaining her with stories from Enid Blyton's Faraway Tree. This Miss Stone – she had tried really hard, Michelle thought, to get her to change her mind before the trial had started. She had liked her for that. Even though it had been pointless.

Miss Stone stood up, clutching several dog-eared pieces of paper.

'Yes madam, I'm here to represent the interests of Grace Jenkins, who, as you are aware, was born just two days ago at Worcester Hospital.'

Michelle was suddenly keenly aware of the soreness between her legs, where she'd torn when Grace was coming out. The nurses had said it would take a while to heal. She felt, really, like the whole of her had been torn to bits in the last few days; who knows when she would heal, she thought. Possibly never.

'As you know, madam, social services have been assessing Miss Jenkins' capacity to care for her daughter during her pregnancy,' the children's guardian continued. 'I should add that at nineteen, Miss Jenkins has only recently left the care of social services herself. I understand that she spent much of her childhood in a children's home, and her teenage years in a series of short-term foster placements. She opted to leave care voluntarily at seventeen, shortly before she moved in with her partner, and the baby's father, Rob Allcott. Social workers made contact with her again five months ago when she was treated for unexplained injuries in hospital during her pregnancy. It was shortly after this that Miss Jenkins indicated that she did not want to keep her baby. She insists, I am told, that she is not capable of caring for her. Since then, social services have repeatedly offered to place her and her baby in a mother and baby unit for observation and help, but she has refused this.' Michelle looked down at her lap and began picking at the skin around her fingers. 'Miss Jenkins says she intends to continue living with her partner Rob Allcott at his home in Malvern. Social services have visited the home and have found Mr Allcott to be aggressive and uncooperative.' Only because you riled him, Michelle thought. He keeps me safe. He was only protecting me against you load of liars. 'By all accounts, Michelle's home life appears to be chaotic at present,' Miss Stone continued. 'It is with reluctance, madam, that I recommend that baby Grace should be placed into the care of the local authority. But I think we should give Michelle every support leading up to the final hearing, so that she can make a considered and educated decision about her child's future.'

Michelle looked behind her to catch a glimpse of her latest social worker, Laura, who had an earnest, pained expression on her face, as if she really cared. She must be a good actress, she thought, because they all lied; it was practically in their job description. *Lying, lying Laura.*

'Very well,' the judge replied. 'I take on board Miss Jenkins' unfortunate circumstances, and thank you, Miss Stone, for your thoughts.'

The judge paused and took a sip of water from a glass on her desk.

'As you all know, we are here because the local authority has asked for an Interim Care Order for Grace Jenkins, under section thirty-eight of the Children Act. I have listened with interest to the evidence presented by the barrister for the local authority, Miss Jenkins' solicitor, and the guardian. There are two key things I need to take into account when reaching a decision today. One, does the safety of the child demand immediate separation from the parents, and secondly, can the issues raised by social services await the final hearing?

'I am very concerned to hear of Miss Jenkins' chaotic home life. It is disappointing that she has refused to co-operate with every effort made by social services to work with her. Her declarations of an apparent inability to care for her child are worrying. However, I have also considered the fact that, despite previously telling social services that she wishes to have her baby adopted, Miss Jenkins has not yet confirmed that she intends to give her consent for it. It is possible, I feel, that she may change her mind. Meanwhile, her partner – the baby's father, Robert Allcott – has refused to communicate with social services at all. Now, I understand that social services wish to pursue "foster to adopt" in this case. This means that they believe Grace Jenkins should be adopted. Given the apparent instability of the couple's home life and the absence of evidence of changed behaviour, I am inclined at this stage to agree. However, I am also keen not to close off all avenues, in the event that her parents do show that they are ready and willing to care for her properly. The court always prefers to keep children with their birth parents if it can, as you all know. So, having listened to the evidence from social services and from the children's guardian, I feel it's best to grant an interim placement order, so that social services can place her with foster carers who wish to adopt.'

Michelle felt a lump rising in her throat and coughed to disguise it. As she did so, she felt five pairs of eyes boring into her.

'Here's how things are going to pan out from now on,' the judge continued. 'Within four weeks, we'll all meet again for the case management hearing. At that hearing, I'm going to need statements from all parties, and an independent parenting assessment. Then in about four months, we'll hold the issues resolution hearing, and if we are unable to resolve things then, the final hearing will take place shortly after that – so some time in February or March next year. In the meantime, the child will stay in foster care. Both parents will be able to see the child two times a week for supervised contact at an appropriate local centre throughout the interim period. That is all for now. I'll see you all again in four weeks.'

All of a sudden, people were standing up, putting folders into bags and donning coats and scarves. Michelle looked up in surprise.

'All done,' her lawyer said, pulling a face which she assumed was meant to show sympathy. Michelle nodded and followed the woman out of the courtroom and into the lobby, which was home to a broken vending machine and a suite of mismatched metal chairs. Michelle wondered what she should do next. Seeing her uncertainty, the lawyer paused.

'Look, Michelle, I'm sorry it's come to this. I *did* try, honestly. But you didn't give me much to work with.' Michelle shifted awkwardly from one foot to the other and did not reply. 'But this isn't necessarily *it*. It's not over. You can contest it, the adoption. If you want to. We're only at the beginning of a long journey. You haven't surrendered parental responsibility yet. But if you want to change things, if you want to get her back, you'll have to trust social services a bit.' Michelle grimaced. 'Hmm, yes, I can imagine how you feel. Look... Anyway... Here's my card. Please call me. We need to get together before the case management hearing.' Michelle took the card that she was holding out. 'I do want to help,' said Sally.

Michelle doubted that. She was only after the money she'd get if she helped her further, she thought. Everyone you met was on the make, one way or another. That was how the world worked.

'Look, I've got another case. I've got to go.' Michelle could see that the lawyer was becoming increasingly anxious, stuck here with her. 'But... ah here we are, it's your social worker, and Marion Stone, the guardian. I'll leave you in their capable hands. And remember... It's not over. You have options.'

Michelle watched her walk away at speed, only to be replaced by *Lying Laura* and the mousy old lady who had just stood up and basically told the judge that she was a waste of space. Laura was probably her 656th social worker, appointed after she'd ended up in A&E a few months ago. She smiled a lot, even when delivering bad news. In fact, she was beaming now.

'Michelle love... I'm sorry. But I think it's for the best. You can use this time to get yourself together now, can't you? We can help you. We can help you get back on your feet.'

Helping me, Michelle thought. *You mean like when you lot told me that we'd always be kept together? Or when you said you'd find me a nice stable, safe place to live?*

Michelle realised she desperately needed to get home to change her clothes. She was leaking blood down below now, and the pad the nurses had given her didn't seem to be holding.

'I want to go home,' she said, quietly.

'Yes, I know, of course you do,' the social worker replied. 'Okay. You go, you need a rest. But look, we'll be round to see you in a few days, to see how you're getting on. Okay?'

'*We?*'

'I'll be coming to see you too, every so often,' said Marion, speaking to Michelle directly for the first time since before the court hearing. She is *very* small, Michelle thought. Now that she was standing up next to her, Michelle could see that she was at least three inches shorter than her already fairly tiny five foot three. 'They didn't really explain in there, but I'm an experienced social worker,' she continued. 'I'm not from the local council – I'm independent, you see, representing baby Grace. I will be writing a report for the final hearing, giving my recommendation, so we need to get to know each other,' she said. 'If that's okay with you?'

Michelle nodded and looked down, keen not to show how pleased she was that this gentle woman was going to speak up for Grace. They hadn't had child guardians when she was younger, but she wished they had. It might have made a difference.

Keen as ever not to engage, even with Miss Stone, Michelle began to walk towards the exit, but then had a sudden thought, and turned around to face her social worker.

'Can I go now to the hospital and say bye to her?' she asked Laura. 'I didn't get a chance this morning. But I want to. To give her a kiss, and that.'

Laura looked pained. 'I'm so sorry, lovely, no. You can't. That's against the rules.'

'But you said, in the hospital...'

'I'm sorry Michelle, I should have been clearer. Once you left her there in hospital this morning, that opportunity passed. You can't go back.'

Yet another of your lies, then, thought Michelle. Her stomach sank, and her eyes began to tingle. Oh no. She was going to cry, she thought, and she hadn't cried since... then.

Marion Stone took a step towards her, and it looked to Michelle like she was about to try to hug her. Michelle took two steps back in response and folded her arms across her chest. She didn't let anyone except Rob touch her. She dug her fingernails deep into the skin on her arms to stop herself from crying, and Marion stepped back.

'... but you'll be able to see her on Thursday,' said Laura. 'The judge has arranged it. You can go to the contact centre and see her, twice a week. We can arrange to pick you up and take you there, if you can't get a lift. Would you like that?'

Michelle nodded frantically, before turning heel and walking away without another word. She had no desire to go to the contact centre at all, but she needed to get out of the court building fast, before anyone saw the tears which were still threatening to fall.

'*Would you like a lift home now*?' shouted Laura as Michelle marched out of the building and onto the street. She didn't want to stay and talk anymore.

It was raining heavily. Michelle stood outside the grand nineteenth-century court complex, watching as parades of cars sprayed filthy water over the pavement. She was getting soaked, and she did not have a coat. She did, however, have a phone. She pulled it out of her pocket and dialled Rob's number. He picked it up after six rings.

'All right, babe. How did it go?' he said.

'I didn't even get to say bye to her, Rob. They wouldn't let me.'

There was a short silence on the other end of the line.

'Oh, darlin'. You must be feeling royally shit. It was always going to be hard, right? Look, you must be knackered. Come 'ome.'

'Can you come and get me? I haven't got a coat and...'

'Sorry darlin', the car got seized yesterday. No insurance. I haven't been down to get it out of the pound yet. I didn't think you'd be out of hospital so soon.'

'Oh... right.'

'Look, if you go get the bus though, I'll make sure I've been to the chippie by the time you get 'ome. All right? How's that?'

Michelle made a vague noise of assent before hanging up and placing the phone back into her pocket. She turned to her right and began the long, painful walk to the bus station, her limbs numb with cold and her heart numb with a pain she had only just begun to process.

3

October 10th

Amelia

Twenty weeks until the final hearing

'Darling, do come over here and meet Mr Joll. You know his son Charles, don't you?'

Piers placed his arm around Amelia's slim waist and guided her over towards the fireplace, where a tall, grey-haired man was standing with a glass of slightly warm, boxed Sauvignon Blanc in his hand.

'Yes, I do,' replied Amelia, smiling, desperately trying to picture the boy in her head as she did so. 'He's…' Ah yes, she thought. He's the boy we caught wrestling with a fellow boarder last week. The other boy had needed a patching up from Matron. 'He's the promising rugby player, isn't he?'

The man's face lit up. 'Yes,' he said. 'Yes, that's him. He loves his rugby. Much more than schoolwork, unfortunately…'

Piers laughed. 'My wife knows all of the boys, Mr Joll,' he replied. 'She treats all of them as if they were her own.'

It was true; Amelia did know all of the boys. She'd made it her job to do so since Piers had been made housemaster two years previously. The extra responsibility – living-in, taking care of the pastoral side for the boarders in Shakespeare House – had brought a welcome boost to his salary as a Geography teacher, and she also knew that the role was considered a stepping-stone for senior management. Piers wanted to be made deputy head before he was fifty, and he was already forty-four. Time was running out and she was determined to support his ambition.

'Do you have children?' the boisterous boy's parent asked, looking first at Piers and then at Amelia. It was a question that she knew was as natural as breathing for many. But not for her. For her, it was like being stabbed repeatedly in the heart with a kitchen knife.

'Not yet, sadly,' Piers replied without skipping a beat, his smile undeterred but his grip on Amelia tightening. 'But we're working on it.'

She had to escape.

'I must go and speak to Mrs Collins…' she said, scanning the room for her. She was certain that their dependable, unflappable matron read her like a book, despite all protestations to the contrary. This meant, unfortunately, that she knew all of her faults. 'I must… speak to her… about the cake. It should be out by now.' She smiled politely at Mr Joll, peeled off Piers' embrace and strode away, placing as much distance between herself and *that question* as she could manage, given the circumstances.

It was their termly parents' evening, and the mothers and fathers of the boarders had finished being given their edited updates by the teaching staff and had retired to Shakespeare for some substandard plonk and stale cheese straws made by the house chef, Colin. He was unenthusiastic about both children and cooking, and it showed. But no matter. It meant that the parents didn't linger. She abhorred small talk anyway, but particularly now.

She felt sorry for the boys, though. In less than an hour, those parents would bid farewell to their children, who they wouldn't see again for another four weeks. There would most likely be tears in the younger boys' rooms later. She dreaded these evenings. She tried so hard to be maternal to console the little ones, but she feared that she was a very poor substitute for the real thing.

Amelia walked out into the hallway of the boarding house and considered heading upstairs, taking refuge behind the door marked 'Private'.

Their two-bedroom apartment was located at the back of the large, red brick Victorian-villa-turned-boarding-house. Their private living room looked out over a granite retaining wall, which was effectively holding back the hill beyond. Amelia could only see the sky if she stood in the doorway; any closer and all she could see was a collection of enterprising weeds, dappled concrete and the little waves of damp which surged down it when it rained, like the tide.

No, Amelia thought, *I don't think going upstairs will help*. Instead, she headed for the housemaster's office, which was on the ground floor at the front of the building, overlooking the broad tree-lined avenue. Furnished with a large wooden desk, two sofas and a coffee table, it functioned mostly as a room for chats with parents, tutorial sessions with small groups and disciplinary meetings for naughty teenage boys. Piers preferred to do his admin and marking in the small study in their private apartment upstairs instead, and she didn't blame him. The boys were always walking in here without knocking.

Amelia stood by the window, which looked out down the gravel driveway, towards the street. Cars and vans were passing with regularity, the once elegant carriage ride now reduced to a rat-run beloved by delivery drivers and shoppers seeking free parking. It was raining again, and a bubbling brook had formed at the side of the road, racing down the hill.

Suddenly, playing in the water, was a dark-haired girl of about three. She had moved into Amelia's view so quickly, she wondered if she'd imagined her. She was clad in red knee-high wellies and a red waterproof jumpsuit. The girl began taking huge, gleeful leaps in the water, flinging her arms around in large circles, landing hard on the road surface, sending spray ricocheting around her. Amelia could see, but could not hear, the shrieks of laughter this provoked, the sound of joy causing the girl's body to shake and her face to change shape almost entirely.

Leila would be her age now, she thought. *Three.*

The sight of the little girl sent Amelia's mind in search of its most desperate desire, a desire she had been trying her utmost to suppress. After checking she was alone, she reached out her hand into the air, where it met another. Not the hand – barely heavier than a piece of paper – that she'd clung on to for hours in the hospital, aware that as soon as she let go, her hopes and dreams would disappear with it. No, this hand was strong, warm and pink. And this time, she would not let go.

'Amelia?'

Amelia snatched her hand back and thrust it into her pocket. She turned towards her husband.

'Sorry, darling. I was just taking a moment.'

'He didn't mean anything by it, you know. People just ask things like that, to be polite.'

Amelia tried to smile.

'I know that. I should be better at dealing with stuff like that by now. Sorry.'

Piers walked towards her and took her in his arms.

'Don't be silly. We've been through hell, haven't we? Both of us. But things are getting better. We're on the right path now. There *are* things to look forward to.'

Neither of them spoke for a few seconds. Amelia focused on the ticking grandfather clock in the hallway, the whine of passing cars and the distant sound of clinking glasses. Anything to persuade the apparition of Leila to fade. She needed to move on. She knew that.

'Mr Howard? The cake is lit. Do you want to come in and do the speech?' Mrs Collins had arrived at the door, and Amelia was grateful.

'Yes, sure,' Piers replied. He was keen, Amelia knew, to get back to the crowds of parents who were all waiting to celebrate the boarding house's fiftieth anniversary. He let go of Amelia and walked towards the door.

'Give yourself a minute to compose yourself, darling, and I'll see you in there, shall I?'

Amelia nodded. When he had left the room, she collapsed into the office chair, her head in her hands. It had taken all the energy she had to maintain her face this evening – she felt like she didn't have any left to do it again.

Then her phone rang. It almost never rang. If it did, it was usually the doctor, or someone calling to try to defraud her. She pulled it out of her pocket and answered it.

'Hello?'

'Oh, hello, Mrs Howard,' said the voice in the receiver. 'This is Gloria Reynolds here. From social services? I just tried your husband's phone, but it's turned off. I have some news for you.'

4

October 13th

Michelle

Nineteen weeks until the final hearing

There was a thudding coming from the direction of the window. Michelle became aware of it gradually as the dank cloud which lurked over her every morning gradually began to clear. When she managed to open her eyes, pain shot through her. Sunlight, which had pierced the bedroom's thin blue curtains, was shining directly into her eyes through a cloud of dust and stale smoke. When she recovered, she could make out the shadow of an adult behind the curtains, but whether it was male or female, she couldn't say.

'*Piss offfffffff*,' yelled Rob beside her, opening one eye and throwing himself onto his side, the springs in the ancient mattress screaming in protest. 'It better not be the bloody pigs again…' he added, in Michelle's vague direction.

Michelle's heart sank. She didn't want to go through that again.

The noise began once more. But now that Michelle was coming to, she realised that it was more of a tapping sound. A gentle tapping, even.

'Nah, Rob, I don't think so. I'll go.'

She pushed herself up and rolled over, wincing as she hauled her legs over the side of the bed. The scars from the birth were healing, but slowly. She looked down and checked for damp patches on her chest. There were none this morning. Her milk must be drying up, finally, she thought; she had been in intense pain yesterday, with boobs the size of footballs, but she hoped her body was now getting the message.

'Can you put the kettle on when you pass the kitchen, Chelle? I could murder a cuppa.'

'Sure.'

Michelle stood up and walked slowly out of their bedroom and through the living room. When she reached the front door, she opened it a crack and peered outside. She didn't want to go out in her pyjamas.

'Hello?' she said, as loudly as she dared. She didn't want to annoy the woman in the flat upstairs again. They'd had enough problems with her already. 'I'm here,' she called out. 'By the door?'

Her social worker Laura appeared seconds later from the far corner of the building, fresh from tapping on their bedroom window. She was wearing a padded, belted black coat and a grey knitted hat with a pom-pom on the top. She looked a bit like she might be about to head up the ski slopes, Michelle thought.

'Ah, Michelle, there you are. I hoped you wouldn't be out.'

Michelle nodded, unable to think of a response to this. They were almost never out. They had nowhere to go. They were both unemployed, for a start. Rob had failed to hold down a job, ever, and she'd had to give up her zero-hours job at a local delivery warehouse when she'd got pregnant. She'd been too knackered to continue.

She folded her arms across her chest and stared down at her feet, shifting her weight from one leg to the other. She shivered. It was the first frosty morning of autumn, and she was in her pyjamas.

'Look, can I come in? Then we can both warm up,' Laura said, marching towards their front door as she did so. Michelle felt a dart of panic. The flat was a tip, she knew that, and Laura probably lived in a detached new-build and had a weekly cleaner. But then, to be honest, they all thought she was pond scum. Why bother to try to change their minds?

'You'd better come in, then,' she said as she walked back into the flat, sweeping aside a pile of takeaway menus and double-glazing flyers with her feet. She shut the door behind Laura and followed her into the flat, noticing, as if for the first time, the smells that she lived with every day – tobacco, dust, dirt, fried food, old food. She saw Laura wrinkle her nose when she thought she wasn't looking. Yep, she definitely had a cleaner. Probably one paid for by an overpaid, under-skilled husband, who felt he was indulging his wife's desire to 'do good' by letting her earn a relative pittance as a social worker. If they ever did any good, which was doubtful, Michelle thought.

'Would you like a cup of…'

'Oh no,' Laura replied, before she'd even finished her sentence. 'Don't want to cause you any bother. I just had a coffee. I'm fine.'

Yeah, right, Michelle thought. You don't even want to touch anything in here, do you? In case you catch something. Like norovirus. Or poverty.

Michelle walked into their small galley kitchen and poured water into the kettle. Laura had followed her in there, so they waited in silence as it came to the boil. Michelle found two mugs in the sink and rinsed them under the tap.

'How are you getting on, Michelle?'

Michelle grimaced and kept washing the cups.

'Cracking. Peachy. Perfect,' she said, her voice dripping with sarcasm. 'I'm fine,' she added, after she'd mentally thrown a grenade in Laura's general direction. 'Fine. I don't need *you*. I don't need no one.'

'But it's the first contact session today, Michelle. I thought you'd like to come. You said you wanted to see Grace? I can give you a lift there, if you like.'

'I don't need a lift. Rob...'

'He's here, is he?'

Michelle nodded in the direction of the bedroom. 'He's asleep, yep. In there. Shall I go and wake him? He can take me...'

Michelle registered a flicker of fear in Laura's eyes, which was hilarious. He'd never even gone near them. Except to tell them to fuck off, of course. But they deserved that, well and truly.

'I didn't see a car outside?' she said. 'Your car is usually in the parking space out front, isn't it?'

Michelle slammed the mugs down and spun around. They still didn't have a car, because Rob still hadn't paid to get it back from the pound.

'Look, you were *wrong*, all right? About the contact thing. I don't want to come anymore. Because she's not mine. She's gonna be someone else's. It's done.'

But Laura didn't seem to be listening.

'Michelle, that's not true. You don't know that. If you get your act together,' she waved her arms around her, gesticulating at the kitchen and the living room beyond, 'there's a chance... The courts...'

'There's no chance, *Laura*,' Michelle answered, baring her teeth, congratulating herself for omitting the 'Lying' from her name when she'd spoken it out loud. 'And you know it. And *I* know it. You are all full of such bullshit. Every single thing you lot've promised me in the past has turned out to be bollocks. *Just move on from here and it'll be the final move, Michelle*,' she said in a sing-song voice, while making a face. '*Don't worry, Michelle, you'll be safe, your roommate will be nice. Michelle, it'll feel just like home, and don't worry, your gran will be back to see you soon...*' Michelle paused and saw puzzlement on

Laura's face, and almost felt sorry that she'd obviously burst her naive little newbie bubble. 'If I go today, *Laura*, all I'll do is… get attached. And that's not good for her… or me. It's best if I stay away. Start over, you know?'

Laura walked towards her and placed her hand on Michelle's arm. She shivered at her touch and moved a step away.

'Michelle, I know that… things have been hard for you. For a long time. What with your own mum and dad… and I wondered… whether you'd like to talk about that? We can set you up with a counsellor?'

Fucking hell, she thought. Another one. They'd tried that once, but he'd been this old guy with bad breath who'd stared at her breasts and tried to feel her up. She hadn't gone back after her first session. She had not reported it, though, because there was no point. Nobody ever believed her.

Laura turned off the tap for her and took the two mugs from her hands.

'Do you have a tea towel?'

Michelle knew that they didn't.

'No, they're all in the wash. But there's some kitchen roll…'

Laura scanned the worktops, found a roll and began to dry the mugs.

'Look, Michelle. I know you don't want to go today,' she said, reaching for two teabags from a box on the counter and dropping them into the mugs. 'But just in case you change your mind – and I know you feel you won't – but just in case, you know – the judge and the children's guardian won't look kindly on you if you haven't been. I am just thinking of you. And Grace.'

Lying, lying Laura, Michelle thought. You have *never* thought of me. You're just thinking of your targets. But still… I do want to say goodbye to her, she thought. I want to see her one more time, just so that I can take a mental photo of her face.

Michelle did that sometimes, when a moment was particularly happy; she would stare, really take in her surroundings for a few seconds, and then close her eyes, focusing on taking in every single detail, every colour, every smell, every shape. That way, she stored it in her brain properly, so that she could relive that moment whenever she wanted. In that exclusive filing cabinet she could feel once more the warm, pink dressing gown she had clung to, and the soft arms which had gathered her into it; and a green, swirly carpet covered in Lego and Barbie dolls, and the smiling face of her companion. There hadn't been too many moments like these in her life, so she hadn't had to do it too often, and the memories she did have in there were regularly accessed. The storage space in her brain had plenty of room.

'I'll come,' she said, before she could change her mind.

Michelle saw a look of relief light up Laura's face.

'Okay, lovely, that's great. Shall we leave the tea then, and head off? The session starts in half an hour.'

'Nah,' Michelle replied, thinking of Rob in the next room. 'I said I'd bring Rob one. And I need to get dressed.'

'Okay,' Laura replied, pouring the hot water into the mugs. 'How about I make the tea, and you go and get changed?'

Michelle nodded and went back into their room. The curtains were still closed, but she could just make out a pile of clothes in the corner. She had last done a wash before going into hospital, and she knew that that pile at least was clean. She sifted through the clothes, locating a pair of jeggings, some pants, a bra and a pink jumper. She pulled off her pyjamas and pulled on the pants, followed by the jeggings, which were maternity clothes, and mercifully had a forgiving elasticated waist. Her stomach was still sticking out – she still looked pregnant, she reckoned – and lined with angry red stretch marks, like a Punch and Judy tent. The bra, however, was a waste of time. It had only just fitted when she was pregnant, but now it dug into her breasts, and rubbed a raw ring around her chest. She'd have to go without. At least the jumper was loose. It covered a multitude of sins.

Finally, she grabbed a hairband from the floor beside the bed and pulled her long, dyed-blonde hair up into a high, messy bun.

She emerged from the room to catch Laura loading their bin with most of the contents of their kitchen surfaces.

'... I just thought I'd tidy up a bit...' she said, with a face that looked like a rabbit who'd just spotted a farmer with a loaded gun.

Michelle raised both eyebrows but said nothing and walked over to the steaming mugs of tea. 'I'll just take this in to him,' she said, taking hold of one, 'and then we can go.' She leaned into the bedroom door to push it open and walked over to Rob's side of the bed. 'Here you go, babe,' she said. 'I'm just off out for a bit. Back later...'

Rob snuffled. 'All right, babe,' he replied.

Michelle picked a pair of trainers up from the floor, sat down on her side of the bed to put them on, and walked back into the lounge.

'Ready?' she said, eager to get Laura out of their flat.

'Of course,' said Laura, who was now washing her hands in the sink.

'You'll need a coat,' said Laura. 'It's freezing outside today.'

Michelle looked around and saw Rob's parka lying on the floor by the sofa. She grabbed it and pulled it on.

'Let's go then,' said Laura, holding the front door open for her and walking towards her car, which was a silver VW Polo. Not a BMW, then, thought Michelle. Perhaps it's in for a service? Michelle sat in the passenger seat and did up the seatbelt, noting as she did so that the back seat of the car was strewn with paperwork, sandwich cartons, chocolate and biscuit wrappers and half-drunk bottles of juice and water.

'I'm so sorry about the mess,' said Laura. 'I don't get many chances to take proper meal breaks. Or much time to clear out all the crap,' she said, smiling one of her big smiles.

Michelle tried to smile back, but only managed something

like a smirk. Smiling was another thing she wasn't very good at, especially in the presence of a social worker.

The journey to the contact centre was mercifully short. Michelle only had to endure ten minutes of awkward small talk punctuated by the banality of a local commercial radio station, before they pulled onto the driveway of a large red brick building in the centre of town.

It was a building that Michelle realised she'd passed multiple times while on the bus or in a car, but she'd never consciously seen. There were so many buildings like that, she now realised; loads of places which your brain happily passed over, filling in the gaps, unless fate found a reason to steer you towards them. This one was double-fronted with large sash windows and elegant, black wrought-iron downpipes. It would have been a very nice house for a very rich someone, once, she thought.

Laura walked up to the front door and pressed the buzzer. Michelle followed.

'Laura King and Michelle Jenkins,' she announced into the microphone. There was a click, and she pushed the door open. They walked down a dark corridor and turned left into a small room, in which a middle-aged, despondent-looking woman sat behind a desk.

'Laura King and Michelle Jenkins,' she repeated, and the woman looked up at her.

'Ah yes. Of course. The foster parents brought baby in just now. Just give me a moment.'

Michelle took a seat on a stained blue seat, which was exactly like every other stained blue seat she'd sat on in government-funded offices over the years. Laura sat down next to her.

'Grace has been with emergency foster carers since the day of the court case,' she said. 'Not the couple who want to adopt. They will meet her soon, though.'

'Oh.' It was the only thing that Michelle's exhausted, hormonal brain could think of to say.

'Look, Michelle. What I was saying earlier... it isn't a foregone conclusion that the foster to adopt parents will get to adopt Grace in the end. There's still a chance... a small one, but still a chance... that you could keep her. If you make changes. The judge said as much, didn't she?'

Michelle chewed her cheek.

'Yeah, but the thing is...' she began to say, before being interrupted by the receptionist, who'd re-entered the room.

'We're ready,' said the receptionist, sounding as if she was a circus master announcing a high trapeze act. She obviously lived for these moments, Michelle thought. Bully for her.

Laura stood up and Michelle followed, her breathing rapid and shallow and her palms beginning to sweat. The receptionist led them into the room opposite. It had large bay windows overlooking a small garden, and was full of toys, bean bags, soft mats and a brightly upholstered sofa. It was as close to being homely as social services could manage, she thought. In the corner sat a woman Michelle hadn't met before, and next to her was a car seat. And in it, a sleeping baby covered in a pink blanket. Michelle froze.

Laura walked over to the woman and went to shake her hand. 'Hi, Gloria,' she said, before turning around. 'Michelle, this is Gloria, Grace's social worker.'

Michelle tried very hard to hate the woman who was sitting down next to Grace. After all, it was her job to take children away from their parents, wasn't it? But she seemed to have a kind face, and she was smiling.

'Hello, Michelle,' she said. 'We were hoping you'd come.'

Michelle felt like she was supposed to smile back at her, but she couldn't do it. And she also couldn't move closer. She stayed rooted to the spot.

'Shall I bring her to you?' Gloria said, exchanging glances with Laura, who nodded encouragingly.

Gloria picked up the handle of the car seat, lifted it up slowly and began to walk towards her. Michelle could now actually hear her own heartbeat and her legs began to tremble.

When Gloria was close enough, she looked down into the car seat. *Yes*, she thought, *that's her*. Grace had her head turned to the left, and her arms, clad in little pink mittens, were resting on top of her chest, which was rising and falling with her tiny, shallow breaths. She could just make out wisps of dark brown hair beneath the pink cap she was wearing. Her nose was small and straight, and her lips full and pink. And she seemed to be smiling, even while sleeping. Yes, that was the little body she'd clung to when they'd put her on her chest, seconds after the agony had subsided, and before the other agony had begun. She would remember that moment forever.

'She's due a feed,' Gloria said, looking at Michelle. 'We need to wake her up for it. Would you like to...'

Michelle thought of her boobs, which, after all of the pain, mess and discomfort, were now dried up and useless. 'I can't...'

'I have a bottle here,' Gloria continued. 'I'll just go and make it up.'

Gloria put the car seat down by Michelle's feet, walked over to her chair, picked up a large bag and walked in the direction of the door. 'There's a kitchen down the corridor,' she said. 'Back in a sec.'

Laura said nothing, and the silence was overwhelming. Michelle could just hear small snuffles coming from the car seat, and the distant rumble of passing traffic.

Michelle came to a decision. She dropped to her knees next to Grace and stared at her, trying to soak up every detail of her face, of her long eyelashes, of the tiny bump she had on each earlobe, of the dimples in her cheeks. She leaned down, right next to her face, and lingered there, listening to her inhale and exhale, smelling the sweetness of her breath. Then she kissed her, softly, just once.

'You can pick her up if you like,' Laura said, walking towards them both.

Michelle considered this for a moment. She had only held her once, just after she'd been born. Would it be so bad if she did it once more?

'Okay,' she said, almost whispering.

Laura knelt down next to her and began to unbuckle the car seat. '*There, there, little one*,' she said, when Grace grimaced at being woken. Then she lifted her up as if she was a priceless antique and draped her onto her chest, Grace's head resting on her shoulder, and her legs curled up underneath her, like a frog.

'I've got your mummy here, little sweetie. Your mummy,' she said, moving towards Michelle, preparing to hand her to her.

Mummy. Mother. Mum. No, she thought. *No. I can't do this. This will make things worse.*

Michelle shot up and bolted towards the door.

'Michelle!' Laura shouted, as soon as she'd registered what had happened. '*Come back!*'

Michelle knew that Laura wouldn't risk running after her, not with a baby, so she stopped running when she reached the gate and walked slowly up the road, panting, trying to work out how she was going to get back to Rob's.

Because she was never going back in there. *Never.* Because Grace was much, much better off without her.

5

October 12th

Amelia

20 weeks until the final hearing

Amelia and Piers turned off the main road into a cul-de-sac cluttered with new-build houses. When they reached No.22, they found its sole designated space taken up by a black Vauxhall Astra.

'I'll just pull up here,' Piers said, pulling up on the pavement in front of No.22's tiny garden, blocking half of the small access road and all of the pavement as he did so. 'Not much choice, really. Right,' he said, pulling the handbrake, removing the keys and opening the car door. 'Let's go.'

Amelia opened her own door and stepped out, clutching the fancy chocolate biscuits they had detoured to buy. She looked around her. The sound of traffic thundering past echoed off the walls of the relentlessly rectangular homes. Each house was constructed from the same orange brick, had four matching uPVC windows facing the street, a postage stamp of turf out front and a tiny wooden porch hanging over a front door, which seemed to come in three different colours: red, black or grey. Perhaps the only distinguishing feature the purchaser was allowed to choose, she thought.

When she turned around, Piers was already at the front door, ringing the bell. She hurried to join him, and he grasped her hand. A few seconds passed before they heard voices, and a figure appeared behind the door's obscure glass. Then the door clicked open, and they were greeted by a smiling woman with a short brown bob. Amelia judged her to be in her early fifties.

'Hello, you must be Piers and Amelia,' she said, still smiling. 'I'm Gloria. I'm baby Grace's social worker.'

'Lovely to meet you,' said Amelia, holding out the biscuits. 'These are for you.'

'Oh, how wonderful, thank you,' Gloria replied, smiling. 'Come on in.'

Gloria led them down a small corridor and turned right into the front room, where two other women were seated on two large cream armchairs. One of them, a woman Amelia judged to be in her sixties, with frizzy grey hair and reading glasses perched on her nose, was sitting on a chair clutching a notebook and pen. The other woman, probably in her forties, Amelia thought, was cradling an infant.

She took a sharp intake of breath at the sight of her, and felt tears begin to form.

'Oh lovey, I know,' said Gloria, noticing her emotional state. 'Isn't she… gorgeous.'

But it wasn't her beauty that had made Amelia gasp. It was simply her existence. Yesterday, there was no baby. There was never going to be another baby. And today, there she was. Like… magic.

'May I hold her?' asked Piers. Startled by his voice, Amelia turned to look at him. She had almost forgotten he was there.

'Of course,' the younger woman said. 'I'm Leonora, by the way. I'm an emergency foster carer. I've just had her for a couple of days.' Leonora stood up with the baby, and held her out for Piers, who walked over to her and proffered his arms. 'Support her head,' Leonora advised Piers, refusing to relinquish control of Grace's body until she could be certain that Piers had a solid hold of her.

'It's okay, I've done this before,' Piers said.

And just like that, Sebastian, Piers' nine-year-old son with his first wife, entered Amelia's mind, unbidden. And why shouldn't he, she thought? It wasn't his fault that his existence was an embolism in her heart. Social services knew about him – they'd asked about him a lot during the application process, naturally – but she had hoped that they wouldn't have to talk about him here, not now. Not when she was finally being given a chance to be a mother in her own right.

'Ah yes, they did tell me,' Leonora said quickly, ignoring the pregnant pause. 'Sorry, I'm so forgetful. I blame the kids. As I say, I've had her a couple of days. She's been good as gold. Really, no trouble. She's a lovely little lass.'

'Shall we all sit back down?' Gloria asked, smiling at Amelia. She directed them to sit on a large three-seater leather sofa – Gloria to the left, Amelia in the middle and Piers to her right, still cradling Grace. Leonora took a seat in an armchair opposite, next to the older woman who had not yet introduced herself.

'So, as you know,' Gloria continued, 'the judge has made a care order for Grace, with the intention that she should be adopted.' Amelia looked to her right, and saw that Grace was now gripping Piers' finger. Of course she was, she thought. Everyone was seduced by Piers as soon as they met him. His charm was irresistible.

'As you said that you were happy to foster to adopt, and you were very near the top of our list, we decided that you were the right couple for her. You've been waiting quite a long time, we know, but hopefully… she's worth the wait?'

'Without doubt,' Piers replied, smiling down at Grace, who was now sleeping. Amelia leaned over, pushed Grace's little cap upwards and began to stroke her hair, which reminded her so much of Leila's. She still had a little snippet of that hair. She'd put it in an envelope in her box of keepsakes in the loft. It was too painful to look at every day, but it was comforting to know it was there.

'Not too hard, darling, or you'll wake her,' Piers said. 'She's just dropped off.' Amelia sprang back, embarrassed by her lack of experience with babies.

'Oh, I shouldn't worry,' said Gloria. 'Babies sleep for most of the time at this stage. If you wake her, she'll soon drop off again. We fed her just before you came, so she'll be out for the count for a bit.'

'It's all very overwhelming at the beginning,' said the older woman, who had laid her notebook down on her lap. She was smiling, and Amelia thought she seemed kind.

'Oh I'm sorry, I should have introduced you,' said Gloria. 'This is Marion Stone. She's the children's guardian – that's the independent social worker appointed by the court to act in Grace's interests. She'll be attending meetings and coming to visit you occasionally, so that she can build up a full picture.'

'I'll try not to get in your way,' Marion said. 'I know it can be strange, being observed and assessed.'

'No, that's fine. You have to do what's best for her,' said Amelia, looking down at her, spellbound. She reached out to stroke her arm, encouraged by Gloria's advice.

'Babies take a while to get used to,' said Gloria, smiling. 'But you'll get there. Everybody does.'

'And I'll help her,' Piers said, grinning. 'Admittedly it's been a bit of a while, but I'll pick it up again I'm sure. Like riding a bike.'

'Yes,' said Gloria.

An awkward silence followed. They don't want to have to talk about Leila or Sebastian, do they, Amelia thought. We Brits always try to avoid talking about difficult things. Anything, frankly, to avoid exposing how we really feel.

'But every baby is different, you know,' Gloria continued, to Amelia's relief. 'They all have their personalities, even this young.'

'What sort of personality does she have, then?' asked Amelia, desperate for just a small piece, any piece, of the infant sleeping next to her.

'Oh, she's an easy baby,' said Leonora. 'Calm. She sleeps well. And she reacts well to cuddles – I've been lying her on my chest, and she just drops off.'

'That's the heartbeat,' replied Gloria. 'Babies listen to their mother's heartbeat while they're in the womb, you know, and when they're new-born, it comforts them. It reminds them of being safe, warm and secure.' She smiled kindly. 'Come on, let's see how Grace reacts to yours, Amelia.'

Amelia took a deep breath in an attempt to slow down her own heartbeat. It had been hammering through her chest since they had received the phone call yesterday. 'Open your cardigan,' she instructed. Amelia did as she was asked, fumbling with her buttons as she did so. 'Good. Okay,' Gloria said, retrieving Grace from a reluctant Piers' grasp, and lowering her gently onto Amelia's chest. 'There you go.'

The baby did not wake. Her sleeping form seemed to mould into her; Amelia had expected her to feel like a weight, but in fact, she felt as light as air. Grace's eyes were still closed, her breathing quick and shallow. Amelia found it impossible to stop her own breathing from synchronising with hers.

Somewhere, there was another woman who must be desperate to be doing this right now, she thought. One whose own heart had lulled this baby to sleep throughout her pregnancy.

'Does she miss her mother, do you think?' she asked Gloria. She had been so focused on her own need – her deep, desperate need for a child – but she could not forget that for Grace to be hers, she had to no longer be someone else's.

'Babies this young don't know who's who, really,' Gloria replied. 'They can't really see.'

'Oh,' replied Amelia. 'But the mother... she must...'

'We can't tell you too much about her,' she replied. 'But to be honest... I'm not sure if she misses her, or not. She hasn't had much to do with her since she was born. She doesn't seem to want to. It's sad. Very sad.'

Amelia looked down at the brand-new human being sleeping on her chest and found it hard to imagine how a mother could possibly behave in that way. What reason could she have? What had driven her to it?

'Are there drugs involved?' she asked.

'No, not that we can tell,' Gloria answered. 'Grace seems unaffected by any drugs, at any rate. All her tests are normal. And the mother's social worker says that she seemed to be clean throughout the pregnancy, despite significant drug use beforehand.'

'That's good,' said Piers. 'Is that rare, amongst mothers who give their children up?'

'I'll just go and make the tea,' said Leonora, standing up. 'And then we can crack open those lovely biscuits you brought. How do you take it?'

'Strong, just a bit of milk,' replied Piers. 'For both of us.'

'Children are put up for adoption for all sorts of reasons, Mr Howard,' Gloria said, as Leonora left the room to make the drinks. 'Drug addiction is just one among many.'

'Of course,' he replied. 'Of course.'

Just then, the baby began to snuffle.

'Oh, I think she might be waking up,' said Amelia, stroking her back. Grace's eyes opened as she did so, and then Amelia found herself exchanging a stare with the most beautiful thing she had ever seen. She had a button nose, luscious eyelashes and piercing blue eyes. Amelia was transfixed.

'So do you have all the things you need?' Gloria asked.

'We have a list,' said Piers. 'You gave us one. We popped into John Lewis this morning and bought it all. It's being delivered tomorrow.'

'Goodness,' replied Gloria, laughing. 'Most of our parents buy a lot of things second hand. There are good markets for this sort of thing...'

'Nothing but the best,' said Piers, 'for our girl.'

Amelia saw then that Marion had taken up her notebook and begun to write. Was she writing positive things, she wondered? Amelia was used to people reacting to Piers' accent in particular, quite often negatively. It wasn't his fault, though; his parents had sent him to private school. She'd met his friends – they all sounded like that. And the fact was, simply, that Piers enjoyed spending money. He loved his car, doted on it, and he lavished presents upon her at birthdays and at Christmas. She just felt embarrassed when people noticed and wrote them off as posh idiots, which she was worried Marion might be doing right now.

'Ah well, that's great then,' said Gloria, her face a practised picture of non-judgement. 'We plan to start the phased introduction tomorrow. I will come over at about ten a.m. with Grace, and you can spend some time getting to know each other then. I'll show you the tricks of the trade, so to speak. Nappies, and so on.'

'Yes, I'll need some tutoring on that,' said Amelia, getting in her response before Piers could refuse the offer. 'And bathing? I'm afraid I haven't looked after a new-born before.'

'That's absolutely fine,' replied Gloria. 'We're here to help you.'

Leonora reappeared at that moment bearing a tray. She placed four mugs of tea on a coffee table in front of the sofa. 'Shall I take baby, so that you can have your tea?' she asked.

Amelia did not want to surrender her, not at all. But she realised that she was in no position to argue.

'Of course,' she said, allowing Leonora to lean down and sweep Grace away with practised ease. She sat down opposite them again, this time with a baby on her lap.

'Leonora is an old hand at this,' Gloria said, picking up her tea. 'How many children have you fostered now, Leo?'

Leonora pondered. 'I think about thirty now, more or less,' she replied. 'Some for short bursts, you know, and some for years. Some became like my own kids.'

'And Leo does have her own kids, too,' Gloria added. 'She has four.'

'Wow,' said Amelia. 'So many! You must love children.'

'Yes,' Leonora replied. 'Most of the time. It's so hard when the foster kids go, though... That's the struggle with it.' She had a funny faraway look in her eye. I wonder what the story is there, Amelia thought. Because everyone had a story, she knew that for certain.

'Do you have any more questions for any of us?' Gloria asked.

'No, I don't think so,' replied Piers without pause, sipping his tea. 'Except – what's the timeline now? When will the court case be heard? When will she be officially ours?'

There was a brief silence.

'Did they not explain this to you when you applied to foster to adopt?' Gloria said. 'It's not a foregone conclusion... I mean, it's highly likely, but...'

'I know there's always a small chance it won't work out,' Piers interrupted. 'But we were told it was a *very* small chance.'

'Yes, in practice, that's true,' Gloria replied. 'Ninety per cent of our foster to adopt babies are eventually adopted by their foster carers. But I think it's always best to be prepared, to know that it's not a given. It's possible a family member might pop out of the woodwork. The baby has not been surrendered – I mean, the mother has not officially handed over her parental responsibilities. Yet. And Marion here will have to make a recommendation to the court, after she's conducted all of her research…'

'No. But the mother… she's not in a good place, is she? That's what they said, the other social workers,' interrupted Amelia, her heart in her mouth.

'We can't share too many details with you, I'm afraid,' she answered. 'But it's certainly true that the mother's home situation wouldn't be in Grace's best interests, currently.'

Piers nodded, as if he heard about these sorts of situations all of the time. Amelia admired his composure. She was far from calm. There was just so much to take in. So many human dramas meeting in one place, in one small child.

'So with that in mind, then – when will the court hearing be?' Piers asked.

'There will probably be three more hearings, Mr Howard,' said Gloria.

'Please, call me Piers,' he said, flashing his disarming smile.

'Okay, then. Piers – there will be three more. There's a case management hearing in a month, a resolution hearing sometime in January, where we hope to settle things, and if we don't manage that, there'll be a full, final hearing after that. The target we work to for it all to be completed is twenty-six weeks,' she answered. 'But this judge seems keen to hold the final hearing in February. She does a lot of family court work, and she feels it's best to have things resolved as quickly as possible.'

So, she may be ours by spring, Amelia thought. Or she may not. She could not, *would not* believe it was a done deal, until everything was concluded. That was the price of having loved and lost before.

'Can I hold her again?' she asked Leonora, putting her mug of tea back down on the table, only half finished. She intended to savour every single minute, while she had the chance.

* * *

Sweet, shallow breaths... Hands unfurling her fingers... a beating heart...

'Are you okay, Mrs Howard?'

Amelia refocused her eyes on Julia, her one and only art student.

'Sorry, sorry, was away with the fairies. I'm fine,' she said, pushing her hair back behind her ears. 'Where were we? *Yes*. Watercolours. Can you show me what you've been doing this week?'

Julia was seventeen. She was the daughter of the college's Classics teacher, but due to her gender, she was not entitled to subsidised education at the school. Instead, she attended the local comprehensive, which was academically excellent, but in which Amelia suspected she was very much at sea. She was a quiet girl, slightly square, impeccably polite and undeniably artistic. Amelia believed that she had every chance of getting into art school, and their lessons, held once a week in the housemaster's sitting room, were designed to help her get there.

Amelia was happy to help Julia out, but she wasn't a qualified teacher. She had given up her attempt at a postgraduate teaching diploma – something that had been her father's idea, not her own – soon after meeting Piers. It had been a lucky alignment of two things: she had been failing the course, and they had both wanted to try for a family straight away. They'd agreed that life as a trainee teacher would not co-exist well with pregnancy.

However, after years of IVF and their eventual heartbreak, Amelia's unemployment had begun to feel more of a burden than a blessing. She'd had far too much opportunity to let her thoughts roam, which was why she'd leapt at the opportunity to teach Julia when Piers had suggested it. She also loved it because it gave her time to focus exclusively on art. Since becoming a housemaster's wife, her life hadn't been her own. She was on show almost all of the time, and even when they were in their flat, the boys' voices seemed to follow them, echoing through the walls. Art allowed her to escape, and this session at least gave her carte blanche to do so, without guilt.

'I walked up British Camp,' said Julia, pulling out her sketchbook, 'and painted this.'

Her work really was exceptional, thought Amelia. She had captured the former Iron Age hillfort beautifully; each deep, sculpted trench and hill sang, and the reservoir at the hill's foot shone in the sunlight.

'This is wonderful,' she said.

'I love it up there,' said Julia. 'It feels like an escape. There's something about the Malvern Hills, their age, the fact they've been there pretty much forever, that makes me feel better...'

'Oh, I agree,' said Amelia. 'I love running up there. Sometimes I stop to snap a picture that I can paint later.'

Julia smiled at her teacher.

'Can I see some of your pictures?' she said.

'Oh, they aren't out on display. I think they're mostly in the loft...'

The truth was, Amelia had previously used the small single bedroom in their apartment as an art room and had hung a few pictures in there just for her own consumption. However, they'd agreed to set it aside for Grace. Piers had spent the past week putting everything she'd had in there into the roof space.

'I'd like to see them, though. To see what I'm aiming for,' said Julia.

'I'll see what I can dig out,' said Amelia, hoping that she'd forget by next week. 'Anyway,' she said. 'This is great, but I think it needs a little more light and shade. Can you set yourself up, and then we'll work on it together?'

She stood up then, and walked over to the window, giving Julia space to get ready. She could see the house's front lawn, which was much prized by the Year 11s, who were allowed to sit on it in the summer term.

Piers was out on the lawn erecting several gazebos with the help of their groundsman, Tony. They were preparing for a party to be held after the school's annual Bonfire Night fireworks display, which was scheduled for Tuesday. If it didn't pour with rain, the boys were set to enjoy hot dogs and candy floss and a visit from those parents who lived close enough. It was always a pleasant event, full of laughter and fun. She enjoyed seeing the boys so happy.

'How long have you been married to Mr Howard, Mrs Howard?' said Julia, having noticed that her attention was elsewhere.

'Oh, six years, nearly,' she replied, smiling at her charge.

'Wow, that's a long time,' said Julia. Amelia reflected that Julia's idea of relationships was probably measured in intense teenage weeks rather than sedate adult years.

Amelia examined her husband. Piers was casually dressed for his task, wearing a fleece top embellished with the school logo and a pair of tracksuit bottoms which he wore for his sporadic attempts at a fitness regime. His light brown hair, usually well-groomed and kept in place with hair wax, had reacted to the damp air and was now sticking up all over the place. But she liked it like that, she thought. He looked strong and capable and motivated, even with just the hint of a middle-aged spread about his girth. He was smiling at something Tony had said; knowing Tony, it was likely to have been a filthy joke. The casual clothing he was wearing today had the effect of smoothing some of his harder edges and she had to fight the urge to sprint outside and run her arms over his broad shoulders. She'd fought the same urge on the first night she'd met him; their physical attraction to each other had been intense.

Amelia felt a surge of warmth towards the man she had married. He was a good-looking man, someone she was proud to be seen with; someone, if she was honest, that she was amazed to find herself married to. What was that phrase – punching above her weight? She had always felt that way about their relationship. She had always been plain and easily missed; he had always been the life and soul of the party, the man in the room everyone noticed.

And yet she now knew that behind that exterior, behind that mask, was a very different man. Their mutual grief over Leila had stripped them both bare for a while. All of their coping mechanisms had failed, hers for far longer than his; but although it had been a brief window, she felt like she'd stared into his soul in those few raw days after the birth, for that period where he couldn't find the energy to resurrect his force field. She had seen vulnerability, insecurity, sadness and pain. She knew it must take an enormous amount of energy to keep that hidden most of the time. She couldn't imagine, in fact, how he did it. So she understood now why Piers experienced life as a series of intensely private peaks and troughs. She understood that she was the only one he could expose those troughs to, and that was fine. That was what partners were for. She had also learned, as their relationship had progressed, to cling on during the troughs, because his peaks were so powerful, they swept away the bad.

'Where did you meet?'

'Online.'

Piers had been her first and only match on the dating app she had downloaded in a fit of madness and desperation, the result of a long night attempting to dispose of her loneliness via a massive bag of crisps and a whole bottle of Prosecco. She had only uploaded one picture of herself onto the app, one of only a few that she was prepared to share with the world. It had showed her sitting on a bench on the Embankment on a sunny day in spring, her thick brown hair cut into a chic bob, her slender legs crossed. She had been wearing a purple knee-length dress and brown cowboy boots, and beside her sat a large tote bag, stuffed full of paper, pens and books. She had been living in a dream when that picture had been taken, she thought. Which was so terribly, depressingly different from living *the* dream.

She had nearly stood Piers up on their first date. Imagine that! She had arrived at the windowless wine bar, seen how empty it was, realised how exposed she felt and nearly bolted back out of its oppressive twilight, into the street. But then she'd looked over to the bar and seen a man smiling at her, illuminated by a bare pendant bulb, its spiral filament a flaming helter skelter. She recognised Piers from his profile picture, which had shown him on a beach somewhere hot, sporting an impressive tan and a large, cold glass of lager. His torso hadn't been on display in the bar, of course, but she could see the same broad smile and shoulders, and his forearms, exposed beneath rolled-up shirtsleeves, flexed as he waved to her. She had spent most of that evening staring at the contours of his arms, examining them as she would if she had been preparing to draw him. Every ridge, dip and dimple on him was like music to her. She had been spellbound. And when he had pulled her towards him later, as the rain had finally begun to fall after weeks of oppressive heat, she had never felt so desired, or so safe. He was strong, successful *and* handsome, and more than that, much more than that, he seemed to want *her*. And that particular miracle felt most incredible of all.

'Did you know he was a teacher here when you first met? I remember Dad saying your father was headmaster of Langland, years ago?' said Julia.

When she'd found out where Piers worked, it had been like the stars had aligned. And when Amelia had seen the joy in her father's eyes, she'd realised that Piers had been met with approval – and so, for once, had she by extension. And as she'd been trying and failing to please her father for her whole life, this magical synchronicity had to be seized upon. Piers had offered her a new beginning, an opportunity to put her string of low-ranking, dogsbody jobs in art supply shops and galleries

– not to mention her failed attempt at a teaching qualification – behind her. They had been married within months. There had been no reason to wait.

'No, not initially. But it was pretty lucky,' she replied. 'We both feel at home here.'

She watched as Piers and Tony worked together to peg down the wayward gazebo, wooden mallets flying back and forth. Piers was a hard worker, undoubtedly, both in the classroom and out. He was also incredibly ambitious, and she was proud of what he had achieved so far. He'd come to the college after a decade working in a school he hadn't liked, but he'd certainly found his calling here. He really might get a deputy headship in the next five years, she thought. And that ambition would be assisted, she knew, by their marriage. It helped to be seen as a stable family man. Private education had endured one too many sexual abuse scandals in recent years.

She considered then the anxieties which had kept her awake the previous night. She had been haunted by feelings of inadequacy and fear. Could she really be trusted to look after a baby? But it also seemed ludicrous to be feeling like this now, two years after they'd started the adoption process, and five years after they'd first embarked on their mission to have their own child. She'd had half a decade to think about having a baby, but now that it was incredibly real, and imminent, why was she feeling so afraid?

But was she afraid, really? Even in the dull, damp light of this particular autumn day, she could see that her nocturnal nightmares were ridiculous. For surely these were just ordinary nerves, the sorts of worries every new parent had, and they were also the sort of worries she had spent a lifetime cohabiting with. She must try harder to ignore them, she thought. Because she and Piers were both more than capable, *more* than ready to become parents. That man out there in the garden, that man who had risen through the junior teacher ranks so quickly at the college, and who had given her so much – *he* would help her through it. And they had been waiting so long, after all. Yes. Like their mutual grief, they would get through this next chapter together.

She spun around and walked towards where Julia was sitting, a renewed spring in her step.

'Right,' she said to her student. 'Ready? Let's get going on this. It's going to be amazing, you know, when it's finished.'

6

October 17th

Michelle

Nineteen weeks until the final hearing

There was a burning smell coming from the kitchen. Michelle had been slumped on the sofa for quite some time, but the acrid scent of smoke was just enough to penetrate her consciousness. She had lost track of how many minutes she had been there, although certainly for long enough to develop a numbness in her fingers and creeping cold in her toes. The heating wasn't on, she now realised. She didn't think they had fed the meter for days.

She stood up, shook her legs to check they were still capable of moving and stumbled into the kitchen. She was greeted by a cloud of smoke so dense she could only just make out their kitchen window. It had no blind and had a streetlamp directly outside, which meant that walking into their kitchen at night was usually like starring in a fly-on-the-wall documentary, exclusively for their neighbourhood. But not today.

'Rob,' she yelled. '*Rob! Come quickly!*'

A groan came from a few metres away.

'Rob? Are you in here?'

'Urrrggghhhhmmmm.'

'*Fuck*,' she whispered, struggling to speak now above the smoke. She grabbed a mildewed tea towel from the plastic hook on the wall and held it over her mouth. Every breath now tasted of mould. She shuffled forwards and her feet discovered Rob lying on the floor, curled up in a foetal position. She took a huge step over him, found floor underneath her feet and leaned over to the window, groping for the handle. She turned it and pushed it open as far as it would go. Then she turned around and searched for the source of the smoke. It didn't take long; there was a particularly dense acrid black cloud ahead of her. Smoke was pouring out of the oven. She slammed its door shut, wincing as its heat seared into her fingers. She groped behind her and found a wet dishcloth swimming in a saucepan full of grease. She grabbed it and used it to turn all of the cooker dials to the off position.

Confident that she had the fire under control, she then knelt down on the floor and approached Rob. Some of the smoke was escaping through the open window now, and she could just discern that his eyes were closed, and that he was lying in a pool of his own vomit.

'*Oh, Rob*,' she said, rubbing her eyes which were now streaming due to the smoke. 'Wake up, Rob. *Wake. Up*.' But his eyes remained shut. She could not tell whether he was breathing.

She assessed the situation. She could leave him there, but what if he had inhaled too much smoke? What if his lungs were no longer working? And it was freezing in here, despite the fire in the cooker. She knew from experience that you got very ill when you got cold. There was nothing for it. She'd have to move him.

She knew she was weak from lack of food and water, but the adrenaline that had surged through her body in the last few minutes had given her a burst of energy. She flung her makeshift mask aside, lifted both of his arms and heaved. Her best efforts managed to move him a few inches, his limp fingers dragging streaks of vomit across the floor. She paused and dipped down towards the floor to take a deep breath, before sitting back up and yanking his arms once more. This time she took them both across the kitchen threshold, and into the living room. There was much less smoke in here, she realised. Thank God for that.

Within seconds, all of her strength dissipated. She only had enough energy left to turn around, grab the blanket they used to keep warm while watching TV and drape it over Rob's corpse-like body. Then she collapsed on top of him, surrendering once more to unconsciousness.

The baby's hand was soft and warm. It was reaching out for her finger. She ran her index finger down its palm and felt its tiny digits enclose it, grasping hard, refusing to let go. She looked over the edge of the cot, inching ever closer to the infant's face.

'Chelle?'

Its eyes were open, and it was looking directly at her, unblinking. She moved her face closer so that she could smell its warm breath. But something was wrong. Its face, at first placid, was now distorted into a grimace. Its eyes had turned dull, and its skin had turned a stomach-churning blue.

'*No!*' shouted Michelle. '*Noooooo!*'

'Chelle? Are you awake?' said Rob, before sitting up suddenly, knocking Michelle off him and onto the floor. Her head thumped into the sofa as she fell, but despite this she was incredibly glad, for once, to be awake. She pulled herself up to a sitting position, her head thumping. She felt her forehead, and noted a bump was growing there.

'Yeah,' she replied. 'Just.'

'You were makin' weird noises.'

'I was dreaming,' she replied, inhaling deeply. She was glad that the air had cleared in the flat. She was glad that they were both alive, come to that. But she was freezing cold, she realised.

'There was a fire, Rob,' she said, reaching out so that she could share the blanket. 'Loads'a smoke. You nearly died.'

'*Shit*,' he said, rubbing his hands through his hair, and looking around. 'Yeah, I can see that.'

Michelle shuffled so that she was sitting next to Rob, shoulder to shoulder. From their position on the floor, Michelle could see that the kitchen walls, inexpertly decorated with a stripey white and blue wallpaper by a previous tenant, were now mostly black. There was also a thick black border of soot around the archway which led into the lounge, making it look like the entrance to a railway tunnel.

'Did you leave something under the grill?' she asked, looking down at her hands as she did so.

'Yeah, maybe,' he replied. 'I was starvin'. When did we last eat, d'ya reckon?' Michelle thought for a moment. She realised she had no idea. 'Ah yeah, that's it. Was cookin' sausages. It was all we had left in the freezer. And then I...'

'You were unconscious, Rob,' she replied. 'On the floor. And then you threw up.'

Rob looked down at his t-shirt, nodding as he took in the vomit stains.

'Yeah, I see that...' he replied, slowly. 'Oh well. Never did like this top,' he added, inspecting the damage.

'*Shit*, I thought I'd lost you,' Michelle said, tears in her eyes, remembering those few desperate minutes the night before when she had thought her only friend, the only person she actually trusted, had been a goner.

Michelle's relationship with Rob had begun on a sweaty summer's night in Worcester. It had been just a few weeks after she'd turned sixteen, the magical age where she'd finally been able to legally instruct social services to leave her alone. Leaving had felt like a better option than staying put. She'd been forced to leave her final family foster placement – a great place, that had been, one of the only places she'd ever felt safe – a year before and the twelve months she had been forced to spend in a home after that had been horrendous. The boys had tried to shag her or sell her drugs, and the girls had been vicious to each other, genuinely frightening. Social services had told her that it was a well-run home, but as usual, they had been lying.

After she'd left care she had tried to find a job – any job – by day, and had slept rough by night. She'd been incredibly naive, she realised that now; not only about her job prospects, but also about her safety. She'd bedded down for the night in the cathedral grounds beneath a huge cedar, feeling (falsely, she now realised) that both the historic building and its religious inhabitants would somehow keep her safe. But Nate, well, he had found her there in the shadows. He was a brute, well known amongst the homeless crowd as a brawler. He'd stank of fags, dried-in sweat and cheap spirits. He'd set himself upon her, ripping at her clothes, grasping her private parts and squeezing so hard, she'd screamed in pain. He'd held her so tightly, she'd felt paralysed. She hadn't been able to breathe.

'*Get off her, you bastard.*'

That had been Rob. Rob, a man she'd hardly even spoken to before. She'd recognised him because he came into Worcester regularly for drugs, and he'd sometimes shared them with her, and had given her money for food. But that was all. Nothing else. But on that dark, dangerous night, Rob had pulled that thug off her and had battered him, hard. Nate had limped off afterwards, back to whichever hellish hole he'd come out of. And then Rob had taken one look at her, at her bruises and her cuts, and suggested that she should come to clean herself up at his place. So, she had done – and she had simply never left.

Rob reached out for Michelle's hand under the blanket and clasped it. 'I'm sorry, Chelle. Honestly I am. I had no idea that I'd got us such shit. I've never reacted like that before, have I? And giving it to you, your first hit for months… That was stupid of me. Fuck knows what was in it. Dave promised me it was kosher, but… I'll be having words.'

Neither of them spoke for a minute. Michelle could hear kids kicking a ball about outside and footsteps on the floorboards from the flat upstairs. They belonged to the old lady who lived there. She complained to the council about them at least once a month. The letter they received about it every thirty days had become almost a tradition.

Then, the sound of Michelle's rumbling belly called her to arms.

'Did we really only have sausages?' she asked Rob, hauling herself up from the floor.

'Dunno. Prob'ly,' he replied, holding out his hand for her to help him get up. He swayed for a few seconds when he reached standing, as if uncertain of gravity.

Confident that Rob was not going to fall over, Michelle walked into their kitchen and began to open their blackened cupboard doors. They had two which usually contained food. Today she found: teabags, a half-empty tub of value mixed herbs, half a bottle of tomato ketchup and a tub of brown mustard, surrounded by a mystery, sticky puddle. Opening the fridge door, she noted an almost-empty milk bottle in the door, two cans of cheap beer and a takeaway box of pizza which was starting to smell. She grabbed it and thrust it in the bin behind her, several ancient, fat-speckled slices of pepperoni slipping out onto the floor as she did so. The freezer was no better. Its sole occupant was a tray of ice, liberally dappled with frozen peas and other sundry gnarled vegetables.

'You're right, Rob,' she shouted into the lounge. 'We've got fuck all.' She walked back into the living room and took a seat on the sofa, where Rob was now sitting.

She sat up and drew her legs beneath her.

'When does that food bank open, Rob? The one in Malvern Priory?' she asked.

'Dunno, babe. But it won't be open today, will it? It's Sunday.'

'No, it isn't Sunday, it's Monday,' she said, with a certainty she did not feel. They'd always managed to avoid using the food bank so far – it felt embarrassing to admit they might even need it – but needs must.

'*Jesus*, was I passed out for that long?' Rob asked, grinning as he scratched his head. Michelle smiled, despite herself.

'Honestly Rob, I'm not sure. That stuff was... *strong*.'

Rob dug into his trouser pocket and pulled out his phone. The screen was smashed into hundreds of tiny, interconnected shards, but by some miracle it was still functioning. 'Ah, I've still got some battery left. Amazing. It's...' he squinted. 'Monday. You win.'

'*Monday*,' said Michelle. 'Okay. Do we have any cash?' she asked, still hoping she might be able to buy something from Mr Chaudhury's, rather than face the long walk up to town.

'Nah, love, I'm sorry.'

'Didn't you get benefits last week?'

'Sanctioned.'

'*Again*?'

'Yeah, I didn't go to the job centre, did I? I was taking you to 'ospital.'

'*Rob*.'

'But you'll get child benefit, right?'

Michelle felt bile rise in her throat.

'*For fuck's sake, Rob. No*. I won't. Think. Because I've given her up, haven't I? You only get that if you've got a baby to feed.'

Michelle leapt up and strode into the bathroom, where she slammed the door shut and slid the bolt across. She sat down on the toilet and thrust her head into her hands. She closed her eyes to try to clear her head but found that Grace's face was burned into her retina.

'Chelle? Can you 'ear me? Chelle? I'm sorry. I wasn't thinkin'.'

Michelle could hear that Rob had sat down on the other side of the bathroom door.

'I should 'ave thought, Chelle. I know you miss 'er. I miss 'er too. That bump of yours was ours, wasn't it? Ours. Just for a bit.'

Still with her eyes closed, Michelle remembered the red Ford Cortina driving away and the woman in the back window, waving. She had been carrying her favourite teddy in her arms and had struggled to wave back. After that car had become a red speck of dust, the skinny old woman had put her hand on Michelle's shoulder and guided her indoors, into the dark hallway beyond. Into the noise.

'We couldn't keep her, could we?' she whispered through the door, asking a question that didn't need an answer. She looked around her at their grimy bathroom, the plastic shower attachment on the taps, the grey tidal marks on the bath. 'We couldn't give her a good life.'

'No, we couldn't. Imagine us in charge of a child, Chelle! Poor kid would have to like her sausages flame grilled.'

Michelle hugged her arms to her chest and tried to smile.

'She'll have a nice home, love, just like you've always said,' said Rob, through the door. 'No chopping and changing. No lies from those bastards at the social. She'll have stability. Everything she needs. And wants.'

'Yeah,' she replied, remembering her tears as they'd driven her away from her final placement. '*Yeah*.'

'Can you unlock the door, babe?' he asked, his voice calming, cajoling.

Michelle opened her eyes, stood up and pulled the bolt across.

'Come in,' she said, retreating backwards.

Rob walked in and stood in front of her, his arms open.

'Come 'ere, babe. I've got you,' he said, beckoning her, and she did not wait. She threw herself into his arms and sank into his bony chest, her tears soaking through his thin t-shirt. But he didn't shrink from her; he never did. He was always there. And this gave her peace. Even now.

They stood there in silence for a minute or so.

'You know what we need to do about the food, babe?' he said, finally.

Michelle did know, but she wished she didn't. She was far too tired to face the walk to the food bank today.

Michelle stood outside Chaudhury's Megamart, playing with the zip on her hoodie and clutching the 20p piece she'd found down the back of their sofa. It was their local shop, only about 200 metres from their front door. Its glass front was littered with adverts for second-hand leather sofas, dubious rubbish disposal services and even more dubious offers of 'adult massage'.

She had been a regular customer here since she had moved in with Rob. She liked Mr Chaudhury, the old man who owned the place. He smiled at you, really smiled, and she liked that. Not many people did that, did they? Almost no one. Not genuinely.

But now she was going to have to steal from him.

She'd done it a few times. It was easier for her to do it – Mr Chaudhury, the owner, didn't trust Rob, and so he watched him like a hawk. But he seemed to like her. She hated doing it though, because, well, she really liked Mr Chaudhury too, and it wasn't as if he ran a huge supermarket and wouldn't notice the difference. She'd have much preferred nicking stuff from a big shop, but they didn't even have money for the bus fare at the moment.

That was her own fault, really. She should never have allowed Rob to give her that stuff. She'd been so long without it. Somehow, the baby had made it so much easier to say no. But now she had no such excuse, and that desire for oblivion, for a ticket out of her messy life and even messier emotions, had been too much to refuse. And now she'd started again, it would be incredibly difficult to stop. She'd learned that from experience.

Rob had told her to get as much stuff from Mr Chaudhury's shop as she could, but she wasn't going to. She was going to get the bare minimum, just enough to tide them over until she could get over to the food bank. And really, how much could she nick without him spotting her? She didn't want to be arrested. She couldn't stand the police. And she'd had more than enough of the courts already.

She took a deep breath and pushed the door of the shop open. A ding alerted Mr Chaudhury to her presence. He was behind the till, pulling bags of sweets out of a large box.

'Hello, love,' he said, smiling.

'Hi,' she said, as quickly and as calmly as she could manage. She looked about her as if scanning with purpose before walking further into the shop, glad that Mr Chaudhury was busy and hopefully distracted enough to not notice what she was doing.

She walked up to the pasta section and took a small bag of fusilli and a jar of pasta sauce off the shelves, putting one in each pocket. Then she approached the fridge and picked up a pint of milk and put this under her hoodie. Finally, she found a small bag of porridge oats and a tiny pack of cola bottle sweets. She put the porridge in her trouser pockets, kept the sweets in her hands, and crossed her arms over her chest, hugging the milk underneath. Then she walked up to the till, praying that Mr Chaudhury didn't look at her too closely.

'Just these, please,' she said, handing over the sweets.

'That'll be 20p, love,' he replied, still smiling. Michelle held the milk up with her left hand whilst delving into her back pocket for the 20p with her right. She tried to smile as she handed the coin over.

'Thanks, love,' he said, looking straight at her. 'How are you doing? How's...'

He's going to ask about the baby, she thought. *Shit.*

'How's… things?' he said, finally.

'Okay,' she replied. He looked doubtful, so she decided to be honest. 'I'm a bit tired,' she added.

'Then you'd best get home and have a rest, love. Enjoy your sweets.'

'Thanks,' she said, before turning and walking out as fast as she could, convinced that she'd hear him yelling after her, accusing her of theft, at any moment. She didn't risk slowing down until she was almost home.

But she'd done it. They had food now. Enough for tonight, anyway. She'd worry about everything else tomorrow. She ripped open the sweet packet and poured them into her mouth, before discarding the packet in a nearby bin, savouring the sour sweetness as she chewed and swallowed. She was hugely grateful for them; she needed them to take away the bad taste in her mouth.

7

October 17th

Amelia

Nineteen weeks until the final hearing

The doorbell rang while Amelia was kneeling on the floor, peering beneath the kitchen units, searching for her car keys. She'd needed to pop out to the shops that morning to get a few last-minute provisions and hadn't been able to find them anywhere. She'd asked Piers if he'd seen them, and he'd reminded her that she was always misplacing things – not exactly a helpful comment, but definitely true these days – and lent her his keys instead. She couldn't think for the life of her where she'd put them. She'd already turned over her bedroom, searched the bin and gone through all of her coat pockets. *Oh well*, she thought, *they'll have to wait. There are more important things to think about now.* She stood up and dusted herself down, ready as she'd ever be, she felt, for what was to follow.

'I'll go,' shouted Piers, out of nowhere. The corner of her eye caught him running from his study at speed, beating her to it. He had been in that room all morning, doing exactly what, she was not sure, but no doubt he'd say it was important. He was addicted to work, something she'd discovered went hand in hand with his ambition. The stupid thing was, though, he'd taken the day off – in fact, he had the next couple of weeks off as adoption leave. The school had brought the deputy housemaster in to run the house while he was otherwise engaged. But Piers always had an eye on his career path, she understood that. Her father had been just the same.

She followed in his wake, hearing him opening the door as she did so.

'Mr Howard,' said the voice at the door. 'Hello again. I have Grace in the car. Are you ready?'

'As we'll ever be,' he replied, sounding like he was gleefully anticipating the delivery of a three-tiered chocolate fudge cake. He smiled and put his arm around Amelia as she reached his side. 'It's going to be fine, darling,' he whispered. 'In fact, it's going to be great.'

The social worker – Gloria, Amelia remembered – walked round to the passenger side of her car and opened the door. Amelia watched as she smiled at the occupant of the car seat in the back row and unclicked the seat from its base. Then she walked towards them both, carrying her precious cargo as if she was a laptop bag, or some shopping.

Amelia looked down. Sitting there, a tiny nucleus in a squishy cell of assorted pink garments and blankets, was Grace. She was asleep, her long brown eyelashes splaying out under her eyes, like sun rays. Piers stepped forward and clasped his hand around the car seat handle.

'I'll take her from here,' he said, with a confident smile. Gloria handed her over without question. No one ever denied Piers anything, Amelia reflected. He just asked, with that charm of his, and got whatever he wanted. Even when that thing was a human.

Piers turned around and began walking up the stairs to their flat and Gloria and Amelia followed.

'How are you?' she asked Amelia as they processed upstairs behind Piers.

'Oh, I'm okay,' she replied, trying to sound more confident than she felt. 'Nervous.'

'That's absolutely natural, Amelia,' Gloria replied. 'The first few weeks will be hard. It's hard for everyone. But remember that I'm here to help you. I'll be coming every day for a bit. Not to check up on you, you understand, but to help. Will your mother be coming to help, too?'

'Oh, no,' Amelia replied. 'She died. A few years back.'

'Oh, I'm so sorry,' said Gloria, colour rising in her cheeks. 'I should have read our notes more carefully.'

'That's okay. I still have Dad. But he's... elderly. I don't think he'll be up to helping.'

They had reached the door of their apartment. The door had locked itself behind them, so Piers had to reach into his pocket for his keys. Amelia could see him debating what to do with the car seat, before turning around.

'Would you mind holding her while I open the door, Amelia?' he asked, holding the car seat out for her. Amelia nodded and took the seat with both hands. She held it in front of her and gazed downwards, marvelling at how heavy it was. *Of course* it was, she thought; it contained a human life. And all the infinite possibilities that came with that.

Piers turned the key in the lock and held the door open. Amelia looked down and gripped the handle hard as she walked past him, petrified that the seat might hit the door frame, or that she'd drop it. She took Grace into the lounge and placed her next to the coffee table. Gloria followed her in and took a seat. Piers sat opposite them in the armchair.

'Shall we have tea?' he asked.

'That would be lovely, darling,' Amelia replied, knowing full well that Piers had meant that she should do it. She usually did, for visitors. But getting to know Grace was more important than anything.

Piers' smile didn't waver. 'Of course,' he said. 'Do you take milk, Gloria? Sugar?'

'Lots of milk, no sugar,' Gloria replied. 'Thanks.'

Piers stood up and strode out of the room, leaving Gloria and Amelia together on the sofa.

'I can sense that you're on edge, Amelia,' said Gloria, turning towards her. 'This is a really tricky thing you're doing. And you've both been through such a hard time.'

This acknowledgement of their grief sent Amelia's heightened emotions into a maelstrom. She tried her best to swallow, to keep the wave of sadness that was bubbling up inside her at bay. She didn't want to cry. Because this was a happy occasion, wasn't it? One of those red-letter days in your life which you need to make an effort to savour and remember. And yet…

'Look, fostering is difficult, even for someone who hasn't been through what you've been through,' Gloria continued. 'It's totally normal, how you're feeling.'

'Is it?' Amelia asked. 'I feel like I should be leaping across the rooftops and dancing for joy. We've wanted a baby for so long… Had so many… disappointments… So much heartache… And here, sitting right there' – she pointed to Grace – 'is a baby. And she's ours. Or rather, she will probably be ours. And that's the problem I suppose. It's the uncertainty. Sorry, I'm rambling horribly…'

'No, no, please go on.'

'I feel like if I open up my soul and love her, really love her, let her into my core, then fate will come along and rip her out, and the hole in my heart will be even bigger when they do that, from the damage.'

'I see.'

'Do you?'

'Yes, I do. This fostering to adopt, it's a relatively new thing for all of us, and unlike standard adoption, it does come with risk. It's a small risk, mind you. But yes, a risk of separation. And I can imagine how that must feel. You mustn't feel bad about it.'

'But I do feel bad. What if I don't bond with her? What if she isn't happy with me? What if I'm not good enough? If I can't... cope?'

'Don't be silly, Amelia. You will be fine. You have only just met her. These things take time. Come on, let's start. She's stirring.'

Amelia looked over at the car seat and saw that Grace was wriggling, her face gurning comically as she did so. Gloria leant over and unclipped the straps, placed two hands underneath the baby's tiny form and lifted her up. Then she held her out to Amelia.

'Here you go,' she said, smiling encouragement. 'Grace, here's your new mummy.'

Amelia felt tears well up in her eyes. She had longed to hear that word for so many years. She put her arms out and Gloria placed Grace into them.

'That's it,' she said. 'Now, try putting her up on your shoulder. Yes, that's right – let her head rest on your shoulder and her body sit close to your heart.'

Amelia felt Grace relax into her. She reached up and rubbed her back gently, listening to each tiny breath she took.

'Tea for three.' Piers announced his return triumphantly, bearing a tray, a teapot they hardly ever used, three mugs and a plate of assorted shortbread biscuits usually reserved for visiting parents. 'Ah, she's awake,' he said, taking in Grace's relaxed pose on Amelia's chest. 'We'd better not give you a hot cup of tea while you've got her,' he added.

'Yes, hot drinks and babies are best avoided,' Gloria replied. 'But I can take her if you'd like.'

'No,' replied Amelia, firmly. She wanted this feeling to last as long as it possibly could. 'I've been drinking tea all morning. But I would love a biscuit...'

Gloria passed her the plate. She chose a large milk chocolate round and took a firm bite. She hadn't eaten breakfast and it tasted divine.

'There you go,' said Gloria. 'You're multi-tasking already! I used to knit with a sleeping baby on my chest. It's amazing what you can do when you get into it.'

'Amelia is amazing,' said Piers, smiling as he poured Gloria's tea. 'She's an excellent surrogate mother to all of the boys in the house, you know. Grace is very fortunate to have her.'

Despite her deep insecurities and fears, Amelia allowed her heart to swell at his words, to hear her efforts being recognised.

'And you will be a wonderful father, I am sure,' said Gloria, beaming at him.

'Oh, I hope so!' he replied. 'I can't wait. We're going to have such fun, aren't we, Gracey?'

'Ah yes, you absolutely are,' Gloria said, before checking her watch. 'Oh goodness, is that the time? I need to get going in half an hour. Can you just show me your set-up for her – where she'll sleep, and so on? And then I can answer any questions you have.'

'Absolutely,' said Piers, looking at his wife. 'Amelia darling, I think you're best placed for that sort of thing. You've been doing most of the nest-making, after all. Shall I take Grace?'

'Yes,' Amelia answered, allowing him to peel the baby off her chest. She felt too light without her, like a helium balloon devoid of a weight. She stood up, feeling unsteady.

'Okay, yes. The nursery is through here,' she said.

Gloria got up and followed her down the corridor into a small bedroom which looked out over the house's driveway. It was the only room in their apartment which faced away from the hill, so it was lighter and brighter than the rest of their accommodation.

Until recently, she'd used this room as her art space, somewhere to retreat to draw and paint.

Now, however, it contained a white wooden changing table, with storage underneath for nappies and creams, topped with a waterproof cushion decorated with giraffes and monkeys. There was a matching cot, too, and a small chest of drawers. If Gloria looked in those drawers, she'd find row upon row of neatly folded vests, hats, dresses and leggings.

Buying those outfits had felt to Amelia like the fulfilment of a dream. When they'd been going through IVF, she had occasionally allowed herself to drift into the kids' clothing sections of stores, window-shopping for a child who only lived in her imagination. She'd only ever actually bought one item, however. It had been a dress for Leila, a beautiful yellow dress, the colour of freshly budded daffodils. She had been six months pregnant then and she had been naive enough to think that they were out of the woods.

She had considered binning it afterwards. But instead, she had placed it in a special box she had for her memories and stored it in their loft, making space for it among the spiders and moths. It was nice knowing it was still there, even if she couldn't face looking at it ever again.

'Wow,' said Gloria, eyeing the room's decoration. 'How beautiful.'

Amelia followed her gaze to the jungle mural she had painted on the room's longest wall over the weekend. Cascades of tropical flowers in bold red, orange and yellow hues contrasted with deep brown trunks and vivid green foliage; a tiger peered out from behind a tree; monkeys swung between trees.

'Did you pay someone to do this?' Gloria asked.

'Oh, no,' Amelia replied. 'I did it.'

'Wow, did you? That's amazing.'

Amelia felt the colour rise in her cheeks. 'Oh, it's just a rough painting really, a sketch. Nothing special. I paint a bit, when I have time. But I wanted to do something nice for Grace…'

'You have talent, my dear,' said Gloria. 'Have you had lessons?'

'I attended the Royal College of Art,' Amelia replied, without inflection. 'But I'm not very good. Not good enough to make money from it, I mean…'

'People pay good money for that sort of mural, you know,' Gloria replied. 'You should look into it. When Grace is bigger.'

'Yes, good idea,' said Piers, suddenly appearing in the doorway, Grace still on his shoulder. 'But for now, Grace will keep us busy, eh? Talking of which, she's grizzling. I wondered whether she has a preferred feeding bottle, Gloria? Or if not, we have bought a selection, they're in the kitchen…'

They all left the nursery. Gloria brought a bag in from her car and showed them how to make up bottles for the baby, and how to feed her, and how to wind her. And just like that, it seemed, her time with them was up.

'So I've left you the folder with the suggested routine,' she said. 'But honestly, don't worry too much. As long as she's fed and her nappy is dry, you're doing fine. I'll be back tomorrow morning, okay? And you've got my number if you need to call. Oh, and don't forget, Marion, the children's guardian, will be calling you to arrange a suitable time to come over. And you need to take Grace to the supervised visit on Tuesday.'

'What if the birth parents don't show up to the contact sessions?' Piers asked.

'Well, the birth mother did visit her on Thursday,' said Gloria. 'And even if she stops for a while, you'll still need to keep bringing Grace, at least for a few weeks. After that, we can reduce the frequency, if both birth parents are really not interested. And of course, the sessions end when an adoption order is made. So this is only for a few months. I know it's a bind, but it's only temporary.'

Amelia wondered how on earth anyone could not be interested in Grace.

Piers nodded and showed Gloria out. Amelia stood at the top of the stairs and waved goodbye to the social worker, trying to appear as confident and excited as she could manage. When the door shut, Piers turned around and walked back up the stairs. Amelia held the door open for him.

'Well, the adventure begins,' he said, grinning at Amelia as he did so, while cradling Grace. 'We're all going to have such fun, aren't we?' he said, nuzzling the baby's nose. 'We're going to be a perfect little family.'

8

October 18th

Michelle

Nineteen weeks until the final hearing

Michelle's phone was ringing, but she didn't need to look at it to check who was calling. She already knew who it was. It was 10 a.m. on a Tuesday, and that meant it was Contact Day again. And this time, she didn't have any intention of going.

There were two reasons for this. Firstly, she didn't think she could go through that pain again. Seeing Grace up close had just been too hard. She had said goodbye, and that was enough. It had to be.

The second reason was far more practical. She and Rob had been surviving on porridge since yesterday, and today the food bank was definitely open. She'd checked, and she'd had a good sleep and felt that she had enough energy to make the journey. And nourishment was, she reckoned, more of a priority than emotionally skewering herself at the contact centre. Grace was fine anyway, wasn't she? She had a new family. Hopefully a family with sensible, clever, clean-living parents who would never leave her.

'Rob,' she called, turning her head in the direction of their bedroom. 'I'm off to the food bank. See you later.'

A grunt of acknowledgement was all that came back. Rob had never been good at mornings; it was one of the reasons he'd never been able to hold down a job. She'd suggested once that maybe he could solve that problem by doing night shifts instead, but he'd vetoed that too, on the basis that he was usually high after sunset.

She slammed the front door behind her and began to stride out of their cul-de-sac and through the warren of residential streets that surrounded them, in the direction of the centre of town. These roads were full of social housing, a mix of privately owned and places still rented out by the council. You could tell the privately owned places; they had new front doors and loft extensions. Her GCSE English teacher had told her that the roads on the estate, built just after the Second World War, were all named after key figures in Malvern's past: Shaw Avenue after the playwright George Bernard Shaw; Nightingale Rise after Jenny Lind, the Swedish Nightingale; and Elgar Close after, well, Elgar. Everyone knew who he was, didn't they? He was Malvern's most famous son. His face was plastered all over town. His statue stood at the top of Church Street. Her secondary school had been named after him. They sold Elgar fudge in the tea rooms. Looking around her as she walked, Michelle laughed. It was ironic that these streets named after such famous, impressive people were now such shitholes. If Elgar could see his namesake he might condemn it, she thought.

Ten minutes later, Michelle emerged from the estate and began walking up Guarlford Road. It was a long, wide avenue surrounded by ample green verges. The Victorians who'd built most of Malvern must have enjoyed parading up and down here in their carriages, she thought. Now, however, it was most enjoyed by young blokes in souped-up vintage VW Golfs busting the speed limit. She wished, not for the first time, that she'd had money for a bus ticket. She'd be there by now if she had, and she'd have been spared the inhalation of all of these car fumes. But there was nothing, nothing at all that she could do about that, so she pressed on into Barnards Green.

It was an odd place, she thought. *Almost* Great Malvern and yet *not quite* Great Malvern, with its parade of off-licences, convenience stores, hairdressers and takeaways and a traffic island shaped like an egg timer. She'd spent a lot of her teenage years here, after school, in the bus shelter. It had a war memorial on the side. It was made of painted brick and had a clock on top. It was decorated beautifully now, with poppies. They had got a grant, the council, to make it nice. But back when she and her mates had been using it as a meeting place, more than five years ago now, the paint had been blue and peeling and it had been 'decorated' with graffiti tags, and the seating area had been strewn with used fags and empty bottles of White Lightning and had smelled of wee. It probably still did smell of wee, though, she thought. All bus shelters smelled of wee.

She pressed on, as the flat pavement became first a slope and then a hill. Bloody Great Malvern had to be on the side of a bloody hill, didn't it, she thought; if nothing else, living here gave you great calf muscles. At least her scenery was changing now. The houses beside this road were getting bigger and they had things like wrought-iron gates and gardens with sheds painted the colour of soft mints.

And then she realised she'd have to pass *the road*. When she came up here on the bus, she just closed her eyes as they passed it. However, if she wanted to completely avoid it now, on foot, she'd have to take a lengthy detour around the tennis club, up and down another bloody hill, and her feet were killing her. No, fuck it; she'd have to go past it.

She decided the best plan was to walk as quickly as she could. She put on a new burst of speed, breathing deeply and urging her battered body to comply. When she reached the dropped kerb, she cast her eyes to the ground, focusing on the pot-holed tarmac, and not on the perfectly ordinary residential street, with its parade of fine trees and its selection of well-tended hedges and roomy, gravelled driveways, all leading to dark houses which estate agents would no doubt refer to as 'elegant' and 'majestic'.

She only raised her eyes when she'd walked a good twenty paces further. Directly ahead was the Worcestershire Beacon, which loomed large over the town's main street. When she had been in senior school, they'd had to climb that once a year, as part of the PE syllabus. A lot of her mates had hated it and gone off to get 'lost' in the woods to have a fag, but she had loved the escape that it had offered. In truth, she had been pleased when they'd played truant; it had allowed her to join the group at the front, with the PE teachers.

They had been nice, those teachers. They had been some of her favourites. Mr Marks, the football coach, had talked to her about all sorts of stuff as they'd made their way to the top; about weather patterns, about proper fitness, about politics, even. He had always treated her as an equal. Two years later, he had tried to persuade her to stay on at school for A-levels. She felt ashamed that she had let him down, because he had been pretty much the only person who'd cared.

She was at the crossroads at the bottom of Church Street now. She was nearly there. She passed elegant, boarded-up buildings that had once contained banks, a lucky dip of charity shops, two coffee shops and several pharmacies, before coming to the gates of Malvern Priory. She automatically stood up a little straighter as she took in the church, smoothing her hair down and brushing it back behind her shoulders. This building had always had that effect on her, because it was so grand.

Unlike those houses further down the hill, it truly deserved to be described as majestic, she thought. She didn't believe in God, but the Priory had stood here before any of the others around it, long before. And that sort of history, all of those stories of the people who'd worked on it and in it – *that* was what impressed her. Its walls told thousands of tales, she could feel it. She walked slowly through the churchyard, past a series of Victorian lamps – they made the place look like Narnia in the winter – to the large stone archway at the entrance.

As she approached the door, her phone beeped. She pulled it out of her pocket. It was a text from Lying Laura, saying how sorry she was that she hadn't attended the contact session that morning. Yeah, of course you're sorry, Laura, she thought. *Whatever*. The text went on to remind her that the case management hearing was in three weeks' time, and would she like to arrange a lift? *No Laura*, she thought, I bloody won't, because I'm not going. She was going to let Grace go without a fight, she'd decided. Whatever way meant the least involvement of social services, the better. She needed to spare her that.

She paused as she walked through the Abbey's porch. She had spent her childhood in the Priory's grounds, playing hide and seek among the gravestones and, later, being played with by boys behind the tombs and trees. But she had never been inside. Until today.

An old lady was standing by the glass doors that led into the church proper. She was wearing a sash which said 'Welcome'.

'Hello,' she said, acknowledging her presence with a smile. 'Are you here for the morning prayers? Or...?'

'Oh, no,' replied Michelle. 'No... the... the... food bank?'

'Ah yes,' the lady replied. 'Of course. Welcome. It's just through here, but I think they're just setting up. Come in. Let me check.'

Michelle followed her into the main body of the church. The woman gestured to her to wait a while and Michelle nodded. It was an overcast day outside, damp and grey, but it was warm in here, and bright. Glowing spotlights were lighting up the centre of the building, drawing her in. She pulled back her hood and walked a few steps so that she stood at the top of the aisle that ran straight through the centre of the church. There were geometric tiles in red and tan beneath her feet; simple wooden chairs were lined up in rows either side of the aisle. She decided to sit in one, choosing the one closest to the aisle, on the back row.

She sat down and looked up. The ceiling above her was like a large grid, with each square individually painted and embellished with gold. It must have taken someone months to do that, she thought. How did they do that? Did they lie down on their backs? And was the scaffolding they were given to do it, safe? They must have been so brave, those people, she thought.

Just then, a horn sounded loudly. She jumped.

'Oh, sorry to startle you.' The lady who'd gone off to find the food bank people had come back, and she'd caught her jumping. 'Mark, our organist, just came in to practise. He does love starting off the morning with something loud. It'll get quieter, I am sure.'

'No worries,' said Michelle, keeping an ear out for the music he was now playing, which was strangely absorbing.

'Well, anyway,' the woman said. 'They're ready for you now. I'll show you the way.'

Michelle stood back up and followed the woman down the side of the church, past a gift shop, a carpeted area full of toys and bean bags and white marble statues reclining on top of stone tombs.

'Have you been before?' the woman asked Michelle, as they walked.

'No,' she replied. 'But I was given a leaflet by the job centre… and…' she found she didn't want to finish the sentence.

'It's fine,' the woman interrupted, sensing her unease. 'You don't have any explaining to do at all. It doesn't matter. Ah, here we are. Gillian! One for you.'

Michelle looked over in the direction she had shouted, and saw another woman, possibly in her fifties, she thought, standing behind a trestle table laden with tins and packets. She had a neat brown bob and her outfit was a dazzling combination of yellow, red and royal blue. She wore long red dangly earrings, and as Michelle approached, she could smell her perfume, which wasn't an old lady smell, like lavender, but something more exotic, like incense.

'Oh hello there,' she said in an upbeat, plummy voice, her face an image of welcome. 'I'm Gillian. I'm here to help you.'

The other woman retreated to her post at the door as Gillian walked towards her, but Michelle was too distracted to note her leaving. Something about the way this stranger – this ludicrously posh-sounding woman – had offered to help her had cut through Michelle's steely resolve. Normally she'd laugh at someone with an accent like that – she had routinely goaded the stiffly-dressed, frightened-looking private school kids who'd wandered past the Barnards Green bus stop when she'd been a kid – but there was something about this woman that made her feel differently. Without warning, tears began to fall down Michelle's face, unbidden and unheeded.

'Oh, goodness. I *am* sorry,' Gillian said quickly, spotting her tears. She rushed around the side of the table, in Michelle's direction. 'I didn't mean to upset you.' Michelle watched as she delved into her handbag and grabbed one of those little plastic packs of travel tissues from its depths. She took one out and handed it to Michelle.

'There you go. Have a mop up and then we can start again.'

Michelle blew her nose, wiped under her eyes and tried her best to rebuild the force field of nonchalance that she had been maintaining since Grace's birth.

'Thank you,' she said. 'Sorry about that. I'm not a crier, to be honest. I don't know what…'

'Don't be silly,' Gillian interrupted. 'Everyone cries every now and then. Now, let's distract you. I always need distraction when I'm sad or cross. Now, what would you like? We have a plethora of delights here,' she said, framing each item on the table as if she was selling goods on a TV shopping channel. Michelle smiled, realising who the woman's voice reminded her of. It was Hyacinth Bucket in *Keeping Up Appearances*. Her nan had loved that sitcom.

'Just some basics,' she said. 'We've run out of… most stuff.'

'Okay,' replied Gillian, without pause. '*Roger that*. Basics. First, let me find you some bags so you can take things home.' She turned around and rifled through several large cardboard boxes, returning with four large bags for life, from a variety of supermarkets.

'Here we go,' she said. 'Now. Cereal first? What do you like?'

'Anything,' Michelle said, conscious of the depth of her hunger and also of her cavernous embarrassment at being there at all. She needed to get out of there, and quickly.

'Righto. Weetabix? Corn flakes?' Michelle nodded. 'Okay. Just stop me if I put something in you don't like.' Michelle watched as she worked her way down the table methodically, adding a bag of pasta, some rice, assorted tinned vegetables, tuna, biscuits and some pasta sauce. 'Oh and I know you just said basics, but just give me a sec,' Gillian added. 'I've got something nice for you under the table. I keep them hidden, for special guests only.' Michelle watched her reach under the table, and spring back up with a large box of chocolate biscuits in her arms. 'Voilà! Delicious chocolate shortbread.' She added it to Michelle's collection of bags. 'And there's just one more section left, the fresh stuff. Shall I just put a selection of fruit and veg in? We had a delivery from a supermarket just this morning, it's in good shape.'

Michelle smiled weakly. 'Please,' she said, intensely grateful for every bit of sustenance this woman was giving her, while also feeling incredibly guilty. She felt unworthy. She'd stolen food yesterday, and yet here she was today, being treated like a special case.

'Oh, hi Bill,' said Gillian, turning to acknowledge an elderly man who was just taking off his coat. 'Bill's another of our volunteers,' she said to Michelle. 'He comes in every week.'

Michelle didn't know what to say. This was so uncomfortable. All of these nice law-abiding people, giving up their time to help her. She didn't deserve it.

'Right,' said Gillian. 'I think that's your lot,' she said, holding the handles of the bulging bags. 'Would you like to stay for a cup of tea and a biscuit? If you have time?'

Michelle was in a quandary. She desperately wanted to get away, but she was also incredibly hungry, not to mention knackered. She had walked a couple of miles to get here, and she had a couple more to cover on the way back. And she hadn't thought they'd give her so much food. Just the thought of the pain she would undoubtedly feel carrying it home made her feel faint. Although she had slept okay the previous night, she still felt weak following the birth, like her body wasn't quite fitting together again properly.

'Yeah, please,' she said, with reluctance. She resolved to eat and drink quickly and go.

'Great,' said Gillian. 'You go over and sit on one of those chairs, and I'll be with you in a jiffy. Do you take sugar?'

'Yeah, one,' replied Michelle, carrying the laden bags over to a circle of plastic chairs which had been assembled in a corner, near a small stone altar and a metal frame made for the sort of candles you bought in memory of dead people. Several had been placed there that morning and lit and Michelle sat there staring at them. Their flickering light calmed her. For the first time that day, she allowed her mind to clear and her body to stop fighting its way through space. She noticed that her breathing was becoming less shallow.

Then, something else seeped into her consciousness. It was the music. Not the loud, triumphant burst of noise that she'd heard before; no, this was different. It was almost like singing, although far more tuneful than anything she'd ever managed. It sounded a bit like the noise she thought angels might make. If angels existed, that was. She closed her eyes and allowed it to sweep over her.

'Ah, thank God for that, Mark has started playing something less boomy.'

Gillian's voice interrupted her daydreams, and her eyes snapped open. Gillian had placed a mug of tea and a plate of biscuits down on a small table nearby, before noticing that Michelle had had her eyes closed. 'Oh, I'm sorry, I didn't mean to interrupt your reverie,' she added. 'It's nice, isn't it? Elgar. The organ sonata. One of my favourites.'

Michelle didn't know what to say. She had gone to a school named after Elgar, but she had never consciously listened to any of his music.

'It's great,' she said. 'I've never heard it before.'

'Ah, well, great pleasures await,' said Gillian, smiling. 'Mark is a great organist, a great musician. Part of the joy of this job is getting to listen to him practise. You can come any time, you know, and sit in here, and listen. Or just think.'

'I don't have… I mean, I'm not a churchgoer. I never…' said Michelle.

'You don't have to be,' replied Gillian. 'There aren't any rules about this place. It's been around so long it has its own soul, I think. And it welcomes everyone, I'm sure of it. Come and use it. It deserves it.'

Michelle nodded and looked down at the plate of biscuits. There were six on there, a mixture of custard creams, bourbons and digestives. Her stomach growled. She wanted all of them, at once. Instead, she took one bourbon, as slowly as she could manage, and nibbled at it, fighting her urge to shove the whole thing into her mouth in one go.

'My favourite, too,' said Gillian.

There was silence then, as Michelle finished her biscuit, washing it down with hot, sugary tea.

'I wanted to say, obviously, that you don't have to tell me anything if you don't want to,' Gillian said, eventually, 'but if you do feel like chatting – I wondered if you wanted to tell me what brought you here? It helps inform our work. We want to help. If we can.'

Michelle almost laughed but thought better of it and grabbed a custard cream instead, biting it in half and rolling it around on her tongue. Seriously, though – what could this obviously quite mad old woman, clearly totally divorced from reality, do to make the slightest bit of difference to her life, except for providing her with food to keep her going? A whole host of people with all sorts of qualifications had tried to help her at various points in her life, and none of them had succeeded.

'I'm okay,' she replied, after a pause. 'Honest. I'm just tired, and hungry. We ran out of food, as I said. We're not great with money. My partner… Rob… he forgot to go to an interview, so he's been sanctioned. But we'll be fine. We always are. In the end.'

'If you need any advice on benefits, or job seeking, or whatever, I can help,' said Gillian. 'Or rather, the charity I volunteer with can. We're a Christian charity, but we aren't teaching Bible stuff, don't worry about that,' said Gillian, chuckling. 'We just want to help people. We have all sorts of people who can offer all sorts of advice.' She dug into her batik shoulder bag, which was hanging over her shoulder, and pulled out a dog-eared card. 'This isn't in the best shape, sorry, but you can still read it. It's got the contact details for the charity on it, and my name and number. If you need help, just give us a call. Or me. Honestly.'

Bloody hell, she thinks she's going to heal me or save my soul, Michelle thought. Time to get out of here. She had said too much already. She grabbed another bourbon biscuit and bit into it. Her stomach was calmer now and she could feel energy and warmth returning to her limbs. Right, she thought, I'll change the subject, and then go.

'My nan used to bring me to church,' she said to Gillian, her mouth still full of biscuits. 'When I was little. For a bit.'

'That's nice. Was that around here?'

'Yeah. I grew up here. In Malvern. I've never left. I dunno which church it was though, it was ages ago.'

'Does your nan still go to church?'

'I dunno,' she replied, looking at the floor. 'I never see her. I don't even know where she is.'

There was silence while Gillian processed this information.

'That's a shame,' she said, but didn't ask why. Michelle was grateful for that.

'I've got to go now,' Michelle said, standing up. She cast a longing look at the remaining biscuits but realised she couldn't risk staying here any longer. She didn't want to have to tell her anything else.

'Why don't you take the remaining biscuits home,' Gillian said, as if reading Michelle's mind. 'If you leave them there, I'll only be forced to eat them myself, and you can see from my hips that I am not in need of any more sustenance.'

Michelle smiled, the first genuine smile she'd managed that day. 'Thanks,' she said. 'I skipped breakfast.'

Gillian smiled. 'Just give me a sec,' she said, walking over to the trestle tables and wrapping the remaining biscuits in a tissue. It seemed to be taking her some time. Bloody hell, Michelle thought. It'll be dark by the time she's finished.

'Come on, let me help you carry the bags out,' she said finally, walking back over to Michelle. 'Are you in a car? Or are you taking the bus home?'

Michelle didn't know what to say, or where to look. She had no cash for the bus, of course. To be absolutely honest, she hadn't thought they'd give her so much stuff. But they had, and she wasn't going to say no, was she? She would just have to carry everything home by herself, and that was that. She steeled herself and reached down to take the handles of all of the bags.

'Nah, don't worry,' she said. 'I'm... walking.'

'Oh, do you live close by?' Gillian asked.

'I live on the Elgar Estate,' answered Michelle, too tired to make up a lie.

There was a pregnant pause.

'That's a long way away,' said Gillian. 'I know it well.' Michelle wondered why she thought she'd believe that. Only people who lived on the Elgar Estate ever went there, and this woman was clearly not an Elgar Estate sort of person.

'S'no prob. I like walking,' she said, hauling the bags up a few more inches and beginning to walk towards the door. 'Thank you for the stuff,' she called out behind her, hoping that Gillian would get the hint. There was no response. Michelle kept on walking, out of the front porch and down the meandering church drive, onto the main high street. By the time she got there, the bags' handles were already digging into her hands, so she decided to put them down and pause at the gate.

It was then that she heard the car engine. A red Ford Focus had drawn up next to her, its window down. Gillian was behind the wheel.

'Come on, lovey, I can't have you walking for miles with all of those bags,' she said, matter-of-factly. 'I've squared it with Bill, they're not busy in there this week. I've got the time to take you home. Least we can do.'

Michelle considered her options. She could keep on walking, but that would be very rude, and Gillian seemed nice, if infuriatingly persistent. And she didn't like being rude. It wasn't in her nature. And walking several miles with these bags was going to take her hours. But they were both taking a risk. What if... she was... crazy? A pervert? You could never tell.

'Are you sure?' she said to Gillian. 'You don't know me.'

The other woman shrugged. 'I'm pretty sure you're not an axe murderer. And I won't tell the charity if you don't.' She raised her eyes, 'Come on, hop in. You can dump the bags on the back seat.'

Michelle sighed and opened the rear door of the car. A large red and blue check blanket was draped over the back seats. It was covered in long brown hair.

'Please excuse the hair, and the smell,' said Gillian. 'Rory is very hairy.' There was a short pause. 'Rory's a German Shepherd, by the way… Not my husband.'

Michelle smiled and opened the passenger door. 'I love dogs,' she said while sitting down. 'We had one at the home.'

If this information shocked Gillian, she did not show it.

'Oh really? What breed?'

'He was a retriever, I think,' answered Michelle, simultaneously doing up her seatbelt. 'A therapy dog, they called him. He was called Joe.'

'I love retrievers,' said Gillian. 'Like German Shepherds, they're very loyal.' Michelle remembered how she had lain down next to Joe on the floor of her room, curling into him, crying into his fur. He had not moved or shown discomfort. He was by far and away the best thing about that place, she thought. Although it wasn't like there was much competition.

'All belted up?' Gillian asked. Michelle nodded, and they set off down the high street, towards Barnards Green. Even in the first few minutes of the journey, Michelle could tell that Gillian was something of an erratic driver. She was talking all the time – she was currently going on and on about roadworks in the town centre – and waving her hands around as she did so, occasionally taking both hands off the steering wheel simultaneously, while looking at Michelle, and not at the road. Michelle wondered whether she'd make it to her destination alive.

'So, do you live alone?' Gillian asked, finally abandoning her rant about the state of the pot-holed roads. They were a mile or so away from the flat. Michelle tried to work out how many minutes that might be, at the very slow, erratic speed they were doing. Three minutes? Five? Oh my *God*, she thought, *please* make it three.

'Nah,' she said, hoping that would satisfy her jailer. 'As I said, there's Rob. My other half. I live with him.'

'Ah,' she replied. They were approaching the edges of the estate: they were almost there. Thank God. 'Do you have anyone else nearby who can help you?' Gillian continued.

'No, not really.'

They were two streets away now. There must be just seconds left, surely?

'Ah. Okay. Well, if you need anything, remember, you have my number. Just call it, anytime. Honestly. I want to help.'

I am beyond help, Michelle thought.

'It's just over here,' Michelle said, pointing Gillian in the direction of her flat. 'By the tree.' She could have said, 'next to the fly-tipped mattress covered in urine stains,' but that didn't seem appropriate, given the company she was in, she thought.

Gillian drew the car to a stop and pulled on the handbrake. Michelle unclicked her seatbelt immediately and reached for the car door handle.

'Thanks for the lift,' Michelle said, meaning it, although she wished it had been less of a white-knuckle ride. She got out of the seat as soon as she could, trying not to meet Gillian's eye as she did so. She opened the back passenger door and removed the shopping bags.

'No problem,' Gillian said, turning her head to speak to Michelle as she cleared the back seat of her food supplies. 'I couldn't in all conscience let you do that by yourself.'

Michelle smiled what she hoped was a convincing smile of thanks, heaved the bags up with both hands and walked towards her front door. She heard the car engine start up as she did so. She put the bags down to find her keys and turned around as Gillian pulled out of the car parking space.

'Look after yourself,' Gillian called out from her window, which she'd lowered. 'And do come back to visit us at the food bank. We love having visitors. Makes us feel useful.' And with that she drove away, her car swerving as it made its way down the road with the wipers on, despite the fact it wasn't raining. She was barking mad, that woman, Michelle thought. Properly barking mad. But she had liked her, all the same.

Michelle turned back towards the door, pulled her house keys out of her pocket, and turned the key in the lock. The curtains were still pulled shut in the living room, and the TV was not on. Rob must still be in bed. *Good*, she thought, *that means that I've got some time to get some brunch together from these bags to surprise him with when he wakes up*. She walked through to the kitchen and laid the bags on the floor. There was no room on the kitchen surfaces. She would clean this room properly today, she decided. Living in this mess was not helping her mental health at all.

She began pulling items out of the bags, putting them away swiftly in the relevant place. Pasta and cereal in the food cupboard. Milk, cheese, butter, fresh fruit and vegetables in the fridge. And then she found the biscuits she'd almost left behind in the church, wrapped up in a napkin. She unfolded the little package carefully, and found, nestling amongst the biscuits, a ten-pound note.

Gillian must have put it there. It can't have been an accident, can it? It must be meant for her. Michelle picked up the plastic tenner and tried to fold it, noting how it kept its form, no matter what punishment she gave it. And then she turned it over, and saw the tiny note on the back, written in pencil. 'For the bus. Come and visit us soon,' it said, in neat, swirly letters.

Michelle smiled. Should she put it in their spare cash tin? That would be sensible, because they had to buy a new electricity token this week. But then she thought of Gillian's smiling face, and her offer of help, and her insistence that Michelle should look after herself, so she folded the note, opened the cupboard door and tucked it into an empty box of mixed herbs. Just in case, she thought. Just in case.

9

November 8th

Judge Joshi

Case management hearing – sixteen weeks until the final hearing

'So, is this everyone?'

Judge Prisha Joshi looked over her bifocals – which infuriated her, as they were always slipping down her nose – at the lawyers and social workers assembled for the case management hearing.

Philip, the barrister for the local authority, was sitting to her right, tapping away on his phone, smiling at the screen. Had he just been given a really well-paid case, or was he having an affair, she wondered? It was definitely one of the two.

Behind him sat Laura and Gloria, two social workers she knew well. Gloria particularly, as they had both been witness to the same human dramas in the family courts for more than two decades. Laura and Gloria were engaged in an intense conversation, which was definitely more about work than play. She was glad they took their role seriously. So many vulnerable lives depended on them, she thought.

Directly in front of her was the ever-colourful lawyer Sally Mucklow. She was wearing a bright red tunic dress today, with lipstick to match. Unfortunately, however, there was no sign of her client, Michelle Jenkins. Damn, thought the judge. Although a refusal to co-operate would make her decision about the adoption easier, she had felt instinctively that Michelle – that young woman who'd been in and out of care for most of her life, who looked like she was fighting to stay afloat in a flood – might decide to change her mind and fight to keep her child. But a refusal to turn up in court was never a good sign.

To the judge's left was the children's guardian, Marion Stone. She was appointed by Cafcass, the Children and Family Court Advisory and Support Service. Prisha had known Marion a long time and she trusted her judgement. She was relieved that she'd have her input. Each adoption case she took on was full of unexpected twists and turns and gut-churning, middle-of-the-night-haunting decisions. It helped to feel like she was sharing the burden.

The judge cleared her throat to get the attention of the assembled professionals.

'Okay. I am assuming that Miss Jenkins is not attending today?'

'Yes, madam,' replied Sally, standing up as she did so. 'Unfortunately, I have been unable to contact her since the first contact session. She is not returning my calls or opening the door to her flat.'

'So she has been attending the contact sessions?' Judge Joshi asked.

'Only once so far, madam.'

'Has the mother officially relinquished the baby?' she asked.

'No, madam. Not yet.'

'Thank you, Ms Mucklow,' she said. Interesting, she thought. That latter fact makes this case far from clear cut.

'Very well. Mr Shelley' – she turned to the barrister for social services – 'The father, has he been attending the contact sessions with his daughter?'

'No, not at all, madam,' he replied.

'I see,' said Judge Joshi, sitting forward in her seat. 'At the first hearing, I asked for a parenting assessment and reports from all of the relevant social workers. Are these ready?'

'Madam, I do have reports from both the baby and the mother's social workers, but we have been unable to complete a parenting assessment so far, because, as you are aware, the mother is refusing all contact attempts currently.'

'I see,' she replied, before taking a deep breath and looking down at her notes, mostly for show, because there was very little written there so far today. As she cast her eyes down, she considered her options. She could go ahead with the hearing today and discuss the case with the assembled lawyers. That would be the sensible thing to do; after all, it was looking as if this might be a cut-and-dried adoption. Or, she could give the mother more time to decide, either way. She could postpone the analysis of the reports until the resolution hearing.

She thought then about her own children, both now at university, one studying law – she suspected mostly out of misplaced duty – and the other, music. She hadn't heard from either of them for at least two weeks now and her heart ached.

'Very well,' she said. 'I think it's best if we postpone the reading of the social workers' reports until the resolution hearing. Ms Mucklow, please can you ensure that a parenting assessment report is ready for that hearing, which will fall in the first week of February, or we will have to proceed without it. I hope that we will also have the mother and her representative at that hearing, so that we can properly assess this case from all angles. And please, do make sure that she is given every opportunity to officially surrender the child, if she wants to do so.'

'Of course, madam.'

Judge Joshi nodded, picked up her pen, and noted the date of the resolution hearing in her notebook. It was the clerk's responsibility to book it in, but she had learned over the years that it didn't hurt to double check these things.

'See you all in early February,' she said.

10

November 8th

Amelia

Sixteen weeks until the final hearing

What time was it? She didn't have her watch on and her phone was still on the bedside table, but she reckoned it must be after midnight now.

This was the second time she'd been woken so far tonight, and she'd only been in bed for a couple of hours. It turned out that Grace – beautiful, beguiling Grace – did not sleep at all well. Leonora, the emergency foster carer, hadn't mentioned any issues with her sleep, and Amelia now wondered whether that was because she hadn't wanted to put them off.

Or perhaps it was just that she was doing all the wrong things. How could that be, though? She'd read every parenting book she could find in preparation for adoption, and she'd made copious notes. She reckoned she had tried every 'trick' recommended by those writers in the past twenty-two days – all 528 hours, for she'd counted them all – that she'd been left in charge of an infant.

Piers wasn't much help either. To her surprise, he seemed more at sea with it all than she was. Grace wouldn't settle in his arms when she was crying, and he'd almost dropped her during a nappy change in the early days. Watching his struggle with her was painful and concerning, so she had now taken over the lion's share of the caring responsibilities herself. It was certainly less stressful this way, but it did mean that she was absolutely exhausted. She was barely getting any rest, because instead of nice, long sleeps, Grace seemed to prefer short, sharp power naps, followed by languid bottle feeds with a generous burping and stroking session to follow. Once fed and comfortable, she then wanted to be held in a sling and gently rocked to sleep. This latter stage could last anything between a few minutes and half an hour, Amelia had learned. Then her challenge was to prise her out of the sling and lower her into the cot as slowly and as gently as she could, her lower-back muscles screaming, before tiptoeing out of the room at speed, desperate to be allowed to sleep herself. If she made it as far as their bed, she had about a fifty-fifty chance of being called back to repeat the sling rocking bonanza, because it didn't always work the first time. It was, she thought, like living with a ticking bomb. She was constantly on edge, listening out for the whimper that would signal the explosion to come.

If those useless parenting manuals were textbooks, then Gloria, the social worker, was Amelia's examiner. She had visited every day for the past fortnight, and Amelia had begun to see her visits as a test which she could pass or fail, and not as a helping hand. She was desperately worried that Gloria might realise her ineptitude and remove Grace, and she knew that she had to prevent that from happening at all costs.

She had tried to hide how tired she was by putting on makeup every morning – she should have taken shares out in concealer. It hadn't been enough, however. Gloria had clocked her exhaustion immediately and offered her even more useless parenting advice, things like 'sleep when the baby sleeps' (so, twenty-minute naps, thought Amelia – how restful) and 'put the baby into a routine'. (Now why didn't I think of that, she thought. If only I could get Grace to agree to adhere to one.)

Gloria had also suggested that she should leave Grace with Piers so that she could have a nap. She had only tried that once. She'd taken herself off to bed but Grace's cries from the next room, as Piers had tried and failed to soothe her, had put paid to any idea of rest. Instead of falling to sleep, her heart had hammered in her chest, and she'd given up within minutes. Motherhood seemed to her to be one enormous dichotomy. You yearned every minute to have time by yourself again, but when you got it, you yearned for it to end.

Standing there in the inky darkness of the nursery, her eyes desperate to close, her legs ready to buckle, tears began to roll down Amelia's face. This was not the motherhood of her imaginings. She realised now that her exposure to other people's children had been heavily edited; she had previously only held fully dressed, recently fed and changed, sweet-smelling babies. Babies who were usually asleep. They had seemed extraordinary to her, like little pockets of magic. And yet here she was, rocking the tiny form of a human backwards and forwards in a bright pink, organic cotton sling, but this particular baby felt rather like a dictator with a finger permanently on the nuclear button and vocal delivery that was a fixed on 'yell'.

Or a jailer, even.

Amelia hadn't been out of the house since Grace had arrived two weeks ago. Piers had given himself the job of venturing out to get food and various bits of baby equipment they hadn't anticipated needing (like endless piles of disposable nappies – they'd given up on cloth nappies within two days). While he had been the hunter gatherer, her role had been to remain, quite literally, holding the baby – for Grace did *not* like being put down.

As Piers set out for his first foray out of the house on day two of parenthood, he'd given her a smile of encouragement, and told her that she was a 'natural' and 'clearly the better parent for the job'. She had so wanted to believe it, even though the evidence to the contrary was all around her. She was almost on her knees. Grace just seemed to scream all day, and their flat looked like it had been ransacked by an incontinent rhino.

She longed to pull on her trainers and set out for a long, slow run, but Piers' apparent inability to watch Grace for anything longer than a few minutes meant that this was not on the cards. Amelia wondered now what involvement he'd had in his son Sebastian's early years. She had never asked him about it, in case he had found the memories too painful. After all, it was unutterably cruel, what his first wife Lesley was doing to him, keeping him away. The thing was, Piers had lost two children, in effect. She must never forget that. He'd been through a great deal.

Amelia had never met Lesley and she didn't want to, either. She didn't even know what she looked like, or what she did for a job, although she did know that it was part-time and for a low wage, as Piers complained about this bitterly. It wasn't so much that Piers didn't want to give her the details, she thought, it was just that she'd never asked. She hadn't wanted to think about Lesley, that was the thing, because she had, after all, been able to give birth to a living, breathing child. Thinking about her and that boy she was now raising alone – albeit with financial assistance from Piers – had been torture, so she had suppressed all brief appearances of them both in her consciousness. But now, for the first time, she wondered what stories they could tell.

Amelia took a deep breath and exhaled, trying to breathe out her negative thoughts as she did so. She attended the occasional yoga class run by one of the school's PE teachers, and the tutor had taught her to breathe out her anger and pain. It was a move she had adopted at home. It helped a little, to feel all of the grief gush out of her into the air, even if she was only fated to breathe it back in moments later.

Taking another deep breath in, she stopped rocking back and forth and assessed Grace's demeanour. She was still now, at last. But was she asleep? Her breathing seemed to be quieter and less agitated. There was no snuffling. *Yes*, she thought. *Bingo*.

She tiptoed over to the cot in the corner of the room, shuffling right and left to avoid the creakiest floorboards. This Victorian house was full of them, and she now knew them intimately. Reaching the cot she untied the sling, cocooned Grace in her arms and bent over, lowering her inch by inch into the super-soft, tempur mattress the lady in John Lewis had convinced them they needed. Not that it made a blind bit of difference to her apparent dislike of being in bed, more's the pity.

Grace touched down smoothly, her arms splaying behind her head, her legs still. Things were looking good. Amelia resisted the temptation to run out of the room, forcing herself instead to tiptoe out like a pantomime burglar, picking up each leg as high as it could go and striding as far as she could with each movement, absorbing the impact by bending her knees.

Reaching their bedroom, the sight of her side of the bed – the duvet folded back, the sheets clean and crisp – felt like spotting the sea on the first day of a beach holiday. She simply couldn't wait to throw herself in. She collapsed into it, pulling the duvet over and around her, hugging it close. This was her time, her only time for herself. And since becoming a 'mother' – she still used inverted commas in her head, because Grace was not yet 'theirs' – she had become skilled at falling asleep quickly. It was what happened when you only had about sixty minutes to rest before the baby needed you once more. Putting Grace down was like turning over an egg timer, and she could almost hear the grains of sand falling down, freely and relentlessly. Amelia sighed, turned onto her side, closed her eyes, and prepared to commit herself to dreams.

'She asleep?' mumbled Piers, turning over in the bed and spooning her. She had thought he had been out cold. He seemed to have an incredible ability to sleep through Grace's cries. But not her return to bed, obviously.

'She is now,' replied Amelia.

'Good morning darling,' said Piers. He was standing in front of the long mirror in their room, adjusting his tie. 'Did you sleep well?'

Amelia opened one eye and saw that Piers was smiling at her reflection.

'Not really, no,' she replied. 'Grace woke me up four times, I think.'

'Oh darling, you must be tired. Let me bring you a coffee.'

Piers left the room and headed to the kitchen. Amelia looked over at the moses basket in the corner of the room, currently home to the sleeping form of Grace. After she'd woken up a few more times in the night Amelia had grown tired of tiptoeing back and forth from her cot and moved her into the bedroom, where she had mercifully fallen asleep for a few precious hours. Bugger it, she thought. Why couldn't he have let her sleep a little longer? She lay back down and stared at the ceiling, willing her anger to remain contained for just a while longer. Nothing good came of letting it seep out, she knew that.

'Here you go,' said Piers, placing a mug of instant coffee down on the bedside table as if it was a platter of caviar and smoked salmon tartlets. 'Coffee for Mummy.'

'Thanks,' said Amelia, picking it up and taking a sip. Then she took in Piers' outfit properly for the first time that morning. He was wearing his work clothes – chinos, a smart shirt and a red and blue striped tie.

'Why are you dressed like that?' she asked. 'You've got adoption leave for another couple of weeks yet.'

'Oh, you know me, I'm terrible at being at home,' he replied, sitting down on the bed next to her. 'I thought I'd get out from under your feet and head into school for a bit. I'll be back in time to watch Grace during your lesson with Julia.'

'Okay.'

'I heard a rumour that the deputy head has been headhunted for another job,' Piers continued. 'It doesn't do to be out of view for too long when there's a potential vacancy arising. I'm just going to show willing.'

Amelia considered this. She was due to see Dad this morning. They had planned to do that together, but now…

'Look, darling,' he continued, misjudging her thoughts, 'I know you're nervous about being on your own with Grace. That's natural. But you'll be fine, I know you will. You are a natural mother.'

Amelia was too tired to contradict him, but inside her exhausted brain, a tiny spark of freedom was ignited. The reality was, she was almost alone with Grace even when he was in the flat, because he didn't really help her. And if he wasn't here, she could maybe get her paints out when Grace was napping… She took a large gulp of coffee and swallowed hard.

'Oh Piers, that's okay,' she said, with all the positive energy she could muster. 'I know what your job means to you. *Go*. I've got this.'

'Great,' he said, standing back up. 'I knew you'd be fine with it.' He walked back over to the mirror and began to brush his hair into a sculpted swoop. 'Oh, and I have a surprise for you,' he said. 'I anticipated that you'd be nervous about being on your own, so I've arranged with one of the other college wives – Caroline, Brian's wife, I think you've met her? She's going to come and pick you up later and take you to a mother and baby group she goes to.'

Amelia's heart sank. She was far too tired to put on a public face, and she had hoped for, no, *pined* for some time alone today. And what's more, she definitely knew Caroline. She was an enthusiastic horsewoman, had gone to Cheltenham Ladies

College, and dressed head-to-toe in Boden. She would have no time for 'arty, liberal types' like Amelia.

'Oh darling,' said Piers, seeing her reaction, 'don't be like that. There's nothing to be scared of.' He sat back down on the bed next to her and began to stroke her arm. 'I know you find social gatherings tricky, but Caroline tells me it's a nice group full of lovely women, all very educated and cultured and supportive and friendly. It sounds fun.'

Amelia could think of nothing she'd like less than spending time with a group of 'lovely', superficial, upper-middle-class Stepford wives, but she said nothing. She knew that Piers felt she needed to make some new friends, now that she had cut ties with the old ones. He had been right about them though, she thought. They had all come from her old world, from her unhappy secondary school years, and her failed attempts at a career in art. It was a good idea to leave them behind and focus on the future instead. But whether she could ever forge a proper friendship with a posh, entitled woman remained to be seen.

'I have to visit Dad today,' she said, still clutching her coffee.

'Ah yes, I remember,' Piers replied, still stroking her arm. 'But you can go later, can't you? Afterwards. I'm sure he won't mind.'

Amelia was about to reply that they'd told him they'd be around before lunch, but she decided not to. Nothing Piers did was ever wrong in her dad's eyes. Piers looked at his watch and shot up.

'Golly, I must go,' he said. 'Now, Caroline is going to be here at nine-thirty, okay? It's eight-thirty now, so you have time for a bit of breakfast and a shower, by my calculation?'

Amelia sighed, placed her coffee mug on the bedside table and swung her legs over the side of the bed.

'Wonderful. Oh, and just *look* at her,' he said, his eyes swivelling towards Grace. 'She's still sound asleep, so that Mummy can have a shower.'

Amelia rubbed her eyes and smoothed her hair with her hands.

'You could wear that grey dress I bought you, couldn't you?' Piers said, as he pulled on his jacket. 'It looks beautiful on you.' He leaned down to kiss her on the cheek. Amelia looked up at him; his hair was well ordered, his frame was strong, and his face was recently shaved. He looked efficient, smart, handsome. She smiled up at him, a momentary dash of pride lighting up her face.

'Yes, I will,' she said. 'Thanks for buying it for me, Piers.'

'You're worth it, my darling,' he said, putting his watch on. 'Right, I must go. See you after school. Enjoy the baby group. Your first!' he said with a dazzling smile. 'But not your last.'

He shut the door as he left, and Amelia exhaled loudly as he did so. She hadn't realised it, but she had been holding her breath.

She sat still for a few moments, listening to the sound of spoons clinking on cheap white bowls in the boys' dining hall, local children shouting as they walked to school, cars driving up the steep local roads and the muffled growls of distant dogs. Then, she launched herself out of bed. If she was going to have to put on a face for Caroline and her undoubtedly perfect mummy friends, she'd have to make a proper effort.

'There you are,' said Caroline, looking Amelia up and down as she did so. Amelia backed away slightly from the front door of the boarding house and returned the favour. On Caroline's hip balanced a blue-eyed, long-blond-haired child of about two, who was mining a bag of organic sweetcorn puffs with some urgency. Caroline was wearing buffed brown knee-high leather cowboy boots, skinny blue jeans and a frilly, floral, gauzy shirt that was probably made by Kate Middleton's favourite designer, Amelia decided. Amelia looked down at her own outfit – the grey, high-collared woollen tunic dress Piers had bought for her to wear at parents' evenings and concerts – and felt matronly in comparison.

'How lovely to see you,' said Caroline, leaning forward for a two-cheek air kiss. Amelia had to dart to the left to avoid hitting the child's snack packet as she complied. 'This is Theo,' she said, introducing her offspring. Amelia was glad she'd said that; she'd taken him for a girl. 'Shall I come in?' she said, walking through the threshold without waiting for an answer. 'Oh, *look* at her,' said Caroline, spotting Grace, who was sleeping in her car seat in the hallway, strapped in. Amelia had decided it was best to have her ready to go. She had not wanted to have to invite Caroline into her home, not even for a brief moment. It was far too untidy for that.

'How old is she? She looks fresh out of the packet,' said Caroline, stooping down in front of Grace, her child still on her hip.

'A few weeks,' Amelia replied, spotting some letters on the doormat where Caroline had been standing. She scooped them up and placed them on the windowsill, noticing that there was one addressed to Piers on the top, with a handwritten address.

Caroline was now stroking Grace's outfit, which Amelia had chosen carefully. It was one of the ones Piers had chosen; it was a red and white knitted dress, with matching stripey red and white tights. Caroline stood back up, demonstrating admirable control of what must be Pilates-honed core muscles, Amelia thought.

'So precious. What's her name?'

'Grace.'

'Is that the name you and Piers chose?'

'No, it was given to her by her… mother,' Amelia said, focusing on Grace as she did so, and absolutely not looking at Caroline. '*Birth mother.*'

'How are you keeping?' said Caroline.

Amelia looked up at her. She had tipped her head to one side, like Princess Diana used to when she was showing empathy.

Should she be honest?

Frankly, Caroline, I am walking through a dark tunnel, and there is not a smidgeon of light at the end.

'Oh, you know,' said Amelia after a pause, 'I'm okay. Coping.'

Caroline had moved closer and was now directly opposite her. She was staring at her intently, and Amelia found both her proximity and her gaze uncomfortable.

'You look a bit tired,' Caroline said, her head tipping once more. Oh shit, thought Amelia. Why do all of these women *know*?

'I am a bit,' she replied. 'She's not a great sleeper. But never mind... Who sleeps when they have a baby, anyway?' She laughed a bit when saying that, knowing that it sounded false, but hoping that the other woman would take the hint and not probe further.

An uncomfortable silence followed.

'Well, let's get going, hey? It starts in ten minutes. My car's this way,' said Caroline, filling the silence.

Amelia sighed with relief, and picked up Grace's changing bag, car seat and the buggy frame that went with it, and followed Caroline out onto the driveway, where a black Range Rover glistened in the weak autumnal sun.

'Is it an Isofix seat?' asked Caroline, pulling open one of the nearside rear doors. 'I've got a spare base here, if so.'

Amelia had no idea. They hadn't taken her out in the car yet; in fact, they'd only begun tentative local walks with the buggy in the past few days.

'I'm not... sure,' she said. 'We haven't...'

Caroline walked up to Grace's car seat and inspected it.

'Yep, looks like Isofix to me. And it's a Mamas and Papas, right? I have the base for that, as luck would have it.' She put her hand on the car seat's handle. 'Shall I?'

Amelia relinquished control of the car seat and watched as Caroline clicked Grace's car seat into position with the minimum of fuss.

'There you go,' she said, emerging from the car. 'Lovely. You can sit in the front with me, and Theo can keep her company in the back.'

Amelia acquiesced, because she couldn't see any way that she could squeeze past the car seats to take a seat in the middle. All the same, it didn't feel right, leaving her there in the back, all by herself.

'She'll be fine,' said Caroline, opening up the boot and placing the buggy frame and changing bag inside, before slamming it back down. '*Honestly*. We've only got to go around the corner, really.'

Amelia nodded and walked towards the passenger door, which Caroline had just opened. She pulled herself up and strapped herself into the leather-upholstered seat, taking in the bamboo takeaway coffee cup in the cup holder, which was green and decorated with black Labradors.

'Right,' said Caroline, opening up the door and sitting next to her. 'Off we go.'

She did up her seatbelt, pressed a button and the car's engine sparked into life. Amelia stared out of the window as they drew away from the house and made their way up the hill. She counted each school building as they drove by: the sanatorium, the sports hall, the chapel, the music centre, and several boarding houses, all named after famous male authors – Shelley, Dickens, Wordsworth, Shakespeare. They'd had a competition to decide the name of a new sixth form boarding house last year, and she had – anonymously – suggested Dickinson and Angelou and Plath. They had not opted for any of her choices.

'So, this is your first baby group, Piers said?' said Caroline, turning briefly to look at Amelia before focusing back on the road.

'Yes,' replied Amelia. 'In fact, this is my first trip out since she arrived.'

'Wow,' Caroline said. 'I'm honoured.'

Amelia raised an eyebrow. Her home counties accent made her sound at best insincere, at worst sarcastic. But she turned to look at her and observed that she had a straight face. Perhaps she'd give her the benefit of the doubt this time.

'Here we are,' announced Caroline, pulling the car into a small, shady car park. Amelia peered out of the car window. There was a large oblong wooden hut to their left, almost obscured by trees. It had a wooden sign board outside, onto which were nailed a number of adverts for local events: on Fridays, a whist drive; on Saturdays, a country music band; on Mondays, a book swap; and on Tuesdays, Bumps and Babes.

Caroline looked over at Amelia. 'We're here,' she said, unclipping her seatbelt. 'Are you okay?'

Amelia shrugged. She had assumed they'd be meeting in an upmarket coffee shop which sold artisan milkshakes and macarons, not in a scout hut on the outskirts of town. 'Yes, sorry, just a bit tired,' she said, undoing her own belt and opening the car door. With Caroline's help, she removed Grace's car seat from its base and followed her up a ramp to the front door, which was wedged open with a grey plastic chair.

They walked through a dingy entrance hall and emerged into a long room which had a lino floor, bare wooden walls and windows at shoulder height running along both sides. Long fluorescent strip lights hugged the hut's wooden vaulted ceiling, casting a sickly yellow pall on the group of women and children who were assembled below. Beyond them, on the far wall, was an open serving hatch, behind which an elderly woman with white hair in a bun was arranging mismatched teacups and placing biscuits onto plates.

'Caz! You made it!'

One of the dozen women who were all sitting in a circle on identical stackable chairs had spotted their entrance.

'Yes, sorry girls, I had to swing by the college to pick up a new member,' Caroline said. This prompted all of the women present to halt what they were doing and turn around and look directly at Amelia and Grace. Amelia blushed bright red and looked down at Grace intently.

'Well, come on over,' said the woman, beckoning them. Desperate to be absorbed into a crowd, Amelia walked forwards, noting that the woman who had called out to them had bright purple hair and a nose piercing. She got up as they approached and pulled out her chair so that they could expand the circle.

'Hello,' the purple-haired woman said, holding out her hand for Amelia to shake. 'I'm Rachel.' She was wearing no makeup and was wearing a t-shirt emblazoned with 'Well-Behaved Women Rarely Make History'.

'Hi, I'm Amelia.'

'Fabulous,' she said, with a broad smile on her face which looked, Amelia decided, quite real, and honest.

'And who's this?' she said, looking down at the car seat.

'Oh, this is Grace,' said Amelia quickly, infected by Rachel's joie de vivre.

'Aww, she's tiny,' said Rachel. 'You forget they were once so small. Come on over here, I'll just go and get you a seat. You must be knackered.'

Amelia looked around for Caroline, not wishing to appear rude to the woman who'd brought her there. However, she could see that she was already ensconced in conversation with a smartly-dressed woman who Amelia vaguely recognised as someone who had something to do with the college.

'Take a seat here,' said Rachel, walking up to Amelia carrying another chair, and putting it down in the expanded circle. 'I'll put you by me.'

Amelia looked around and saw that inside the circle of chairs was a large area lined with padded mats, and filled with an assortment of babies, toddlers and toys. Grace was clearly too small to play, but she followed Rachel's suggestion, and carried the car seat over to the circle and sat down.

'Ah, the joy of a seat,' said Rachel, pulling up another chair, and closing the circle so that none of the children could escape. 'Some days I realise I never ever get to sit in one, you know?' Amelia smiled, engaged by her companion's warmth. She had no personal experience of looking after a toddler, and Rachel clearly knew that, but saying things like that made her feel like she'd been accepted into the club. 'So, sorry, I got all excited about finding chairs there and got a bit flustered. Now that we're both seated, let's rewind. I'm Rachel, you're Amelia' – she looked down at the car seat – 'and this is Grace?'

'Yep.'

'And over there, currently eating a large piece of red Brio, is my daughter, Ella,' said Rachel. 'She's one next week.'

'Wow, and she's walking?' said Amelia, looking over at the toddler, who had a mass of brown tight curls, and was wearing blue leggings and a white t-shirt with a rainbow on it. She was sucking the red block, depositing dribble all over it.

'Yep, has been for a few weeks,' said Rachel. 'And now I'm even more tired than before. Each stage of motherhood, you think you have it sorted, and then, boom, they change, and you're completely floored all over again.'

Yes, that's how I feel, Amelia thought; *floored*.

'You'll be feeling completely banjaxed at the moment, I'm guessing?' asked Rachel, turning towards her.

Amelia smiled through the hazy aura which seemed to encase her at all times. 'Yes, I'm… banjaxed,' she said. 'Sorry, I'm just not myself at the moment. You know?'

'Yes, I do know,' replied Rachel. 'Now, can I have a cuddle?'

Amelia thought she was asking her, and she looked up, shocked, only to realise that Rachel was looking down at Grace.

'Oh, of… course,' she said, hesitating. She had not let anyone other than Piers hold her so far.

'Brilliant,' said Rachel, leaning down and unclipping the straps, before cocooning Grace safely in her arms, and lifting her up onto her lap.

Amelia watched as she brought Grace's face closer to hers, and inhaled. 'Oh, that new baby smell,' she said, laughing. 'They should bottle that.' She then ran her right hand over Grace's arms, trunk and legs, as if inspecting a horse.

'She's really small. Was she premature?'

Amelia thought for a moment. She could lie about being a foster mother. But then, Caroline had probably already spilled the beans, and anyway, Rachel's demeanour didn't invite that sort of thing. Something about her inspired her to be honest.

'The truth is, I don't know,' she said, looking at Rachel.

'Ah,' said Rachel, still smiling. 'Was she born to a surrogate?'

'No. Well, she was born to another woman. No, we're fostering her. To adopt. We're hoping she will be ours officially in a few months.'

'Ah, so you're extra special,' Rachel said, addressing Grace. 'Your parents really, really worked hard to have you.'

Amelia could feel a tear forming in her right eye, but she didn't try to prevent it falling, which surprised her. She always had to have a tissue on hand when at home, just in case.

'Yes,' replied Amelia. 'We waited a long time for them to place a child with us. And we've had a long road – IVF, and so on…'

'Ah, I had IVF, too,' said Rachel, looking over and clocking Amelia's tears. 'Oh shit, sorry, I didn't mean to make you cry! Mind you, I know that tears are a pretty constant feature of this stage of motherhood, so I don't know why I'm surprised. Look, let me get you a drink. And a biscuit?'

Amelia nodded. 'That would be lovely, thanks. Tea?'

'Coming up,' said Rachel, holding Grace out for Amelia to hold. She took her from the other woman, happy to see that

Grace was still happily asleep. She'd fed her just before they'd left the house, hoping she could avoid having to make up a bottle for her whilst out – she hadn't done that yet and the thought of it made her nervous.

While she waited for Rachel to return, she surveyed the other mothers present. Aside from the ever-glossy Caroline, there were a couple of other ladies of her ilk; Piers would probably refer to them as 'yummy mummies'. It was a term that managed to be both flattering and insulting at the same time, Amelia thought, labelling women as gorgeous whilst inferring that they had little personality to match it. She knew that she did not fit into that category, anyhow. She had never been considered gorgeous, not by anyone, although Piers had made her feel it sometimes, in the early days. She had been plain at school, a bit too tall, a bit too skinny, and that theme had continued into adulthood. She had always felt that her height – five foot ten – made her stand out too much, and in recent years she had dressed accordingly, to try to blend in, even though she had always secretly devoured fashion magazines and wished she could indulge her secret desire to wear radical shapes and colours.

'Here you go,' said Rachel. 'One tea. I put milk in it, is that okay?'

Amelia nodded. She didn't care, as long as it was a drink, and she didn't have to make it. 'Oh, and I got you a custard cream. Here, take one.' She held out a plate with two biscuits on it, and Amelia looked embarrassed. She had Grace in one arm and her free hand was holding the cup of tea.

'Oh silly me, the joy of holding a baby. Look, I'll put these on the floor while you drink your tea, and then you can swap the mug for a biscuit. I promise not to eat mine until you get there. I know how rare food is at this stage. You're probably starving.'

Amelia smiled and turned to the side so that she could take a sip of tea without risking dropping it on the baby.

'So how are you finding it?' Rachel asked between slurps of her own tea. 'The new-born stage is hard.'

'Yes!' said Amelia. 'She doesn't want to be put down. She only falls asleep after a feed, and if she does, only for about an hour, even at night. She screams all the time when she's awake.' Amelia paused and took a deep breath. 'I think... I *think*... I'm just no good at this. I think maybe she knows that I didn't give birth to her...'

'Don't be silly,' Rachel replied. 'Everyone thinks they're shit at the beginning.'

'Do they?'

'Yes. Really.'

'Oh.'

'Look. I know everyone gives you uninvited advice, and that's infuriating,' said Rachel, making Amelia laugh, 'but – for what it's worth – here's some more. This is what saved me...'

What followed was far from infuriating. Amelia got out her phone, opened the notes app and typed up every tip Rachel had, including the use of a dummy ('Ignore all the dummy snobs,' she said, 'those things are amazing'), to feed Grace only when she woke, not to help send her to sleep, and a swaddling blanket ('seriously, you'll be checking her for a pulse').

'Thank you so much,' said Amelia, really meaning it. 'I'll be straight on Amazon when I get home, ordering a dummy and a blanket.'

'Good,' said Rachel. 'You can do it, honestly. You're just in a sort of grieving period for your old life at the moment. But your new life will be great, honestly. When you adjust.'

Amelia thought of her dark flat, of her surrendered art room, of Piers' misplaced confidence in her. Doubt began to creep back in.

'Oh, don't cry again,' said Rachel, spotting Amelia's fall back down into the rabbit hole. 'Now, let's distract you. Who here don't you know?'

Amelia looked around. 'Well, I know Caroline. And I sort of know the woman she's chatting to.'

'Yes, that's Becky. She's married to one of the groundsmen at Langland College.'

Amelia felt awful. Of course she was; she'd seen them chatting to each other over the low wall around the boarding house, presumably on the way to and from nursery.

'And over there, that's Belinda – she's a primary school teacher – and then there's Natalie, she's a stay-at-home mum, and then there's Lorna, she works in a supermarket, I think.'

'I feel really bad,' said Amelia, putting her tea down and reaching down for a biscuit.

'Why?'

'Before I came here, I thought… not very nice things about baby groups.'

Rachel snorted. 'Ha, I love your honesty. Let me see. Did you think we would all be sitting here eating almond croissants and sipping pumpkin spice lattes?'

'How did you know?' said Amelia, laughing for the first time in weeks.

'Well, I'm guessing you extrapolated from Caroline and your mind went wild.'

Amelia looked guilty.

'What's funny though is that Caroline, despite her glossy exterior, had it worse than all of us, for a while.'

'Oh?' said Amelia, her ears pricking up.

'Yes, she had a diagnosis of postnatal psychosis. She's really open about it. She had a short spell in a supervised mother and baby unit. She was sectioned.'

'Oh… God.'

'Yep, pretty horrendous, really. But she came out of it. And she's fine now.'

'I had no idea.'

'No, I know. I don't think her husband talks about it. He's

quite senior at the college, isn't he? Probably thinks it looks bad.'

Amelia suddenly felt incredibly guilty for every snide thought she'd had about Caroline.

'Look, so that's the thing. We all struggle, even if we don't look like we do. You'll be grand. Honest.'

Amelia realised she felt buoyed up by the women around her – probably, she reflected, for the first time in years.

'Now,' said Rachel. 'Let's get down on the mat, and Grace can meet Ella. She loves tiny babies. She thinks they're living dolls.'

'Dad?' Amelia pushed open the heavy oak door, and stared into the gloom beyond. '*Dad*?'

There was no reply, so Amelia pushed the door open further and walked in, carrying Grace's car seat inside and placing her down on the hall floor. She walked down the hallway and into the living room. The heavy blue damask curtains were closed. She went over to the windows and threw them open, coughing as clouds of dust took flight. When she turned around, the light from the south-facing windows illuminated a pile of blankets on the sofa.

The pile of blankets coughed.

'Dad!' said Amelia, running to the sofa and pulling the blankets back. 'Dad! Are you okay?'

'Eh?' he said, rubbing his eyes. 'Amelia, is that you?'

'*Dad*. You didn't answer when I called.' She bent over and held her arms out to her father. He took them and allowed her to pull him up to a seated position.

'I didn't hear you,' he said, his voice deep and stern.

Amelia looked at him more closely. His thin white hair was hanging in all directions, like a miniature mop; his moustache was straggly and appeared dirty; his loose, freckled skin was sallow; and his large, floppy ears were… naked.

'Dad, where are your hearing aids?'

'Eh?'

'*Your hearing aids*,' she repeated, so loudly this time that she fancied she could see his hair moving, her words reached him with so much force.

'They're uncomfortable,' he answered. 'I only wear them when I'm meeting people.'

Amelia was tempted to answer 'and don't I count as a person?' but decided better of it.

'Right,' she muttered to herself, as she smoothed the blankets over his knees and placed cushions behind his back. 'So I drove you all the way to Worcester to get them, but you're not going to use them.'

'Eh?'

'Nothing, Dad.'

Cries erupted from the hallway. Grace was awake. Not that her father had noticed, of course; he had his noise-cancelling equipment already installed.

'Just a minute, Dad,' she said, leaving him to go and retrieve Grace. She was unsure how he'd react when he met her. It was fair to say that he was not particularly enamoured with babies. Or, in fact, children up to the age of forty, she thought.

'Here she is, Dad. I've brought Grace to see you.'

'Ah,' he said, sounding a bit like he'd just chanced upon the answer to a particularly cryptic crossword clue.

Amelia put Grace's car seat down, unclipped her and lifted her up onto her shoulder, before taking a seat at the other end of the sofa from her father. They sat in silence for a few seconds.

'Why are you asleep in the middle of the afternoon, Dad?'

'I thought you were coming this morning. I just sat down for a bit, Amelia, and I had a nap,' he said, sounding every inch the retired headmaster he was. He had always been good at chastising people.

'But you were in the dark.'

'The sun was coming through the window and blinding me,' he said. It was autumn, and the sun's appearances were weak and fleeting, but Amelia decided not to push the point.

'How's that chap of yours?' her father asked. 'Has he been promoted again?'

Amelia knew they were on solid ground now. Her father loved to ask about Piers' job. It was a 'safe' topic, unlikely to provoke emotions, or political views, or anything else that might cause embarrassment. And talking about Piers' job no doubt reminded her father of his own career in education, which had always dominated their family life, in tandem with her mother's illustrious scientific achievements. Ambition had always been a prized personality trait in their family, which had made it so much worse when she had failed to achieve pretty much everything.

'He's doing well, Dad,' she answered. 'He said that one of the deputy heads is leaving. So he's ingratiating himself there this afternoon.'

'Good man,' he said. 'That'll do it.'

Amelia looked at the floor and saw there were several dirty plates by the sofa and a number of stained mugs were lying on their sides by her father's slippers. She was taken aback; he'd been fastidious since her mother's death. Every time she'd come over in the past year, she'd found the house clean and ordered, despite the fact he'd refused any home help. But not today.

'Are you feeling poorly, Dad?'

'No, Amelia. Just old.'

'Okay. Well, hang on. Let me put Grace back down,' – she placed her back in the seat – 'and I'll just tidy up a bit.'

Her father sighed, but she didn't acknowledge it. Instead, she picked up the plates, balanced the mugs on top of them and walked into the kitchen, leaving a sleeping Grace on the floor next to the sofa. She was neither reassured nor worried by the knowledge that she'd be exactly where she'd left her when she got back.

She walked into the small galley kitchen of her parents' small retirement flat, a flat she had tried very hard to persuade them not to buy. It had seemed so pokey and so anonymous after the rambling, Georgian house in West Malvern they'd occupied for the previous four decades, but her mother in particular had insisted. 'It'll be easier for us to keep clean,' she'd said, despite having had a cleaner for most of her life. Amelia was fairly confident that she'd never so much as used a duster in anger.

It had felt to Amelia as if by moving to this flat they were preparing for their imminent demise, and it had depressed her greatly. She'd had dreams of pushing her own child on the rope swing on the old oak tree that her father had strung up for her in the garden of their old house, the house she'd grown up in, but her inability to carry a baby to term had put paid to that. Her parents had moved house a few years ago, just after…

'Are you okay in there, Amelia?' her father shouted from the lounge. He had never liked to leave her unattended in the flat, although she couldn't imagine what he thought she'd unearth if left unsupervised.

'*I'm just washing up, Dad*,' she shouted back, putting the dirty plates in the sink and turning on the hot tap. 'Won't be a sec.'

While the sink filled with water, she checked the contents of the fridge. There wasn't much in the way of food in there; it was mostly old condiments and aged vegetables, well past their best. Then she checked the cupboard where he kept his tins and jars. She counted five tins of stewed beef, a tin of oxtail soup and a jar of pesto. Hardly enough to feed a grown man for a week. Had he stopped going to the shops? She walked back to the sink, quickly scrubbed and rinsed the plates and cups and left them to dry on the drying rack.

'All done,' she said, walking back into the lounge. 'Shall I get you some more food from the—' Amelia broke off. Her father's head had begun to nod forward once more; Grace snored gently on the floor next to him.

Amelia considered offering to stay to help him make dinner, to try to evoke some sort of familial feeling for an hour or two. What point was there, though, she thought. He would never say yes.

'*Okay Dad, we'll leave you to it*,' she said loudly, so as to wake him up.

His head snapped back up.

'Eh? Ah, yes, thanks. I'm feeling a bit tired. Sorry.'

Me too, Dad, she thought, *me too*. 'That's okay. But Dad, have you got enough food? When did you last go to the supermarket?'

'I'm not very hungry,' he mumbled.

'*Dad*.'

'I'm fine. Look darling, I know you have enough on your plate, what with this baby and everything. I'm okay. Don't fuss.'

'Dad, you are not okay. I tell you what, I'll organise a food delivery for you. They'll bring it right to your door. I'll do it when I get home, okay? I'll call you when I've done it.'

'But what if I don't like what they bring?'

Amelia smiled, despite knowing that she was making more work for herself. 'I'll order everything you like Dad, okay? Why don't you fire up your computer and send me an email later with a shopping list?'

'All right,' he replied, still mumbling.

'Great. We'll do that.'

'Okay,' he said. Before taking a deep breath. 'Thank you.'

She leaned down to kiss him on the cheek. He'd never been a hugger; an air kiss was usually her lot, and so it was today.

'Goodbye darling,' he said. 'Thank you so much for coming.'

'That's all right, Dad. I'll be back in a couple of days, okay? And I'll put that order through tonight. Send me your list. Or

I'll order you pilchards and smoked mackerel.' Her father had never, ever liked fish.

'Will do,' he said, managing a smile.

'I love you, Dad,' she said, picking up Grace and walking towards the door. Her father made no response, either because he couldn't hear her, which was likely, or because he didn't know what to say in response, which was also a possibility. He had never been one to show emotion.

As she walked down the hall, her phone rang in her pocket. She put Grace back down and picked it up. It was Piers.

'Hi darling,' she said, mustering up some jollity from the far reaches of her energy reserves.

'Where are you?'

'I'm at Dad's. I told you I was going to see him.'

'Oh. I thought you'd come home first,' he said. 'I came home for lunch, and you weren't here.'

'Well the baby group ran over, and one of the girls from the group suggested we grabbed a sandwich in town, so I joined her. So…'

'Caroline?'

'No, not Caroline. Rachel. Her name is Rachel.'

'Oh,' he said, as if confused. 'Right. Are you coming home now? You've got your session with Julia?'

'I'm done now. We'll be back in a few minutes.'

'Good. I expect Grace will need a feed and a change,' he said. 'She won't know what's hit her, with all this coming and going.'

She's a *baby*, Piers, she thought. She doesn't care where she is.

'See you soon, then. Bye.'

She ended the call, noticing that she had a text message from Marion, the children's guardian, asking whether she could visit in the next few days. Bloody hell, Amelia thought. When will I ever have any peace?

11

November 27th

Michelle

Thirteen weeks until the final hearing

It was late November and the sky above Michelle was packed with dirty-dishcloth clouds. They were depositing a deluge so heavy that it was hard for her to see. Her long blonde ponytail was clinging like a fat slug to her face and neck, and the temperature – not quite cold enough for snow, but chilly enough to make her lack of a proper coat now a major issue – was making her hands numb. Her stomach growled and her muscles throbbed. She couldn't stand here a minute longer, she realised.

The sweeping canopy of the superstore loomed in front of her. Shoppers were running with trolleys for the entrance, as if taking part in a combination of *It's a Knockout* and *Supermarket Sweep*. She thrust her hands into the pockets of her now soaking wet hoodie and began to walk forward, swerving left and right as necessary to avoid the trolleys swarming through the doors.

She clocked the security guard as soon as she walked into the shop. He was a big guy, over six foot, she guessed, wearing a black and white uniform designed to make him look a bit like a police officer. He looked bored. He was standing staring blankly into space, not paying any attention to the screens in front of him on his standing desk. Long may that continue, she thought.

She walked past the escalator and towards the fresh produce aisle, scowling at the few shoppers who stared at her as she passed them. She knew she looked awful, but she hadn't eaten anything not out of a tin or a packet since she'd finished the last of the stuff she'd brought home from the food bank, and so she didn't care. Fruit safely stowed in her pocket, she took a pint of milk from the fridge and a small box of cereal from the shelves before moving towards the cakes, reasoning that, given her limited hiding space, the food she took needed to pack a calorie punch. She stood for a moment eyeing up the options, her eyes drawn to the Battenburg. Her gran had always served slices of it on her best porcelain plate, on a little metal trolley she rolled into the living room in the afternoon, crowned with a large teapot concealed beneath a tea cosy embroidered with roses. Yes, she thought, I'll get some of that. She reached for the packet, looked left and right to check to see if anyone was looking, and hid the pack under her top, alongside the cereal she'd chosen. She now looked a little bit pregnant, an irony she did not allow herself time to dwell on.

It was time to leave. She had no money to buy even a small tube of sweets this time, so she was going to have to walk out of the shop without buying anything, a situation she was not at all comfortable with. As she approached the doors, she saw a middle-aged man with a small boy, and she sped up to join them, hoping it might look like they were together. She reached them just as they were going through the doors, falling into step just behind them.

She felt a blast of warm air as they passed underneath the air-conditioning unit, and then the chill of the outside air as they moved into the atrium. And then she felt a hand on her arm.

'Mam, please come with me,' the man said, his hand increasing its grip. The other man and his son carried on walking, oblivious, and she was left there, marooned amongst a sea of shoppers, several tutting loudly at the obstruction she and the security guard were causing.

Michelle considered her options. This man was big and bulky, but he was unlikely to be fast. If she ran, she might be able to lose him. But his proximity to her was triggering memories which she had worked hard to suppress, and the effect of their surfacing was temporary paralysis. She simply couldn't move.

'Mam,' he said, tugging at her arm. After a deep breath, she allowed herself to be pulled back through the doors to his station, where a female member of the supermarket staff was now waiting. Michelle stood in front of them both, her eyes starting to blur. She was feeling dizzy and everything now seemed to sting.

'Mam, we have reason to believe that you have been shoplifting,' he continued. 'Can you please empty your pockets?'

She found she couldn't move her hands, so the security guard nodded at the female staff member, who moved forward and began to remove, bit by bit, all of the food that she'd stashed away. She hadn't eaten for so long that her hunger had mostly left her, but the sight of her nourishment for the week being taken away was more than she could take. Before she knew it, she began to cry.

'Mam, do you have a receipt for these?' asked the security guard despite her tears, his certainty in the answer clearly reflected in his voice.

Michelle couldn't move her mouth to speak. Her head was swimming and her legs felt like broken matchsticks.

'Miss?' asked the female shop worker. '*Miss? Are you okay*?'

As Michelle's legs buckled and she headed for the grimy lino floor, she replayed in her mind the image of a fist heading for her stomach, of blood leaking, and a chunk of hair floating downwards. And then it went dark.

***

'Hello there? Are you with us?'

Michelle opened her eyes a crack and took in a neon strip light, a tiled false ceiling and a hard bed. Oh great, she thought, a police station. She had a thumping headache, every muscle in her body seemed to be screaming, and despite lying flat, she felt like she'd just stepped off a merry-go-round.

'Hello? I don't know your name because you haven't got any ID on you, so I can't use your name. But if you can hear me, please squeeze my hand.'

I could just lie here, Michelle thought, and pretend to be dead. It would make everything much easier if I was.

'Hello?'

But she's not going to stop asking me, is she, thought Michelle. She's going to just keep going on and on until I answer, so that she can read me my rights, and then sign me up for some stupid community service programme, or some other pointless shit.

'Hi,' she replied, finally, her eyes still closed. What was the point in putting this off? 'I'm… Am I under arrest?'

'No, sweetheart,' replied the other woman, her voice kind and calm. 'You're in hospital.'

Michelle opened both of her eyes and looked at the woman for the first time. She was wearing blue scrubs, and a badge that said 'Adrienne, Staff Nurse'.

'I don't get it,' said Michelle, trying to sit up, but finding that her stomach muscles felt like they'd been severed. She howled in pain.

'Hang on, hang on, don't rush to sit up,' said the nurse, guiding her back down onto the bed. 'Let me press the button on the bed and sit you up a bit.'

The nurse reached for the remote beside the bed and pressed a button, and the top of the bed began to rise.

'Why am I here?' Michelle asked, as her view began to shift.

She could now see that she was in a curtained-off section of a ward of some kind, and there were all sorts of medical noises around her – assorted beeps, cries and the screeching wheels of trolleys.

'Because you've been in the wars,' said the nurse, returning the remote and retrieving a machine from the shelf behind her. 'Can you put your arm out? I'm just going to take your blood pressure.'

Michelle did as she asked. 'No, I mean, I thought I was going to be arrested for shoplifting,' she said.

'The supermarket told the paramedics that they weren't going to press charges,' the nurse said as the cuff began to tighten. 'So you don't have to worry about that. Okay?'

Michelle felt relief flood through her. She would not have to face the police again. Thank fuck for that. But then she thought about the food, the food that was going to keep her going this week, being taken away, and she felt a flood of emotion that she was unable to control.

'Oh, lovey, don't cry,' said the nurse. 'It will be okay.' She handed Michelle a tissue, and removed the cuff from her arm. 'Right, that's fairly normal, maybe a little low,' she said, responding to the read-out on the blood pressure machine. 'Do I take it you've not been eating much? The paramedic told us that you... had some food in your pockets?'

'I haven't had much to eat recently,' Michelle admitted, looking down at her hands, which were very pale, and shaking. 'I feel... a bit funny.'

'Right,' said the nurse. 'I'll take a little prick of blood from you to check your blood sugar, but before that, I'll get some toast and tea on the go for you.' She walked up to the curtain. 'Marie? Could you be so kind as to bring my lady some toast and a cuppa? Thank you.' She returned to her seat next to Michelle.

'So let's go back a bit,' she said. 'Can you tell me your name? We couldn't find any ID on you when you were brought in.'

If I give them my name, Michelle thought, they'll call Lying Laura. And she didn't need that shit today.

'I'm... Helen,' she said. Helen had been the name of her childhood teddy bear.

'Helen?' said the nurse, implicitly asking for her surname while putting a machine over her finger. 'Sharp scratch.'

Michelle winced as she squeezed the tiny hole she'd made to draw blood.

'Just Helen,' she replied, eventually.

'Right then, Helen,' she said, waiting for the machine to give a blood sugar read-out. 'That's a little low,' she said, after a beep. 'As I'd expect. Are you known to social services?'

'No.'

'Okay. Can you tell me how you got these injuries?'

'Which ones?' Michelle asked.

'When you fell in the shop, they took your hoodie off,' she replied. Michelle did not answer. 'We have found bruises all over your stomach,' she said. 'And on your wrists, too.'

Michelle shrugged. 'I fell over in the supermarket, didn't I? I must have got them then.'

'We also found some cigarette burn marks. How did you get them?'

A memory of searing pain struck Michelle hard.

'I'm clumsy. I drop fags sometimes,' she said, stumbling slightly over her words.

'Helen, in my long career as a nurse, I've learned a lot about people, and about people with injuries,' said the nurse. 'And those bruises are of varying ages, I'd say, but they are definitely not from this morning. And I don't think you're telling me everything.'

She wasn't, of course. She had no intention of telling her that a 'mate' of Rob's – to be honest, his dealer – had been hoping to use her as payment the previous evening. She had refused to play ball, of course. No way was she doing that, even with Rob.

She wasn't ready for anything down there yet, she was still too sore.

A woman in a maroon uniform opened the curtain and walked over to Michelle, bearing a mug of steaming tea and a plate of white toast, doused with butter. Michelle nodded her thanks, put the mug on the side table and then fell upon the toast, mainlining it into her mouth and swallowing it so fast, she could taste very little apart from salt. Her stomach made loud, appreciative noises as it absorbed its first food in days. When she'd finished, she put the plate on the side table, and picked up the mug of tea and took a sip. It was the colour of her face powder and very sweet.

'Helen?'

'Hmm?' said Michelle, continuing to sip the tea, which was incredibly hot.

'As I was saying, I don't think you're being entirely honest with me.'

Michelle shrugged.

'Okay,' said the nurse. 'Fine. I'll leave you in peace for a bit. Would you like some more toast?'

Michelle nodded, too shell-shocked to look up or speak.

When the curtain closed, Michelle let out a long breath. She was relieved. Relieved that she had got away with not saying who she was; relieved that she hadn't been arrested; relieved that she had a warm, safe bed here, at least for today. She hadn't always had one, so she knew its value.

She felt incredibly tired. All that adrenaline she'd had circulating earlier was going now, she supposed, and all she had left to run on were the calories in that toast. She closed her eyes once more, pulled up her blanket, and turned over onto her side, wincing as her muscles screamed in protest. Then she curled up in a foetal position and drifted off to sleep.

★★★

'*Michelle*?'

Woozy with sleep, Michelle mumbled something incoherent, and tried to turn over onto her back, before remembering how much it hurt.

'Michelle, it's me.'

I know that voice, Michelle thought. It's...

'Laura.'

Bloody hell. Michelle decided not to bother turning over. She did not want to acknowledge her presence.

'Michelle, I know you can hear me,' said Laura, sitting down on the chair next to the bed. 'Look, I didn't know it was you. The staff just called us saying they had a female patient who needed our help.'

'I don't need any help.'

'I think you do, Michelle. The nurses have told me you have heavy bruising again.'

'*I fell.*'

Michelle clamped her eyes tight again, trying to block out the memories which were threatening to surface; memories of sirens, and shouting, and much, much worse later on.

'There are bruises all over you, Michelle. And they say you have cigarette burns and that you aren't eating.'

'That's the bloody job centre's fault. They sanctioned Rob, didn't they? Bastards.'

'We've been here before, Michelle. Look, shall I ring the woman who lives above you, the one who reported the incident last time? She could probably help clear things up.'

'That bloody bitch needs to get her nose out of our business,' said Michelle.

'Look, here's another cuppa for you. Shall I put it on the table?'

'Whatever,' said Michelle, although in truth, she'd have loved another drink. And something more to eat. She was still starving.

'Michelle, I think you're in pain.'

'No shit, Sherlock. I fell, and it hurts like hell.'

'No, I mean emotional pain, and you know it. You only had a baby less than two months ago, and you've only seen her once.'

'It's for the best.'

'Is it?'

'Yeah.'

'If you leave Rob, I reckon there's a good chance you could convince the judge at the next hearing to let you keep her.'

Michelle laughed, even though her ribs hurt.

'Oh, don't be so fucking *naive*, Laura. I know you're new to this job, but really, I've been "looked after" by social services for a long time now. I know how much you all lie. I have no chance of ever being able to keep… her. I'm damaged goods. I was raised in care. My own family didn't want to keep me, did they? And you've seen me here twice now, each time in a right state… How could I ever look after a child? I couldn't. I'm a fucking disaster.'

'That's not true at all. Your family…'

'I don't want to talk about them,' she said, making the effort to turn around so that she could face Laura. She wriggled up the bed, trying to raise herself up a bit so that her eyeline was a little higher than the social worker's. She needed to feel in control.

'They left me, didn't they? So that's it. Done.'

'I really think we need to meet properly and talk about this…'

Michelle drifted off into her memories to block out Laura's yammering.

She remembered another meeting, one where she had been ushered into the front room of the home, which had been full of toys; toys that she was not allowed to play with normally. She'd been knee deep in Lego and Barbie dolls when she'd heard a distant cry, a very familiar cry, coming from the hall. 'Chelle,' that little voice had called, her voice strangulated. 'Chelle…'

She had tried to open the door to get to her, had tried to yank it open, but the woman she was 'meeting' had held it shut, and tried to distract her with a doll. She had thrashed and thrashed at that door, had kicked and screamed, but it had not worked. She had not managed to get out of the room. She had been too young, too small to fight. When she was finally let out into the hall, her sister had gone. Forever.

'Michelle, I know that social services made some terrible mistakes in the past. But we can help you now,' said Laura. 'Honestly. I joined up so that I could help people like you.'

'*You. Are. Fucking. Dreaming*,' said Michelle, her voice getting louder, more confident with every word. 'You, and the others just like you, have done nothing for me, ever. I have had a parade of women like you take my "case" over the years, and you're all useless, or even worse, actually *evil*. Do you ever wonder why I haven't taken your "help"? Because I know that the end result will always be the same. That's why I want nothing to do with you ever again. In fact, can you just leave now? Just leave me. I've had enough of you.'

'Michelle. Please. I…'

'*No*.'

'We can offer you a place in a hostel…'

'And what then? Because I know that now I'm out of care, I'm pretty easy to wash your hands of. I *have* somewhere to live, anyway. With Rob. There's nothing to worry yourself about.'

'Rob is abusing you, Michelle,' said Laura, getting up to leave.

'That's your opinion,' she said. 'Now *fuck off*.'

Laura seemed to take that calmly. She picked up her coat and put it on.

'You know my number,' she said to Michelle, as she slung her bag over her shoulder and made for the exit. 'I do know that nothing I can do will make up for mistakes in the past. But I do want to help you. And there is a chance, Michelle. If you want to take it.'

* * *

'Let me in, Chelle.'

'*No.*'

Michelle had drawn the bolt across the door when she'd heard him wake up. She'd been allowed out of hospital late the previous night, and she'd slept on the sofa so she didn't have to be near him. She was confident that he wouldn't push the door hard enough to remove it, because he wasn't high. He was a very different man when he was sober.

'Let me in. Come on. We need to talk. I'm sorry...'

'I know you are.'

The problem was, he was always sorry.

Michelle stood at the bathroom sink and stared at herself in the mirror. Her face looked about as normal as it ever did – she had a zit coming on her chin, and her skin looked slightly grey. It was a different story, however, when she lifted up her top. She stood back and inspected her reflection. There were several red marks across her stomach. Experience told her they would turn grey later – the colour of an angry sky – followed by shades of green and then finally, yellow.

'Chelle, I'm serious. I *am* sorry.' There was a pause, during which Michelle imagined him taking a deep breath and rubbing his eyes. 'I was wasted, wasn't I? I wasn't thinking straight. That stuff he brought round was strong.'

Rob's addiction was real and serious, she knew that. It was like a resident monster in his brain. He'd gone several days without a fix, and frankly when he was in that state, he'd have committed murder for the drugs he wanted.

'And I think what with the baby being taken... I'm not copin' very well with it. Not as well as I thought I would. I just needed somethin'. I know that's not an excuse...'

His acknowledgement of Grace's existence made Michelle feel like she was being hit in the stomach all over again. She let go of her top and leaned forward, bracing herself on the sink. When she closed her eyes, she could see her baby's face clearly.

She could remember her thick eyelashes, her dark velvet hair, her soft warm body. She was so desperate for that image to be real that her body actually began to ache, well away from where his fists had impacted only a couple of nights ago.

Giving Grace away was the right thing to do, she thought. That poor child deserves far more than me. Far more than *this*.

'You were going to buy drugs with my body, Rob. Give me away like a fucking prostitute!'

Michelle remembered the man lunging at her, the foul stench of tobacco as he got close enough for her to smell his breath. She had fought back, pushed him away, kicked him where it'd hurt. The memory of it made her hackles rise. Rob *knew* that he was the only man she trusted. And he'd broken that trust.

'I was... I were... not thinkin'. Like I said. I'm sorry, Chelle. So sorry.'

Michelle let go of the sink and pulled herself up, tightening her ponytail as she did so. She stared at herself in the mirror. Maybe she deserved all of this, she thought. Every punch he landed on her, every cigarette burn. Feeling that pain felt like recompense for letting both her Graces go.

'Chelle? Chelle?' said Rob through the door. 'Please say somethin'.'

Michelle looked in the mirror and saw how she really was. She saw someone who'd failed at life before they'd even really started. She'd failed to keep her sister safe; she'd failed to get a proper education; she'd failed to get a job; she'd failed to provide a home life that a child would be not just safe, but happy in. She was hardly better than her own mother, and that thought made her want to vomit.

Michelle moved over to the toilet and lifted up the seat. She stood over it, fighting nausea. And then she looked up, and she knew what she needed to do.

***

'Michelle, love? Michelle?'

Someone, somewhere, was calling her name. But she had no idea who it was.

'*Michelle*?'

There were footsteps walking towards her. But where was she? And why was she… still here?

'*Oh! Oh no!* Michelle, Michelle, it's Mr Chaudhury. Your door was open. Can you hear me?'

Michelle tried to speak, but only managed a moan.

'Okay, okay. I'll call an ambulance, okay?' She heard a rustling, followed by tapping on a keypad.

'Hello? Ambulance please… Yes, she is breathing, although very fast… She's sort of… blue… She's not waking… Please come quickly… Yes, we're in the flats behind my store in the Elgar Estate, Chaudhury's, do you know it? The door of the flat is open. Okay?'

She felt someone sit down on the floor next to her and take hold of her hand.

'Michelle, I'm here, okay? I won't leave you until they come.'

It was too much effort to focus on waking up, so Michelle allowed herself to sink back down into her dreams. In them, she was playing with a little girl, a toddler. They both had Barbie dolls, and they were pretending to be doctors, taking turns to wrap toilet paper around their limbs, in place of bandages. The little girl's dark brown hair was in bunches, and the bottom of each bunch ended in ringlets. Michelle leaned forward to feel one of the curls, to wrap it around her fingers and feel it spring back as she did so.

'Michelle? Hello. My name's Mike, I'm a paramedic. What have you taken, Michelle?'

They *took* her, she wanted to say. *They took her from me.*

'She looks a funny colour,' said Mr Chaudhury.

Michelle felt a blood pressure cuff being wrapped around her arm and it began to tighten.

'Are you her partner?' the paramedic asked.

'Oh, no,' said Mr Chaudhury. 'I am a local shopkeeper. I was just walking past on my way to work, you know, and I saw the door was open. So I came in, and... found her... Like this. The bathroom door was off its hinges.'

'Ah, I see,' said the paramedic, before ripping off the cuff. 'Her blood pressure is very high. Michelle, we're going to put you on a stretcher and take you into hospital, okay?'

Michelle tried to protest but only managed a laboured breath and a cough. She felt tugging and pulling as her body made the transition from the bathroom floor to something metallic. Then there was loud screeching, a mechanical whine and a series of clunks.

'I'll leave you with them now, Michelle, okay? But I'll check up on you later,' said Mr Chaudhury.

Then there was the slam of a door and an engine started. Michelle prepared to leave all the noise behind once more, and head back into her...

'*Stay awake, Michelle*,' said the paramedic. 'Stay awake. Can you open your eyes?'

Michelle opened her eyes a crack and was dazzled by bright neon light. She shut them immediately. Then she tried to take a breath and panicked when her lungs seemed to fail her.

'Your body is struggling a bit, Michelle. Hang on, here's some oxygen...'

A mask was placed on her face, and she felt a cold breeze on her lips. She tried to breathe again, and it felt a little easier.

'Can you speak, Michelle?'

Her mouth tasted of metal, or maybe ash, she thought. But this was what she deserved, wasn't it? This was what she had wanted. And it might still work, if she kept quiet.

'If you can speak, could you tell me what you've taken? I need to tell the doctors.'

She would not tell them. And then she might still be allowed to die.

'Michelle, I really do need to know. You might have caused serious damage to your organs.'

Good, she thought. *Good*. There was silence then, and she just had the ambulance sirens and the hum of the engine to entertain her. She wondered how long it would take to reach oblivion. Soon, she hoped. She conjured up the memory again – back to that room with the Barbie dolls. She released the long, brown curly bunches and cupped the girl's chin in her hands, before sweeping her hands over her face, remembering every ridge and every curve.

'Okay, Michelle, we're here. There'll be a bit of noise while we lower you out of the ambulance, okay?'

Michelle heard a rustle, a hum and a click and then she felt herself being propelled along a bumpy surface. She could hear their breathing beginning to labour as they went up an incline, and then the distant hum of conversation. Then a conversation started right next to her.

'Hi, this is Michelle. We don't know her surname. We think she's in her late teens or early twenties, although no exact age as yet. A neighbour found her unconscious about half an hour ago. We don't know how long she'd been like that. We suspect a drug overdose, but she won't tell us what, even though she seems to be conscious. She's tachycardic, her blood pressure is one-sixty over a hundred, she's having trouble breathing, she's vomited and she's lost bladder control.'

'Great, thank you. Okay everyone, let's treat this as a cocaine overdose. Let's do an ECG and bloods, check her urine, and give her a benzodiazepine IV. *Michelle, I'm James*, I'm one of the doctors here. We are giving you a sedative to help you go to sleep, okay?'

Whatever, Michelle thought. It's too late, anyway. Give me an extra dose for good measure, if you like.

She felt them stab her arm with a needle and shortly afterwards, she felt a wave of calm come over her. It was welcome. It swept her backwards, back into that room, where the sunlight was flooding in, lighting up her companion's face. She reached forward now and took her hand.

'Chelle!' she said, in a voice full of joy. 'Chelle! I love you.'

I love you too, she thought. I love you so much. But I let you go.

12

December 3rd

Amelia

Twelve weeks before the final hearing

'Why didn't you pack them in the changing bag? Am I going to have to unload the whole bloody car?'

Amelia winced. They were in the car park of Exeter services and Piers was absolutely fuming. He was pulling bag after bag out of the boot of their Volvo Estate, hurling them onto the frozen tarmac by Amelia's feet. Wrapped Christmas presents were tumbling out of supermarket shopping bags, showering glitter, and she had just spotted a pair of her knickers and her toothbrush by one of the tyres. People were walking past, staring.

She had dressed Grace just after dawn that morning. She was wearing a beautiful knitted dress and tights combo, bought by her mother-in-law. Unfortunately, it was now stained the colour of mustard yellow, thanks to a particularly spectacular explosion of poo, which had seeped through the tights and transferred a knitted pattern, painted in faeces, to her car seat.

'I thought she'd manage the journey without needing a change of clothes,' she said. The whole situation was her fault entirely. She should have foreseen that she'd need to change her, but she'd never done a journey this long with Grace before. She'd simply had no idea what to expect.

Grace was now sleeping in her arms, blissfully unaware that she was the cause of so much fuss. Amelia's hands were also now covered in poo and she urgently needed to take Grace inside to get her changed and tidied up, but she couldn't do that until they'd located a change of clothes for her. And those clothes were in a small red holdall, one of the first bags Piers had loaded into the car that morning.

They had been on the road for four hours already. It should have taken them two and a half hours, but a combination of heavy traffic and stopping to feed Grace had delayed them considerably. Piers liked to set off early for trips down to see his mother, ideally before 6 a.m., but they'd discovered it was practically impossible to do anything swiftly with a baby in tow. And so here they were, at nearly midday, surrounded by swarms of harassed motorists, only halfway through their journey down to Falmouth. It was, she acknowledged, a recipe for disaster. They were both knackered and in a foul mood.

The thing was, they were only going for a night. That was partly due to Piers' school commitments and partly due to their twice-weekly sessions at the contact centre, which they still had to attend, even though Grace's birth father had never turned up, and her birth mother seemed to have stopped attending. Gloria had told them that they might be reduced to once a week in January if this continued, and Amelia prayed that it did. It meant they couldn't go away over Christmas, and the sessions swallowed up two whole mornings each week.

The sessions were also a regular reminder, if in fact she needed one (which she definitely didn't) that Grace was not yet theirs. This reality gnawed at her most of the time but taking her to the centre really rammed it home. She thought, far too often, about the court hearing that they both knew was looming.

Piers, on the other hand, didn't seem at all bothered about

it. She admired his confidence. He pointed out that the birth parents' inability to turn up to contact sessions would count against them in court, *if* they decided to contest the adoption, which they had shown no signs of doing so far. And that was true, she thought. It was definitely a point in their favour. He also said he'd found the first visit of the guardian, Marion, a few weeks previously, reassuring. He believed they'd made a great impression and was convinced that no court in the land could decide Grace was better off anywhere other than with them. Amelia wanted to believe him, but Marion's first, brief visit had passed in a blur of exhaustion and fear for her, and she often woke up at night now – even when Grace was asleep – torturing herself about how limp and defeated she must have appeared during that meeting. Anyhow, she thought, Marion was due to visit again soon, and this meant that she could make amends. This time, she needed to be sorted and settled. She needed to ensure that the report she would send to the court painted them in the best possible light.

Amelia now realised that she had vastly underestimated how fostering to adopt would make her feel. It had seemed such a no-brainer when they'd first discussed it. She had focused so much on its ability to deliver a new-born to them, a child without an abusive past, that she'd batted away any niggling concerns about whether that baby would eventually become theirs. Now, however, the uncertainty of it all was eating away at her. She had been certain about things in the past that had turned out to be as solid as shifting sands. She trusted nothing, and no one, not even herself, now. She needed certainty to keep her steady.

'Ah, *finally*,' said Piers, pulling the red bag out of the boot, and holding it out to Amelia. 'What do you need from here?'

Amelia took a deep breath, heading off a small voice inside her head which wanted to ask him what *he* needed from the bag.

'I think I packed a blue and white striped knitted dress, and some navy blue tights,' she said. Piers nodded before crouching down and beginning to search, Amelia swallowing hard as he messed up her carefully folded, logically arranged packing. *Jesus* she was tired, she thought. She always got ratty when she was tired. She needed to keep it in, though, otherwise this day would get even more stressful than it already was.

'These?' he said, holding up the two items.

'Yes,' she said, walking over to take them from him, before squatting down to pick up the changing bag. 'I'll just be a few minutes,' she said, turning towards the entrance to the services.

'Fine, yes,' Piers replied, his head already in the boot. 'It'll take me at least as long to sort out the car, anyway.'

The services was absolutely packed and it smelled of coffee, bacon sandwiches and sweat. As Amelia walked to the toilets she passed long, snaking queues for takeaway food outlets, all offering dubiously priced, frankly disgusting-sounding Christmas 'specials' like minced pie lattes and turkey and stuffing pasta bakes.

Christmas was not a time of year Amelia liked. It seemed to her to be a celebration of all that was wrong with the world – consumerism; cheap, unnecessary tat; and a whole load of hollow emotional promises and inevitable let-downs. A bit like this ludicrous 48-hour whirlwind trip to see Catherine, her mother-in-law. Piers had styled it as a pre-Christmas 'break' for them both when he'd told her he'd agreed to it, but they both knew that this visit was actually just about duty.

Catherine lived alone in a small, nineteenth-century terraced house in Falmouth with a view of the harbour. It had two small rooms on each floor, a postage-stamp sized garden up a steep flight of steps and it was damp in the winter and cold in the summer. Her ex-husband, a wealthy banker named Philip, had left her when Piers had been at prep school, and while he'd continued to pay for his son's education – Piers had been sent to boarding school at eleven – he had provided little for his wife.

Piers' father had gone on to remarry, produce two daughters who Piers had never got to know, and died twenty years later, loudly and extravagantly, during a day out at the races. The entirety of his estate had been left to his second wife.

Coming from a generation of women largely expected to give up any idea of a career after marriage, Catherine had found herself divorced aged thirty-three, without useful skills or qualifications and very little confidence. Thus, she had decided to move down to Cornwall to be near her parents, who'd owned a small hotel on the seafront, which Catherine had helped them to run. The hotel had limped along for a couple of decades, buoyed by nostalgic coach tours and amateur magic shows, before finally closing in the 1990s, laden with debt. It was now flats. Catherine's parents had bought the house she now lived in with the very small sum they'd got left over after the sale, and she remained there now, long after their deaths.

Amelia found her mother-in-law's home incredibly depressing, but she had grown to love Falmouth, with its bustling main street, busy harbour and diverse population of arty students from Falmouth University. She loved spotting them walking by, their hair coloured pink or jet black or blue, with multiple piercings in their noses, eyes and God knows where else, wearing tiny crop tops or enormous kaftans in all the colours of the rainbow. They reminded her of herself, but in a previous life that she could barely believe had existed. She looked down now at the outfit she was wearing – high-waisted blue jeans and a blue polo neck jumper – and realised that she no longer recognised her younger self.

When she reached the baby changing room, she was relieved to find it unoccupied. She pulled the door open and shut it behind her, breathing through her mouth to avoid smelling the delightful cocktail of baby poo and wee which was emanating from a bank of overfilled nappy bins in the corner.

She pulled the portable changing mat out of the bag, threw

it over the padded mat that was provided – which she was relieved to see looked at least superficially clean – and then laid Grace down on it. Her eyes began to open as she did so, and she started directly at Amelia, who had begun pulling off her dirty clothes and placing them, one by one, in tied nappy sacks. Distracted momentarily by the challenge of removing her tiny dress without redistributing poo all over her hair, it took her a while to notice that Grace was smiling. They'd had a few false alarms over the past few weeks, when she'd grimaced with wind, but this seemed like the real thing. She was beaming at Amelia, with her eyes as well as her mouth.

Amelia was stunned and felt a surge of love so strong that it felt like a physical embrace. She stopped what she was doing, leaned down and kissed Grace on the nose. Grace smiled, so Amelia did it again. And again. And then she kissed her stomach and blew a raspberry. Grace's little legs kicked out as she did so, her arms flapping wildly. It felt to Amelia as if they were the only two people in the world. This, she thought: this is what motherhood is. This is what makes everything worthwhile.

She finished cleaning her up, snapped and buttoned her new outfit into place, and then put everything else back in the bag. There was a small sink in the corner of the room, so she held Grace over her shoulder as she washed and dried her hands.

She was about to leave when a thought occurred to her. She got out her phone.

She smiled at me! The most gorgeous thing. I don't even feel that tired anymore! she wrote, sending the message to Rachel.

Rachel had been a pillar of strength for her in the past few weeks. She had been on the end of the phone at all times to answer queries about odd rashes, feeding issues and sleeping queries, and Amelia had relished her private chats with her in the coffee shop after baby group. She was so honest, so straightforward and so fun, and she had made all of her worries, fears and inadequacies feel normal.

As Amelia pulled the door open, her phone beeped. She slung the bag over her shoulder, kept a grip on Grace, and pulled her phone out of her pocket.

Awesome! It begins. Enjoy.

She felt a warm glow and held Grace, who had fallen back to sleep against her shoulder, more tightly. She returned to the car with a spring in her step.

'Piers, guess what?' she said, approaching the car. She was desperate to share her joy. Piers was standing against the car boot staring at a piece of paper.

'What?' he snapped, folding the paper up and putting it in his back pocket, his face one giant scowl. It must be one of the letters she'd seen on the dresser that morning, placed there by Matron. School related, maybe? He'd tell her what it was about in time. It didn't seem like good news, anyway.

'Nothing,' she said. 'Nothing to worry yourself about.' She opened the passenger door and strapped Amelia into the car seat, which Piers had given a perfunctory clean with baby wipes, tell-tale traces of yellow still visible in the corners. But it would have to do, Amelia thought. They needed to get going. Piers started the car as soon as she had got in the passenger seat.

'Right,' he said. 'Let's finally get going. Should be there for a late lunch. I texted Mum. She wasn't too upset that we're delayed, which is good. Onwards.'

'Amelia, dear,' said Catherine, craning her leathery neck so that Amelia could lean down to kiss her cheek. 'How lovely to see you. And this…' she said, her eyes darting towards the car seat Amelia was holding, '… must be Grace?'

Amelia watched her take in Grace's sleeping form and saw that her eyes had begun to water. 'How wonderful. Just wonderful. Won't you come in?'

Amelia followed her down the short stone path to her front

door and into her living room. 'Come and sit down over here, both of you. I'll make tea.'

There was a small artificial Christmas tree in the corner of the room, next to the fireplace. It had been decorated with a string of multi-coloured lights and an assortment of garish plastic baubles which Amelia guessed must date back to the 1980s. On the mantelpiece were a few Christmas cards, showing scenes of snowy churches, choirboys in ruffles and Mary, Joseph and Jesus beneath a star. Amelia knew that churchgoing was an important part of Catherine's life. She was glad that her mother-in-law had that sense of community around her, even if she didn't share her religious belief. She was keenly aware that Catherine had scant communication from her busy, work-addicted son.

'How've you been, then, Mum?' said Piers, sitting down on one of Catherine's battered cream sofas, which were topped with lace antimacassars. 'Been busy?'

'Oh, you know, this and that,' said Catherine, speaking from her small galley kitchen, which was through an arched doorway off the lounge. 'Doing the flowers. Choir practice. Going for walks. And I help Jim down the way, you know. He's ninety. He needs lifts to the hospital sometimes.'

'Sounds like you have lots going on then,' said Piers.

It was incredibly clear to Amelia that the very opposite was true. They had last seen Catherine in the summer. They'd rented a large seafront apartment in Padstow, which was a considerable drive from Falmouth. It had been Piers' choice; a treat, he had said, for them both, after everything they'd been through. They'd only been to visit Catherine a couple of times on that trip. Amelia still felt guilty about it. Piers was Catherine's only son. How must she feel, knowing that he had come all of that way for a holiday, but not really been bothered enough to drive a tiny bit further a bit more often to see more of her?

'Don't worry about the tea, Catherine, come and have a

cuddle of Grace,' she said, calling out in the direction of the kitchen.

'Hang on, just a minute, and I'll be with you.'

Amelia felt embarrassed, just sitting there waiting, so she got up and went into the kitchen.

'Look, let me help you,' she said to her mother-in-law. 'Shall I get a tray?'

'Oh yes, thank you dear. It's behind the toaster.'

Amelia retrieved a plastic tray decorated with poppies and put it down next to the kettle. Then she helped Catherine assemble cups, saucers, milk and sugar, and found her a tea cosy for the pot she had just made. Then she put it all on the tray and carried it back into the lounge, Catherine following behind her. As she put the tray down on a side table, she saw that Piers was now cradling Grace.

'Now, let me see her more closely,' said Catherine, sitting down next to her son and leaning over Grace. Amelia could see that she was soaking up every little detail with her eyes, while her hands assessed her tiny feet, her striped dress, and her wisps of brown hair.

'She's... beautiful,' said Catherine, her voice reedy.

'Isn't she,' said Piers. 'She's going to be a stunner.'

'May I hold her?' Catherine said, looking over at Amelia and not at Piers. Amelia smiled.

'Of course! Just make sure that you support her head.'

'Ah yes, it was a long time ago, but I remember,' she said. 'You never forget that sort of thing.'

Piers handed over Grace to his mother.

'How old is she now?' asked Catherine.

'Eight weeks,' replied Amelia.

'And how does she sleep?'

'She... doesn't,' replied Amelia, trying to make light of it. 'She is a *stinker*. She sleeps for maybe an hour or so at a time.'

'Oh, that's so hard,' said Catherine. 'You can cope with

almost anything when you've had a good sleep. But when you're tired… that's another thing entirely.'

Amelia nodded in agreement. She leaned over and began to pour three cups of tea, dashing milk in beforehand, as she knew Catherine expected her to do. Catherine had Irish roots, and tea was practically ceremonial in her household.

'So when is the court case? The one where you get given her, properly, I mean?' she asked Amelia.

'Oh, that's three months away, probably,' said Piers. 'But it might be earlier. The birth parents aren't turning up to the contact sessions. If they don't contest any of it – and it seems to me that they won't – it should all be just a formality. The social workers have done their reports now, I think. They could schedule it for a couple of months' time.'

'I see,' said Catherine. 'And that would be a real relief for you, wouldn't it?' she said, looking over at Amelia, who thought, not for the first time, that her mother-in-law might be psychic.

'Oh, we're not worried,' said Piers, idly stroking Grace's head. 'We know we're a good, solid prospect: loving parents in a stable relationship with a stable income and a nice home. I'm sure the judge will see that.'

'Yes, of course,' said Catherine, pausing to sip her tea. 'Is she a good feeder?'

'Yes,' said Amelia, grateful for the change of subject. Piers' confidence felt to her like tempting fate. 'She guzzles. Actually, she's due a feed about now. We last fed her in Exeter. Can I use your microwave to sterilise a bottle?'

'Of course,' said Catherine, getting up. 'Come this way. Hopefully I have everything you need.'

Amelia got up and followed, leaving Piers cradling Grace. He was making cooing noises, rubbing noses with her. Amelia carried the changing bag into the kitchen, which she'd now become accustomed to packing in her sleep. It contained: three nappies, a portable changing mat, a pack of nappy sacks, nappy rash cream, baby wipes, spare dummies, a muslin, pre-portioned formula powder, a microwave steriliser and two milk bottles, with teats.

She pulled the steriliser, the bottles and the teats out of the bag, and walked over to the kettle to add a small amount of water to the base of the steriliser. Catherine watched her with interest. 'It's all changed so much since my day,' she said. 'We just boiled bottles in a saucepan. And I think I gave Piers cow's milk from young. I always struggled with breastfeeding.'

Amelia suddenly felt her nipples twinge; muscle memory that refused to die. She needed to keep talking about something else to prevent herself going down that particular rabbit hole.

'Right,' said Amelia, putting the bottles in the steriliser and placing it in the microwave. 'This needs four minutes. Can you set it going for me?'

'Of course,' said Catherine. 'You just turn this dial and press...'

They were interrupted by ear-piercing screams from the lounge. Grace was bawling her eyes out.

'Heavens!' said Catherine. 'She's got a pair of lungs on her.'

'Ha, yes,' said Amelia. 'That's the noise that wakes me up several times a night. And yet Piers seems to sleep through it.'

'He's always been a solid sleeper,' said Catherine, staring at the steriliser revolving inside of the microwave. 'I suppose that might be because of boarding school. I think he had to sleep through lots of noise every night, sharing a room with eight other boys.'

Amelia thought of the boys who lived in their boarding house. The dorms were smaller now, with no more than three in each, but even then, she wondered what it must be like to have so little privacy from so young. She had gone to the local state school – being a girl, she hadn't been eligible for a place at the college and her parents couldn't afford the fees at the nearest private girls' school, anyway – and she was glad. Her parents had not been overly affectionate, or particularly empathetic, come to that, but at least they had given her a room of her own to return to each night.

That room, the smallest in the house and sandwiched up against the hill that had risen behind their large Victorian villa, had been a merciful escape from the world. She had covered the walls with pictures cut out from fashion magazines and had bought an old easel from a second-hand shop. She had spent most of her free time painting and drawing on it, creating new landscapes, new rooms, new worlds in which she was entirely comfortable, and never ignored, or disappointing.

The microwave pinged and Catherine held the door open for Amelia, who was distracted by the loud cries still emanating from the lounge. She took the steriliser out of the microwave, placed it on the side and walked back through to check on Grace.

Piers was pacing backwards and forwards across the small lounge, bouncing Grace up and down with vigour. Her face was red, and so was his; it was clear from his expression that her screams were now inflicting something akin to pain.

'She just won't stop,' he snapped. 'Whatever I do. She just *won't*.'

'She'll be hungry,' said Catherine, suddenly surging past Amelia and lifting Grace out of her son's arms. 'We've got the bottle here, I'll feed her. Why don't you go for a walk, darling?' she said, looking at a somewhat shell-shocked Piers. 'Clear your head after the long drive? Get us fish and chips for dinner?'

Piers, whose face was still red and etched with pain, took a step towards the door.

'That might be good, yes,' he said, mumbling a little. 'I'll be back… in a bit.'

He walked towards the door, took his coat from the hook, put it on and closed the door swiftly behind him, with a click.

Then there was silence for the first time in about ten minutes.

Amelia looked across at the sofa where her mother-in-law was now sitting, angling a bottle of warm milk into Grace's grateful mouth. They were the picture of serenity. It was an extraordinary contrast with what had gone on just minutes before and it took Amelia a while to adjust.

'Sit down, won't you, Amelia?' said Catherine, noting Amelia's discomfort. 'Take a break. I know this stage is tough.'

Amelia sat down at the other end of the sofa. She was mesmerised by the ease with which Catherine was taking care of Grace. It was like they had always known each other.

'I blame myself,' said Catherine.

Amelia's head snapped up. 'What do you mean?' she asked.

'About Piers. His temper. I blame myself.'

Amelia was blindsided. She had never discussed Piers with his mother. It had never occurred to her that Piers had ever been angry with anyone but herself. Catherine had always seemed so proud of him.

'I...'

'When his father left us, you see, I didn't fight hard enough to keep control of him, the care of him. I didn't try hard enough to keep him at school near me, and I didn't explain things that had happened to him properly. And then he got angry, so very, very angry about it all... And I think he has never stopped being angry since,' she said.

Amelia's first instinct was to defend her husband – he was usually thoughtful, gentlemanly, generous. And after all, the drive down had been hellish for them both. But she examined her mother-in-law carefully. Although Catherine's words were profound, her face was calm, as if she had come to terms with what she was saying years ago. She seemed to be speaking the truth, or at least, her version of it, anyway.

'I had hoped that after he and Lesley... well... I had hoped he had recovered a bit. After meeting you.'

For the second time in recent weeks, the spectre of Lesley

loomed large for Amelia. Piers had always shut down all lines of enquiry, but now, she wanted answers. She seized the chance.

'Were you close to him? Sebastian, I mean?' she asked Catherine.

'Oh yes. I looked after him when he was tiny. I even babysat him for weekends. He was a lovely little chap.'

Amelia looked closely at Catherine and could see that her eyes were threatening tears.

'I'm so sorry, Catherine,' she said.

'Not your fault at all,' she replied. 'In any way.'

They sat in silence, the only sounds Grace's rhythmic drinking and the distant calls of seagulls.

'Do you keep in touch with Lesley?' Amelia asked, emboldened by Catherine's shocking admission.

'Only via email, and Christmas cards,' Catherine replied, quickly.

'But you must miss…'

'Yes, I miss Sebby, yes,' replied Catherine. 'Very much. But Piers was so angry after he and Lesley parted, and he would see me still seeing him as a betrayal. And I have let him down enough, I think.'

Amelia was stunned. She had never heard anyone describe Piers as anything other than charismatic; capable; clever; an excellent leader. He didn't seem the sort of man who'd ever been let down.

'You haven't let him down,' said Amelia, automatically. 'You have been a wonderful mother to him…'

'I *have*. I let his father take him and put him in that awful school, and most of all, I failed to stop his father leaving and taking all of the money,' she said. 'And Piers has never forgiven me for that. Although he now says he liked the school, in the end.'

Amelia struggled to decide how to respond.

'… but he has done so well…' she said.

'Yes, he has. And he met you. And I'm delighted about that,' said Catherine. 'And now we have little Grace. Which is wonderful,' she said, beaming as she looked down at her.

Amelia felt a cloud come over her. 'Yes, she's amazing,' she said, 'but has Piers explained – she isn't officially ours yet? At the moment, we are just her foster parents. There has to be a court hearing, before they grant the adoption.'

'… but Piers says that's just a formality?'

'We hope so, yes. It should be. But I just feel… so anxious…' Before she knew it, Amelia was crying. She tried not to cry in front of Piers, because it upset him, but she had always felt a connection with Catherine, and so this time, she let them flow.

'After… losing Leila…' she continued. 'I just can't… believe… that anything will ever be right again.'

Catherine shuffled further up the sofa, trying not to disturb Grace as she did so, and put her hand on Amelia's.

'What happened to Leila wasn't your fault, Amelia,' she said. 'And all of this bad luck you've had since, trying to get pregnant, that's not your fault either.'

Amelia gulped as a particularly large shudder of tears and rage ripped through her, then coughed several times to try to clear her throat. She could barely see.

'Oh, lovely girl,' said Catherine, patting her arm. 'You've been through so much. Look, take Grace. She needs her mummy.'

Catherine shifted the still feeding Grace into her lap, and Amelia stared down into her crystal-clear blue eyes and immediately felt calmer. She smiled at Grace and the baby's eyes brightened, as if replying to her.

'I am quite sure that the court case will be cut and dried, and you'll be her parents officially very soon,' Catherine continued. 'But in the meantime, just try to enjoy the experience. If you can, I mean. I know it's exhausting. It was years ago for me, and I still remember.'

Amelia smiled through her tears, feeling the same relief she felt at the mums' meeting in the hall. Knowing that her experience was shared reduced her pain.

'She won't sleep...' she said.

'Ah. One of those,' said Catherine. 'Piers was similar. I felt like he was torturing me.'

'It does feel a bit like that, yes,' said Amelia, with a laugh. It felt good to laugh, she realised. She didn't do it anywhere near often enough.

'Look,' said Catherine. 'When she's finished that bottle, why don't you pop upstairs for a nap? You must be exhausted, particularly after the journey. I'll look after Grace.'

'Really?' said Amelia. No one had offered to do this so far and she had felt almost imprisoned by Grace's constant presence and constant needs, and guilty about having those feelings, too. But the warmth her mother-in-law exuded was also drying her tears. She wondered then what her own mother would say, if she was still alive. Would she be offering to look after Grace? Or would she have opted for a more worthy project in retirement, as she had done throughout her working life?

'Yes, of course,' Catherine replied. 'Piers will be back soon, anyway. Go on. *Go*. Grab some sleep.'

Amelia didn't ask twice. Grace had reached the end of her milk, so she handed her over to Catherine, who began to rub her back to burp her. Then she stood up, smiled her thanks and headed up the stairs towards Catherine's spare bedroom.

She pushed the door open, noting the white bed linen, the pale blue anaglypta on the walls and the slender, tall bedside lamps with shades embroidered with cornflowers, before collapsing into the bed, closing her eyes and sinking into welcome oblivion.

'Blimey, where are all of these people staying?' said Piers, as he tried to weave Grace's buggy through a particularly dense crowd of shoppers on Church Street. 'I didn't think there were this many houses in Falmouth.'

It was a Saturday afternoon three weeks before Christmas and Amelia wasn't even slightly surprised that it was busy, but she nodded and smiled in agreement with him, anyway. She felt rejuvenated by her nap and she was determined not to let anything ruin their trip to Cornwall, which so far had been much more enjoyable than she had anticipated.

It was 4.30 p.m. and already dark. Small, sharp jabs of hail were spitting from the sky, making the multi-coloured lights strung across the street judder. Amelia folded her arms across her chest and pulled her woollen hat further down over her ears to try to keep out the cold.

They were walking into the town centre to buy Catherine's Christmas present. Amelia had been so absorbed by looking after Grace that she'd had very little time to think about buying presents for anyone this year, let alone a mother-in-law they hardly ever saw. She felt incredibly guilty.

Piers pointed the buggy in the direction of a shop selling an eclectic mix of handmade jewellery, Cornish fudge and wistful original paintings of beaches and lighthouses. Amelia waited for a slow train of shoppers to pass in front of her before joining them.

A little bell rang above the door as they entered the store, which was a merciful oasis of calm and warmth. They were the only customers and the assistant beside the till appeared glad to see them.

'Can I help you?' she asked. 'Are you looking for anything in particular?'

'We're looking for a present for my mother,' said Piers. 'Maybe jewellery?'

The assistant nodded and directed Piers to a glass case on the left of the shop. Amelia was about to join him when she spotted an eye-catching painting on the wall. It was of Pendennis Point, the headland just outside the town. St Anthony's Lighthouse and the village of St Mawes were in the background, but the main focus of the painting was a seagull, its wings spread wide, soaring above the sea. The style was striking and familiar.

'Who painted this?' she asked the shop assistant.

'Oh, that's by one of our resident artists,' replied the woman. 'I mean, she lives in Falmouth. But she sells art all around the world. That picture is here as a favour. She doesn't usually sell her stuff in little shops, you see, but she's friends with our owner. Her name's Sophie. Sophie Slade. Do you know her work?'

Sophie. Yes, Amelia knew Sophie. And her work.

Amelia had been working night and day at art college in London in preparation for a display of her year's best work in a local gallery. The event had been a jovial, drunken affair. She'd attended wearing a charity-shop find she'd fallen in love with – a puffed shoulder, silk knee-length dress in bright yellow – and she had felt, just for that evening, as if she had been floating. The public were finally seeing her work and she had felt exhilarated.

But that feeling had not lasted long. That evening, long after dark, she'd felt her phone vibrate in her pocket, and she'd opened it up and found a link to a review of the display in the *Evening Standard*. She hadn't even known that a reporter had been there.

As she clicked the link and began to read it, her stomach sank to the floor.

'*Amelia's work*,' it read, '*is brutal. Not in the modernist sense, but in its lack of refinement. It stood out for all of the wrong reasons. It is vulgar, slapdash and verging on obscene.*'

Amelia had run to the toilets and vomited copiously. Then she had taken the bus back to her student halls, stopping off at a local off-licence just around the corner and buying a large bottle of vodka. Then she'd drunk it until she'd passed out.

She'd repeated this process daily for weeks, spending her days comatose in her dingy, stale room, rather than in the art rooms finishing her portfolio, and her nights unconscious, rather than in the pub with friends.

Discovering several months later that the review had been written by a critic who Sophie – the very glamorous Sophie Slade, her closest rival in their year – had been sleeping with at the time, wasn't enough to rescue her. She had been far, far too destroyed by then. She had almost dissolved and ceased existing.

Why let one dreadful review ruin a promising career? Amelia had been asked that by one of her tutors a few weeks afterwards, when she'd told them she wanted to drop out of the course.

Amelia had given that question a lot of thought in the years since. The thing was, she now realised, that that review had simply been the tipping point for a mental health crisis that had been brewing for years. It hadn't been about just one bad review. No, it was every single negative thing that anyone had ever said about her: the kid at primary school who'd laughed at her sticky-out ears; the dance examiner who'd commented on her lack of rhythm; the recruiter at the cinema who'd said she wasn't outgoing enough for the weekend ticket sales job. She'd stored away every single criticism and castigated herself with them regularly.

But art – art was one of the *only* things she'd ever really been praised for and so she'd allowed it to define her, allowed herself to use it as a prop. And so that 'one review', that extremely negative assessment of her only acknowledged talent, had been catastrophic because it had destroyed the only self-worth she had.

She had abandoned her degree and returned to Malvern soon afterwards. Every bit of hope she'd conjured before her move to London, every bit of colour, design or joie de vivre, had dissipated when she'd returned. It had taken a huge amount of bravery to pursue an art degree in the face of her parents' disapproval and leaving it in those horrendous circumstances, in that fog of self-harm, had almost knocked her into oblivion. She had clung onto life with her fingernails, resisting the voice in her head which had whispered to her that she had no purpose on earth, no reason to exist.

After months of self-imposed isolation at home with her parents, her mother had managed to coax her out slowly, encouraging her to get dressed and get washed, and, bit by bit, she'd put a semblance of herself together again. She'd eventually found a job working at an art supplies shop in Worcester, the first of several unskilled roles on the very edges of a career she'd dreamed of. She'd gone through the motions to earn her wage, just treading water.

So when she met Piers a decade later, his confidence – which he apparently had in abundance – had drawn her in like a moth to a flame. And more than that, his desire for her had seemed miraculous.

She hadn't told Piers, or anyone else for that matter, ever, but she'd still been a virgin when they'd met. She'd been ashamed of this because it had seemed to confirm something she had long been convinced of: that she was entirely unattractive.

She had felt uncomfortable in her body since puberty. She was tall, skinny and almost flat chested. She stuck out in crowds. Clothes that were meant to hang elegantly from an ample bosom swamped her. And her face, well, it seemed to her to be plain on a good day, and on a bad one, it needed to be hidden. Accordingly, she'd dismissed the boys who'd tried to kiss her at school, and the ones who'd tried to talk to her in noisy pubs in London, as either desperate or drunk.

So when Piers had asked her to marry him, it was like he'd been a fairy godmother offering her a brand new life. In that moment she had been instantly transformed from an unwanted, unattractive shell into a fully-formed, desired woman. And so it had never occurred to her to say no.

★★★

'Yes, I know Sophie,' replied Amelia then, looking at the shop assistant. 'I went to art college with her.'

This drew Piers' attention.

'That could have been you, eh?' said Piers. 'Selling your wares in tourist gift shops.'

Amelia smiled at him, despite noting the assistant's scowl. Piers knew about Sophie's boyfriend's review, and what it had done to her.

'She's very well known,' the sales assistant added, her voice insistent. 'She's very successful.'

'I'm sure she is,' said Piers, his smile lighting up the shop. 'How wonderful to make a living from art.'

The shop assistant appeared satisfied.

'I think those would be nice,' said Piers, his attention now back on the jewellery. Amelia walked over and saw that he was pointing at a pair of silver drop earrings. They were pretty, but nothing special, she thought. They were also priced at 15 pounds, which she thought was pretty cheap for a Christmas present for his only parent.

'Yes, yes, I think they will be lovely. Can you put them in a box?' he asked the assistant. 'And do you take cards?'

The shop assistant nodded and brought out the card machine. Piers tapped in his pin number while the assistant lifted the earrings out of the display case and put them in a smart navy box.

'Brilliant, thank you,' he said, taking the box and putting it in a bag he'd strung over the buggy's handlebars. 'Let's go, darling,' he said to Amelia. 'I think if we're lucky, we might catch the Sally Army. Mum said they are going to play carols in the square this afternoon.'

Amelia followed him as he opened the door of the shop, pushed Grace through and headed in the direction of the Prince of Wales pier.

Should I, thought Amelia. And can I? And is it worth it? Sod it, she thought. I've had a sleep. I can cope.

'Do you think that's enough for your mum, Piers?' she asked, as gently as she could. 'We could get her something else...'

'It's plenty,' he replied, as they walked past a busker singing 'A Fairytale of New York'. 'You know we can't afford extravagances, not since spending everything we have on the IVF.'

Ah, the IVF again, Amelia thought. It was as if he hadn't chosen to spend that money too, she thought; as if he'd forgotten that.

They walked in silence along the street, turned left at the pier and found themselves in the town square, where, as Catherine had suggested, the local Salvation Army band were assembled. Piers reached for her hand as they stood waiting there in the cold and she took it.

'You look lovely today, by the way,' he said. 'I love that coat on you.' Amelia considered her outfit. She was wearing blue skinny jeans, a grey jumper, long black boots and a grey button-up high-necked coat, which Piers had chosen with her. She thought she looked a bit like a Russian soldier, but she was glad he liked it.

She moved closer to him and rested her head on his shoulder. He leaned into her as the brass band began to play 'Once in Royal David's City', which Amelia remembered from countless school carol services growing up. It had always been accompanied by candlelight and the smell of pine trees erected in the church and draped with tinsel, and the rustling of hundreds of orders of service, and a hope that this year, *this year* would be a lovely, calm, joyful family Christmas.

It had stopped hailing now and the Christmas lights decorating the square were reflected in the puddles gathered in the cracks on the stone paving beneath their feet. It was like being surrounded by hundreds of tiny stars. As the familiar wrapped itself around them, Amelia looked down at Grace, who was asleep in the buggy.

Suddenly, she felt at peace. It's going to be okay, she thought to herself. We're going to be fine, the three of us. I am *sure* of it.

13

December 3rd

Michelle

Twelve weeks until the final hearing

'Michelle? It's me. Laura. Well, obviously. You can see that. We meet again. Sorry.'

Fuck, Michelle thought. Despite being on a ward full of other women, Michelle had managed to keep her own counsel since she'd woken up again, having tried and failed to leave the world for good. She hadn't told the nurses anything about anything, and all of the other patients had left her alone after she'd glared at them like a hungry guard dog. She'd done that because she hadn't wanted to talk about stuff. She was still working it all out in her head.

'The doctors called social services to say they had someone in who'd taken an overdose and might need our help. So here I am. They tell me you had a lucky escape.'

Lucky? That really depends on your perspective.

Michelle looked her social worker up and down. It was now Saturday night, and she'd heard one of the nurses moaning about missing out on an early Christmas party because she was on shift. It seemed that Laura was missing out on an event too; she was wearing a sparkly red top emblazoned with a reindeer with a red pom-pom for a nose, a short black shirt and black knee-high boots, and her eyes were smoky, with eyeliner artfully applied.

'I'm just going to sit down next to you, okay?' she said, wafting a floral scent as she did so.

Suit yourself, thought Michelle. *But it's your time you're wasting.*

'So first of all, I want to say sorry, about last time we met,' Laura said, taking a seat on the padded blue chair next to her hospital bed. 'I didn't get to say what I wanted to say, and I should have tried harder. I do want to help you, Michelle. I really do.'

Leave me, Laura, she thought. *Leave me. Everybody else has.*

'Don't you have somewhere better to go? Santa will be missing Rudolph,' said Michelle, noting Laura's smile wavered slightly as she said it.

'Look, Michelle,' said Laura, ignoring the jibe. 'When you left care and you didn't take the support you were offered, we all – the team, I mean – we all felt like we'd failed you. And I know we did, I know social services have seriously failed you over the years.'

Michelle was singing songs silently in her head, trying to block out her words.

'But things have changed, times have changed, and even though you've left care, we can still help you. And we want to, believe me. And I'm here because… I can't quite get over what I've read in your files, and what… untruths you've been told over the years. I want to put it right. That's why I'm here tonight, and not drinking two-for-one festive cocktails at Fat Harry's.'

La la la la la laaaaa. La la…

'You know, what you said last time, about your family not wanting you, I think maybe there was a… miscommunication about that, and I wanted to clear it up. So the thing is, your grandmother...'

'Don't even think about talking about *her*,' said Michelle, her voice hoarse. 'She left us. She took us to a children's home and she abandoned us. Just like our parents did.'

'She didn't have a choice,' said Laura.

'Yes, she did! She could have brought us up. She had a big house with bedrooms for each of us.' Michelle's had been pink, with fairies on the wallpaper. 'But she thought I was too much of a handful, too naughty, too difficult to look after...'

'It wasn't anything to do with you,' said Laura.

'*What*?' said Michelle, looking at Laura in shock. She was sitting to her right on a chair, her hair pulled back into a neat high ponytail, her face sincere.

'It wasn't anything to do with you,' Laura repeated. 'For some reason, they didn't tell you the truth about that. I suppose they thought they were trying to protect you.'

'Then what was it to do with?' asked Michelle, trying to sit up, but finding that she ached all over.

Laura looked uncomfortable.

'I think we need to talk about this properly, at the office. I'm not really supposed to be here, you see. They were going to write to you, but I thought you might not read that... If you do come to the office, I have documents I can show you.' There was a short pause while Laura inspected her fingernails, which Michelle noticed were covered in chipped red varnish. 'The thing is, I didn't know that you... didn't know. I'm so sorry.'

Michelle wanted to hate her, wanted so badly to dismiss the suggestion and her apology, but she wanted this information very badly.

'Can't you just tell me *now*?' she asked, her voice pleading. She had abandoned her attempt to sit up. She hurt too much.

'You're just recovering, Michelle. I think you need to be well for us to talk properly. But I'd love to have you come along to meet me soon, if you'd like?'

'Is this a ploy just to get me to accept your help?' Michelle asked, staring at the ceiling, which was home to islands of peeling, shiny paint.

'No,' said Laura. 'I promise. *No*.'

What should she do? She refused to be manipulated anymore by these *freaks*. Wasn't this just another of their games? But... she sounded sincere, thought Michelle. And she desperately wanted to know what had happened to Nan, and why she and Grace had been abandoned like that. Wasn't finding out worth the risk? Maybe they'd even be able to tell her where Grace was? The very thought of that made her heart soar.

'I'll come then,' said Michelle, trying to sound cool and disinterested. She didn't want them to think they'd won. 'But just for a meeting. Don't pull any other shit. Okay?'

'Okay,' replied Laura. 'But we also need to sort you out with somewhere new to stay.'

'I live on the Elgar Estate,' Michelle replied. 'I'll go back there.'

The reality was, of course, that Michelle wanted to go back to live with Rob about as much as a fly wants to land on a spider's web. But it was the only place she could realistically go. Her current plan, such as it was, was to go there when she was feeling better, grab as much of her stuff as she could, and to try to find a hostel bed somewhere. And then, maybe a job? She could try to get her old warehouse job back, maybe. But it was hard to get a job without a permanent address, she knew that, so maybe she'd have to stay with Rob for a bit after all?

'Michelle, the thing is, we can't find Rob. He's not at the flat.'

Michelle suddenly felt acutely nauseous.

'He wasn't there when Mr Chaudhury found you, and he's still not there. Did he give you the drugs?'

Michelle turned over and retched into the cardboard bowl a nurse had left by her side.

'Oh, I'm so sorry, Michelle. We shouldn't be trying to talk when you're poorly,' said Laura, who was clearly feeling uncomfortable.

Michelle thought of the stash of cocaine she'd found in the toilet cistern, the stash Rob had clearly thought she was unaware of. The stash he'd probably bought with his universal credit payment, which he claimed he hadn't even received. The stash she'd decided to take, all in one go, to put an end to everything.

'No. He didn't,' said Michelle, turning back to face Laura.

'Okay. Well... Whatever happened, he isn't around, and you need someone to take care of you. Is there someone else who can come and stay? If not, we'll find you a temporary placement with a foster carer. Just as a lodger, I mean.'

Michelle thought of the line-up of foster carers she'd had over the years; all firmly middle-class folk, all very well meaning, but almost all of them had been too gullible, too formal, too... condescending. Only the couple she'd had at the end, Leo and Mark, had been any good, and they'd kicked her out of there, anyway.

Then she thought of a card which she'd been keeping in her pocket, folded up tightly, for reasons that she had not yet processed.

'There *is* someone you can call,' she said.

14

December 8th

Amelia

Eleven weeks before the final hearing

Amelia was standing at the window of their living room looking out at the retaining wall, which was now home to frozen rivulets of rain. It was below freezing outside, a bright, crisp cloud-free day, by all accounts, although it was hard to tell this from their quasi-subterranean lounge.

Amelia had spent most of the past hour trying to decorate a small Norway Spruce which Piers had bought from outside the fruit and veg shop in town. She had pulled their small box of decorations out from beneath their step ladder and assorted ironing in their storage cupboard and carried it into the lounge. There, with Grace strapped to her chest, she had lit a scented candle which promised 'festive smells' and asked Alexa to play carols. It was as much as she could do to conjure up the cosy Christmas family scene she had in her head, which seemed destined to remain fiction.

The school term had ended, but Piers had been locked in his private study since the post had arrived that morning. He'd stomped into there clutching a pile of letters and he hadn't re-emerged. He seemed to be angry about something, although

Amelia couldn't work out what she'd done to annoy him. He'd promised a couple of hours ago that he'd emerge for a ceremonial lighting up of the tree, but this had not materialised, so she'd left the lights on throughout the whole procedure, in defiance. It looked rather nice, she thought, despite its small stature. It was homely and cosy.

She had chosen some retro-style lights made to look like gas lamps and their bright colours made the room seem warmer and more welcoming. She'd picked out some decorations she'd brought with her when she moved in, treasured remnants of her own childhood, including a pair of rather moth-eaten little doves and a tiny porcelain Father Christmas figure. Sitting down now on the sofa and looking at the tree, she was momentarily transported back decades, back to a similar apartment, also owned by a school, where she was also alone.

Rain had been thrashing at the windows. Her mother had been delayed at work, and her father was sitting at the dining table in the next room, writing reports. She had removed a VHS from the cupboard beside the TV and placed it in the video player. The opening bars of *The Snowman* soundtrack had sung their way around the room and she had sat up straighter, sinking into the familiar film like an embrace. She had watched, enraptured as ever, as that solitary small boy gloried at the snow, overjoyed at the beauty that awaited him in an ordinary garden of an ordinary house. And then his mother had beckoned him inside for tea, back into a warm family unit, toasting bread on the fireplace.

She had thought then of her hopes for that evening, of the snacks she had assembled on the coffee table, and the cherished decorations she'd saved to unwrap and, maybe, *just maybe*, laugh about together.

Her father had only emerged that evening to make a cup of tea in the kitchen and she knew there was no point trying to persuade him to join her. He was always too busy. Her mother, on the other hand, had not made it home until 8 p.m. that night, long after Amelia had made herself a sandwich, turned the Christmas tree lights off and headed to bed, dreams of family games and laughter doused with tears.

Back in the twenty-first century, the doorbell rang in Amelia and Piers' flat.

'*She's here*!' shouted Amelia in the direction of the study door, as she walked down their stairs to open the front door of the boarding house.

'Hi,' she said, smiling as she opened the door to the Scottish lady who held their fate as parents in her well-scrubbed, tiny hands.

'Hello again, Amelia,' said Marion. 'You look lovely. *And little Grace, of course*,' she said, greeting the baby who was still dangling from Amelia's chest in the baby carrier, 'you look wonderful too.'

'Come on up,' said Amelia, walking back up the stairs in the direction of their living room. 'Would you like a drink?'

'Just a cup of hot water, please, if you could,' she said. 'Caffeine makes me jittery.'

Amelia winced and thought back to the coffee she'd served Marion on her first visit, a month previously, when she'd been so exhausted after sleepless nights with Grace, that she couldn't even remember what they'd talked about, let alone whether she'd even asked Marion for her preference of hot drink.

'Really? I've got some herbal tea somewhere, if you'd prefer?' Amelia asked.

'No, really. Hot water is just fine. I've been drinking it for years. Hasn't killed me yet.'

Amelia nodded.

'Okay! Well, take a seat in the living room, and I'll be with you in a minute. Piers is just finishing up some work, I think, but will be with us shortly.'

As Amelia flipped the kettle on and searched for clean,

unchipped mugs, she thought back to that previous meeting. Just remembering it made her heart thud. She was certain that she'd made a terrible impression on Marion and that was something that she absolutely had to remedy today. Piers, she thought, had acquitted himself well last time – he had been, after all, still getting his sleep – so she was less worried about what Marion had made of him. No doubt, she had found him charming. No, it was the impression she had of Amelia that really needed to be improved if they were to stand any chance of keeping Grace. Because that was how Amelia saw it: this was an exam, and she simply had to pass it, for their future as a family depended on it.

'Here you go,' she said, walking into the living room holding out a mug of hot water with her arm outstretched, demonstrating that she was keeping it at a safe distance from the now sleeping Grace. 'I'll just go and get my tea, and then we can chat.'

When Amelia had claimed her mug from the side of the kitchen and returned to the living room, Marion was examining the Christmas tree ornaments Amelia had left out on the table.

'Och, we had some like this when I was young,' she said, lifting a small feathered, multi-coloured bird, with sequins sewn into its plumage. 'Lovely wee things. We covered our silver tinsel tree with them.'

'Yes, that's from my childhood,' said Amelia. 'My parents told me I could take some of their Christmas decorations when I got married, for my own tree. I'm about to put them on, with Piers.'

'How lovely,' said Marion. 'Christmas traditions are so powerful, aren't they?' Amelia smiled and took a sip of her tea, listening to an a cappella version of 'Silent Night', which was currently being broadcast by their smart speaker. 'Now, Amelia, as you know, I am Grace's advocate. I felt last time that you might have been a bit on edge, having me around, and

I understand that it might feel that way. But I want you to try to relax. I just want to get a feel for how things are going here, really. That's all.'

Amelia smiled. 'I'm sorry if I seemed a bit odd last time,' she said. 'The thing is, I was very tired – Grace wasn't sleeping well – and it was all new. I feel a lot better now. We're in a rhythm.'

'Yes, of course. It takes time. And really, I can already see that Grace is happy and safe here. She seems content, and you are doing all the right things. My main job is to assess the birth parents' situation, really, so that I can make the right recommendation to the court, armed with all of the facts.'

'Yes. I think about her – the birth mother – a lot.'

Marion looked up from her steaming cup of water.

'I can't tell you much about her, I'm afraid,' she said.

'I know that. But I do know what it's like to lose a child. We had a stillborn baby, a few years ago. She was born after several IVF cycles…'

'Ah, yes, social services told me about that. I'm so sorry.'

'Thank you. Some days, now, it seems like it happened to another woman. Other times, I'm right there, you know? Right there in the delivery room, with those shocked faces and that horrific silence.'

'I can imagine.'

Jesus, thought Amelia, catching herself. She's going to think I'm mentally unhinged. Time to change the subject.

'Have you visited the birth parents yet?' she said, eager to change the subject. 'Sorry. I suppose you can't tell me that.'

'I haven't been able to fix a date yet, no,' said Marion, her eyes fixed and unblinking. 'But I'm sure I will soon.'

'Great,' said Amelia, glad that their main opposition was currently doing itself down. And then in an instant, she felt guilty for feeling that. 'I mean, great that you're going to see them soon.'

'Ah, hello, welcome back, Marion,' said Piers, arriving at the doorway. 'Sorry I took a while. I've been writing the end of term reports for the boys. Always takes me days. Apologies.'

'No worries at all, Piers,' said Marion. 'Amelia and I have just been catching up.'

'Ah, good! As you can see, Grace has settled right in,' he said, sitting down next to his wife. They all looked at Grace then, at her long eyelashes splayed out over her plump porcelain cheeks, her tiny chest rising and falling like a slow waltz.

'Yes, she seems very happy indeed,' said Marion. 'Very happy. Now tell me, how are you both managing with the demands of a new-born? Has the transition been tough?'

Piers reached over to grasp Amelia's hand. 'I think the first few days were a shock for all of us, Marion,' he said, 'but that passed, and we are so happy. We love her completely. I mean, who couldn't? She's part of our family now.'

Amelia heard Piers' words, and every sinew in her body ached to believe them. She looked across at Marion and judged that she, at least, was convinced. Thank heavens for that, she thought; I have one less thing to worry about.

After Marion left, Piers went back into his study, leaving Amelia in the lounge. She felt exhausted. It was so hard, trying her best to appear perfect. She walked over to where she'd left the Christmas decorations and sat down. Then she looked down on the table and noticed that one of the decorations was missing.

Her childhood miniature Father Christmas was nowhere to be seen. How strange, she thought. She stared at the table for a minute or so, as if by doing so, she could force it to materialise, before setting about searching the cracks between the sofa cushions, underneath the rug, and even on the tree, looking for it. Where on earth could it be? She had had it there when Marion arrived. She couldn't have taken it, could she? Bloody hell, she thought, I'm so tired, I'm actually losing my mind.

At that moment, her phone bleeped. Rachel had sent her a text.

Hey you. Are you busy? There's a Christmas fair thing on at the church. Do you want to join?

Amelia looked down at Grace, who was just waking. She walked into the hallway and saw that Piers' office door was still shut. What the hell, she thought.

'*I'm going out*,' she said, as loud as she could.

There was a clattering inside the room, followed by footsteps. The door handle opened.

'Are you?' said Piers, standing in the door frame, sweeping his hair back with his hand. 'Where?'

'To the Priory,' she said. 'There's a Christmas fair on. I'm meeting Rachel.'

'Oh. Remember you have a session with Julia this afternoon.'

'Yes, I'll be back in time for that. I'm only going out for an hour or so.'

Piers took a deep breath through his nose.

'Oh. Okay. Right. But I thought we were going to finish decorating the tree together?'

'We were, darling, hours ago. But you've been busy. So I thought...'

'Ah yes, sorry, I've been madly busy.'

'I know, don't worry about it. I get it. Look, it's a funny thing, but did you happen to notice my Father Christmas tree ornament? I could swear that I left it on the coffee table for us to put on the tree together later, but it's vanished...'

'No, darling, I'm afraid I haven't. Perhaps you put it on the tree, and forgot about it?'

'No, I don't think so.'

'How odd.'

'Yes.'

'Well maybe it's still in the loft? Or in one of the other boxes. I can have a look up there for you. We'll find it, I'm sure. I know how much it means to you.'

'Yes,' replied Amelia, feeling wrong-footed. She'd had that ornament for most of her life, and it had become something of a talisman to her.

'Oh and Amelia, I meant to say, actually – I saw you put the lights on by yourself. That's quite dangerous, you know, my mother once got a horrible electric shock from lights. I'd rather I'd done that myself. I don't want anything happening to you or Grace.'

In previous times, Amelia would have responded positively to something like this. It had felt, for years, like she was being cared for. But this time, something inside her snapped. Maybe it was tiredness, maybe it was motherhood, or *maybe*, she thought, just maybe, she had had *enough* of being smothered.

'I'm not a child, Piers,' she said, her face on fire.

Piers looked like he'd been slapped.

'Goodness, Amelia. What has got into you?'

Amelia clenched her fists. He sounded like he was chastising one of the boys.

'I'm going out, Piers,' she said, avoiding the question. 'I'll walk into town with Grace. I'll be a couple of hours. I'll see you later.'

She turned, grabbed her coat and the changing bag from the hat stand, and walked down the stairs, where Grace's buggy was parked. Piers said nothing more, although she could feel his gaze boring a hole into her back.

15

December 8th

Michelle

Eleven weeks to final hearing

The house looked a bit like a public toilet from the front. Built of granite and topped with terracotta tiles, it had just a large oak door and a couple of small, frosted windows either side when you looked at it from the road. Michelle wondered if the social worker had driven her to the wrong place. After all, Gillian clearly had money, and she'd imagined that she might live in a large house in the countryside, not a bungalow the size of a shed.

Laura walked up to the door with her and rang the bell. It wasn't one of those plug-in doorbells; instead, it made a deep drilling sound, like a school bell. A few seconds later there came a clip-clopping of shoes on what sounded like tiles and the door swung open. Gillian was wearing a deep red tunic over black leggings, long twisted silver earrings and a red and white spotted scarf in her hair, giving her the look of a wartime factory worker.

'Michelle, how wonderful,' she said, as if she was a much-anticipated dinner guest. 'I'm so glad to see you again. Won't you both come in?'

Michelle crossed the threshold and walked into a tiled hallway which had a large picture window at its end. She caught a glimpse of the view and caught her breath. The whole of Worcestershire lay before her; it was as if the house was clinging to the edge of a cliff.

'Quite the view, isn't it?' said Gillian. 'It's what sold the house to us. It's amazing. I never tire of it. Despite all of the stairs.'

Michelle turned around to see Gillian and Laura heading down a flight of stairs, flanked by polished oak banisters, which were wrapped in ivy, secured with red ribbon. She followed them down, taking in the pictures that hung next to the staircase, among them a Parisian square, a windswept beach and a bustling street, somewhere in Asia. All of them were abstract, colourful, draped in more ivy, and at least a metre wide.

At the bottom of the flight of stairs was a living room. Unlike the hallway, which was clad in dark wood panelling, this room was painted white and light was flooding in through an enormous rectangular window which ran almost the whole way across the space. In front of it was a huge Christmas tree, adorned with silver and gold baubles and strings of little silver bells. The wall nearest Michelle was lined with shelves, groaning under the weight of hundreds of books. On the furthest wall was a log burner, and a blazing fire was under way behind its glass door. Above it, a polished metal chimney made its way through the wall to the outside of the house, and in front of it sat three high-backed armchairs, each upholstered in different fabrics, all in primary colours.

'Take a seat over there,' said Gillian, gesturing in the direction of the wood burner, 'and I'll ask Mike to bring us some coffee.' As Michelle and Laura walked over and picked a seat, Gillian went down a further flight of stairs which Michelle had not yet noticed, and called out.

'*Could you bring coffees up, darling*?' she shouted. '*And some of my cake*?'

Michelle heard a murmur of assent from below. Gillian then walked over to where they were sitting and took a chair. Then Michelle heard the noise of little feet coming in their direction.

'Ah, Rory,' said Gillian. Michelle leaned forward to look past the wing of her chair, and saw a large, hairy German Shepherd, currently tolerating kisses from his owner. 'This is, obviously, Rory,' said Gillian. 'He basically runs the house. We are but his servants.'

Michelle could see Laura smiling, falling under Gillian's spell, just as she had when she'd met her at the food bank. Gillian seemed absolutely batty, but there was something special about her, definitely.

'So, you said on the phone that Michelle is looking for somewhere to stay for a bit?' Gillian said to Laura. 'That's fine by us. We have plenty of room.'

Michelle was astounded. She had thought they had come here to discuss help from the charity Gillian worked for, not to secure her accommodation. She felt incredibly embarrassed.

'You don't have to...' she said, speaking for the first time since entering the house. 'I mean, it's nearly Christmas... I can go...'

Where could she go, though? She could go home to the flat, if the council let her keep it, but she'd just been there with Laura, and Rob had clearly left. It was in a terrible state, totally stinking, and Rob had taken – or maybe, sold – the TV and the microwave. Anyway, she couldn't afford the rent on her own, and she knew that social services didn't want to let her go anywhere unless there was someone to keep an eye on her, given what she'd just done. And she knew that if she was going to find out about her grandmother, and all the stuff social services had been keeping from her, she'd have to play along. At least for now.

'Oh, don't be silly. It will be nice. It's just the two of us here anyway, plus Rory of course, so it will be nice to have someone else to cook for.'

Michelle wondered where Gillian's family was. She seemed the type to be surrounded by a huge brood of children and grandchildren, all tugging at her earrings and wiping their noses on her expensive clothes, which Gillian wouldn't mind at all, of course.

'It would be wonderful if you could offer Michelle a bed for at least a couple of weeks,' said Laura. 'So that she can recover from her… illness, and so that we can have a meeting in the new year, when the office is open again, to talk about the way forward.'

'*And the past*,' interrupted Michelle.

'Yes. And the past,' said Laura. 'I promise.' She then turned to face Gillian. 'So, I understand that you've fostered?' she said.

'Yes, that's right,' answered Gillian. 'We fostered for about twenty years.'

Wow, thought Michelle. That's… amazing. She thought about the hard time she'd given a lot of her foster parents and was astonished that anyone could stick it for that long.

'What sort of ages?'

'All sorts,' she replied, 'but latterly, lots of teenagers. I liked having them around. They livened up the place.'

Michelle thought that the house looked pretty lively as it was.

'So, you'll know that we can give you an allowance, to cover Michelle's food and things,' said Laura.

'Yes, yes,' said Gillian. 'But no hurry. We're not exactly impoverished. And anyway, this isn't a foster situation, is it? This is just helping out a friend.'

Michelle looked down at her feet. She felt incredibly guilty for every single negative thought she'd ever had about Gillian. Not that there had really been that many. But she still felt bad.

'Great,' said Laura.

At that moment, footsteps sounded up the stairs, and a man

with closely cropped silver hair appeared next to them, carrying a tray.

'Everyone, this is my husband Mike,' said Gillian. 'He comes bearing slices of my patented Christmas cake. He usually guards it closely, but he decided to make an exception for you lot.'

Michelle looked more closely at Mike. He had dark eyes, long eyelashes and a round face, with wrinkles that suggested he smiled a lot. He was smiling right now, in fact. 'Yep, it's pretty special stuff,' he said, in an accent Michelle recognised as Geordie. 'But I am prepared to share this morning.' He held the tray out to Michelle. 'Michelle? Take a slice of cake and a coffee.'

Michelle peered over the side of the tray and took a steaming mug of coffee and a white porcelain plate, upon which she found a rich, iced fruitcake, the sort her nan used to make when she was little. As the other women made their choices, she put the coffee down on the small side table beside her, broke off a small piece of cake and put it in her mouth. It was an explosion of everything Christmas tasted of, she thought. It was spicy, nutty and fruity and there was booze in there too, probably. And Mike was right. It was delicious.

'Good, huh?' he said. 'And the great news is, there's more where that came from.' Then he bid them goodbye and headed back down the stairs.

'So, will you be okay for a couple of weeks?' asked Laura, resuming her earlier conversation with Gillian.

'Oh, yes,' she said. 'No bother. We are looking forward to it.'

'That's wonderful,' said Laura. 'Are you happy with the arrangement, Michelle? It's important you feel comfortable.'

Michelle looked around her at the warm room, at the food on her plate and the coffee in her hands, and her decision was made. She was so tired and so hungry. She didn't have the energy to go anywhere else, anyway. She could be sitting on a park bench and she wouldn't want to move now. She was done.

'That would be great,' she said, putting her coffee and cake down on the table, and feeling her eyes beginning to close. Then the room began to swim, and the heat from the fire reached out to cocoon her and she was aware of only the rhythm of her own heart.

It was dark outside when Michelle woke. The lights on the Christmas tree and the embers of the fire were the only lights in the room. She stood up gradually – her body still remembered the birth, even if she had tried to forget it – and walked to the window. The lights of the distant towns sparkled down below, and streetlamps lit up the local 'A' roads, making them look like long, thin runways. What would it be like to jump on a plane to get out of Malvern, she wondered? She'd never done it. Hadn't had the money to. But she intended to, one day.

'Oh, you're awake,' said Gillian. Michelle jumped; she hadn't heard her coming up the stairs. 'I'm sorry, I don't mean to frighten you,' she said. 'I just left you to have forty winks. You looked so peaceful.'

'Thank you,' said Michelle. 'I needed it.' Gillian came to join her at the window. 'You didn't need to take me in, you know,' she said. 'I feel bad… I didn't mean for you to have to do it.'

'Don't be silly,' said Gillian. 'I *want* to. *We* want to.'

They stood there in silence for a moment, both staring at the view. About a mile away, Michelle could make out the distinctive, garish sight of an inflatable Father Christmas figure on someone's roof. That was in the direction of the Elgar Estate, she thought. Somewhere down there, is the flat. With my stuff in it. She was glad not to be there, however; the power had been disconnected a few days ago. It would be freezing in there.

'Are you hungry?' asked Gillian. 'I've been cooking dinner.'

Michelle thought for a moment. She hadn't eaten properly

for so long, she wasn't even sure what it felt like to experience normal hunger. But she decided that dinner would be great.

'That would be nice,' she said, conscious of a need to be polite. After all, she was a guest, and Nan had always said you were polite when you were a guest. She'd never been a guest before, either.

'Perfect. Come on down, then,' said Gillian. 'Come and see Rory. He's had his dinner, luckily, so he won't try to eat you,' she said, with a wink.

Michelle followed Gillian down the stairs, into a large, modern kitchen. A massive stainless-steel lamp hung in the centre, dangling above an island topped with white granite. On the other side of the island, Mike was standing in front of a giant metal extraction hood stirring something on a large gas hob, steam rising and disappearing into the vent. The white kitchen units surrounding him on all sides were sleek and shiny, and the whole feel of the space was modern and clean – the very opposite, she thought, of their dingy, mouldy kitchen in the flat, which probably dated back to the 1980s. The only thing not polished or ordered in this kitchen was Rory, who was napping in a large, soft brown dog bed in the corner.

'This room really reflects Mike, more than me,' Gillian said. 'He's an architect, you see. He has to have everything in its place, you know?' she winked in the direction of her husband. 'I, on the other hand, like things a bit more rough and ready. But I do love it... it was a present to each other, last year, for our thirtieth wedding anniversary.'

Thirty years, thought Michelle. *They've been married longer than I've been alive. How on earth does someone do that?*

The smell of the food Mike was cooking made Michelle's mouth water. She hadn't eaten a proper cooked meal for a long time, not a balanced one, with vegetables and stuff. Her stomach began to rumble.

'Goodness, you sound hungry,' said Gillian. 'It won't be

long now. I think Mike's made us his king prawn risotto. It's delicious, I promise. Do you want to take a seat?'

Michelle looked longingly at Rory. 'Do you mind if I stroke Rory for a bit?' she asked. 'If he is okay with that…?'

Gillian laughed. 'He'll be in heaven. He reckons that he gets nowhere near enough attention as it is.'

Michelle walked over towards the dog and sat down on the floor in front of him, her legs crossed. He watched her approach, and as soon as she was on his level, he raised himself up onto his legs and padded over to her, resting his head on her legs. She felt his warm, wet nose nuzzle against her hand and she could feel his heart beating against her leg. Following an instinct seeded long ago, she leaned forward and draped herself over him. He did not move, apparently happy with the arrangement. And suddenly, she was back in the children's home, and she was crying into the coat of a golden retriever, grasping it tightly, to make sure that it could not leave her alone.

'Wow, he loves you,' said Gillian, walking over to them both. 'I've never seen him do that with a guest.'

Michelle raised herself back up to sitting position and looked at Gillian, her eyes glistening. 'He's brilliant,' she said. '*Brilliant.*'

'Dinner's ready,' said Mike, turning around from his position at the stove.

'Come and get it while it's hot,' said Gillian. 'Then you can resume your communing with Rory afterwards.'

Michelle nodded and stood up, unfurling herself from Rory's embrace with care.

'How old is he?' she asked, as she took the seat Gillian indicated at a large glass table.

'Rory? He's eight now. We got him as a puppy, but he's still a puppy at heart now, really. He goes mad on his walks. He's so loyal, and a lot of fun. It's nice to have him around the place, otherwise, now we've stopped fostering, the house would be rather empty.'

'Do you guys have family?' asked Michelle, as she accepted two large spoonfuls of steaming food ladled into a large white porcelain bowl. A silence followed that lasted longer than was comfortable. Michelle looked up from her food, and saw a look of pain puncture Gillian's warm, friendly face. 'I'm sorry,' Michelle said. 'Me and my big mouth.'

'No, that's okay,' said Mike, placing his hand over Gillian's. 'It didn't happen for us, even though we wanted it to. So that's why we fostered. We call them our foster family. Most still come to visit us, and some of them have kids now, so we have foster-grandkids, too.'

'That's amazing,' said Michelle. 'I mean, I was sent to a few families to foster, and none of them were as nice as you.'

Gillian and Mike both laughed. 'You hardly know us, darling, we might turn out to be utter bastards,' said Gillian, chuckling into the wine which her husband had just poured her.

'Would you like a glass?' he asked Michelle, holding out the bottle.

'I don't... drink,' said Michelle.

'Ah, no problem at all,' said Mike, not skipping a beat. 'I've got some elderflower fizzy stuff in my fridge. Would that do?'

'Yeah, fine,' said Michelle, before checking herself. 'Thank you.'

'No problem,' said Mike, walking over to the fridge and retrieving a green bottle. 'And I should probably have asked, before serving up food for you – is there anything you don't eat?' He poured Michelle a glass and she took a sip of the sweet, scented drink.

'Nah, I eat pretty much everything,' she said, looking down at the risotto, which contained prawns, bright red peppers and brown, nutty mushrooms. 'This looks amazing.'

'Thank you,' said Mike. 'I'm glad.'

They all began to eat, the only sounds in the room being Rory's breathing, and the gentle clicks of jaws and teeth as

Mike's risotto filled their stomachs. The impact of the food hit Michelle in particular. She felt more grounded in reality somehow, more awake. She had finished it within minutes.

'That went down well,' said Gillian, looking at Michelle's empty plate. 'Would you like seconds?'

Michelle shook her head. 'Sorry, I eat really quickly, it's such a bad habit,' she said. She didn't say why this was; that in the past, if she hadn't eaten quickly, other kids might have stolen it, along with any seconds, or pudding, first. It had been the law of the jungle sometimes, at dinner times.

'Not at all, I take that as a compliment,' said Mike. 'I hope this appetite continues. You look like you need some more meat on those bones.'

Gillian jabbed her husband with her elbow, playfully. 'Mike! Sorry, Michelle. He can't stop himself.'

Michelle looked down at her plate, trying to smile. 'I will do my best,' she said, before sitting back in the chair, her eyes heavy, her body aching for sleep.

'You look so tired, Michelle,' said Gillian. 'Sorry, we should have thought, and not eaten so late. Let me show you to your room.'

'It's okay, please, just finish your dinner,' she said, knowing it was the right thing to say, even though she wanted to pass out right where she was sitting. It was something to do with the warmth in there, and the dog, and the food, and the laughter, and the locked door upstairs. She finally felt safe enough to sleep.

'No, no, I'm done anyway,' said Gillian, laying a fork down on a half-eaten bowl of food. 'Come down with me, I'll show you what's what, and then you can settle yourself in.'

Michelle stood up and followed Gillian as she walked over to the stairs and began to walk down to the floor below.

'This is where all the bedrooms are,' she said. 'We're in there' – she pointed at an oak door on her right – 'the bathroom you can use is here' – she pushed open another door, revealing a large room with a big white bath which had feet, and big gold taps at the centre – 'and down here, on the left, is the spare room. Which will be yours, while you're here.'

Michelle walked into a room which had cream walls, wooden floors, a large double wooden bed frame, and a duvet cover embroidered with hundreds of tiny daisies. There were two windows, each flanked by curtains which matched the bed linen. There were two wooden bedside tables, upon which sat two tall lamps, topped with large white shades.

'*Wow*.' The bedroom was the nicest she'd ever seen.

'Thank you,' said Gillian. 'I chose the bed linen in here. I wanted to keep it simple but make it pretty. Hopefully that's the effect, anyway.'

'It's lovely. *Really* lovely.'

'Right, well, I'll head off and let you sort yourself out. I've put a towel out for you' – Michelle turned and saw that a large white fluffy towel was folded at the foot of the bed – 'and I know you haven't got your things with you, so for now, I've put a pair of my pyjamas there. I hope you don't mind.'

'No...'

'It's totally fine. Just borrow them and use what you find in the bathroom. There's toothpaste and a spare brush by the sink and use all the shampoo and potions and creams as you like. Okay?'

Michelle smiled, hoping that it conveyed her thanks adequately. She felt momentarily suspicious about this couple's hospitality – were they going to murder her when sleeping, or try to persuade her to join a cult? But then she felt incredibly guilty for thinking that and tried to brush it off. Maybe, just maybe, she thought, some people behaved like this.

'Thanks,' she said. 'Can I have a bath?' She had a nagging pain in her abdomen and she thought that submerging herself in hot water might help.

'Of course. It's all yours. Do you remember where it is? Out here, turn left?'

'Yeah, I do. Thanks. Again.'

'Don't be silly. Sleep well, and we'll see you at breakfast.'

Gillian left the room, leaving Michelle to take in her surroundings. She pulled one of the curtains back and saw that it looked out onto the side of the house, where she could just make out a garden of some sort, through the darkness. Then she walked over to the other window and pulled its curtains back, and found the Severn Valley spread out below like a magic carpet. She contemplated sitting on the bed for a while and just staring at the view, but two things – her tiredness, which was now undeniable, and the pain she was feeling down below – called her to action. She picked up the towel and pyjamas – they were navy blue and made of soft jersey – and walked down the corridor to the bathroom.

She shut and locked the door behind her before pulling off her clothes – black leggings, a white vest and a blue hoodie – and twisted both bath taps, ushering in a rush of warm water. A column of steam rose above the bath, twisting its way towards the spotlights which were dotted around the ceiling. There was a wire rack at the end of the bath, which held bottles filled with purple, green, pink and yellow liquid, giving the place the look of an old-fashioned apothecary. Michelle looked closer and chose a bottle which promised 'relaxation and calm'. It had been a long time since Michelle had felt either. She poured a generous amount into the bath, replaced the bottle in the rack and stood there for a moment, watching as the liquid began to form bubbles. Nan had poured bubbles into their baths, from a bottle made to look like a sailor. She remembered sticking the bubbles onto her face and pretending to look like Santa.

Shit, she thought, suddenly; I bloody need a wee. She couldn't remember when she'd last been – it had probably been before she'd taken the drugs. She took her pants off, noting that they were starting to lose their elasticity – she'd have to hide them from Gillian, she didn't want her thinking that she was a hobo – and went and sat down on the loo. What followed was a piercing pain, like someone had shoved a knife up her urethra, followed by blessed relief as the warm urine had started to surge out. Afterwards, there was a residual stinging, but that would be sorted by the bath, thought Michelle; it had worked well on the stinging she'd had after the birth.

She stood up, wiped herself and stepped into the bath, the warm water a longed-for embrace. She let out a sigh as she lay down, feeling at least some of the horrors of the past days dissipate as she did so. Images of nurses and doctors peering down at her flashed across her vision; lights being shone, needles being inserted, and a feeling of overwhelming, gut-wrenching nausea.

These images were fleeting, however, and what followed was a blissful calm, a numbing – both of her emotional state, and of her body, which, for that moment at least, was no longer causing her pain.

She soaked for about twenty-five minutes, until the water had cooled a little and her skin had started to wrinkle. Then she pulled the plug, stood up, wrapped herself in the fluffy towel, gave her teeth a perfunctory clean with the spare toothbrush that had been left out – it had been wrapped in plastic, like it had been provided by a hotel, or something – picked up her clothes, and walked back down the corridor towards her room.

There, she changed into the blue pyjamas – they felt so soft, it was almost as if she wasn't wearing them – turned on the bedside light, switched off the main light and sank into the bed, pulling the covers up to her chin. Back home, she would have had to pile a couple of coats on top of the duvet to ward off the cold, but the central heating was on here, so there was no need.

She lay there for a few seconds, listening. She could hear footsteps above – presumably Gillian and Mike, tidying up after dinner – and there was a hum of traffic from a distant road. But there were no sirens, no screams and there was no yelling, and that was a gift. She turned the bedside light off, curled up in the darkness, and fell asleep instantly.

16

December 8th

Amelia

Eleven weeks until the final hearing

Amelia opened the church door and was hit by an explosion of festive cheer. A large speaker to her right was blasting out Christmas carols played on the Priory organ; at least six large trees, dotted around the nave, had made the air smell of pine forest; and at a trestle table on the other side of the church, someone was stirring a large steaming saucepan of what looked – and smelled – like mulled wine.

'*There* you are,' said Rachel, spotting Amelia through the crowd which had gathered in front of a stall selling personalised Christmas baubles. 'I wasn't sure you were going to make it.'

'Sorry, it took me ages to get Grace ready, and then I decided to walk,' said Amelia, instinctively not telling her friend about her argument with Piers. She didn't want anyone to know that her marriage was anything less than perfect, because she knew that marrying Piers was her only real achievement, ever.

'Ah, well, you're here now,' said Rachel, whose daughter was halfway through a chocolate lollipop, in the shape of a Christmas pudding. 'I've got to go in a bit – it's time for her nap,' she looked down at her daughter, and made a face '– but in the meantime, let's go and get some hot chocolate, shall we?'

Amelia smiled in agreement and they made their way through the crowds towards the front of the church, where a small army of elderly women were doling out hot chocolate in polystyrene cups.

'I'll get these,' said Amelia, digging into her bag and pulling out a ten-pound note which she'd had floating around since Catherine had sent it to her, in a pretty card, for her last birthday.

'Thanks,' said Rachel, grinning. 'Mine's one with cream and marshmallows. I'll take both kids over to the pews and grab us a couple of seats, shall I?'

'Thank you,' said Rachel, as Amelia returned from the stall and handed her a cup, before sitting down on the pew next to her with a sigh. '*That bad*, is it?'

'She's still not sleeping very well,' said Amelia. 'Although she's got a lot better since I bought the swaddling blanket. She loves that thing.'

'What did I say?' said Rachel. 'Magic.'

'Yep.' Amelia thought back to the incredible transformation she'd observed in Grace after she'd swaddled her. She had gone from absolute rage to perfect stillness in ten minutes. In fact, she'd been so quiet, she'd had to go and check that she was still breathing. That thing was magic, all right.

'How are you getting on with Christmas stuff?' asked Rachel. 'Got everything already?'

'Crikey, no, not this year,' said Amelia. 'I haven't had a moment to myself since Grace arrived. I'm going to have to do everything last minute.'

'Ah well, there's lots of good stuff here,' said Rachel. 'Why don't you have a good look when I've gone? There are some nice foodie gifts and plenty of smelly stuff. Do you have much family to buy for?'

'No,' replied Amelia. 'Just my dad. Mum died a few years ago…'

'I'm so sorry.'

'Thank you. It was cancer. Hideous. Quick. I think Dad is still reeling from it.'

'I bet.'

'I want to help him out more, see him more, but he's so incredibly independent, you see. He and Mum were such a successful unit, they excluded outsiders – even me. And now he's just continuing like that, just by himself. He just doesn't seem to want me there. He can be outright rude. And in terms of gifts, he's crotchety and curmudgeonly and generally difficult to buy for. So I usually end up buying him a bottle of whisky, which he will probably put away with the other bottles of whisky I've bought him over the years,' she said, with a raised eyebrow. 'And then there's Piers, obviously. His dad is dead, and my mother-in-law, we bought her something when we were down there visiting recently, in Cornwall.'

'Cheap to buy for then, at least,' said Rachel. 'Meanwhile I have two siblings and five nieces and nephews, two parents, two in-laws and aunties and uncles galore. I start saving for Christmas at New Year.'

To Amelia, who had become accustomed to having a tiny family, Rachel's situation sounded wonderful.

'Are you all getting together for Christmas?' she asked.

'Oh, some of us, not all,' she replied. 'We don't all fit in one house, and my brother lives in Germany now. But there will be fifteen of us around the table come Christmas Day, I think.'

'Does Jake have a big family, too?'

Amelia had yet to meet Rachel's husband Jake, but she had heard good things. He ran a record shop in Malvern, selling vinyl to the town's hipsters and millennials.

'Ah no, his is relatively small, thankfully, and mostly they are still back in Jamaica. But he's pretty tolerant of mine, which is a relief, frankly. We'd be divorced, otherwise.'

'My dad gets on really well with Piers,' said Amelia. 'They have a lot in common. They're both literally old school, I suppose. Dad's a retired headmaster. He ran Langland College for a decade. That's why we moved to Malvern. So it's sort of amazing that Piers is a housemaster at the same school now. He's hoping to be promoted to the senior leadership team soon.'

'I've been meaning to ask,' Rachel said, sipping on her hot chocolate, 'what being a housemaster actually means. I don't really know what you guys do there, what the job entails.'

'Ah, yes. I forget that other people didn't grow up in a boarding school,' said Amelia, smiling. 'Well, in practical terms it means he's responsible for all of the boys who live in Shakespeare, the house he's in charge of. He oversees all of their pastoral care, discipline, stuff like that. And in the daytime, he still has teaching duties at the school.'

'Oh right. So you have to live there?'

'Yes, it's compulsory in term time. In the holidays, we don't have to, but we don't have our own place yet. We spent so much money on IVF, we are a way off having a deposit, I think.'

'I see. Do they pay you for the work you do at the boarding house?'

Amelia laughed. 'Heavens no! They take me well and truly for granted. Housemasters' wives always end up being treated as unpaid employees, like vicars' wives, I suppose. We are well and truly part of the package.'

Rachel's eyes widened.

'We need to get us all together,' she said, finishing the last of her drink. 'For a dinner sometime. I'll text you some dates, shall I? We could try to get something in before term starts again? I imagine things get busy again then for you both.'

'How will we manage with the babies?' asked Amelia.

'Oh, you can bring her to ours,' she said. 'Babies are really portable at this age. You can just put her down for the night at our place, while we eat. I have a travel cot you can use.'

Amelia had always been nervous when they were invited out as a couple, even before Grace's arrival. She had worried that she would say the wrong thing, that Piers' friends would detect her lack of a degree or guffaw at her uninformed views. But this felt better because this time, it would be on her terms, and not his.

'That would be lovely,' she said. 'Just let me know when.'

'Brilliant,' said Rachel, standing up and looking around for a bin, and spotting one over by the hot chocolate stall. 'Right, I need to shoot off now, sadly. But I'll text you some dates. Okay?'

'Great,' said Amelia. 'Look forward to it.'

'Are you coming with, or are you staying to do a bit of shopping?' asked Rachel.

Amelia considered what remained of her ten-pound note, which was in her pocket. It was all she had with her. She didn't have a bank card, and Piers hadn't given her the week's housekeeping money yet.

'I might do a bit of shopping,' she said. Which was sort of true. She might be able to afford a little thing for Grace's stocking.

'Okay, cool.' She leaned over to kiss Amelia on the cheek. 'Brilliant. Talk soon.'

Amelia watched as Rachel headed off towards the door, her purple hair sprouting out of a messy bun, and her coat – a shiny yellow padded number – drawing stares, mostly of the admiring kind. Rachel could probably have walked in dressed like a Copacabana showgirl, and no one would have thought the less of her.

Amelia, meanwhile, was wearing a black woollen coat, black jeans and black boots, and if placed in a dark corner, she could probably be mistaken for a shadow, she thought. Which was a good thing, as far as she was concerned.

She peered into the buggy. Grace was still asleep, a minor

miracle. Amelia was amazed she could manage it with all of this noise. There were children laughing, adults chatting and babies crying all around them, all of it to the backdrop of loud Christmas music. The current carol, 'We Three Kings', was one of her favourites.

She wasn't a churchgoer by any means, but an annual carol service was an immovable feature of every school's calendar, and it had been one of the rare rituals that she had truly enjoyed, growing up. She had yearned to escape throughout her youth, so much so that the reference to exotic foreign climes at these services – the 'Orient', Nazareth, Bethlehem, Judea – was not so much of a religious experience, as a reason to dream. It was incredibly ironic, now she was an adult, to realise that the furthest she'd managed to escape to had been London, and then, only for a short period of time. Her younger self would be bitterly disappointed in her, she thought.

She stood up and began to walk in the direction of the choir stalls, leaving the crowds behind. She didn't really want to spend any more money today. Having a bit of cash in her pocket felt more comfortable, somehow, and Piers had said he would take her shopping for Christmas presents tomorrow, anyway. She knew that they would buy Grace some beautiful presents, together; they had already bought her a little reindeer teddy, which they'd seen during their trip to John Lewis. Piers would give her his credit card so that she could go out and buy something for him, too. This year, she had planned to buy him a nice shirt from T.M. Lewin and maybe some cufflinks.

When she reached the altar, she found relative tranquillity. There was one woman kneeling at the rail, so Amelia moved away from there and towards the side of the stalls, where there was a row of standalone chairs, all empty. She took a seat there, parked Grace to the side, and looked up at the magnificent painting immediately behind the altar. It depicted the wise men laying their gifts before Jesus. Jesus himself was looking both jolly and saintly, she thought, standing up on his mother's lap, pointing at the gifts, as if to say, 'yes, thanks, put them down here please'. If she had been the recipient of parades of people bringing gifts after Grace had arrived, she wondered, what would she have wanted? Definitely not frankincense or gold. Probably dummies, or snap-on vests, or IOUs for babysitting. Oh, blessed uninterrupted sleep, she thought. How I miss that.

And yet she looked down to check, and Grace – who never normally managed to sleep for longer than an hour – was still asleep. She was amazed, particularly given that the music was significantly louder here. In fact, it was so loud that Amelia could feel the floor by her feet vibrating.

The final verse of 'We Three Kings' reached a crescendo, and after that there was a silence, of sorts. People were still chatting and transacting and arguing down in the nave, but where Amelia was sitting was quiet, save for the footsteps of a woman walking from the altar and towards the exit. Seconds later, there was another noise – footsteps coming from behind her.

'Oh, hello,' said a male voice. 'I'm sorry, do you mind if I move the buggy a bit?'

Amelia turned around, and saw a man – tall, a little gaunt, his blond hair somewhat dishevelled, wearing a creased linen shirt and ill-fitting grey trousers – coming towards her, carrying a large pile of what looked like scrap paper.

'Oh, I'm sorry,' she replied, standing up and moving Grace down in front of the choir stalls. 'I didn't realise I was in anyone's way.'

'I've just been up in the organ loft,' said the man, looking, she thought, unnaturally startled. 'The entrance is just there. See?'

Amelia looked and saw that one of the wooden panels had a handle and saw stairs rising behind it. Above her, huge metal pipes soared towards the roof.

'Oh,' she said. 'I see. Were you… playing? I thought it was a CD…'

'Ha, I think that's a compliment,' said the man, chuckling as if she'd just delivered a hilarious joke. 'I'm Mark?' he said, with a quizzical expression. 'I'm the organist here? And you are... Amelia, I think. Piers' wife?'

'Yes! How did you know that?'

'I see you at college chapel services,' he replied, quickly.

'Ah, yes,' she replied, embarrassed that she had not consciously ever seen this man before.

'So you're a full-time organist, then?' she said, trying to show interest.

'Yes, well, that and a choirmaster, along with a bit of piano and organ teaching on the side,' he said. 'None of it pays very well, sadly. I'm poor as a church mouse. But I do love it.'

'It must be amazing to do something you have such a passion for,' said Amelia.

'Yes,' he answered, with a sigh. 'I wish we were appreciated a bit more, but... yes... It's amazing in many ways.'

'And in such a beautiful place,' she said, realising how calm she felt. There was something about sitting there, in that exact location, that had worked wonders both on her mood and Grace's – for she was still, against all odds, asleep.

'How old is your baby?' asked Mark.

'She's two months,' she said. 'She's called Grace.' Now was not the time to go into details about Grace's provenance, Amelia decided. It was too complicated to explain succinctly.

'How lovely she is,' he said. 'And how peaceful.'

Amelia could only laugh. 'She howls most of the time,' she said. 'But she seems to like it in here, for some reason.'

'Perhaps it's God's influence,' said Mark, with a wry smile.

'I'm not... a church...'

'Oh, I'm not really either,' said Mark, whispering and leaning in conspiratorially. 'But don't tell my boss, because faith kind of goes with the job.' Amelia smiled with relief. 'It might just be the organ,' he said, looking at Grace. 'Maybe she likes loud noises?'

Amelia pondered this. 'You know, you might be right,' she said. 'How funny.'

'There are a couple of my CDs for sale in the shop, if you want to try it out at home,' he said. 'You'll find them covered in dust, I expect.'

'I'll be sure to check them out,' she said, with a broad smile.

'Lovely,' he said.

There was a pause then: an embarrassing pause that made Amelia squirm.

'Are you playing the organ for the college carol service?' she asked. It was in a couple of weeks, on December the 21st.

'Yes, I play whenever they need music,' he said.

'Of course. Right. Well, I'm going to be there, as usual,' she said.

'Great. Well. I look forward to seeing you then, then,' said Mark, moving towards the end of the pews. 'Lovely to see you,' he said, before turning and walking away. And then Amelia watched as he appeared to trip over his own feet. He emitted something like a yelp, followed by what was probably a swear word under his breath. Then he held up his hands in an embarrassed wave afterwards, before marching off down the aisle without a backward glance. As she watched him leave through the side doors of the church, Amelia was still smiling.

'Ah, you're back,' said Piers, his face flushed with what Amelia assumed was anger. 'Julia is here. For her lesson? We missed you.'

'I'm only a couple of minutes late,' she said. She knew that Piers hated poor timekeeping. She had jogged all the way back from town. She'd simply lost track of time in the Priory. 'Where is she?'

'She's in the housemaster's office. Shall I take Grace?'

'Yes please,' said Amelia, noting that she was now stirring. 'She'll be hungry. She's had a long sleep,' she said. '*Amazingly.*'

'Well, that's unusual, certainly,' said Piers. 'Right. I'll get a bottle going. *Go*, Julia is waiting. I've got things here.'

Piers kissed her quickly on the cheek, and Amelia responded with a smile which she hoped expressed gratitude. She headed downstairs into the main body of the boarding house.

Julia was sitting on the sofa in the office, her hair tied back in a neat ponytail, and her hands on her lap gripping her phone, her fingers frantically flicking through some sort of social media app.

'Julia. Hi. I'm sorry I'm late. I lost track of time. Shall we go?'

'Sure,' said Julia, still looking down at her phone. How rude, Amelia thought. And how unlike her. She wondered if there was some sort of bullying going on at school. It was hard, she knew, being a bit different.

'Come on, Julia,' she said, her voice soft. 'Put that away. It's time to paint.'

Julia looked up, chastened. 'Sorry,' she said. 'I'm... sorry.'

'That's fine. Come on, let's go out to the conservatory. I set a surprise up for you there earlier.' Amelia set off down the hallway, and Julia followed two steps behind. She was never a particularly chatty girl, but today she was much quieter than usual. The silence clung to them both and Amelia walked faster, as if to escape it.

'Right. Here we are. Ta-da!' she said, as if announcing an exciting trapeze act, although in reality, it was just an easel and a blank canvas, another easel holding one of her paintings of the hills, some paints, and some brushes. She had asked Piers to bring them down from the loft that morning when he'd been up there searching for her missing ornament.

'Great,' said Julia, her voice dense with ambivalence.

'I thought you'd like it,' said Amelia, chastened. 'You said you wanted to see some of my work...'

'I do,' said Julia, her eyes earnest. 'I do. Sorry. I…'

'That's okay. Look, is something up? Do you want to talk about it? Is it something to do with school?'

Julia shook her head vigorously. 'No,' she said, her voice insistent. 'Nothing.' She surged forward to the easel containing Amelia's picture.

'When did you do this?' she asked, sounding artificially light. 'It's amazing – the texture, the light, the depth…'

'Thank you,' said Amelia, baffled by Julia's demeanour. 'I'm sure you can do similar.'

It was then that she heard the tears. They were quiet to start with, but then they became sobs, with loud gulps interspersed between them.

'Heavens,' she said, walking towards her. 'What *is* the matter?'

But the girl didn't respond; instead, she threw herself into Amelia's chest, her tears now cries of anguish. Amelia stood stock-still, blindsided by Julia's outburst. She tried to think of something to say but decided in the end to remain silent. Without knowing what the cause was, she knew her words would be empty platitudes. Instead, she rubbed the teenager's back, hoping that simply her presence would reassure her, and that in time, she'd tell her what was wrong.

'There, there,' she said. 'It can't be as bad as that. It simply can't.'

Julia's continuing anguish, however, hinted at the opposite.

'Piers?'

'In the lounge,' he called out.

Amelia walked in to find her husband and Grace lying on the floor together. Grace was chuckling as Piers tickled her. It was a perfect scene, Amelia thought, and a sign that Grace was getting used to Piers, and Piers to Grace. If she could leave her with him for longer periods, she knew her life would get much easier.

'Did Julia seem strange to you when you saw her earlier?' she asked, deciding to sit down on the floor next to them. Piers continued to play with Grace.

'No, not particularly,' he replied in the same baby voice he used for Grace, who he was currently playing peekaboo with. 'Maybe she was annoyed you were late?'

'No, it's not that. She was really upset. Crying. It's something else.'

'How odd,' he said. 'Maybe hormones? It's a difficult age, isn't it, for girls? Look, shall I talk to her dad about it tomorrow? See if he knows anything?'

'Yes, that would be good,' she replied, nodding to herself. That would put her mind at ease. 'Shall I put dinner on, if you give Grace a bath?' she asked, standing up. She might as well get on with things. Her presence was clearly not required here.

'Perfect,' replied Piers.

17

December 8th

Michelle

Eleven weeks until the final hearing

'Nan?'

'Yes, Michelle, love.'

'Are we staying with you?'

'Yes, love. Mummy is poorly.'

'Okay. But I meant, can we stay with you… forever?'

'Yes. I hope so. Yes.'

Michelle reached up to her grandmother's neck, looped her arms around it and clung on tight.

'I love you, Nan.'

'I love you too, pet.'

But then Nan's neck began to melt.

Michelle tried so hard to cling on, but her hands sank into the sticky, lumpy mass and when she pulled them away, the foul mixture clung to her hands. It had hair attached to it, too, lots of matted, thin grey hair, and when she looked up, she saw that where there had previously been a kind, loving face, there was now a rotting skull. Pink and red sludge was dripping off the nose bone. And then, it opened its mouth, and…

'*Noooooooooo*!'

Michelle woke with a start. It was pitch black, so she fumbled for the switch on the bedside lamp and flicked it on.

She was incredibly warm. She threw off the duvet and lay there spreadeagled, sweating.

It took her a few minutes to realise that the heat, however, was not coming out of the radiators – it was coming out of her. Her body seemed to be on fire. And the pain she had been feeling all day, that dull ache, was now a thud, and my God, it stung down there, too. Shit, she thought; that excruciating birth was a gift that just kept on giving. She must have an infection where they had sewed her up.

She wondered what she should do. She definitely didn't want to wake up Gillian and Mike to ask for help; they'd been so kind, and they might change their mind about offering her a bed if she disturbed their sleep on the first night, like a needy toddler.

No, she needed to handle this alone. Where did they store their medicines, she wondered? There had been a mirrored cabinet above the sink in the bathroom. Might they keep their paracetamol and stuff in there? It was worth a try, she thought.

She got out of bed and padded down the corridor, closing the bathroom door as gently as she could. She pulled the light cord, opened the cabinet and peered inside. There were lots of tubes and tubs of face cream and hair styling products, and then to the right, several boxes of what promised to be painkillers. *Bingo*. She reached for a box but nudged a glass jar of face cream as she pulled it out. It tumbled out of the cabinet and down into the porcelain sink, shattering as it made impact, glass and cream fanning out in a splatter pattern that looked like modern art.

'Shit, *shit*,' she said under her breath, looking around for something to clean it up with. She spotted a spare toilet roll beside the loo, grabbed it, took out a large swathe of paper and started mopping up the broken glass and cream, which probably cost more than a meal at a posh restaurant, knowing her luck, she thought. She'd definitely chuck her out now. *Fuck*.

Suddenly, the door opened. Michelle acted on instinct and scooped up the mess in the sink and held it behind her back.

'Are you okay? I heard a noise.' It was Gillian, wearing red and white spotted button-up pyjamas, her blonde hair a halo of frizz.

'Yes, sorry, I fell over,' said Michelle, leaping for the first excuse she could think of. 'I'm sorry I woke you up.'

Gillian's eyes shifted to the cupboard above the sink, which was open, its collection of ointments and medicines – minus one large pot, obviously – very much on display.

'Have you been in the cupboard? What were you looking for?'

'Some... soap?'

'But there's soap on the sink.'

'I didn't...'

'What have you got behind your back, Michelle?'

Shit, she thought. Here we go. I am an idiot and I cannot be trusted. I've been told this so many times, and it looks like they were right.

'Nothing.'

'I'm not a fool, Michelle.'

Michelle paused while she considered her next move. Should she own up? But if she did, she was in shit for sure.

'Nothing...'

Gillian walked forward, and stood directly in front of Michelle, almost nose to nose.

'Were you looking for drugs in the cupboard? Because we don't have any codeine, we never have any.'

Michelle was astonished at her assumption, and angry.

'*No*.'

'Then what is it?' she said, reaching around to try to grasp Michelle's hand. 'What have you stolen?'

'*Nothing*!' said Michelle. 'Oh my *God*, nothing! I wouldn't steal from... Look, it's your face cream, all right?' she said, bringing the collection of glass, cream and tissue around her front once more. 'I broke it. It fell out of the cupboard. I was trying to tidy up. I know you'll be angry. I know you won't want me to stay now…'

'Why were you in the cupboard?'

'I wanted some paracetamol,' said Michelle, aware that she was feeling increasingly weak. She needed to sit down. 'I feel a bit…' She deposited the tissue into the sink, and then sank onto the closed toilet lid. '… shit.'

Gillian came and stood next to her. Michelle sat there, her head bowed, waiting for the impending diatribe to begin.

Instead, however, a cool hand reached down and touched her forehead. 'You are *boiling*,' said Gillian. 'Hang on, I'll get my thermometer.' She walked over to the mirrored cupboard, retrieved a small digital thermometer, took it out of its plastic case, turned it on and handed it to Michelle. 'Put this under your tongue,' she said.

Michelle complied without saying a word. As she sat waiting for it to beep, Gillian went back to the cupboard. 'Did you manage to take any paracetamol?' she asked her. Michelle shook her head. Gillian retrieved a pack and walked back over to her as the beep sounded. 'Thirty-nine centigrade,' she said. 'You have a high fever, darling. Right. Okay, come over here, take a swig of water from the tap, and down these two pills.' Michelle watched as she grabbed the remains of her face cream and dumped it in the bin by her feet, before turning on the tap and dropping two paracetamol tablets into her hand. 'That's it,' she said, as she leaned down to take a sip, 'down the hatch. That will help. Now, let's get you back in bed.'

Michelle followed her back down the hall and into her room, where she watched Gillian pull back the duvet and plump up her pillows.

'Hop in,' she said. Michelle did as she asked, largely because she was exhausted and also because she was so incredibly delighted and surprised not to have been turfed out onto the street. She allowed Gillian to pull the duvet over her, give her a pat, and then sit down near her feet.

'Does anything hurt?' she asked her. 'I reckon you've got an infection of some sort.'

Michelle considered whether to tell her the truth or not. She'd only just met the woman, and it all seemed a bit personal, but then, she had forgiven her for breaking something really dear, so...

'It's down there, I reckon,' she said. 'Between my legs, like.'

'Do you mean, like a sexually transmitted disease?' asked Gillian, with a perfect poker face.

'Shit, no...'

'Oh, I'm sorry, I didn't mean to...'

'Look, it's from giving birth, okay? I've got some damage down there, I think...'

'You have a baby?'

'*I don't have it*, no. I gave it up. Better for her.'

'When? When did you have this baby?'

'Two months ago. It was a girl. I called her Grace.' Had she said too much, she wondered? Michelle looked at Gillian, trying to study her reaction. 'You'll hate me for it, won't you, for giving her up? I know you and Mike wanted kids. You probably think that people like me are scum,' she said.

'Heavens, no,' said Gillian. 'I'm sure your reasons are sound. But you have had such a horribly tough time. I just can't imagine how you've got through it.'

'Well, I haven't, have I?' she said. 'I ended up trying to kill myself. I'm a total fuck-up, that's what I am.'

'You are *not* a fuck-up, Michelle,' said Gillian, sounding more comfortable swearing than Michelle could have imagined. 'And you're still here, thank heavens. That's what matters. Now, this infection. You say it hurts down there?'

'Yes. It thuds, and it stings when I wee.'

'At two months postpartum, you wouldn't really expect a new infection,' she said. 'Do you want to wee more than usual?'

'Yes. I feel like I need to go again now, actually. But man, it feels like there are knives down there.'

Gillian smiled. 'I think you have a UTI. A urinary tract infection. Have you ever had one of those before?'

'Not that I know of.'

'Well, this may be your first. I'm going to get you a large jug of water. I want you to drink as much of it as you can and then keep drinking. The more you wee, the more the infection is cleared. And we'll drop a sample of your urine into the doctor in the morning, and most likely, they'll start you on some antibiotics.'

'How do you know all this?'

'Two reasons, my dear Michelle. One, because I was plagued by UTIs for a lot of my twenties – and two, because I am actually a nurse. I work in the community.'

'Oh.'

'I work with a lot of people near where you live, in the Elgar Estate.' So that's how she knew the area, Michelle thought. That makes sense. Gillian stood up. 'I'll go and get you the water, okay? But first, I must say, I'm sorry that I jumped to those conclusions. About the drugs, and the stealing. It was an appalling thing to do. I try to be better than that.'

'S'okay,' said Michelle. 'I'm not perfect. To be honest, I'd have thought that about me, as well.'

Gillian smiled. 'Right. Well. We can confess our sins to each other another time. I'll go and get you the water, okay? And a hot water bottle. That will help with the pain.'

'Okay.'

Gillian turned and opened the door.

'I'm sorry, though,' said Michelle.

'What for?'

'For dropping your cream,' she said. 'When I get a job, I'll pay you back. I am going to try to get a job, now I've had the baby, and that.'

'Oh, don't be silly,' said Gillian. 'My sister-in-law bought me that stuff last Christmas. Costs more than myrrh, probably, but makes my eyes sting and brings me out in zits. Better off in the bin.'

As the sound of the footsteps faded, Michelle surrendered to her battling body and her extreme exhaustion. She closed her eyes and dropped back off to sleep, and for the first time in months, she did so with a smile on her face.

18

December 21st

Amelia

Nine weeks until the final hearing

'When are they letting us in?' asked Amelia, the freezing wind whipping through her thin tights, burning her skin.

'Any minute now, I think,' said Piers. 'The choir are just doing a final run-through. I *told* you you should have worn trousers. It's the depths of winter, after all.'

Amelia had chosen a red and black tartan A-line skirt tonight, which finished mid-thigh. She had owned it since university – it had a strong Nineties vibe about it – and putting it on again had felt great. But now she doubted her choice. Was it too short, maybe? Did it, in fact, make her look like a slut? Would Piers' colleagues judge them both harshly as a result, as he had said they would? Maybe. She pulled the belt of the grey coat tighter, like a corset.

She looked down at the buggy, where Grace was revelling in her early-evening sleep, gloriously cocooned in layer upon layer of thick, soft, warm fabric. She probably had no idea that they had had to wait outside the church in minus one degree centigrade for the past twenty minutes (and counting), and that was really just as well.

'Ah, looks like they're opening the doors now,' said Piers. 'Come on. We have reserved seats near the front.'

If we have reserved seats, why do we need to arrive so *bloody early*, she thought. The queue began to shuffle forwards. Amelia followed Piers, who was pushing Grace with great emphasis in the direction of the West door.

As they entered the ancient church, decked out with hundreds of flickering tea lights, fairy lights and greenery, her heart soared. This was one of her favourite annual events, and even better – this year, they had Grace with them. This was their first Christmas as a family and this evening was going to be magical, because, honestly, how could it be anything but that, when you were in a place like this?

'Ah, Mr and Mrs Howard. You're down there at the front, on the left. I thought maybe you could park the buggy in the side aisle?'

'Thank you, Virginia,' Piers said, beaming at the school secretary, who was sixty-five, always wore a ponytail tied with a bow, and had lost her husband to cancer around the same time Amelia's mother had died. Virginia smiled back, before turning to the next guest at some speed. As they walked to their seats, Amelia wondered whether she had detected a smidgeon of disgruntlement from her husband that Virginia hadn't festooned Piers and his wife and new baby daughter with more adoration.

When they sat down, however, any sign of that was gone. Piers was back to his sociable self. They were seated next to the other housemasters and their wives and he joined in with their conversation effortlessly, exchanging opinions on the rugby team's recent performance, the Year 12 play (*The Importance of Being Earnest*, this year) and recent changes to the teachers' pension scheme, which everyone seemed to agree were resoundingly bad.

Amelia, on the other hand, was focusing on Grace, who seemed to be waking up. Should she get her out of the buggy, she wondered? She could feed her now, but she had planned to do that during the service, to try to keep her quiet. She never had much success at that, but she was going to try, as she knew how important tonight was for Piers. It was the first time they'd brought Grace to a school event and she knew that he wanted to show her off.

'Hello again.' Amelia looked up. Mark, Malvern Priory's accident-prone organist, was standing by the buggy.

'Mark! Hello. How lovely to see you,' she said, glad that she had remembered his name, and recognised him. He looked different. He was dressed very smartly in a dark suit, white shirt and red tie, and he seemed to have had a shave and brushed his hair, too. He was carrying a tatty leather bag, out of which several pieces of sheet music were apparently making a bid for freedom.

'You too. I can't stay – got to play, you know – but I hope you enjoy it.'

'I'm sure I will,' she said.

'I'll play as loud as I can,' he said, with a conspiratorial smile. 'To help the baby sleep.'

'Brilliant,' she said. 'If you could manage that, it would make my evening a whole lot easier.'

'Then I shall try,' he said, shifting his weight from one leg to the other, a little too often. 'Watch out, 'Silent Night'! No one's ever played that extra *forte*, have they, ha? We could start a new trend.'

Amelia laughed. This prompted a change of colour in Mark's cheeks, from porcelain to rose pink.

'Well, bye then,' he said, turning and disappearing at speed up towards the organ loft, his shoes squeaking as he walked.

'Who was that?' asked Piers, turning around after concluding a chat with a fellow housemaster about the relative quality and availability of school kitchen staff.

'Oh, that was Mark. You know him, I think?'

'Yes, I do, of course I do,' he said. 'He plays for all our services, and he teaches music, the organ and piano, at the college. But how do *you* know him?'

'Oh, I met him here, when I came to the Christmas fair,' she said. 'He seems nice. Funny. Friendly.'

'One of life's failures, if you ask me,' said Piers, reaching into his pocket for a handkerchief and blowing his nose. 'Child prodigy, would you believe, Oxford, the Royal College of Music, and then all he ends up doing is being the organist of a minor church in the Midlands, teaching a few private pupils to make ends meet. I mean, was it worth all that effort?'

Amelia paused before replying, formulating her words carefully.

'I think if you love something like music – as he clearly loves music – it's reason enough, whatever you get paid,' she said.

'But you can't *live* on your art. I mean, you can't eat it, can you? It's absolutely fine as a hobby. You could even make a little money from it, like you do, but honestly, pursuing it as a career is downright daft.' Amelia did not respond. She'd have agreed with him previously, but now, something inside her was inciting rebellion. At that moment, the organ struck up, playing something loud and Christmassy, with the pipes sounding a bit like bells. 'And Christ! How are we supposed to talk over that racket?'

Out of the corner of her eye, Amelia could detect that Grace had stopped wriggling. She looked down into the buggy and saw that she was lying in repose, her eyes wide, and fixed straight ahead – a precursor, Amelia had learned in recent weeks, to sleep. Perhaps organ music was the magic cure she'd been looking for! Extraordinary. Well, that was one reason to come to church, at least.

A few minutes later, the lights of the church dimmed and sidespeople came to the end of each pew bearing a lit taper, holding it against the wick of the candle held by the person seated nearest to them. Then began a chain reaction of light, snaking around the church, into each and every corner and cavity.

As Amelia held her thin white candle with its white cardboard hand guard, the flame sending flickers of warm light onto Grace's angelic face, she felt a lump rise in her throat. And then, the solo voice of a young chorister began to sing a carol she had known since childhood. '*Once in royal David's city, stood a lowly cattle shed…*'

She felt a tear begin to gather in her eye. For the past few Christmases, she had been immersed in a darkness she felt she would never emerge from. Losing Leila had tested her beyond measure.

'*Where a mother laid her baby, in a manger for his bed.*'

And yet here she was, with her husband by her side, and a baby, a living baby, asleep in a pram beside her. So as the familiar words and melody reached out and entwined themselves around her heart, she let the tears fall, for unlike those spilled in previous years, these were happy.

'Well, that went well, I thought,' said Piers, as he pushed Grace's buggy towards their car, which was parked beneath one of the giant cedar trees in the Priory grounds. 'George Saunders did a good reading. He'll be an excellent Head Boy next year, don't you think?'

'Pardon?' said Amelia, her thoughts elsewhere. 'Sorry, I didn't quite hear you.'

'Saunders. I said he'd be a good Head Boy.'

'Oh yes, he seems charming,' she said, as she transferred Grace into her car seat and strapped her in.

'So, how far away is this place?' asked Piers, as they both opened their respective doors and took their seats in the car.

'Only five minutes, I think. I've got the postcode. Hang on.' Amelia took her phone out and began to scan her emails for the address.

'So how long are we staying? Because I wanted to get some final marking done tonight.'

'Until dinner is finished, Piers. It would be rude to leave before that,' she said as she typed the address into their car satnav.

Piers pulled out of the parking space quickly, but found his way blocked by an elderly lady who was struggling to drive her Vauxhall Corsa out of a disabled space in front of them.

'*Come. On*,' shouted Piers, slamming both hands onto the steering wheel. 'Seriously, you old bat, it's time to surrender your driving licence. *Do. The. Decent. Thing*,' he added, jabbing his finger through the air repeatedly in the direction of the exit as he did so. That poor woman, Amelia thought. I dearly hope she can't lip read.

'I don't think it's far,' she said, ignoring his frustration, hoping that if she did that, it might go away. 'We won't be too late.'

Amelia exhaled in relief as the woman managed to squeeze out into the road without scraping any cars. When his path was clear, Piers slammed his foot onto the accelerator and roared off towards the exit.

There was something about being behind a steering wheel that transformed all men – at least temporarily – from humane, rational adults into tub-thumping toddlers, she thought. Her father had been hideous in the car, too. On one baking hot summer's day, when they'd found themselves imprisoned in a motorway tailback on the way back from holiday in Devon, he had actually got out of the car and abandoned Amelia and her mother, apparently to go in search of the reason for the delay. He had been gone for almost an hour, and when he had returned to their car – which two other drivers had helped them push onto the hard shoulder – he had offered no explanation or apology, either for his actions or for the hold-up. But Amelia had understood. She knew that he had never been able to cope with not being in control.

'I do wish you'd cleared this with me before agreeing to go,' said Piers, as they drove onto Church Street.

'It's the end of term. I assumed you'd have finished all of the work you have to do.'

Piers sighed. 'I wanted to set Year Ten a mock GCSE before they break up. To get them geared up for next summer. Anyway, never mind. So, who are we meeting?' he said. 'Is it just this Rachel, and her husband?'

'Yes, it's just Rachel, my baby group friend, and her husband, Jake. It'll be really informal and friendly. Rachel's very relaxed about things.'

'Right. Okay. What time are we due?'

Amelia checked her watch. It was 7 p.m. 'About now,' she said.

'Just as well we didn't stay and endure Mrs Sutton's overbaked mince pies, then,' said Piers, managing a small smile. Amelia softened a little. He worked incredibly hard. She resolved to try to be more understanding. Her own fatigue levels had made her tetchy, she knew that.

They drove to Rachel's house largely in silence, the satnav chirping its instructions intermittently, and the local radio station filling the conversational void with a steady diet of Christmas songs, each one jolting Amelia back to a certain stage of her life. Wham!'s 'Last Christmas' – the song that her mother maintained was playing on the radio when she had entered the world, on an icy December day in 1984. 'Stay Another Day' by East 17 – gruesome memories of an awkward school disco in the final year of primary school. Michael Bublé's version of 'Santa Claus is Coming to Town' – a song that had been played, without mercy, every hour, on a loop, during the long four weeks she'd worked as a sales temp at a large department store in Worcester. She turned the volume down as they turned into Rachel's street. She didn't want to listen to it anymore.

'It's here I think. Number three.' They pulled up outside a yellow brick semi-detached house, which looked to have been built in the 1960s. It was on a street of similar houses, all with large, square, mostly unfenced gardens out front, and concrete paths leading to a small flat-roofed porch with a front door on one side. Piers pulled their car onto the drive and parked it behind Rachel's car, a Ford Focus.

'Did you bring the bottle of wine?' he asked, as Amelia reached in to remove Grace's car seat.

'Yep. It's in the boot.' Amelia had bought a nice bottle of Rioja and had put it in a special red paper bag, which she'd decorated herself.

'Got it,' said Piers, joining her beside the car, and walking with her to the front door. Amelia rang the bell, carrying Grace's car seat in her left hand. A light flicked on in the front porch, and a tall man wearing a blue and white chunky jumper and jeans opened the door.

'Hi,' he said, his smile broad and welcoming. 'I'm Jake. You must be Piers and Amelia.'

'Yes!' said Amelia. 'And this –' she looked at Piers, and the bottle he was holding '– *is for you*.' Piers handed over the bottle.

'Oh, brilliant, I love this stuff. *Rach! Your mates are here*,' he said, shouting into the house. 'She's just upstairs, putting the littl'un to bed. Come on in.'

They walked into a narrow hall, from which a flight of carpeted stairs led up to the first floor. Jake led them into a room on the right, a lounge diner, which spanned the full depth of the house. In the corner by the window was a large artificial Christmas tree, decorated in shades of silver and gold, and topped with a silver star. On the room's white walls were framed black and white photos of icons from music history: Bob Marley, Eric Clapton, Joni Mitchell. Amelia and Piers took a seat on a black leather corner sofa, which faced a TV, flanked by large speakers. On the other side of the room was a glass dining table and chairs and in between them stood a colourful wooden storage cabinet, bulging with toys. Amelia unclipped Grace from her seat and cradled her on her lap.

'What would you like to drink?' Jake asked. 'We have some mulled wine on the go, if you fancy that?'

'I'd love one,' said Amelia, determined to make the most of the first evening out she'd had in months.

'Just something soft for me. I'm driving,' said Piers. It was a well-rehearsed line. He always drove them everywhere, and tonight, Amelia was glad of it. Particularly because she knew that he hated mulled wine.

'She's asleep! Thank God for that.'

As Jake disappeared to make drinks, Rachel had appeared in the room. She had her purple hair thrust up into a messy topknot, and she was wearing a pair of blue jeans and a large red and white striped jumper, which was covered in damp patches. 'She kept chucking her flannel at me in the bath,' she continued, pointing to her outfit, '– as you can see. But she was absolutely knackered by the effort of that at least, so she's out for the count.'

'What I'd give for Grace to go to sleep at seven every night,' said Amelia, with emphasis. Rachel gave a sympathetic smile.

'Oh lovey, I know. But she seems asleep now?' said Rachel, looking at Grace resting in Amelia's lap. 'That's something...' Then she looked over at the sofa. 'Oh... bugger, I haven't introduced myself, have I? How rude of me. You must be Piers,' she said, walking towards him with her hand outstretched.

'Yes! That's me, by a process of elimination,' he said, standing up and taking her hand, and shaking it firmly, with a broad smile. Amelia watched her friend, noting her own genuine smile in return. 'Yes, unusually, she's been really good tonight,' said Piers. 'Which was a relief, as we've just sat through the school's annual carol service. But she didn't make a peep.'

'Ah yes, Amelia said you're a teacher?' said Rachel, sitting down next to Amelia.

'Yes, I teach Geography at the college. And I'm a housemaster, as Amelia has probably also told you.'

'Yes,' she said. 'She tells me you all live above the shop.' Amelia caught a mischievous twinkle in Rachel's eye as she said that, but Piers' smile didn't flinch.

'Ha, yes, you could put it like that. We live in an apartment in the boarding house. I'm responsible for the boys' pastoral needs. In loco parentis, as it were. But it's a situation Amelia knows well, of course. What with her dad being headmaster at the school when she was growing up.'

'Yes, and now I'm bringing up my own baby in one of the boarding houses,' Amelia said, smiling. 'There's a sort of symmetry to it.'

'Well, you must like it, then,' said Rachel. 'Rather you than me. I can't stand teenage boys. Bleh.'

'Are you being rude about teenage boys?' said Jake, entering the room with a tray full of drinks. 'That's pretty rich, given that you met me when I was a teenager. You must have thought I was okay?'

Jake placed the tray down on the coffee table, handed them out, and then pulled a chair out from the dining table, carried it opposite the sofa, and sat down on it.

'Oh, you were passable,' said Rachel, her expression conveying her understatement.

'So did you meet at school, then?' asked Amelia.

'Nah,' said Jake, laughing. 'No, man. We met at a rave. On Castlemorton Common. The illegal one – do you remember it?'

Piers, who'd grown up elsewhere, shook his head, but Amelia nodded. She had been banned from attending, of course, but the distant thud of the drum and bass that had been played 24 hours a day from multiple gigantic sound systems had kept her awake for days. But she hadn't minded; it had been thrilling, the only exciting thing ever to happen in Malvern. She had been glued to the news bulletins that week, soaking up the flagrant rule breaking and free living that was going on just a few miles away. She had lived vicariously through teenagers like Rachel and Jake.

'Yes, we were both a bit wild, back then,' said Rachel, sipping from her steaming glass of mulled wine. 'But look at us now! Totally dull. All settled down, with a kid and a mortgage.'

'It comes to us all,' said Piers, chortling. 'Although we technically still don't have a mortgage.'

'That's right! Ha. How funny. So you have a bit of immaturity to cling to, at least,' said Rachel.

An awkward silence followed, and Amelia was not surprised. She knew that Piers prized his mature, schoolmaster image above all else.

'So, Jake, how's business?' said Amelia, changing tack. 'Rachel tells me you run that new record shop on Bellevue Terrace. Dropped Beats?'

'Yep, that I do,' he said. 'It's the fulfilment of a lifelong dream of mine. I used to love shopping for vinyl when I was a kid. I asked my mum for a DJ rig on my sixteenth birthday. And its rise in popularity spurred me on. It's tricky, like, money-wise, but we do a lot of sales online. We're making it work.'

'I'm really proud of him,' said Rachel. 'He's created it from nothing.'

'Yeah, like, literally nothing,' said Jake. 'I left school with nothing but a collection of angry reports. Did a bunch of crap, low-paid jobs. Relied on Rachel to keep us afloat for years. But finally, I'm doing something, and it's working.'

'So what do you do, then, Rachel?' asked Piers, re-entering the conversation, and changing the subject.

'I'm a graphic designer,' she replied. 'I'm freelance. I design greetings cards, posters, adverts, things like that.'

'She's being modest,' said Jake. 'She's in great demand around here. This,' – he spread his arms wide – 'here is the house that Rachel built. Well, paid for. She's awesome, is Rach.'

'Don't be daft, Jake.'

Amelia watched Rachel and Jake smile at each other then, and she fought jealousy. Piers didn't ever look at her like that now, she realised.

'So, what do you do, Amelia?' asked Jake. 'When you're not bringing up a baby, I mean.'

'Oh, nothing really,' she replied. 'I teach art a bit, privately. That's it.'

'So you're an artist?'

'Yes, I suppose so.'

'Did you study art?'

'Yes…'

'Where?'

'The Royal College.'

'Wow.'

'I shouldn't be too impressed. I didn't finish. I gave it up.'

Amelia was now staring at the floor. She had revealed more than she'd meant to. She took an urgent sip of the mulled wine, which was sweet and spiced with cloves.

'You don't need an art degree to be an artist,' said Rachel. 'It's not about a certificate, it's about talent. I'm looking forward to seeing your work, Amelia. *And Piers*, you need to nag her to get her work out. She tells me she's stored it away.'

'Ah yes, well, we have less space now we have Grace,' he said, grimacing. 'Babies take up so much room, don't they…'

'They sure do,' said Rachel, pointing out the large box of toys next to the sofa, before continuing her diatribe. 'Amelia, you know, you should look at getting a job, related to your art. When Grace is bigger, I mean.'

'Oh, I don't know… I had a go at training to teach, but I just didn't like it…'

'You could even start your own business. It's such a shame to see someone letting their talents go to waste.'

'Amelia is using her talents as a mother at the moment,' said Piers, pulling himself up in his seat.

Amelia's first response was to be pleased that her husband was defending their joint decision to shelve her teacher training. But then her eyes darted to Rachel and Jake. Their faces were hard to read.

'Grace is still settling in, and we also have the boys in the house to consider,' added Piers, clearly, Amelia felt, feeling his counter-argument needed fleshing out. 'It's a big job, running a boarding house.'

'Yes, but not one Amelia gets paid for,' said Rachel, her face impassive. 'Surely it might help your finances if you both worked?'

'Our finances are fine,' Piers snapped, his face reddening, his features on high alert. 'They are *fine*.' She watched as he took a series of deep breaths; his skin colour lightened with each, and his ever-present smile returned after a couple of seconds. 'Sorry, I didn't mean to snap,' he said, after a long pause. 'It's been a long term, and Grace doesn't sleep well. We're both a bit…'

'Knackered?' suggested Rachel. 'Understandable. Look… let me check on dinner. It's just a casserole and mash, followed by shop-bought mince pies and cream, I'm afraid.'

'That will be lovely,' said Piers, sounding like he actually meant it.

Rachel stood up just as Amelia's mobile phone began to ring. She picked up her handbag, fished around inside it for the phone, and saw an unfamiliar number flash up on the screen.

'I'm sorry, I'd better take this,' she said to the others, as she stood up, accepted the call, and made to leave the room.

'Hello,' she said.

'Is that Mrs Howard?' a woman's voice asked.

'Yes,' she said, walking into the hallway and closing the lounge door.

'Mrs Howard, my name's Gabriella, I'm one of the nurses at Worcester Royal.'

'Oh…'

'I don't want you to panic, Mrs Howard, but your father has had a fall. He was brought in by ambulance a couple of hours ago. He's broken his ankle and he's a bit shaken up. A bit confused, too. Could you possibly come in to see him tonight, to reassure him?'

Why hadn't he called her, she wondered. He had her number stuck on the wall by the phone. Oh Dad, she thought. *Dad*. He was so bloody private about everything, even medical emergencies like this.

'Yes, of course,' she replied. 'I'll leave now. I'll be with you in about forty-five minutes.'

The hospital corridors were almost empty, save for a small army of cleaners, who were mopping the shiny lino with a neon-coloured liquid scented with the nauseating aroma of chemically created citrus. It was a smell which carried with it dreadful memories. Amelia rushed onwards, dodging a number of sandwich boards which warned of slippery surfaces, passing notice boards strung with shiny plastic bells and streamers and plastered with adverts for 'Xmas sales' and 'festive meals', and climbing two flights of dimly-lit stairs before she reached the ward.

She pressed a buzzer on the wall and the swing doors opened, wafting an oppressive mix of toast and toilets as they did so. Then she walked towards what she assumed was the nurses' station – a bright source of light at the far end of the corridor.

'Hello?' she said, to attract the attention of a nurse who had his eyes firmly focused on a pile of paper on the desk.

'Oh, hi. Sorry, it's not visiting hours. Can I help you?'

'I had a call, about an hour ago, from a woman. She said she was a nurse here. Sorry, I can't remember her name... it was all a bit of a shock...'

'Was it Gabriella, maybe?'

'Yes, maybe.'

'Are you –' he checked on the computer in front of him '– Mrs Howard?'

Amelia nodded.

The man stood up and craned his neck, looking left and right, finally spotting a woman emerging from a side room further up the corridor.

'*Gabriella*,' he said, in a half-shout, half-whisper. 'Your gentleman's daughter is here.'

A short, slim woman walked down the corridor towards Amelia, a glossy dark brown ponytail swishing behind her head. As she got closer, Amelia saw that she was Asian, although she couldn't pinpoint exactly where she might be from. She hadn't travelled enough to know.

'Mrs Howard, thank you so much for coming,' she said, her face a picture of welcome and reassurance. 'I know your father will be pleased to see you.' The nurse turned and walked back up the corridor, bidding Amelia to follow.

'How is he?' she asked as they walked.

'Oh, I think a lot better. He was very worried when he came in, very upset, but he seems calm now. And when I told him you were coming, he looked much more happy.'

'Really?' Amelia had said it before she could censor herself. Gabriella turned around, looking surprised.

'Yes,' she replied. 'He was calling for you a lot. You are Amelia, yes?'

'Yes,' said Amelia, astonished that her father had asked for her. He never phoned her, and never said thank you when she visited. When she went a couple of days without calling in to see him, as she had just done – Grace had consumed all of her energy – he never even mentioned it. She had concluded that he didn't even notice.

'You said he had a fall?'

Gabriella reached the entrance to a small ward, stopped and turned around. 'Yes. The paramedics found him in the hallway. He had crawled there to reach the phone.'

'Why did he fall?'

'We don't know yet. He said he lost his balance. Does he have trouble with balance?'

Amelia thought. She hadn't seen her father standing up for several weeks now. He had always been sitting on the sofa whenever she had visited.

'I don't know.'

'It might be a new thing,' said the nurse. 'I notice he is a bit deaf. That can make people lose balance. Or maybe it is to do with not taking his medication?'

'What medication?'

'Oh I'm sorry, I thought you would know. He said you were his carer.'

'Did he? Not really. I pop in most days to bring food and clean up a bit, but he mostly looks after himself. Mum died three years ago. He doesn't like company.'

'Well, maybe you can talk about it. He is in here.'

The nurse led her into a room filled with six beds, each with its own small TV screen, plastic chair and ring of curtains for privacy. It was nearly 10 p.m. and several of the patients appeared to be asleep. At the end on the right, however, she found her father sitting up in bed, a reading light illuminating his face and chest, a book lying unopened on his lap. At first, she thought he seemed normal, but then she noticed that his eyes were closed, that his habitually Brylcreemed hair was askew, that his face was an odd colour – in fact, she thought, it was almost yellow – and that his chest was rising and falling at a rapid clip.

'Dad?' No response. She tried again, louder this time. '*Dad*?' She watched as his eyes opened slowly.

'Amelia?'

'*I'm here Dad*,' she said with emphasis, trying to strike a balance between speaking so that he could hear, and not waking the other patients. 'They tell me you've hurt yourself.'

Gabriella walked past Amelia and stood at the top of the bed.

'I'm back, Mr Darke,' said the nurse, her voice soft and light. 'I told you I'd get her, didn't I? Now, I'll just check you over while you chat. Okay?' Amelia watched as she noted his oxygen read-out and took his temperature using an ear thermometer. 'You can take a seat,' she said to Amelia, pointing to the chair beside the bed. Amelia did as she suggested.

'So what happened, Dad?' she said, leaning over to take hold of his hand – which felt strange, as she couldn't remember the last time she had done so. Had she been a child? In fact, had she ever actually reached out for his hand? The thought that she might not have done so shocked her. She saw little girls holding their fathers' hands every day on her runs and walks. She realised now that her relationship with her own father had always been at best dysfunctional, and at worst, actually emotionally damaging. And yet, he had asked for her. Called for her, in fact.

'Where am I?' her father asked, his eyes wide.

She looked across at the nurse with discomfort. Her father, despite being almost ninety, had always maintained possession of his faculties.

'You're in hospital, Mr Darke,' said Gabriella. 'Do you remember? You had a fall?'

'Oh yes,' he said, as if someone had corrected his manners. 'Of course. Yes.' Then he snatched his hand away from Amelia, and grabbed hold of the nurse's arm, his eyes pleading, his mouth wide.

'*Where. Is. Amelia*?' he shouted at the nurse, at the top of his voice. '*A-mee-lee-aaah*. Don't you speak English? Where is she?'

'She's here, Mr Darke,' she replied, unruffled. 'Sitting beside you. Look.'

Amelia felt deeply embarrassed at her father's treatment of the nurse. She mouthed the word 'sorry' in her direction. She smiled in response, as if to say – 'please don't worry, I get it all the time'.

'Ah, there you are. Amelia. Thank heavens. I need you.'

'Why, Dad?' An ordinary daughter might have assumed her father needed her there for moral support. But theirs was no ordinary relationship. His eyes darted towards the nurse, and back to Amelia.

'Ah, well… erm…' he said. The nurse took the hint.

'I'll just be behind the nurses' station if you need me, Mrs Howard,' she said, withdrawing. Amelia smiled her thanks.

'What is it, Dad?' she said, as soon as Gabriella was far enough away.

'I need you to get a message to your mother,' he said. She looked at him closely. He was not joking. Definitely not. 'Tell her that I've decided. I don't want the job. It doesn't matter.'

'Sorry, Dad? Which job?'

'The school job in Malvern. I know it will make her unhappy leaving the city, you see. So tell her it's fine. We can stay in London.'

Amelia knew that her parents had moved to Malvern a year after her birth. She had always assumed that it had been a mutual decision. But if what her father was saying – in his addled state – was correct, then she had been wrong. Amelia sat there in silence for a few moments, trying to decide how to respond. Should she correct her father, or not? Would it distress him if she did? After all, remembering that his wife was dead would do nothing to improve his state of mind. In the end, she decided that doing nothing was the best policy.

'Okay, Dad. I'll do that.'

Her father exhaled loudly as she said it, as if he was releasing a breath he'd been holding for decades.

'Thank you, Amelia. You've always been such a good girl.' Her father reached out and patted her arm, before putting his own arms under the covers and closing his eyes. It seemed that he was done for today, and she had been dismissed, like one of his students.

Amelia sat back in her seat and stared, unfocused, into the Stygian darkness of the ward. She was overwhelmed by what had happened in the last few minutes: her father's confusion, this apparent new insight into her parents' relationship, and the final sting in the tail – hearing an absolute, undeniable truth repeated back to her – yes, she had always been a *good girl*.

She had spent her whole life trying to please her parents – particularly her father – trying to make up for her failures. For she had never been intelligent enough, or technical enough, or pretty enough for him. But here she was, aged thirty-six (but frequently taken for ten years more than that) with an instantly forgettable face, no career, and married to a man almost exactly like her father. For, like her father, Piers had absolutely no interest in her art – or any creativity, in fact – and he prized academic achievement above all things. And, just like her father, he liked women to be *good*. The realisation hit her hard.

Had her mother, her clever, achieving mother, moved to Malvern to be *good*? Would she actually have preferred to stay in London with her friends and family close by, and to keep her promising academic career at Imperial College intact? She had never considered it as a possibility before but doing so now brought up so many questions.

Amelia saw that her father seemed to be sleeping. She took a deep breath, reached for her handbag and walked slowly out of the ward to the nurses' station. Gabriella, the nurse, was sitting behind the desk.

'Nurse... I'm sorry... I mean... Gabriella,' she said, fumbling for her words. 'I wanted to say... My father isn't usually like that. He was so rude. Unpardonably.'

'Oh, Mrs Howard, that's fine,' she said. 'He is not himself, is he?'

'No. He is not at all normal. He seems very confused. In fact, he thinks my mother is still alive.'

'I see,' said the nurse, standing up and walking around the front of the desk. 'He is definitely anxious. Perhaps he is suffering delirium. That's quite normal after a fall, at his age. He was a little dehydrated when he came in. I'll bleep a doctor to ask them to come see him, okay?'

'Okay,' said Amelia, almost choking on tears which she had not realised were falling. She looked down and saw that Gabriella was holding out a box of tissues.

'Take a few of these,' she said. 'And we'll go to the relatives' room, shall we? You've had a shock.'

Amelia followed her down the hall and turned left into a small windowless side room which was furnished with four soft green chairs, a few mismatched cushions and a couple of prints showing scenes from rural Worcestershire. Amelia sat down opposite Gabriella.

'I'm so sorry to take up your time,' she said, looking at the nurse.

'Oh, don't be silly. Most of the patients are asleep. You are giving me something to do,' she said.

'Are you on shift all night?' she asked.

'Yes. But I like nights. I have time to think,' she said.

'But it must be difficult, for family life?'

'My family live a long way away, my dear.'

'I'm sorry. You must miss them,' said Amelia, feeling guilty for her assumption. 'Where are they?'

'My daughter is in the Philippines. She lives with my mother.'

'How old is she?'

'She's eight.'

'Oh.'

'It's okay. I earn good money here, and I can send it home. And if I stay here longer, I can apply for citizenship, and she can grow up here. It's worth it, for me.'

The nurse watched Amelia intently as she blew her nose and used another tissue to wipe under her eyes.

'Do you have children, Mrs Howard?'

'I…'

Suddenly, Amelia couldn't breathe. It felt like her throat had closed over and her heart was pounding so fast, she could feel it in her chest. She felt sweat rise all over her in a tidal wave, and when it began to subside, she started to shake.

'Mrs Howard? *Mrs Howard*. I think you are having a panic attack,' she said, moving swiftly to sit next to Amelia. 'Try to breathe deeply, to the count of four. With me. Okay? Breathe in – one – two – three – four – and then out – one – two – three – four.'

They sat there for a few minutes, Gabriella monitoring Amelia as she continued to focus on her breathing; in, out, in, out, deeper each time. Finally, her heart began to slow, and she stopped shaking. But then those feelings were replaced by something else. Shame.

'I'm so sorry,' she said, as soon as she could speak again. 'What a state I'm in.'

'Don't be sorry. You have had a shock. Your father…'

'No, it's not about my father. Not really. You asked about… children.'

'Yes,' said Gabriella, moving back in her seat, as if to give Amelia space to speak. And Amelia took it, because she was tired of keeping everything inside. And most of all, she was tired of pretending that she hadn't existed.

'I managed to get pregnant once. Only once. IVF. She was called Leila.'

'I see.'

'No, you don't. Because she wasn't a real person, not really. Because she died, before she was even born. She died in me, and I didn't even know.'

'I'm so sorry. But she *was* a real person, you know. We are all God's creatures, even if we only live for a minute.'

'But she didn't breathe. She never... she came out blue. But she was so beautiful. She had this mass of dark brown hair, and a button nose, and a tiny chin. I remember wrapping her little fingers around my own, just to see what that might feel like. They let me hold her for as long as I wanted. They wrapped her up, and I just lay there in that horrible room, staring at her, willing her to breathe.'

'If she grew inside you, she lived,' said Gabriella. 'That's what I believe. I am Catholic, and that's what we believe. She was a real person. Leila. She is in heaven, too, I'm sure.'

Although Amelia had no faith whatsoever, the nurse's words were warm and heartfelt, and she was grateful. And just being able to talk about Leila was an enormous relief.

'How many weeks was she when she was born?'

'Thirty. I went into labour quickly and unexpectedly. The doctors still can't tell me why. No one can.'

'How long ago was this?'

'Three years ago,' Amelia answered. 'Just before my mother died. And I haven't been able to get pregnant since. We have tried and tried, and I had three rounds of IVF. Ridiculously expensive, exhausting. I got pregnant on the last round, with Leila. That was my one chance.'

And then Amelia felt immense guilt, because she knew that Grace was at home, right at that moment, with Piers. Grace, a living baby, a baby who was, most likely, hers to keep. She was immensely lucky to have this chance. So why wasn't she euphoric about it? Why couldn't she ignore that nagging voice in her head which kept telling her not to love Grace, in case she had to let her go too?

'There is always another chance,' said Gabriella. 'You mustn't give up.'

Amelia dabbed at her eyes with a tissue. She thought of the other nurse who had kindly, gently removed Leila from her arms that evening and given her a sleeping pill to usher in oblivion.

And then she thought of Grace, who she enveloped in her arms every night as she paced the room, feeling her little chest rising and falling, her tiny hands grasping Amelia's fingers so hard, she had to unfurl them when it was time to put her in her cot.

'Yes,' she said, nodding at the nurse, the words. '*Yes.*'

19

December 24th

Michelle

Nine weeks until the final hearing

'Just roll it. That's it. Not too hard, or it'll be tough as old boots. Spread it out at the edges. We want to get as many out of this as possible.'

Michelle lifted up the rolling pin and examined her efforts. She'd got half of it stuck on the rolling pin and the pastry was far from being a uniform pound-coin width throughout, as ordered, but she still felt a tiny burst of pride. These would be her first home-made mince pies, ever, and her nan would be proud of that, she thought. She had made delicious cakes – fruit ones, mostly, like Christmas cake.

Gillian and Mike's kitchen smelled of spice and booze and wet dog. Mike had just taken Rory out for a walk to a nearby quarry, and he'd apparently thrown himself into the murky water with wild abandon, despite the fact it must have been zero fucking degrees in there.

It was frozen solid outside. She had almost fallen arse over tit on a frozen puddle when they'd walked out to the car that morning, going to pick up party supplies. It seemed astonishing to her now that she'd once spent a winter sleeping out in this sort of temperature. She remembered that a sort of numbness had set in eventually, when she could no longer shiver, and she recalled the true value of the piece of cardboard beneath her that had prevented the tiled doorway floor she'd bedded down on turning into her very own mortuary slab.

'Right, so now you need to take a cutter,' said Gillian, reaching into a box in one of the cupboards beneath the counter, 'and cut out the lids.'

'Gotcha,' said Michelle, taking the cutter and setting herself to the task.

'Are you going to be all right, this evening?' asked Gillian. 'I can imagine you might not feel up to being sociable.'

Michelle paused. She was still recovering from her overdose. Frankly, she still felt like she could sleep for days, and she was not a sociable person. In fact, she suspected most people went out of their way to avoid her. However, she was so grateful to Gillian and Mike for their generosity, and a part of her was also incredibly curious to meet their guests.

'Yeah, I should be fine,' she said.

'Okay. But if you're feeling tired at any point, just go to bed. Honestly, we won't mind.'

'Got it.'

Michelle had now cut out circles from almost all of the pastry and had deposited them delicately on the top of deep pastry cases, filled with a spoonful of mincemeat each, and a tiny slice of marzipan. 'That's my mother's secret,' Gillian said. 'They taste delicious.' Gillian nodded and smiled at Michelle's work, picked up a brush, dipped it in milk and began to coat the pies. 'I'm glad you're feeling better,' she said. 'And I wanted to say – if you want to talk about anything more – about the things we discussed when you first arrived – I am here, okay? We can chat, whenever.'

Michelle watched as Gillian picked up the tray of pies, opened the oven door, placed them inside and snapped it shut. She had been so relieved to talk about Grace, she really had, but now she'd said it, she kind of wanted to shove it back in the box. Grace had gone, and that was it. Done.

'So tell me again who these people are that are coming?' she asked.

'There will be a few people from church, the food bank, and some of our ex-foster kids,' she said. 'We always get them round on Christmas Eve every year. It's become a sort of tradition.'

'Ace,' said Michelle, meaning it. 'Will they think it's weird though, me being here? I don't really want to explain stuff.'

'Don't be silly. They don't expect anything at all, either way,' replied Gillian. 'We have fostered a lot over the years. They won't even question it. Or we can just say that you're a family friend, and that you've come to stay with us, if you like.'

'You didn't have to do this,' said Michelle. 'Put yourself out…' In truth, she feared feeling like a fish out of water amongst a crowd of well-to-do people who'd never met someone who didn't have a mortgage or a credit card, let alone someone who'd spent most of their childhood in care. But knowing that some of their foster kids were coming had reassured her a little. She reckoned she could handle this, for Gillian.

'You silly girl. I'm enjoying this. I'm doing this for me,' said Gillian, reaching out to pull Michelle in for an unexpected hug. Michelle winced and pulled away.

'I'm sorry…' she said. 'I don't really…'

Gillian looked crestfallen. Crap, Michelle thought; I upset everyone in the end, don't I?

'No, I'm sorry,' said Gillian, pulling away. 'I shouldn't push you to do something you aren't comfortable with. Apologies. I should have thought. Let's forget it happened, shall we? Now. Shall we have a well-earned cup of coffee?'

***

'Gillian! So wonderful to see you. And dressed in red and green for the season too! What do you remind me of...?' From her position at the top of the stairs, Michelle could see a large man with a booming voice had arrived at the door, bearing a bottle of red wine.

'An elf?'

'Bah humbug. No. You look like a personification of holly and ivy; the evergreen life of our Lord and saviour.'

'Hugh, you are ever the priest, and ever the gentleman,' replied Gillian, turning around to Michelle as she did so. 'Hugh, this is Michelle – she's staying with us for a while. Michelle, this is Hugh – he's the vicar of Malvern Priory.'

Michelle took in the enormous presence of the man who'd now walked through the door. He was wearing polished pointy brown shoes, rose pink trousers, a pink and blue check V-neck jumper and a chunky blue knitted cardigan. There was no sign at all that he was a priest, aside from his voice, which she reckoned would easily fill Westminster Abbey, without the help of a microphone.

He walked over to Michelle, his face a picture of interest and welcome, holding out his hand. 'Michelle. A pleasure to meet you.'

Michelle smiled and took his hand, fascinated by his flamboyant personality, and oddly, not at all afraid. She had spent most of her life being frightened by strangers, but something about this house, about Gillian and Mike, seemed to be giving her an invisible armour. And it felt great.

'Hugh, you're first to arrive,' said Gillian. 'Which means you get an exclusive preview of our mince pies. Michelle and I spent all afternoon making them. Won't you come down?'

The three of them walked down the stairs into the kitchen, its cupboards and surfaces newly festooned with ivy Michelle and Gillian had spent the afternoon picking in the garden, white fairy lights entwined amongst its leaves and stems. The aroma of mulled wine, sweetened with honey and sugar and spiced with nutmeg, ginger and cloves, filled their nostrils. Even Michelle, who'd been sworn off alcohol for years, was tempted to try some. Mike, meanwhile, was removing trays of mince pies from the oven, placing them on a wire rack to cool, and sprinkling them with icing sugar.

The doorbell rang once more. Gillian ran up the stairs to answer the door, leaving Mike, Hugh and Michelle in the kitchen.

'So Michelle, how do you know these two cracking people?' asked Hugh, as he walked over to the hob to inspect the vat of mulled wine.

Michelle froze. She had had all afternoon to think about her response to this question, knowing that it would surely come, but had failed to come to any conclusion.

'Michelle is a new volunteer for the food bank,' said Mike. The statement had been delivered with speed and conviction, and Michelle was so grateful to him, she fought the urge to run up and kiss him. Which was extraordinary. She never wanted to kiss anyone.

'Ah, wonderful,' replied Hugh. 'That food bank is very close to my heart. It's incredibly shaming that it needs to exist at all, but I'm so very glad it does. Our church is open to everyone, and I feel that strongly.'

He was about to launch, Michelle thought, into a well-rehearsed sermon, but he was interrupted by Gillian coming down the stairs with more guests in her wake. There was a young white bloke, about twenty-five, maybe, with a goatee beard and closely clipped hair, wearing a hoodie and loose jeans. Behind him there was a slim black woman, also in her early twenties, Michelle thought. She was holding a toddler, a little girl of no more than two, who was fast asleep on her shoulder.

'Steve and Cecily! How wonderful to see you again,' said Mike, walking towards the couple, beaming.

'And you, Mike,' said Cecily, her voice warm but muted, in an effort, Michelle reckoned, not to wake her child.

'Why don't you come over here and take a seat?' said Gillian to Cecily. 'You could put her down in our bedroom, if you like? Or on the sofa here, with a blanket?'

'Nah, don't worry, Gill. She sleeps much better on me. I don't mind. As long as I have wine,' she answered, her rich laughter filling the room.

Michelle looked around her. Mike was now chatting to Steve and she knew that just behind her, Hugh was standing silently, waiting to resume his earlier conversation. She needed an out. And wine gave her the answer.

'I can get the wine,' she said to Gillian, who'd just heard the doorbell go once more. 'Don't worry. You go.'

Gillian smiled her thanks and rushed past her. Michelle took a deep breath and walked over to where Cecily and her daughter were sitting.

'There's some mulled wine, or some bottles of white or red,' she said.

'Oh, a glass of white would do me fine, thanks. And I'm sorry… I don't think we've met before?'

'Nah. I'm Michelle. I'm just staying here for a bit,' she said, hoping that that would be an end to it. 'I'll go and get your wine.'

She walked over to the kitchen, grabbed a glass from a pack they'd apparently borrowed from the supermarket, poured wine in from an open bottle and carried it back.

'Here you go,' she said, presenting it and standing back, uncertain what her next move should be.

'Why don't you get a glass and join me?' asked Cecily.

'I don't drink.'

'Oh go on, have a glass of juice with me, then? I'll be lonely, otherwise. And bored. Steve is talking to Mike, and they get on so well, those two, I probably won't see him for the rest of the evening.'

Michelle remembered Hugh and his need to spout forth about his church and decided that perhaps she would be safer with Cecily.

'All right, then. Okay. I'll be back in a minute,' said Michelle, feeling embarrassed at her stilted speech and awkward demeanour, next to a woman who clearly felt at home in every setting.

'Great.'

Michelle returned to the kitchen briefly to source a glass of cranberry juice (Gillian would be pleased) and returned to the lounge, sitting down on the other end of the sofa to Cecily.

'What's her name, your little girl?' she asked.

'Oh, this is Alice,' she said. 'She's really, really shit with babysitters, so we have to take her with us everywhere. It's exhausting.'

'It must be,' she said, deadpan.

There was an awkward silence.

'So you're staying here with Gill and Mike?'

'Yeah... I'm... volunteering at the food bank.'

'The one at the church?'

'Yeah, that's the one.'

'You'll see me there, then.'

'Do you volunteer there as well?' she asked.

'No, lovey. We use it. Steve and me.'

'Oh. I thought...'

'Steve's got a job now, which is brilliant – at a garage in Malvern Link – but his wage isn't enough to get by. And I can't work, because of Alice. Childcare costs too much.'

'Oh, right.'

'Are you shocked? That we use a food bank?'

Michelle considered her instinctive judgement about the couple. They were smart, presentable – and yet they used the same service she had. She was shocked, yes, but not in the way Cecily had meant.

'Nah. But now I feel guilty,' she said, staring at the floor, clenching and unclenching her toes. 'Because I lied. I don't volunteer there. I use it too. The food bank.'

'Ah, right. Well, welcome to the club, then. There's loads of us in Malvern. Hundreds, probably. There's no shame in it, honestly. I thought there was, to start with, but seriously, if it keeps Alice fed, and we can still afford the rent, I'm cool with it.'

Michelle looked at Cecily, who was sipping her white wine from her left hand, while rubbing the back of her sleeping daughter with her right. She looked so assured. She definitely didn't seem to give a second thought to what anyone thought of her. She envied her that.

'So, are you here on a fostering basis, or whatever they call it, these days?' asked Cecily.

Both disarmed and comforted by the other woman's candid nature, Michelle decided to tell the truth.

'Yeah, sort of. I mean, I'm an adult now, so I'm not being fostered, but social services know I'm here, and they're paying Mike and Gillian a bit to feed me, and stuff.'

'Why are you here, if you don't mind me asking?' said Cecily. 'And before you answer – I was here, too, for a bit. I ran away from home as a teenager. My mum was an alcoholic, and my dad beat me. So I left. And so I ended up here. Best thing that ever happened to me, actually. Alice aside.'

Cecily bent down and kissed her daughter lightly on the top of her head. Michelle's stomach turned over with a sudden attack of jealousy at the sight. Not angry, vicious jealousy – just the kind that caused a really visceral, physical ache, an ache which filled the invisible but tangible void where Michelle's arms should also have been holding a child.

'Are you okay?' said Cecily, looking at Michelle with a worried expression. Michelle realised, too late, that her anguish was showing on her face.

'Yeah. I'm all right. Sort of. It's been... a really shitty few months.' Michelle reached for her glass of juice and took a large gulp.

'It's okay. You don't have to tell me anything. Honestly. I'm sorry I'm prying. Steve says I'm too nosy, and that I talk too much. And I think he's probably right on both counts.'

Michelle swallowed. 'S'all right. It helps to talk about it, I'm finding. I told Gillian a bit last night, and it felt good. Strangely.'

'She's a good listener. She listened to a hell of a lot of crap from me over the months I stayed here.'

'Yeah, she didn't seem too shocked.'

'Nah, she's heard it all, and seen it all, I think, what with her nursing.'

'Yeah.'

They sat there in silence for a minute, both watching the interactions between the growing crowd of revellers in the kitchen. They were beginning to spill into the living area, and the volume from the hubbub had grown louder. It felt to Michelle like a perfect smokescreen. No one except Cecily would hear what she had to say, and what did it matter that Cecily knew? She didn't know anyone Michelle knew. She was a safe vessel for Michelle's worries and nightmares.

'I had a baby,' she said, finally. 'Grace. She will be three months old now, almost. I gave her up. For adoption.'

'Why?' There was no accusation in Cecily's voice, just a gentle questioning.

'Because I'm a fuck-up. I've always been one, like my own fucking useless mother. There's no way I can take care of a child. I can barely take care of myself. And you know, adoption means that they'll find her a nice family, wealthy people, maybe, and she won't have to spend half her childhood in care, like me, being passed from pillar to post, never feeling wanted anywhere. I want her to feel secure. I really want that.'

'I can understand that, that feeling of not belonging. And

leaving care is hard too, isn't it? It's like you're just sent out on your own, with no back-up. Although I think they're better at it now, social services? With the care covenant and stuff.'

Michelle knew about the care covenant, the arrangement where social services had promised to support care leavers until they were twenty-five. She didn't want to let Cecily know that she'd opted out of it. Even given their shared background, she didn't think she'd understand.

'Well, the thing is, whether I'd wanted to keep Grace or not, I couldn't've. The judge would have taken her away anyway, because they didn't like where I was living.'

'What was wrong with it?'

Michelle took another gulp of juice.

'It wasn't the place, to be honest. We could've cleaned it up. It was my partner, Rob. He's into drugs, you know? And we fight sometimes. But it's my fault, as well as his. The fighting.'

'I see.'

'Do you?'

'Yeah. I've met a few other mums at the Sure Start centre I go to, who had a similar thing happen. But they got the babies back in the end.'

'Oh, right.'

Michelle had no appetite for a lecture. They sat in silence for a moment, Cecily looking at her in expectation, but not, she thought, in judgement.

And then suddenly, a realisation came to Michelle like a bolt of lightning.

'*I want her back*,' she said, speaking as quickly as she could, to get it out before she could change her mind.

I. Want. Grace. Back.

Wow, thought Michelle. I really do. I want her back.

That ache she felt, that ache she'd been suppressing with the help of Rob's drugs, that stabbing in her heart that had driven her to try to take her own life – it was an ache to hold her daughter again, she now realised.

'What will you need to do to get her?' asked Cecily.

'I dunno. I think I have to do what social services say,' she said. 'And that's the problem. I don't trust those bitches.'

'Why?'

Michelle raised an eyebrow.

'Stuff. Just… stuff. They never tell me the truth. Do *you* trust them?'

Cecily shrugged.

'Dunno. Kinda. They were annoying, sure, but they sorted me out with a placement here, so…'

'They betrayed me,' said Michelle.

'Wanna talk about it?' said Cecily. Michelle looked across at her. Her glass was empty. She took her chance.

'Refill?' she said.

'Yeah, sure. Another white, if you could.'

Michelle got up and walked over to the kitchen, relieved to have bought herself a bit of time. She had only ever told Rob what had happened and that had taken months. She walked over to the kitchen, where a large group of people had gathered. She spotted Gillian and Mike among them, talking animatedly to their guests. She noticed that Gillian had spotted her out of the corner of her eye, and it looked to Michelle that she was about to call her over. She wanted to avoid this at all costs; she felt too knackered and too out of place to make polite conversation. Cecily's straightforward talking, while unnerving, felt easier to deal with.

She grabbed an open bottle of white wine from the kitchen surface and retreated at speed to the sofa in the lounge, and Cecily.

'Here you go,' she said, pouring wine into Cecily's glass, which she'd been carrying in her other hand. 'And you've got your very own bottle, for when you need a refill.'

'Ace,' said Cecily, taking the glass and the bottle, and putting them both on the floor by her feet. 'Good thinking.'

Michelle sat down next to her once more.

'I'm sorry for asking so many questions,' said Cecily. 'I get that you probably don't want to talk about it. Sorry. And thanks for the wine.'

'No bother. And yeah, you're right, I don't want to talk about it. I never do… But…' she paused, and took a breath, 'I'm starting to wonder whether I'm getting that wrong.'

'What do you mean?'

'I mean, I told Gillian about the baby… and I've felt a bit better since, you know? I feel a bit lighter.'

'I think talking does help,' said Cecily. 'I had counselling after I left home. It helped, telling someone else about all of the crap I went through.'

'Yeah. I've never done that. It felt safer just to try to forget it all.'

'But that shit doesn't really go, does it? No matter how much you drink, or party, or take drugs, or sleep with random people…' Michelle could see that Cecily had a faraway look in her eye. '… Sorry, that's probably more about me, ha,' she added.

But Michelle felt understood for the first time. This woman *got* her.

'Nah, most of that is me, too,' she said, looking up at Cecily and smiling, even though their conversation was about her past. Her fucking awful, so bad she'd tried to erase it, past.

'It's not just about my baby,' Michelle said, finally. 'It's about more than that. Social services and I go back a long way. Like I said before, *they betrayed me*.'

'Go on,' said Cecily. 'If you want to.'

Michelle picked up her glass of juice and cradled it.

'I had a sister. I *have* a sister. But I don't know where she is.'

'Wow. That's a pretty big thing to carry around.'

'Yeah. She was – is – called Grace. That's why I gave the baby that name, see? It felt right. I last saw Grace – my sister Grace – when she was three, and I was six. We were both in care, in a children's home, and they – social services – they took her away from me, without giving me warning, or letting me say goodbye. I could hear her calling out to me in the hallway, but they locked the door of the playroom, and I couldn't get out. She was crying so loudly, and I couldn't comfort her.'

Michelle felt a lump rise in her throat, and gulped juice down to try to subdue it.

'You don't know what happened to her?'

'I know she was adopted. They told me that. But they wouldn't tell me who had adopted her, so that was that. And it was from then on that I got really bad, really difficult to handle, I think. I was angry, you see. No, I mean, I was *furious*. Mostly, I was angry with Nan. She'd looked after us after Mum left us – she was an alcoholic, Mum, she couldn't even look after herself – but we loved it there, with Nan. She had a lovely three-bedroom semi in Malvern Link. We each had our own bedroom. Mine was pink and it had a border running around the walls, full of Disney princesses and fairy-tale castles. Grace and I used to love running around the garden, playing hide and seek in the wardrobes in their house, playing dress-up in Nan's clothes. It was like a proper childhood.'

'So, what happened?'

'We packed our bags to go on holiday once – she had a static caravan near Weston, and we thought we were going there – but she drove us to a children's home instead. We didn't know immediately that it was a children's home, of course – for a bit, we thought Nan had surprised us by booking us a hotel, or a B&B. It was a huge place in Great Malvern, one of those massive Victorian villas, with high ceilings and massive windows. But it wasn't a hotel, obviously. And she left us there. She just got into her red Ford Cortina and left us. I still remember watching her drive away.'

'Oh my God. How old were you?'

'I was five. Old enough to know what was going on. Grace was two though, and although she cried for a bit, the old woman who ran the home managed to bribe her with dolls and biscuits, eventually. She didn't cry for anywhere as long as me. I cried on and off for weeks. In between raising hell.'

'So you don't know why she left you there?'

Michelle wrinkled her nose. 'I always thought she'd decided I was too hard to handle. I blamed myself for us ending up there, and for Grace being taken away. But now, I'm not sure. Something Laura, my social worker, said…'

'Oh?'

'When I was in hospital a couple of weeks ago, she said that it hadn't been Nan's choice. And she promised me she'd tell me all about it, if I agreed to stay here, and come to meet with her after New Year to talk about things.'

'Oh, I see. Wow. You've had it really rough, Michelle. Really rough.'

Michelle thought about that. She had always blamed herself for where she'd ended up – her behaviour had, after all, hardly been stellar – but she could see that, seen through someone else's eyes, her story looked very different.

'Thank you,' she said. 'Thanks.'

'What for?'

'For telling me it wasn't all my fault.'

'From where I'm sitting,' said Cecily, waving her glass of wine around for emphasis, 'none of this is your fault at all.'

Michelle caught her breath.

'But I was the one who got expelled from school. I was the one who ended up homeless. I was the one who gave my baby away.'

'Sweetheart, it seems to me you've had zero support in your

life. Nada. Zilch. People have fucked you over time after time. It's not at all surprising that you've gone off the rails a bit.'

Michelle felt her eyes beginning to water. She was close to crying, she thought. She gulped down the remainder of her juice and stood up quickly.

'Another refill?' she said.

'Hang on a sec,' said Cecily, eyeing her. 'Sit down, lovey. You've had a shitter of a time. You need a rest. Let's see if I can call Steve over – he can get us another drink. We have unfinished business.' Cecily waved in the direction of the kitchen until she caught Steve's eye. 'There. So. You are here, ahead of a meeting. That's exciting, isn't it?'

'Is it?' said Michelle, drawing her legs up beneath her. 'I dunno. Maybe they'll tell me something I don't want to hear. Maybe the truth is worse than I've imagined?'

'But they might tell you where Grace is,' said Cecily, taking another sip.

Michelle froze. 'Do you think they could?' she said. 'I thought they couldn't, that it was against the law, or whatever?'

'If she's asked about her family, I think they can,' said Cecily. 'Anyway, it's worth asking, isn't it?'

'Yeah.'

'Does your nan still live in that house?'

'Nah. I ran away from the children's home once, but when I got back there, I found the house empty, and a For Sale sign outside. She's long gone.'

'So they might be able to find her, too.'

'Yeah, maybe,' said Michelle, unable to overcome or ignore the anger she'd directed at her grandmother for the best part of two decades. 'If she's still alive.'

'She might be. How old would she be?'

'Dunno. Mid-eighties, maybe?'

'It's possible.'

'Yeah...'

Michelle's thoughts were interrupted by the sight of Gillian walking towards them bearing a plate of mince pies.

'Hello, both of you,' she said. 'Steve said you might be in need of nourishment. He's headed off to the loo, but he'll be here in a sec. In the meantime, I thought you might like one of our mince pies, Cecily. Michelle and I made them. They're fresh out of the oven.'

Cecily reached over and took one, but Michelle, her mind still in a place she had never previously dared to go, shook her head.

'Oh, go on. You worked hard to make them,' said Gillian, sitting down next to her.

Michelle took a deep breath, leaned over, and took one. 'Ta,' she said, taking a bite quickly and gulping it down, feeling the hot mincemeat sear her throat. Then she began to cough, deeply and profusely, so hard that she thought she might vomit.

'Oh golly, are you okay Michelle? Do you want a lie down? Do you want to go to bed?'

Michelle could feel the gaze of the two women either side of her meeting over her back. 'She's in a state,' those eyes would be saying. 'The poor thing.'

Jesus, how she hated pity.

'I'm fine,' she said, her voice hoarse. She sat up straight and swallowed several times, to try to clear her throat.

'Michelle and I have been getting to know each other,' said Cecily, stepping in to save the atmosphere from swallowing Michelle whole.

'Oh good. I hoped you would,' said Gillian.

'She tells me you are both going to a meeting with social services in a week or so.'

'Yes – well, I'll only attend if Michelle wants me to,' replied Gillian. 'It's not my meeting.'

'I want you to come,' said Michelle, speaking with a sudden

confidence. Sometimes, she realised, you needed to reach rock bottom before you began to see the way out. 'Because I want to find out about my family, and I want you to make sure I stick to my guns when I'm in there. They have a way of twisting things, social services.'

'Of course,' said Gillian, taking a seat on the sofa between Michelle and Cecily. Both Gillian and Cecily sat in silence, waiting for Michelle to continue. They were good people, Michelle thought. And good listeners.

'But anyway, Gillian, I need your help,' she said, finally, after a deep breath. 'Because I want to get my baby back,' she said, pulling herself up straight. 'That's even more important than the past, isn't it? I want a future. With *her*.'

She looked Gillian straight in the eye.

'I want Grace back.'

PART TWO

20

January 1st

Amelia

Eight weeks until the final hearing

'How are you feeling, Dad?'

Amelia raised her voice as much as she could, to compensate for the mechanical whine of the minibus tail-lift.

'I'm fine, Amelia. You don't need to shout,' he replied, his voice gruff.

The driver, who was currently operating the lift, pointed at his own ears, and mouthed: '*He's got his hearing aids in.*'

Ah, thought Amelia. Obviously the nurses made him wear them. Good on them. It was more than she'd ever managed to do.

'Great. That's wonderful. It's so lovely to have you back,' she said, as the driver pushed his wheelchair off the lift and onto the pavement outside his flat.

'*Yes*,' said her father, his voice now soft. 'It *is* good.' Amelia was taken aback by his tone, which was entirely unfamiliar. She took a deep breath to mask her surprise and took hold of the handlebars of his chair.

'I'll take him from here,' she said. 'If you could bring his bag?' The driver nodded and followed her up the concrete path and ramp to her father's front door. She turned the key in the lock and pushed the door open, struck as she did so by the familiar smell of the apartment – a mixture of dust, polish and tea. When her mother had been alive, it had only smelled of the latter two. She pushed her father over the past fortnight's post – she'd deal with that later – and into the lounge.

'I'll just put this here, then, shall I?' said the driver, leaving her father's holdall beside the sofa.

'Yes, that's fine, thank you,' she said. 'I've got it from here. Thank you. I'll show you out.'

She led the man back along the hallway to the front door.

'He's a nice man, your dad,' said the driver, as he walked through the doorway and turned around to say goodbye. 'He was telling me all about you on the way home.'

'Was he?' she asked, stunned.

'Yes. Wish my dad spoke about me like that,' he said, with a chuckle. Amelia couldn't think how to reply, so she merely smiled. 'Well, I'll be off then,' he said.

'Bye,' she said, closing the door swiftly. And then, as an afterthought: 'Thank you.' She leaned against the door then for a moment, considering what he'd said. She'd been to visit her father most days since he'd been admitted to hospital, and he'd recovered from his confused state after a day or so. The doctors had put it down to dehydration. But here he was, apparently telling all and sundry how great she was? She walked back into the lounge, where her father was waiting in his chair, staring into space.

'Sorry about that, Dad. I was just saying goodbye to your driver. Would you like to get out and sit in your armchair? It would be more comfortable I think.'

'Yes, thank you, Amelia.'

'Do you need my help?' she asked, tentatively. He never usually accepted any physical assistance, but she knew that he was considerably weaker now, after ten days spent in bed.

'That would be helpful,' he said. She leaned down, pulled up the footrest of the wheelchair and offered her arms to her father, who pulled himself up to a standing position, shuffled a few feet to the left and lowered himself, with her help, into his chair.

'There you go,' she said. 'Shall I get you a cup of tea? And a fig roll?' They'd always had fig rolls on caravan holidays when she had been a child. She'd spotted them in the supermarket when she'd been there to pick up supplies for him that morning and bought them on impulse.

'Yes, please,' he said, his voice still soft and breathy.

She busied herself in the kitchen, which she'd cleaned in anticipation of his arrival, and returned with a mug of strong tea and two fig rolls on a small plate.

'There you go, Dad,' she said, placing them on a side table. 'Now, is there anything else I can get you before I go? I've left Grace with Piers, but I should go back to check on her. He's not great being left with her for too long. But a carer is coming to help you at bedtime, and in the morning. I've set that up, okay?'

She walked over to the sofa and retrieved her coat from where she'd dumped it when she'd first arrived.

'Amelia?'

'Yes, Dad?'

'Come and sit down here for a minute. If you have time?'

Amelia was shocked and chastened. Perhaps she should have realised that he would need company for a while, but she had become so used to him not really wanting any, that a swift departure had become routine. Particularly because he had actually appeared to resent her daily visits in the past.

'Of course, Dad.' She sat down on the edge of the sofa, nearest to her father's armchair.

'Now. Will you have a fig roll?' he asked. She nodded with a smile, and they sat there in companionable silence for a minute or two, the only sound in the room being the clicks of their teeth meeting as they chewed, and the ticking of her parents' grandfather clock, which stood tall and proud in the hall, the ceiling a good four inches too low for visitors to fully appreciate its beauty.

'Thank you for coming to visit me so often in hospital,' said her father, his biscuit now chewed and swallowed.

'Of course I visited, Dad. I always visit you.'

'But you have a baby to look after now, too. I know that's hard work. You don't have to come so often, you know. I will be fine, with the carers.'

'But I want to.'

'That's kind, Amelia. So very kind.' Amelia didn't know quite how to respond to this new, soft, thoughtful, thankful version of her father, so she remained silent, and let him fill it. 'The nurses tell me I was quite doo-lally in hospital there, for a bit.'

'Yes. You were a bit,' she replied.

'Quite. Did I… Did I…' he paused – 'did I say anything about your mum?'

'Yes. You thought she was still alive, I think.'

'Ah. I wondered about that. I dream that she is, sometimes. I think maybe I was partly asleep when I was talking to you.'

'Yes, I think perhaps that you were.'

'Amelia. I don't think I'm going to live much longer…'

Amelia's head shot around to look straight at her father, the shock at what he'd just said registering in her face.

'*Dad….*'

'Now come on, you and I both know that I'm on my last legs. I'm getting on a bit. I can see it, and so can you.'

'But…'

'And oddly, it is making things clearer for me. Perhaps, as we approach our meeting with our maker, we are given the opportunity to see where we went wrong in the past. A bit like an appraisal, if you will.' The grandfather clock ticked on in the distance, as Amelia sat, frozen, on the sofa. 'And I think I have to apologise to you. And to your mother, if she was still here. Both of you.'

'Why?' asked Amelia, her voice catching.

'Because I realise I have been incredibly selfish, Amelia. I have put myself and my blessed career first, always, and my family second. And I am realising, now, far too late, that I had things the wrong way around. And I am deeply sorry for it.'

'But Mum was happy!'

'Your mum, your incredibly talented, clever mother, was ripped away from a job she loved in London and brought here. Because of my ambition. And she made the best of it, of course. And she did well, yes, but I think she found it much harder to progress here, so much harder to get taken seriously as a scientist. Because she was a woman, you know, and it was the Eighties, and things were different then. So she worked all the hours that God sent to get on, and the result was, of course, that you didn't have either of us around very much. You were just left to your own devices. And that was not what we should have been doing.'

'But I was fine…'

'*Were you?* Were you happy? I don't remember seeing you laugh much, or play.'

'I was fine, Dad. I did what made me happy. I drew. I painted.'

'Yes. That's the other thing I wanted to say,' he said, swallowing down a sip of tea.

'What?'

'Your art. We were dreadful to you, both of us, about that. We were always a very practical couple, you see, very goal focused, and we just didn't try hard enough I think, to try to understand.'

'But you were right, Dad, weren't you? I couldn't have made a living from it. It was never a sensible idea. Never a realistic future.'

'You know what, Amelia, I'm not so sure. Your mother… she did what she loved, and it made her happy. She adored pushing the boundaries of research. But she and I, we both made the mistake of imposing our own talents and expectations on you. We never gave you a chance to shine in your own right, did we? We should have encouraged your art.'

'But it was my choice to leave art college. *I* failed it, Dad. *And* I failed my teacher training, too. That wasn't down to you.'

'Hmmmm,' he said, taking a deep breath. She noticed now that his breathing was laboured. 'There is great joy, Amelia, in doing what you love. We should never have convinced you to do otherwise.' Amelia was staring into space, her eyes unfocused, struggling to fully comprehend the shift in her father's outlook. 'The only satisfaction I have is that in coming back here, you met Piers, and now you have a family, too,' he continued. 'Marrying your soulmate is life's greatest joy, Amelia. But you know that of course. I miss your mother every day. I am nothing without her. Nothing.'

'Oh, Dad,' she said. Her father then held his hand out to her, and she grasped it, tears rolling down her face. They were tears that mourned her mother; tears that mourned a career she had never even started; and tears that mourned a marriage which had promised so much, but which, she was coming to realise, had delivered pitifully little.

She had not wanted to go home, so she had come here instead. It was because, she reasoned, Malvern Priory's utter majesty made her problems and pains feel small. She needed that perspective now more than ever. Her father's dramatic change of heart – brought about, she supposed, by his recent brush with death – had knocked her off her feet. She didn't want to go home to Piers and Grace feeling like this, because she was afraid of what she might say, and what she might do.

She took a seat a few rows back from the front, closed her eyes and sat in silence. She wasn't going to pray – she never prayed – but something in her needed to be here, in this time and space. She tried to empty her mind of everything, ushering her worries for her father out of an imaginary white room, and slamming an imaginary door. Instead, she let the gentle hubbub around her – volunteers chatting quietly near the entrance, tourists walking solemnly around in a self-guided circuit – lull her into a state of calm. She sat there listening to her own breathing and the disconnected noises around her, and felt anger, confusion and fear flood out of her. It felt both exhausting and exhilarating.

Please, she thought, as she prepared to open her eyes to rejoin the world, *please* let me carry this feeling with me when I leave this place. Then she opened her eyes, and…

'Oh!'

'Oh sorry, I didn't mean to startle you,' said Mark. 'I just saw you there, and I came over to chat, but I saw you were praying. So I just thought I'd wait.'

'Oh, I wasn't praying.'

'Weren't you?'

'No. I was meditating. Sort of. To be honest, I'm so tired, I was probably just falling asleep,' she said, with a smile on her face.

'Ha. Fair enough,' he said, beaming back, his smile all teeth, some of them crooked.

'Are you here to practise?' she said.

'Yes, and then I have a lesson to teach. A rather keen boy in Year Eight. Precocious. Plays all of the right notes but doesn't seem to actually feel it. He just plonks his fingers down. If you know what I mean?'

Amelia nodded, although she had no idea really what he meant.

'How are you doing, you and the baby?' he asked.

'We're… fine,' she said. 'I'm knackered. Really tired. But that's par for the course I think.'

'Yes, I hear it is. And your father? I haven't seen him here for services for a bit?'

'You know my dad?'

'Oh yes, he comes to Evensong on Sunday afternoons, every so often. I think he's been coming for a few years? He talks about you and Piers a great deal.'

Since Mum died, she thought. *He's been coming to church since Mum died.*

'Dad has been in hospital,' she said, trying to mask her shock.

'Oh, I'm sorry to hear that,' he said. Amelia examined his expression. He seemed to genuinely mean it.

'Yes. He's back now, though. Got back today. But I do worry about him, all alone in that flat.'

'Yes, I have similar worries about my mother,' said Mark, sitting down on the next chair but one, his music case on his lap. 'She lives alone in Evesham. But she has her church community too, so that helps.'

'The thing is, I don't think Dad really gets out that much,' she said.

'Well, he has his friends here, at Evensong. There's a pretty regular crowd. And has he looked into joining one of our clubs? There's a Sunday lunch club once a month, and a local history group he might enjoy. One of our vergers organises it. It's lots of fun, so I hear.'

'Thank you. I'll suggest it to him.' Her father had never really socialised much outside of work, but it was worth a try, she thought.

'Great. So will I, if I see him after a service.'

'Thanks. I'll have to see if I can find someone to bring him, though. He's a bit unsteady on his feet now.'

'Ah, I see. I tell you what, I'll ask our leadership team if they can find him someone to drive him in. We have a few older members of our congregation who attend church that way. Would that help?'

'That would be a tremendous help,' she said, relief flooding her face. 'Yes, that would be great. Dad needs to get out.'

'That's a plan, then,' he said, getting up. 'I must go. Work calls. But the other thing I wanted to say was – we are totally baby-friendly here, you know. We have a whole soft play area over in the side aisle during the family service. Babies can chirp all they want. If you wanted to come, you'd be welcome.'

'Thank you, but I...'

'Don't pray. Yes. Fair enough. As you know, I'm a bit ambivalent about Big Church myself. But you know... it is what it is. Anyway. I'm off. See you again soon?' he said.

'Yes,' she said. 'And... thank you. About Dad.'

'My pleasure,' he replied, as he walked away. 'He's a lovely old chap. Speaks fondly of you.'

21

January 6th

Michelle

Seven weeks until the final hearing

'We're going to be late,' said Michelle, her hands twisting in her lap.

'No, we're not. It'll be fine. There's a car park just around here which usually has spaces.'

Michelle looked out of the window at Worcester's familiar landmarks – the Commandery, the Cathedral, and the city's medieval shopping street, the Shambles – and shuddered. She'd once spent a night in a doorway in the Shambles, but she'd been woken by a man pissing on her head. He'd been laughing uproariously, as if dousing her with his cloudy, stinking urine had been a brilliant joke.

'Here we go,' said Gillian, as she pulled her car into a small space in a car park behind the university. 'Right. I'll pay for a ticket, and then we'll set off ASAP. We'll make it. Promise.'

As Gillian got out of the car, Michelle reflected on how far she had come. She had, at least for now, a safe, comfortable place to sleep, clean clothes, a full belly and a future, of sorts.

That's what she was here for, after all. To put to bed some

agonies in the past, and to plan for a future. A future, she hoped, with her child.

'Miss Jenkins, thank you so much for coming,' a woman said. She was tall, in her sixties, Michelle reckoned, angular, short haired and wearing small metal-rimmed glasses. Beside her sat her social worker, Laura, and the old woman with the Scottish accent, Marion Stone, who Michelle remembered from the court hearing, because she'd recommended that Grace should be taken away.

They were all sitting in a relentlessly beige room in what she reckoned would once have been a posh, Georgian townhouse housing well-heeled professional people. Now, it had peeling paint several layers thick, carpet squares littered with old gum and tea stains, clanging central heating and steamed-up single-glazed windows – all the hallmarks of a government-run building, in Michelle's extensive experience.

'I'm Mary Evans. I'm the senior social worker here in Worcester. Your social worker Laura asked me to chair this meeting, as we have a lot of very complicated matters to discuss.'

Michelle nodded. 'Also with us is Marion Stone, the children's guardian, who I know is keen to catch up with you, Michelle. She's going to listen in and take notes, and then talk to you afterwards, if that's okay with you?'

Michelle nodded, but inside, she was in turmoil. Shit, she thought. She's left me at least five messages over the past month, and I never called her back. *Shit.*

'This is Gillian,' Michelle said, once Mary Evans' introductions were out of the way. 'I'm... staying with her at the moment. She's... helping me.'

'Yes, Laura informed me of the arrangement, which I hope is working well?'

Michelle smiled at Gillian. Yes, Michelle thought, it's working far better than anything you twats have managed to cook up for me, that's for certain.

'In a moment, we're going to discuss how we can help you,' Mary Evans continued. 'But first, I think it might be good to begin with a short recap of where we are. You left care voluntarily when you were sixteen, I understand?'

'Yeah. That home you put me in was a shithole.'

Mary Evans didn't even flinch. *What a pro*, Michelle thought.

'And after that, you were homeless for a while, and lately, living with your partner, Rob?'

The woman's tone was formal and did not seem to invite argument. But Michelle felt her bile rise at each statement.

'Yeah,' she said, bidding her anger to recede.

'And you had a baby in October, a baby you decided to put up for adoption?'

'Yeah,' Michelle said, automatically, before a flash of anger caused her to change tack. 'Actually – *no*.'

'I'm sorry?'

Michelle's attempts at subduing her reactions failed.

'I mean, I did originally say I wanted to, yeah. And Rob went along with it, because I felt so strongly about it. But it seems now like all of my reasons were wrong, you know?'

'Go on,' said Mary.

'I decided I had to give her up because my life is – was – such a fucking mess,' – she looked at Gillian, apologising silently for swearing – 'and because I didn't trust myself. Because of my sister. They took her away from me, too. Because of me and the way I was behaving. So…'

Mary blinked twice.

'Yes. I want to talk to you about that, Michelle.' She paused, lifted her glasses off her nose and rubbed her eyes. 'I've looked at your files, and there were significant failings in the past.

Mistakes we wouldn't make now, I hope. I want to talk to you about them.'

'What failings?' Michelle asked, the heat rising in her face.

'The thing is... I see that your grandmother offered to care for you and your sister when your mother became too ill to do so herself,' she said. 'And you were placed there for a couple of years. But then you were removed from there and placed in a care home...'

'Well, your notes are wrong. We weren't removed. She dumped us there. She gave us up. Because I was too much trouble.'

'*No*,' said Laura, speaking for the first time. 'Sorry for interrupting, Mary. But no, that's not right, Michelle. Your grandmother had no choice.'

'Really?'

'Yes...' said Laura, looking to Mary for support.

'Yes. Your grandmother became ill,' said Mary.

'Ill?' Michelle asked, her throat tightening. 'What kind of ill? Is that why she never even came to see us in the home, even though she'd promised us she would?'

'Yes,' replied Mary. 'She had been diagnosed with an aggressive form of breast cancer. She'd hoped she'd recover and be able to get you back, but doctors had found it too late, and she declined rapidly. She didn't want you to see her like that, and she knew that you'd end up in care anyway, if she died. She wanted stability for you both. She felt you'd been through enough, had too many changes in your life up to that point and didn't want to unsettle you.'

'Why didn't you tell me that was why?'

'She made us promise not to tell you. I'm sorry, I really do think we should have. I apologise for the decisions that were made. The staff felt you were too young.'

'So... she died? The cancer killed her?'

Michelle looked at Mary and Laura. Their faces were pale.

'I'm so sorry, Michelle, yes. She died,' said Laura, gently. 'A few months after she took you to the home. I'm so sorry. I really, really wish they'd told you at the time.'

Michelle felt the floor fall away from beneath her. She'd spent most of her life hating a woman for something it turned out she had not actually wanted to do. She had actually wished her grandmother dead on many occasions. And now she realised that she'd been innocent of all charges she'd laid against her. But she was dead, anyway, despite that. Which meant she'd never see her again, to say sorry. Michelle wept freely, the memory of the only woman who'd ever really loved her, a woman she'd wholly misunderstood and absolutely wronged, stabbing at her heart.

'And of course, a few months after you arrived at the home, just after your grandmother died, adoptive parents were found for Grace...' said Mary, almost whispering.

'*You took her from me*,' Michelle shouted. 'You took my little sister from me. And I didn't even get to say goodbye.' Her face crumpled then and she began to cry quietly.

'We should not have separated you,' said Mary, choosing her words carefully. 'We would not do it now. But in those days, it was much harder to find new parents for older children, and it was felt better to adopt out a younger sibling, than for you both to grow up in care.'

A tissue was held out under Michelle's nose and she accepted it. She blew her nose loudly and mopped up the tears from her cheeks and chest.

'Take deep breaths,' urged Gillian. 'And here, take a sip of my water.'

Michelle drank, increasingly thankful for the wise woman by her side. She was struggling to process what she'd been told.

'Another thing,' she said, when the tears had subsided. She had decided to ask a question she'd suppressed long ago, as today seemed to be the day for unearthing things long buried.

'I lived with a couple for a while. The last foster carers I lived with. They were nice. Friendly. They were called the Richardsons. Leo and... Mark, I think they were? I got kicked out of there though. Because I was naughty. I was wondering whether I could get a message to them? I want to say sorry. I've always felt guilty about mucking them around...'

Michelle was aware of another silence that had flooded into the room.

'I'm so sorry, Michelle,' said Mary, pulling down her shirt to smooth out some non-existent creases, 'that they didn't tell you the truth about that, either.'

'What do you mean?'

'I didn't know this, Michelle – it wasn't in my files. I thought you knew. You were not removed because you were badly behaved. Leonora and Mark were very experienced foster carers, they have looked after many troubled young people over the years. The file says you were moved for logistical and financial reasons.'

'For *what*?'

'There was apparently a spare place in the care home, your social worker was visiting there regularly anyway, and... so it made sense for you to go there instead. I'm so sorry. I was unaware they had told you something else. I will make a note and follow that up immediately. But of course you can write to them, I'm very happy to pass on anything you wish me to. They are still well, still fostering and still living in Malvern.'

Michelle felt a mixture of relief that she was not to blame, combined with a rage she didn't know what to do with.

'You liars,' she said, tears rolling down her cheeks. 'You never thought to tell me any of this, did you? Just left me wondering. *Fucking liars*.'

'Do you want to continue this another time?' asked Mary, her voice now soft. 'I appreciate this is a huge amount to take in.'

Gillian was now rubbing Michelle's back. Normally she'd try to shrug her off, but right now, it was kind of comforting.

'*No*. I want to talk about this *now*,' Michelle said. 'I hate coming in to see you bitches.' She saw Mary flinch, but Laura, to her credit, did not. Marion was still sitting placidly in the corner, writing the occasional few words down in her notebook. What was she writing, Michelle wondered? '*This girl is a complete fruit loop*,' maybe?

'Where is my sister, then? *Where the fuck is she? Is she dead too?*' she shouted, not caring that everyone in the entire building could probably hear her, and not caring that this set Marion off on a flurry of writing.

'We're not sure,' replied Mary.

'Not... sure?' asked Michelle, her stomach churning.

'Oh, we know who adopted her. That's not the issue,' said Laura, quickly. 'But we've looked into it, and the family emigrated to Australia about twelve years ago,' Laura continued. 'We've sent out feelers to our counterparts in Australia. We're confident we'll find her,' she said, noting Michelle's distress. 'We will let you know as soon as we do.'

'But it's important to stress that we can only put you in touch with her if she wants that to happen,' Mary added, her voice calm and measured. She's done this before, Michelle thought. How many times?

Michelle considered how her sister might be feeling. What if she had spent her whole life blaming Michelle for not preventing their separation – just as she had blamed their grandmother? Or what if she couldn't even remember her, and had no interest in finding her at all?

'So, she could say no,' said Michelle. 'I mean, she might not want to see me. But could I write to her too? To explain? Could you give it to her?'

'We could certainly try to give it to her, when they find her,' Mary said.

Michelle thought then of her failed attempts at passing her English GCSE. She didn't find writing easy. Or reading, for that matter. She was useless at both. What chance did she have of writing something her sister would even be able to read, let alone be convinced by?

'Right,' she said, sounding less convinced. Her initial burst of optimism at the news that her sister was still out there, somewhere, on the other side of the world, had faded fast. This wasn't going to work, was it? She was never going to see her sister again. Even if they found her, she might be so happy in her new life, she'd have no interest in meeting her deadbeat older sister.

'We can discuss this when we have an idea where she is,' said Mary, her voice gentler. 'There's plenty of time to get something together. We can help you write it.'

'I'll help,' said Gillian. It was the first time she'd spoken during the meeting. 'If you want me to?'

Michelle nodded, relief flooding through her. She definitely needed help.

'Good,' said Mary. 'Now, I appreciate that this is a huge amount to take in, so please tell us to stop the meeting if you feel like you need to. But we wanted to take the opportunity to talk to you about the support that's available to you now. We want to help you. As you know, under the Care Covenant, we will offer support to you until you are twenty-five. We can offer drug rehab if you need it? Drug counselling?'

'I don't need none of that,' said Michelle. 'I didn't take any when I was expecting. I got myself off them. I can keep away, 'specially now I'm with Gillian and Mike.'

Michelle was trying to calm down and be polite, as Gillian had told her to do. She was still furious underneath, but she had a higher prize to think about now – Grace. She had to keep it together for her.

'Okay. That's good, and impressive, if you don't mind me saying so. That shows real commitment.' Michelle shrugged. It hadn't been easy – Rob had kept offering her stuff – but the baby had somehow trumped everything. Even her own needs. 'Then how about support finding accommodation? Training? You could go back to college? And we could help you apply for benefits?'

Michelle took a deep breath and pulled herself up in her chair. 'I dunno about that. Maybe. The thing is – I've made up my mind. I want to get my baby back,' she said. 'I'll do whatever I have to do to get her.'

Michelle saw a meaningful look pass between Mary and Laura. Marion stopped writing and looked up from her notes.

'Okay. This is good,' said Mary. 'But a big change. Have you thought it through properly? You would need a parenting assessment, a suitable place to live, and Rob would need to be out of the equation. The judge would have to be convinced that the baby would be safe.'

Michelle thought about Rob's protective embrace; his arm around her at night, guarding her from harm; his resolute support for her when she had decided to give Grace up for adoption. But then she remembered the cigarette burns she'd tried to hide with makeup; the bruises on her thighs and her stomach; and the empty flat, devoid of anything worth selling. He had well and truly left her now, hadn't he. She would have to manage without him from now on.

'Yeah, I'll do whatever it takes. Anything.'

'Okay. Right. Well, what we'll do is have a look at housing options. There might be a room available in a mother and baby unit, where you could have some support from the staff there? Would that work?'

A look of misery crept over Michelle's face. That sounded suspiciously like a care home. She felt sick at the thought of returning, but if it helped to get Grace back, she'd have to do it.

'If I have to...'

'They can stay with us,' said Gillian, suddenly. 'We can give them a start, at least. Until you can find them a flat.'

Michelle gasped and her hands flew to her mouth. No one had ever done something like that for her. Ever.

'Well, that would be acceptable to us, pending an independent parenting assessment,' said Mary, making notes. 'That would be an independent social worker, who'd visit you where you're living, and talk to you about how you'd care for Grace. Okay?'

Michelle nodded, fearing that if she opened her mouth, a sob might escape from it.

'We will be ready,' said Gillian, picking up the mantle. 'I've cared for several babies over my fostering career. We'll be fine.'

'That's wonderful,' said Mary. 'Thank you so much for supporting Michelle. But I must sound a note of caution. Even if Michelle passes the parenting assessment, the judge may still order the adoption to go ahead. She's only seen her at the contact centre once, she missed the second court hearing, and her history of returning to an abusive partner may also count against her. I'm not saying that's what's going to happen, but it could.'

Michelle heard those words and tears began to flood down her face once more. Her mouth emitted a noise that sounded to her like a howl. At that moment, she felt the full impact of her weaknesses and her trademark obstinacy crash down upon her. Because she was a moron. A total loser. A fucking idiot. She had royally messed this up. She deserved everything she got.

'She'll get legal aid though, won't she?' said Gillian, glaring at Mary. 'I did a small bit of research before we came. She is entitled to it.'

'Yes, she will. But that's not for now. The first thing is the parenting assessment,' replied Mary. 'Then you can meet with a solicitor. We have a list...'

Michelle remembered the list that had been thrust at her before the first hearing, and her random choice of Sally Mucklow. She'd been kind, Michelle thought. And she was clever.

'And the assessment will be fine, no problem,' said Gillian. 'It will need to be soon though, won't it? When is the adoption hearing scheduled for? It must be coming up fast.'

'Yes, I was just getting to that,' replied Mary. 'The date has just come through. The courts have only just gone back to work after Christmas. The resolution hearing, where the judge will try to get everyone to reach an agreement, will be on the second of February. And if that doesn't work, there will be a final hearing on the sixteenth of February. That means that all of the statements and reports need to be ready by then.'

Michelle, who was sitting next to Gillian with her eyes closed, grasping the now sodden tissue in her fist, made a mental calculation. They had just shy of six weeks to turn this around.

'We'll be ready,' said Gillian, passing Michelle another tissue. 'I can promise you that.'

22

January 9th

Amelia

Seven weeks until the final hearing

It was snowing; the first snowfall of winter. Through the sash window, Amelia could see some of the younger boys, clad in their regulation school winter coats, bobble hats and woollen gloves, trying to make snowballs from the tiny layer which had begun to settle on the lawn. It wouldn't be long before those gloves were soaked through, she thought, although they didn't seem to care. Boys that age seemed to be weather-proof.

She turned around and looked down at Grace, who was asleep in her cot, her arms thrown insouciantly above her head and her legs gathered in like a frog. She seemed to be smiling. She hadn't a care in the world, Amelia thought, except, perhaps, a small concern about when her next feed was due. And she definitely didn't care – unlike Amelia – about the unscheduled visit from a social worker which was due any moment. Amelia cared very much about that, because usually she was given several weeks' notice. In fact, the very thought of the visit was making her tremble.

'Hello Mrs Howard. Are you and Mr Howard around this morning?' Gloria had asked, quite formally; her use of 'Mrs

Howard' stuck out like a sore thumb. They were usually on first-name terms now.

'He's teaching. Can it wait until later?'

'I'm afraid not, Mrs Howard. Would you mind seeing me alone?'

'No... I suppose that's okay. Is there something wrong?'

'I'll fill you in when I come to see you. See you in about an hour?'

An hour had now elapsed and so Amelia had assumed this position in the nursery, because it was the room that allowed her to monitor their driveway. She'd already tidied up the lounge and wiped down the surfaces in the kitchen, but now her nervous energy was spent and all she could do was stand at the window and wait.

At that moment, a small white hatchback turned into their driveway. She could make out a familiar woman with a finely coiffed head of brown hair behind the wheel. Yes, that's her, she thought. That's Gloria.

As the car's tyres turned over the gravel and came to a slow stop, she walked slowly across the room and down the hall. The doorbell rang as she approached the top of the stairs. She briefly considered not answering it, but that would only postpone whatever news Gloria had come to share. Better to get it over with, she thought. It was coming, whatever she did.

'Hi,' she said, opening the door and putting on her bravest face.

'Hello, Amelia. Thank you for seeing me at such short notice.'

'That's okay, Grace is napping. Shall we go up to the living room?'

The social worker nodded and followed Amelia back up the stairs. She gestured to Gloria to take a seat on their two-seater leather sofa.

'Can I get you anything to drink?' she asked, robotically.

'No, I'm fine, thank you, Amelia.' Amelia considered making

herself a strong coffee to cradle – she felt freezing, despite the fact the central heating was on at full blast – but she could see that the social worker was already taking some paperwork out of her bag. Obviously, she wanted to get on with it, whatever 'it' was, she thought.

'So – you'll be wondering, of course, why I've come at such short notice,' said Gloria, as Amelia sat down opposite her in an armchair. 'I'll just go straight ahead and tell you, Amelia. I can't sugar-coat it, as much as I'd like to. Grace's birth mother has informed us that she intends to contest the adoption.'

A wave of nausea surged through Amelia. She considered racing to the bathroom, afraid that she might actually vomit, but a desire to find out how on earth this had happened kept her rooted to the spot.

'But-she-hasn't-been-attending-contact-sessions,' she said, her words coming out so fast, they ran into each other.

'Yes, I know. But it appears she's had a change of heart. She intends to begin attending immediately, I'm told.'

'Oh. But will that be enough to persuade them?'

'It really might not be. It depends on how her solicitor presents her case. And there isn't much time for her to prepare it, anyway. The resolution hearing is scheduled for February second, and the final hearing for February sixteenth.'

That was just seven weeks away, thought Amelia. Grace could be taken away from them in just six weeks.

'Will she win though? I mean, surely the judge will see that she has been playing games…'

'I know it might feel like it, but this isn't a game for her, Amelia. Grace's birth mother seems very serious about it. This isn't something we foresaw, I must say, and we are desperately sorry that it's come to this, because we understand how this must make you feel. But we have to follow procedure here. The welfare of Grace is our priority, as ever.'

'But how can it be in her best interests to take her away from us, where she's settled and loved, and to put her into the care of someone who until very recently seemed hell-bent on giving her up?'

'The birth mother's original desire to surrender Grace, and of course her personal circumstances, will all be taken into account by the judge. She'll also have to pass a parenting assessment before she even gets to court. It's far from a done deal. You have every chance of keeping her.'

And every chance of losing her, thought Amelia, gripping the end of the seat cushion with both hands.

'So can we get legal aid for the court case?' asked Amelia.

Gloria looked startled. 'Did no one explain?' she asked. 'You won't be able to attend court. You're not part of the proceedings.'

'Why on earth not?' Amelia said, her voice raised. She had given up being polite. What was the point now, anyway?

'The court case is between the birth mother and social services; not between her and you,' Gloria replied. 'I'm sorry. Someone really should have told you this before. You are simply considered to be foster carers by the court, in this circumstance.'

So we don't even bloody matter, she thought. We're not prospective parents in the eyes of the law – we're just useful temporary carers.

'Oh my God,' said Amelia, almost choking on the words. 'Oh *God*. So how do we find out the verdict? Will someone come to see us, like now? Or will we get a phone call? Or a bloody *text*?'

Gloria had a look of genuine compassion, but her expression did nothing to calm Amelia's anger.

'I know this is hard, Amelia,' she said, leaning in. 'We can talk through all of this at another time, perhaps with Piers present. But look, try not to panic. As I say, your chances are still good. Judges rarely find in favour of birth parents at this stage. We wouldn't be taking the action unless we had a good case. Just carry on doing the sterling work you are doing with Grace, and fingers crossed, it will work out.'

'Fingers crossed? I'd like to have more to cling to than that,' said Amelia, her legs shaking.

'That's just a turn of phrase. Perhaps I chose the wrong one. Look, I really do think this will turn out to be a failed effort on her part. The signs are good.'

Amelia didn't reply. She was now staring in the direction of the garden retaining wall. She imagined one of the bricks shifting, and tonnes of cold, hard earth collapsing onto her – because her greatest fear had just been realised. She had been right all along; Grace was not really theirs. She had never actually been theirs, and soon they could lose her, forever. And there was nothing at all she could do about it.

'I have to leave to go to another appointment, I'm afraid,' said Gloria, standing up. 'Are you going to be okay, Amelia? Should I call Piers?'

'No. I'll be fine. I have things to do before he gets back,' she said. And as if on cue, they both heard Grace begin to cry. Amelia stood up. 'I need to go to her. Could you show yourself out?'

'That's fine. Of course. Ask Piers to call me with any questions, okay? And we are available to talk at any time.'

'Okay,' she said, refusing to meet Gloria's eye. 'See you soon then. Bye.'

Then she set off at pace for the nursery, not looking back. When she reached Grace's cot, she leaned down on it, so that it took her entire weight. And when she heard their front door close, she let go of the cot and tumbled onto the floor, her legs giving way beneath her. As her body crumpled on the floor, she let out a guttural howl of anguish.

'Melia! You okay love? Haven't seen you for ages. Are you free this afternoon for a coffee or summat? I miss you. R

I can't. I just can't. A

Amelia? Are you okay? Do you need help?

I think they are going to take Grace. Please come.

'Heavens, Amelia, you poor thing. Hang on. Let me get you a tissue and a cuppa.'

Amelia had managed to stumble to the door to let Rachel in, but once she'd made it, she found she was struggling to stand, so she'd just sat down where she was in their dark hallway, sobbing. Down the corridor, Grace was continuing to cry.

'Okay, the kettle's on. I'm just going to go and pick up Grace, okay Amelia? And see what she wants.' Amelia heard her walk down the corridor, talk to Grace in an easy maternal patter, before walking her down the hall. 'I think she might be hungry,' she said. 'Can I give her to you to hold, while I make her up a bottle? I saw that you have the stuff out on the side in here.'

Amelia nodded. She wanted to hold Grace more than anything at that moment. And more than that, she desperately wanted to never have to let her go. She could hear Rachel in the kitchen – finding a mug, sterilising a bottle, locating the powder and the teabags – but her real focus was the little girl in her arms. She counted her eyelashes and sniffed the top of her head, inhaling her distinctive smell. She knew every inch of her. And that meant she was hers, didn't it? *Hers*. Not anyone else's.

'There you go,' said Rachel, holding a bottle out in front of her. 'I hope this is to her liking. Look, shall we go into the lounge? It might be easier to feed her in there. And much more comfortable for you.'

'Sure,' said Amelia. Rachel leaned down to pick up Grace so that Amelia could get to her feet, before following her as she stumbled into their lounge and threw herself down on the sofa.

There, Rachel returned Grace and her bottle, before heading back into the kitchen for the tea.

'Here you go,' she said, returning with a strong cup of tea and a biscuit, and then sitting down opposite Amelia and Grace, who was now feeding with great enthusiasm. 'So... tell me... what on earth is this all about?'

'They –' said Amelia, getting up the strength she needed to articulate the horror inside her, '– or rather *she*, the birth mother, *she* is contesting the adoption. She wants Grace back.'

'I see. But surely it's too late for that?'

'No, I don't think so. The courts favour birth families, always. If she gets her act together, and convinces them that she's a safe pair of hands...'

'That's a lot of ifs.'

'... *if* she does that, they will take Grace from us. And we don't even get to fight for her. It's not our case to fight.'

'What?'

'Yeah, I know. We don't even get our day in court. The whole system is just treating us like foster parents. We have no rights. No actual claim on her...' Amelia started to cry again. 'God, I feel sick...'

'Hang on a minute. Let's backtrack. Who told you this?'

'The social worker. This morning.'

'Okay. But the council put her up for adoption. Fostering to adopt is exactly that, right? You're on the path to it?'

'Yes, but there is always a risk. They did tell us. I knew it. So did Piers. But we chose to ignore it, saw it as small print. I... We were so desperate for a baby. After Leila...'

'Leila?'

'Leila. The daughter I gave birth to before her time. She was born still. She never lived.'

Rachel looked shocked.

'I'm so sorry, Amelia, I didn't know.'

'That's okay. Very few people know. We prefer it that way.'

'So you prefer not to talk about her?'

Amelia didn't reply, because the reality was that it was Piers who didn't want to talk about Leila, not her. It was different for him. He was fine, because he had Sebastian. He had a child he could call his own, whatever happened with Grace.

Rachel stood up then and sat down next to Amelia, flinging her arms around her.

'I'm here for you,' she said. 'All the way. And for what it's worth, I'm sure social services can see what a fabulous parent you are. That will count for something. I'm sure of it.'

'I hope so. But I have a horrible feeling…'

'Now come on,' she said, rubbing Amelia's back. 'None of that. It's not a done deal, is it?'

'No.'

'So it could go either way?'

'Yes, but…'

'Look, no buts, okay? Let's be positive.'

Amelia reached into her pocket and pulled out a tissue and dabbed her eyes.

'I'm so sorry,' she said.

'Don't be daft. What for?'

'For needing rescuing.'

'Stop it. Now. Look, there's no point in sitting here crying. You've done enough of that today. Here's what we'll do instead. We'll finish Grace's feed, you'll finish your tea, we'll mop up your face, and then I'm taking you out for an afternoon on the town. Yes! Malvern is where it's at, as you know. And I'm talking… clothes. I'm talking… hair. And not a blue rinse. We'll make sure we avoid Elsie's Hair Parlour.'

Amelia smiled, despite herself. Rachel always made her feel better.

'You look fabulous in that,' said Rachel.

They were in Bohemian Bazaar at the top of Church Street. The shop, which had recently replaced an outlet selling Chinese herbs, now sold an eclectic mix of kaftans, tunics, dungarees and dresses in every colour of the rainbow. Amelia was currently trying on a bright pink tunic which was embroidered with hundreds of tiny pieces of mirrored glass.

She stared at her reflection in surprise. It skimmed her slim body in all of the right places and its dipped neckline made the most of her tiny boobs. All in all, she thought she looked – *not bad*, which was an unusually optimistic verdict for her. Usually, she felt – *not grim*. Or, *not awful*. But *not bad* was promising. And the shop itself, which smelled of joss sticks and incense, reminded her of her student days – or the good bits of it, at least. She was sold.

'Please tell me you're going to get it,' said Rachel. 'You look divine. I love colour on you. You wear so much grey and black, but colour really lifts you.'

But Amelia's heart sank, because she had no way of buying it. She'd spent the spare cash she'd had, and Piers had both their debit and credit cards. It never usually bothered her that Piers always had to be present when she went clothes shopping, but suddenly, this particular relationship foible bothered her immensely.

'I haven't got any money with me,' she said, deciding to be honest. 'I'll have to come back and buy it tomorrow.'

'Did you leave your wallet at home?'

Amelia wasn't ready to answer that question. Her heart sank. So she took a deep breath, and lied.

'Yes. It was stupid. I'm sorry, today has been appalling…'

'Understood. Look, I'll buy this for you, okay? It looks so great on you, and you've had a shitty day. This is on me, okay?'

Amelia almost cried with gratitude. Oh my *God*, she thought, this is so embarrassing, and so awful. Why had this never bothered her before?

'Thank you,' she said. '*Thanks*. And Rach...?'

'Yes?'

Amelia decided to voice the niggling worry she'd had following their dinner party.

'I'm so sorry that Piers was a bit short with you when we came over to dinner. About me not having a job. As he said, we're both exhausted...'

'Don't give it a second thought,' said Rachel, taking the tunic and swivelling around to place it on the counter, ready to pay. 'Now, just wait until you find out what excitement I've got planned for you next.'

'Piers?'

It was 5 p.m. She'd normally be home and preparing dinner by now, and Piers would usually be back, too. She had hoped, however, that he'd decided to stay on at school for afternoon tea and networking, because she desperately wanted to put off telling him the bad news. Every minute he could live without knowing that Grace might be taken away was a gift, she thought. She wished *she* didn't know. It wasn't as if she could do a thing about it.

'Darling?' he replied, from his study at the top of the stairs. Shit, she thought. *Shit*.

'Sorry I'm late,' she called up. 'I was in town with Rachel, and we got waylaid...'

'What on *earth* has happened to your hair?'

He'd appeared at the top of the stairs and was staring down at her as she removed Grace from the buggy and began to carry her up. Amelia reached up and patted her new short bob, which had been dyed with a temporary red rinse. Rachel had egged her on, emphasising the difference it made to her face shape and her colouring. And she had been right, Amelia thought; she felt renewed. Different.

'Oh, Rachel treated me to a haircut. Wasn't that nice of her?'

'Well, it's certainly… different,' he said. She prepared to receive the onslaught of criticism which she had been anticipating for the whole walk home. He had always told her he liked her hair as it was, and that he never wanted her to change it. Not to mention how he'd feel about her accepting a gift like that from someone. And she hadn't even told him about the tunic. But…

'Well, you know I prefer your hair long,' he said. 'And I'm not sure about red… but if you like it, then, fine,' he said, opening his arms to take hold of Grace, with a smile.

Amelia was astounded at how calm he was being about it. And she was so relieved, that she didn't stop to question why. Mostly because of her preoccupation with how she was going to break the news about the adoption challenge to him.

'Piers, shall we go into the lounge and sit down?' she said, as he cuddled and kissed the baby he believed was his daughter. 'I have something I need to tell you.'

23

January 10th

Michelle

Six weeks until final hearing

'Sit down, Michelle. Honestly, sit down. Relax a bit. You won't make her come any quicker by pacing.'

Michelle and Gillian were in the mock-living room at the supervised contact centre, the scene of Michelle's previous flight. This time, however, she was not going to run away. In fact, she had almost felt like running towards it, instead.

The anticipation of what was about to happen meant that she had eschewed the admittedly dubious comfort offered by the threadbare sofa and stained armchairs, and instead was pacing backwards and forwards, awaiting Grace's arrival. She paused at the window occasionally, looking out over the centre's neglected garden, which seemed to consist mostly of a very weedy lawn and a tall, dense hedge. They had been placed in this room, she reckoned, so that they couldn't catch a glimpse of the foster parents, who should be arriving on the front driveway any moment with her daughter.

Michelle had now begun to view those foster parents as an enemy, rather than Grace's salvation. She felt a bit guilty about that. After all, it had been her choice (now very much regretted) to put Grace up for adoption that had created this mess. And how she felt about them wasn't personal; they had never met each other, after all. They might be lovely people. In fact, she was sure they were. And she understood absolutely the deep desire for a child. They both had that in common. But that couple, they were trying to make Grace theirs, and that meant Michelle losing her forever. So, she had to fight. It was a war.

It had taken a long while for her to openly acknowledge that gnawing feeling she'd been suppressing for months; that feeling, that knowledge, that she desperately wanted Grace back. After a lifetime of self-hatred and of viewing herself as a liability, she was gradually beginning to see things from a new perspective. Gillian had told her to repeat a mantra whenever she doubted herself: 'I am not to blame'. The first few times she'd said it, she'd felt ridiculous, but now she said it to herself all the time: when she woke up from a nightmare; when she saw the effort Gillian and Mike were putting into her care; when she felt guilty for being so determined to give Grace away. She still felt that a lot of the shit that had happened to her was at least partly her fault – she'd done it, after all, hadn't she? But some of it, well, she was prepared to accept that some of it had been out of her control. And it had made a huge difference to the way she felt. Because she was Grace's mother, and she would always be her mother. She knew that now, with a certainty she could no longer deny. She was absolutely not going to let social services take *this* Grace from her. No way.

'Here she is!' said a familiar voice, as Gloria entered the room, holding a car seat in her left arm. She placed her down in the middle of the floor, and Michelle ran to her, unable to even fake nonchalance, should she have even wanted to.

She knelt down in front of the car seat and unclipped the safety straps, taking in every inch of her daughter as she did so: her short brown hair, which curled at the ends; her neatly clipped, tiny fingernails; her tiny body, clad in a smart, knitted red and white dress and white tights. She picked her up gently, Gloria and Gillian watching her intently as she did so, ready, she assumed, to issue any instructions if necessary, but it seemed that none were required. Michelle stood there in the middle of the room for a minute or two, cradling Grace in her arms, her own intense stare mirrored by the gentle, brown eyes of her baby daughter, which were wide open and clearly taking her in. Michelle wiped away a tear which had formed in her right eye and retreated to the sofa, her eyes never leaving Grace's face.

'Amazing,' said Gloria, taking a seat on the other side of the room. 'She recognises you.'

'Do you really think so?' asked Michelle, not looking up. 'I've only even seen her twice...'

'It doesn't always happen,' she replied. 'Sometimes, there's no recognition at all, especially with babies this young. But I think she knows who you are.'

'Wow. I thought... I thought she'd think I was a stranger.'

'Sometimes that happens, yes,' said Gloria. 'But other times... it's instinct I think.'

'Wow,' she said, holding her daughter's gaze, afraid to blink in case the moment passed, feeling the invisible thread that had connected them since her birth begin to tighten.

'Can I see her?' asked Gillian, moving over to sit down next to Michelle and Grace.

'Of course,' replied Michelle, despite the fact she was loath to let her go.

'It's okay, I'll just look for now,' said Gillian, smiling, sensing her unease. 'You carry on bonding. You've got lots of things to catch up on.'

Gillian then shifted her focus towards Gloria. 'So Michelle can see Grace twice a week here, until the court case?'

'Yes, that's right,' she said. 'So that's in just over a month, I believe?'

'Yep,' replied Gillian.

Michelle felt, rather than heard, the invisible message that passed between the two older women at that moment. They were both acknowledging the unavoidable elephant in the room, she thought – the fact that, if the judge decided against her, she could be in this room in just over a month, saying goodbye. For good. The thought made her clutch Grace even harder.

Six weeks, she thought. I have only six weeks to prove I have a right to be Grace's mother.

Michelle could smell coffee and could hear the gentle hum of the espresso machine. Ordinarily, she'd turn over in bed and grab another hour or so of sleep – she was still struggling to break the habit of a lifetime of late nights and late rises – but today, she decided against it. She had slept fitfully. Snapshots of Grace's face yesterday, together with flashbacks – unwanted postcards from her own childhood – had been haunting her all night, as if the devil had taken charge of the slideshow and refused to let her close her eyes.

And that wasn't all. She had two other vitally important things demanding space in her already addled brain. One, there was a social worker visiting later that day to carry out a parenting assessment, which was a vital cog in the wheel which might, just might, bring her baby back to her. And two, she still hadn't written the letter to her sister, or the letter she planned to send to her old foster carers. This was partly because she was worried about the replies she might receive – if, in fact, she actually received any – but there was something else, too. And it was that thing that was really holding her back.

Michelle swung her legs out of bed, grabbed the dressing gown Gillian had lent her, and padded along the corridor and up the stairs to the kitchen. There, she found Mike standing in front of his polished chrome coffee machine, a large cappuccino cup in his hand.

'Oh, hello Michelle, love. You're up early.'

Michelle looked at the clock. It was 6 a.m.

'Oh shit, yeah, it *is* early,' she said, realising that she was intruding on Mike's usual morning ritual of a newspaper on his iPad and several cups of coffee.

'Ah, no, it's the best time of the day,' replied Mike. 'Would you like a coffee?'

'Only if you don't mind...'

'Of course I don't mind. I dropped about a year's worth of hints to Gillian about wanting this machine. I'd like to get my cost per cup ratio down a bit more, to justify the expense.'

Michelle smiled. It was hard not to, as Mike had a disarming personality. He positively radiated warmth, which was a personality trait she had yet to find in anyone else she knew. Except Gillian, of course. It was no surprise to her that they'd found each other.

'Did you have a bad night?' asked Mike, as he turned the coffee machine back on. The machine hummed, as the water in the tank was heated.

'Yeah,' Michelle answered. 'Yesterday... it was big, you know. And today...'

'Ah, the parenting assessment? You'll ace that, love. Gilly has been rushing around like a blue arsed fly over the past few days, getting all of the stuff ready, as you know. They'll love you and they'll love the set-up here. Honestly. Don't worry about it.'

Michelle shrugged.

'Maybe,' she said.

'Definitely,' said Mike, as he retrieved his box of coffee from the fridge and placed a scoop of it into the machine's filter arm. Michelle took a seat at the table and watched him as he worked his way through his well-practised barista routine.

'Is there something else, love?' he said, noting her silence.

'No...' said Michelle, realising that she was struggling to convince even herself.

'Right,' said Mike, in a tone that told Michelle that he knew there was something else, but that he wouldn't press her on it.

'Do you want something to eat as well, pet? I've just made myself some porridge.'

Michelle thought back to the days when she'd eaten only porridge, because that was all that they'd had in the house.

'No, you're all right,' she said.

'Sure?'

'Yeah. I might have some toast later,' she said. Her whole system was drowning in nervous energy, and it was making her feel nauseous.

Mike walked over to the table and presented her with a large cup of steaming coffee. It was topped with frothy milk, and a sprinkle of chocolate powder.

'I'm thinking of getting a job in Costa,' he said, with a smile.

'Thanks,' she said, smiling back. She blew on it to cool it a little and took a sip, as Mike picked up a steaming bowl of porridge from the kitchen surface, spooned a couple of teaspoons of sugar into it, and sat down opposite her.

'Now, pet. Why don't you tell me what else is bothering you?' he said, as he dived into his breakfast. 'Gillian's sleeping, so it's just you and me, and I have been told now and again that I'm a good listener. Go on. Give me a try.'

Michelle put her cup back down on the table.

'It's the letters,' she said. 'The ones I told social services I'd write. To Grace. My sister, Grace, and the last foster carers I had.'

'Ah.'

'I haven't done them yet.'

'Do you want to?' asked Mike, spooning thick, milky porridge into his mouth between sentences.

'Yeah. But…'

'But?'

Michelle heard the question, and then felt a door inside her shut firmly. She suddenly didn't want to talk about it anymore. This was very uncomfortable territory for her.

'Dunno,' she said, focusing on finishing her coffee, so that she could get out of the kitchen and head back to her room. When she'd taken a final swig, she put her cup down, and saw that Mike had – somehow – finished his porridge. Shit, that guy eats quickly, she thought. I like that in a person.

'Do you fancy coming on a walk up the hill with me and Rory?' he asked. 'It's a lovely morning. I mean, it's cold, mind, but it's lovely, too. Fresh. Clear. If we go now, we'll see the sunrise.'

Michelle thought about it. He'll ask me again, won't he, she thought. He won't let it go. But then, it might be nice to get out and breathe some fresh air, today of all days. And she loved the dog, really loved him. Spending time with him was a tonic.

'Go on then,' she said. 'I'll just go and pull on my jeans.'

'Almost there,' she said, striding ahead of Mike, towards the summit of Summer Hill. It was amazing, she thought, the effect the fresh air and greenery had had on her. She'd felt like death warmed up when she'd left the house, after such a crap night's sleep, but now she felt like she had enough energy to walk the whole length of the hills, if she'd wanted to.

Although Mike had struggled to keep up with her for the past few minutes, the dog had not, and Rory was hugging her shadow as the sun rose. 'Come on, boy,' she said. 'Let's get there before the sun comes up.'

As she took the last few steps before the summit, she looked behind her and saw that Mike was about twenty metres away.

'Blimey, pet, you're fitter than you look,' he shouted. 'You're a veritable mountain goat.'

Michelle laughed and looked east towards Evesham, where the sun, weak with winter, was beginning to rise above the horizon.

'Isn't it spectacular,' Mike said, finally catching up with her. 'That's why I get up early every morning.'

'I thought it was because you wanted to be left alone with your paper,' said Michelle, elbowing Mike.

'Ha, yes and no. I do love this time of day. It's nice to have company for a change up here, though, I must say.'

'I liked walking up here, when I was little,' said Michelle, watching as the morning's first rays lit up a patchwork of fields and ancient hedgerows. 'And we used to have to do it once a year for school, as well. Up the Beacon.'

'I bet that wasn't very fun,' said Mike. 'Being made to do it?'

'Oh, I liked it. It meant no lessons,' said Michelle, stroking Rory, who was sitting by her, panting.

'Not a fan of school then?'

'Nah.'

'It's not for everyone.'

'Nope.' Michelle thought of the teachers who'd tried to encourage her, even when the words had swum in front of her, and she'd sworn in frustration and thrown something, and been chucked out of class, and, eventually, out of school for good.

Mike sat down on a rocky outcrop then and Michelle did the same, pulling Rory onto her lap as she did so. They sat there in silence for a minute, watching the sun try to bring warmth to the frozen earth.

'Are you cold?' said Mike. 'I should have thought and lent you a hat. It's freezing up here.'

'Nah, I think I got so warm walking up here, I'm strangely okay,' said Michelle.

'That's good,' he said, staring straight ahead. Michelle saw that he was watching a ground fog form over a field, the expansive, swirling mist gathering together like an immense army of ghosts.

'I can't write,' she said suddenly, saying it quickly so that she could get it out before she could change her mind.

Mike didn't reply for a few seconds. While Michelle waited, her stomach flipped over and she felt bile rise in her throat. Would he think less of her now? Probably, she thought. People always had done, when they'd found out.

'Well, that's easily fixed, pet,' he said. 'We can sort that, no bother.'

'*No*,' she said. 'They tried, at school. And I tried, I really did. But I just… can't.'

'It'll likely be just shit teaching, pet,' he said. 'But if it's something more than that, we can help with that, too. Don't you worry. Now, you must be getting cold, with all that sweat you worked up chilling your bones. Shall we head home?'

Michelle nodded, noticing that she had lost some sensation in her fingers.

She stood up, held out her hand to help Mike stand back up, and, flanked by Rory, they began the walk back down off the bare summit, through the treeline, past frozen rivulets of natural springs in the hillside, back into Malvern's awakening residential streets. They were almost entirely silent during the descent, but as they approached the house, Mike turned to Michelle.

'Those letters you have to write, love? I'm happy to write them down for you, if you'd like. You tell me what to write, and I'll just type it for you, verbatim. Only if you want me to, of course.'

Michelle smiled. 'Ta. But I know you have to go to work now. I don't want to take up your time.'

Mike put his key in the front door, turned it and pushed it open. Michelle was hit immediately by the warm air that emanated from inside, and the mouth-watering scent of bread and coffee.

'Don't be daft. I have half an hour now. Let's make a start. I'll get us another coffee and some toast, shall I?'

* * *

'Please stop polishing, Gillian. You're making me nervous.'

Several hours after Michelle's dawn hike up the hill with Mike, she and Gillian were standing in the kitchen, surrounded by a scene worthy of a show home. The kitchen surfaces were gleaming; a vase of lilies graced an otherwise unadorned island and a cafetiere, a set of yellow coffee cups and a plate of fondant fancies were arranged enticingly on a wooden tray.

'I know, I'm sorry,' replied Gillian. 'I just don't want to give them any reason to mark you down, that's all.'

'Like they said on the phone, the parenting assessor is coming to see *me*, not you,' said Michelle. 'They just want to see if Grace will be safe with me. They won't care how tidy the kitchen is.'

'They might say that, but they always care. Anyway, first impressions count. They always count,' said Gillian, wiping invisible dirt off her hands with her jeans.

Michelle looked hard at the woman who had given so much to her, without ever being asked; who had, it would be fair to say, brought her back from the brink. And she realised for the first time that Gillian was every bit as invested in Grace's return as she was.

'Why are you doing this?' she asked.

'Like I said, I want you to have the best chance of keeping Grace.'

'Yeah, but why?' said Michelle, a suppressed anxiety bubbling to the surface. 'Because this is just going to mean more work for you and Mike. It'll either be me and a baby, or you dealing with how I feel after they take her away. Either way will be shit, for you. Hard. Tiring.'

For a brief moment, Michelle wondered whether this was all part of some crazy plan of Mike and Gillian's, to get hold of a baby of their own. Could they be that devious? Could they actually be planning to get her shipped off somewhere, written off as an unfit mother, later? But no, surely not. Because they had been so kind. But then, lots of other people in her life had seemed kind, at first…

'Because I think it's time someone gave you a fresh start,' said Gillian. 'You see, over the years, I've seen the gargantuan mess irresponsible parents *and* social workers have made of so many children's lives… And it's made me angry. Furious. Mike and I, you see, we took care of a teenage boy for a bit. Will, he was called. Lovely boy, really. He was so soft underneath, but he had an exterior that was hard as titanium. We tried and tried, but we couldn't get through to him properly. He left us after a few months, and we lost touch with him. But we were told, months later, that he'd killed himself a few weeks after he'd gone.'

Michelle looked closely at Gillian. There were tears gathering in her eyes.

'I just… I feel like I need to take some responsibility for this particularly dark corner of society,' she said. 'I want to take some action, shine some light into it. As I told you when we first met, I want to help.'

'Okay. But that boy's death, it's really sad, I know, but it wasn't your fault, was it? And you have helped so many people already. Don't you want a break?'

Gillian sighed.

'I'm due to retire in five years. In fact, I could retire now, if I wanted. Mike, too. We've got the money to do it. But we don't want to, either of us. We haven't even discussed retirement, because we don't want to acknowledge the elephant in the room. And that elephant is silence, Michelle. We have had a house filled with young people for a couple of decades, but since we stopped fostering, it's been empty. That's why we like hosting parties, you see; it fills the house. Not having any children of our own means that we have no grandchildren to look forward to, no children seeking refuge with us in between relationship break-ups or periods of unemployment. But we wish we did.

In short, Michelle, we like people, and we like looking after people. And to be frank, we have grown fond of you. Very fond.'

Michelle didn't know where to look. She couldn't remember the last time someone had told her they cared for her, and really meant it.

'I'm sorry. For doubting,' she said. 'It's just… I can't really believe anyone really likes me.'

'I wish I could give you a hug,' said Gillian, smiling. 'Because we do like you, and that's a fact.'

Michelle looked at Gillian and returned her smile. She was amazed at the energy she had. She was also astonished to find that putting her trust in someone else for the first time in years hadn't made her feel like she'd lost control; conversely, she felt more in control than ever.

The two women both jumped when they heard the doorbell. Gillian was already jogging up the stairs as the two-tone bell reached its final note.

'Here we go,' she said, as she reached the top step. 'Ready or not.'

24

January 15th

Amelia

Six weeks until the final hearing

'Are you really going out dressed like that?'

Shit, thought Amelia. She had been hoping that he wouldn't hear her walking past his office, but clearly, despite his long, sulking silences over the past six days, he was still as alert as ever. She had made it to the bottom of the stairs, a sleeping Grace in her arms, before he'd emerged from his office, unshaven, still wearing his pyjamas.

She was desperate to get out. The atmosphere in the flat was more oppressive than ever. Outside, it was a dark, dingy, damp January day, but even that was preferable to the whirling fog of anger, frustration, sadness and blame that was clouding her reality. She needed fresh air. She hoped it would give her a fresh perspective. If that was even a thing, when you were facing the possible loss of another child.

She was amazed Piers had been able to pull himself together sufficiently to go to work over the past week. When she'd told him about the birth mother's decision to contest the adoption, she had watched his confident, charming demeanour melt away in seconds. What was left was ragged, furious and enraged. She had known that Grace meant a great deal to him, but even she had been taken by surprise by the strength of his feelings. It was as if he'd done a deal with the devil for a second chance at fatherhood, and now that it was being threatened, his condemned soul was raging.

He had retreated to his office a few minutes after she'd told him the news, and he'd only emerged since to work, find food or go to bed. In truth, she'd been glad of his silence, because it had given her a chance to process how *she* felt. And that was... numb, she thought. She didn't doubt that the reality of things would hit her eventually, but for now, she was mechanically going through the motions of caring for Grace and herself – washing clothes, changing nappies, making up bottles and food – and it was helping. Maybe, she thought, she felt like this because there was only so much grief one person could handle at once? She felt she'd cried all of the tears she could ever possibly cry over Leila. Maybe she had?

'Yes, I'm going out like this,' she said, too tired to pander to Piers and his views on female clothing. She was wearing the tunic Rachel had bought her, and in a brief moment of inspiration that morning, she'd tied an old purple scarf around her new red bob, with a large bow at the top. She'd also put on a small amount of makeup – just some lipstick, blusher and mascara – as she'd found the colour in the material had made her face look far too pale. She felt good in this outfit. So good, she'd even smiled at herself briefly in the mirror as she had applied the makeup.

'Tell me again who paid for this... outfit?' he said. 'Was it that Jake guy?'

'No, Piers, it was Rachel. You know that.'

'And she doesn't want you to pay her back?'

'No.'

'I wonder what she wants, then?' he said, his presence looming over her from the top step.

'She doesn't want anything, Piers.'

'Why don't I give you the money, and you can pay her back?'

'You don't need to do that.'

'I can't have people thinking I can't afford to support my wife,' he said. 'Can I?'

'No one knows she bought it, Piers. Come on. Be sensible.'

'Fine. Whatever. So where are you going?'

'To the Priory. I thought I'd take Dad to a social club thing there.'

Piers was silent for a few seconds. Even he couldn't find anything bad to say about that, she thought.

'Okay.'

'What are you going to do while I'm gone?' She was beginning to wonder what he was doing for all of those hours in his study.

'I'm going to write a letter to those bloody social workers,' he said. 'And their bosses. I will not be treated like this. They have *used* us, Amelia. They've used us as bloody foster parents. They probably knew that this was a possibility all along.'

Of course social services had known that, thought Amelia. They had both known that too. It had said so in all of the literature, admittedly as a small caveat. But they had both, to various degrees, chosen to ignore it.

'Okay. But don't send it yet, please? I'd like to read it,' she said.

Piers raised his eyes to the ceiling.

'If I must, I'll wait. What time are you coming back?'

'Oh, in a couple of hours, I suppose.'

'You're not going to go gallivanting off for coffee with one of your new friends afterwards, then?'

Amelia thought of Rachel. She wished she could be heading off to meet her. She desperately needed to talk to someone about how she felt. And unfortunately, that person definitely wasn't Piers. She decided to send her a text and let her know she needed a chat as soon as she'd managed to leave the flat.

'No, Piers, I'm going to take Dad out, that's all. I'll be back as soon as I can. Are you going to be okay while I'm gone? I know that this is… hard.'

Amelia saw Piers soften.

'Look, Amelia, sorry… I am finding this all very difficult. I'm sure you are, too. What with Leila, and now this… Go on with you, go and have a trip out, and I'll see you later, yeah? I have some work I need to do, anyway. And I'll draft that letter. But I won't send it yet, I promise.'

Amelia was relieved. She really didn't want to go out after they'd had a row; it took hours to bring Piers back from the brink when he got angry. It was why she always tried so hard to avoid it.

'Okay,' she said, taking hold of the buggy, which was parked at the bottom of the stairs. 'So I'll see you later, yes?'

'Yes. Don't rush back. Enjoy yourself,' he said, managing something approximating a smile. 'Say hi to your father for me.'

'Are you sure this is going to be my sort of thing?' said Amelia's father as she pulled into one of the disabled parking bays outside Malvern Priory.

'Well, Dad, given that it turns out you've started to attend church every week, perhaps you could tell me?'

Amelia hadn't meant her statement to sound so accusatory, but she had little patience today for her father's complaints and obfuscations. There was a short silence, during which Amelia focused on the steady, sleepy breaths of Grace in the car seat behind her and not on her father, whose breathing was still very laboured and who had a guilty expression on his face.

'Yes,' he said, finally. 'How did you find that out? I have started attending Evensong occasionally. For the music.'

Amelia's upbringing had been entirely, resolutely atheist, with trips to school chapel maintained strictly for appearance's sake. The idea of her father attending church, proper church, regularly, and not telling her, had unsettled her. And she found his excuse incredibly dubious.

'It doesn't matter how I found out, does it? So – just the music, then?'

'Well, yes, I love choral music. I always have. And also, I love the building. I have always loved it, you know that. All those school services, all of those years here, with your mother...'

'Oh, Dad.'

'Anyway,' he said, opening his door. 'Let's get this over with.'

It's a social club for pensioners, Dad, not your bloody execution, Amelia thought, as she opened her own door and lifted Grace out of her car seat and into her buggy. Then she offered her father her arm, which he took in preference, she knew, to the only other options – a walking frame or a wheelchair.

'Now, I think it's over here, just to the left,' she said, as they entered the church, their pace glacial. She looked down the aisle and saw a group of people sitting around small trestle tables, drinking hot drinks from mismatched china and munching on slices of cake. 'Yes, here we are, Dad,' she said. 'Do you recognise anybody?'

She looked around at the group of pensioners seated in front of her. They were at least seventy per cent female, but there was a smattering of men amongst them, some of whom were playing cards together. Amelia looked at her father's anxious face and searched around for the face of someone who might be in charge. Then she lighted upon a woman in her late fifties, with sleek brown hair. She was wearing a striking red knitted dress and black boots. She was definitely, *definitely* not a pensioner, thought Amelia.

'Excuse me,' she asked. 'My father is new here. Is there somewhere he can sit?'

'Oh, of course,' said the woman. 'Yes. Apologies, I should have come over as soon as you arrived. How rude of me.' The woman looked towards Amelia's father and smiled. 'Hello, my name is Gillian. I think I recognise you, but you'll have to excuse me, I can't quite remember your name.'

Amelia looked at her father, who she could see was wrestling with a desire to bolt out of there as soon as possible, mixed with a desire to please this woman, who was both good looking and charming.

'I'm... David,' he said. 'David Darke.'

'Well David, you are very welcome here. As it's your first time, how about I come over to sit with you, while I introduce you to one of our other gentlemen? I think Derryck would love to chat.'

Amelia watched as the charming, persuasive woman managed the impossible and led her father through the crowd to a spare seat on the far side. When he'd sat down, the woman, Gillian, gave her the thumbs up. Amelia knew that the session lasted an hour; that was one whole hour of peace away from the flat, one whole hour of time to think. She decided to go and take a seat at the back of the church, hoping that Grace would remain asleep for as long as possible. She needed to silence the many different voices in her head.

She walked up to the font, and selected a seat on the far side, near a pillar. She parked Grace next to her, checking as she did so that she had all the equipment she needed if Grace needed a feed. Reassured that she did, she sat back in the pew, and closed her eyes.

Please, please, please let me keep Grace. I have failed at so much. Please let me succeed at this, at least. I'm only just beginning to learn how to do everything properly. And please, please let us both cope with this period of uncertainty. We have been through more than enough already.

Shit, she thought, *I'm praying again. What on earth is wrong with me?*

'Hello.'

Peace, it seemed, continued to elude her. She opened her eyes and saw that Mark, the organist, was standing next to her. 'Oh I'm so sorry, I didn't mean to disturb. I just saw you there, and thought I'd say hi,' he said. 'And I wondered what you thought of the carol service?'

'Oh goodness, that feels like a lifetime ago,' she said, rubbing her eyes. 'But it was lovely, yes.'

'I played a piece for you. Well, for Grace, really. I wasn't sure if you'd spotted it or not.'

Amelia looked at him blankly.

'Obviously not,' he said, laughing nervously. 'Oh well, ha… I have to practise, so…'

'I'm sorry,' said Amelia, recovering herself. 'I didn't mean to be rude. I'm just having a shit day. Sorry, make that *week*. *Year*. Please do tell me. Do you want to take a seat?'

Mark looked awkward at this suggestion, she thought, but he nodded and sat a few feet away on the same pew, as if she had a disease that might be catching.

'Ah well, I changed the voluntary, to something written by Grace – Harvey Grace, that is. A tribute to the little one, if you will. As she seems to be a fan of organ music.'

'How lovely,' said Amelia, feeling her throat tighten and then tears begin to fall.

'I'm so sorry, I didn't mean to make you cry…' he said, still rooted to his spot on the pew, his hands wringing.

'No, no, don't worry, I think anything would set me off at the moment. It feels nice, actually, in a way, to cry. I have spent the past week in a kind of hell, where I felt like someone had stabbed me in the chest, left the knife in, and then kept twisting it every few minutes. I haven't even been able to scream in pain yet, because it isn't over.'

'Oh golly, that sounds bad. Do you want me to go? Or should I stay?'

Amelia looked up at him. He had a kind face, a friendly face. Perhaps he would be someone she could tell.

'Please stay,' she said. 'If you're not in a rush?'

'Oh no, I have all morning,' he said. 'Hours.'

'Good,' she said, almost laughing. 'Hopefully it won't take that long.'

'So, what is it?' he asked. 'I mean you don't have to go into detail if you don't want to, I don't want to pry.'

'No, it's okay. It's nice to talk about it, actually,' she said, reaching into the baby changing bag for a tissue. 'The thing is,' she said, blowing her nose, 'Grace isn't really mine. I mean, I'm looking after her legally, but I'm fostering her, fostering with the intention of adopting her.'

'I see...'

'Piers and I waited a good year on the adoption waiting list to be matched with Grace, after years of trying and failing to have a child of our own. We were told that there was almost no chance that her birth parents would contest the adoption order, and that she'd be ours in a matter of months. But on Monday...' she wiped her nose again, '... on Monday, we were told that the mother, the birth mother, is contesting. She's going to go to court to try to get her back.'

'Oh, I see.'

'And so she might... she might be taken from us,' she said. 'And I can't bear it...' A further wave of sobs took her over, and Mark waited patiently for her to regain her composure, before saying anything more.

'Well, that is absolutely shit, isn't it,' said Mark. Amelia looked up at him, surprised to hear such an apparently mild-mannered man swear. 'I don't think there's much I can say, except I'm truly sorry. If that happens, she will clearly miss out on being brought up by a lovely woman.'

'You don't know that,' she said. 'You don't know anything about me.'

'You really don't remember me, do you?' he said.

'I'm sorry, I...' Amelia's head snapped up.

'I was at your school, for a bit. For a few years, from the GCSE year until A-level.'

'Oh God, *were* you? I'm so sorry.'

'That's okay. I was a lot fatter then. With lots of spots.' Amelia looked at him and decided that he wasn't joking.

'I have always remembered you, because you were so kind.'

'Was I?'

'Yes. When I arrived, you made sure that I knew where lunch was served, where the lockers were, that sort of thing. You anticipated what I'd need to know, and you told me, so I wasn't embarrassed. And I've never forgotten that.'

Amelia searched her memory for a boy who looked a bit like Mark, and eventually lighted on a quiet, podgy, tall shy boy who she'd seen occasionally in Physics, Music and English. Ah yes, she remembered him now; he was a musical wunderkind. The school had boasted loudly of his achievements. How could she have forgotten him? But then of course, the man sitting next to her now was twenty years older, about five stone lighter and had clear skin. And his blond hair, once divided into two enormous floppy curtains, was now kept relatively short and peppered with grey.

'Oh God yes, I do remember you now. I'm so sorry. I must seem so bloody rude, and also, incredibly self-absorbed.'

'Don't be silly. It was years ago. And we were hardly friends.'

'I feel like an idiot. Sorry.'

'Please, don't be sorry. I only told you because I wanted you to know why I'm so confident you'll be a great parent.'

'If… she stays,' said Amelia, her face full of grief.

'Yes,' he said. 'But even if she goes, think what an amazing start you're giving her. You'll always have been her mummy for this period, won't you? Whatever happens.'

Amelia looked at Mark with renewed interest. She was suddenly incredibly glad she'd invited him to stay and talk to her.

'Yes,' she replied. '*Yes*. Thank you.'

'If there's anything I can do, you know, just let me know,' he said. 'I'm boringly available. I don't have any responsibilities, except for the church services and a few lessons. I can provide a willing ear whenever. Or potentially, really badly made, cheap coffee? I live in college accommodation, near the playing fields. Look,' he said, reaching into his pocket, 'here's my number,' he handed over a business card. 'I have these in case I come across any middle-class parents with aspirations to make their children organists,' he said, with a smile. The card read: 'Mark Monvid, organist and organ teacher.'

Mark Monvid. Yes. That was his name, she thought. She was so embarrassed that she hadn't recognised him. It was not as if she'd been one of the cool kids at school – she had probably been just one step up the ladder from Mark. Or probably, not even that.

'Thank you,' she said. 'I really appreciate that.'

'Any time,' he replied, standing up. 'Right, I need to go and practise now. We've a wedding on Saturday, and they are determined that they want a rendering of Ed Sheeran's "Galway Girl" as the bride walks down the aisle. Should be interesting, on the organ,' he said.

Amelia smiled. He was a funny guy, Mark. Why hadn't she noticed that at school? It made her wonder who else she'd missed out on over the years when she hadn't been paying attention. She watched as he ambled down the side aisle towards the organ loft, his weight balanced slightly too much on the balls of his feet, his satchel swinging by his side. And when he disappeared behind a small door, she switched her attention to the other corner of the church, where her father was – she hoped – still enjoying some company.

She stood up and unlocked the buggy and pushed it over to the area where the social club was meeting. As she did so, however, Grace woke up and began to wail. Amelia frowned.

She had only meant to check up on her dad – the club had twenty minutes to go yet. But now the entirety of the social club – or at least, those who actually wore their hearing aids – were staring at her. She felt a rush of heat in her face, and began frantically pushing the buggy back and forth, simultaneously searching her pockets for Grace's dummy.

'Oh, poor thing,' said the woman who'd greeted her earlier – Gillian, she thought her name was. She was standing a few feet away, serving cake to a lady with a very neat top-bun. She had the look of a retired ballet dancer.

'She's hungry, I think,' replied Amelia. 'Or maybe just tired…'

'I meant you,' said Gillian. 'You, poor thing, having to hang around here with an anxious baby. Look. Shall I get one of the volunteers to run your father home? He's having a good time, I think…'

Amelia looked over to where her father was sitting. He seemed to be engaged in a very intense game of cards with two other men. Her father was laughing. It had been years since she'd last seen him laugh out loud. Despite her concern about the noise Grace was generating, she was mesmerised.

'Yes…'

'We drive several of them home. We have a minibus. It's no bother.'

'Really?' asked Amelia, keen to get Grace out of the church and also keen to give her father a little more time doing something he was obviously enjoying.

'Of course. Look, give me your number, and I'll text you later to let you know he's home safely.'

Amelia followed Gillian over to a small table where she put her number on a signing in and out sheet, next to her father's name.

'Lovely,' said Gillian. 'I'll ask your father if he wants a lift here next week, too? Will spare you the bother?'

'That would be great. Thank you.'

Amelia nodded her thanks and waved at her father, who waved back absent-mindedly before returning to his game. Then Amelia pushed the still-screaming baby back up the aisle and out of the church, where she sat on a bench under a huge oak tree and fed a very hungry Grace a bottle.

Once she was fed, Amelia took a deep breath, packed up their things and headed for the car. She didn't particularly want to head home already, but she realised that there was little point putting off the inevitable. Piers was clearly going through another difficult patch, and he would need a lot of support and understanding, and she'd just have to muster it from somewhere. He would never tell anyone else how he was feeling, and that felt like a huge weight for her to carry. But carry it she must.

Amelia was momentarily distracted by the bleep of a text message as she turned into the drive of the boarding house, so she almost missed seeing Julia bolt out of the side door of the house and disappear down the path that led to the house's side gate. Fortunately, she was a conscientious driver, so she only glanced at her phone screen for a second – it was a message from Rachel asking if she was coming to baby group next week – and so looked up just as Julia slammed the door behind her and ran for the exit at speed.

What was she doing there, she wondered? Her first thought was that she'd messed up her diary. Had she missed a lesson? She pulled the car up into the housemaster's parking space, and picked up her phone, opening up her calendar. No: she was due to see her on Wednesday evening. Odd. Very odd, she thought. Well, no doubt Piers could tell her. She turned the car off – using Piers' keys again, for she had never found hers – removed Grace's car seat, and carried her across the threshold into the house and up to their apartment door.

'*Piers*,' she shouted up the stairs. '*We're home*.'

There was no response, so Amelia hung up her coat, and carried Grace upstairs, and walked towards Piers' office.

'*Piers*,' she said, as she turned the door handle.

'Yes darling,' he said, opening the door wide with a broad smile. He had got dressed in her absence and had a shave. 'You're back! Great.'

'Didn't you hear me?' she said, irritated. 'I was calling up to you.'

'Oh sorry, were you? I had some music on. Apologies. Anyway, how was it? Did your dad like it? And how are you, little munchkin?' he said, cooing in Grace's direction, his energy vibrant and joyful. It was like he was a completely different man, Amelia thought.

'It was good. Dad liked it. Piers… before I get distracted and forget – do you know why Julia was here just now?' she asked, putting the car seat down and removing Grace.

'Oh, was she?' he said, his voice still jovial.

'Yes. I saw her leave from the side door as I drove up,' she said, turning to look at him, with Grace in her arms.

'Oh really? I can't imagine why she'd have been here. Maybe she got the day of your lesson wrong and felt embarrassed?'

'Yes, maybe,' said Amelia, as Grace began to grizzle. 'I'll have to ask her.'

'Yes, or maybe ask the staff?' said Piers, reaching out to take Grace from Amelia, who had already decided to ask Matron about Julia's visit later. 'They might know. Now, little one, let's get you fed. I recognise that moany noise you're making. You're a hungry little girl, aren't you?'

Amelia watched him walk Grace into the kitchen and go through the now well-practised motions of making up a bottle of milk for her. And as he did so, she stood in the kitchen doorway, observing her husband. When she'd left the house earlier that afternoon, it had been like his world was ending, and just two hours later, he seemed like a man who was entirely contented with his lot. What on earth had happened in the interim?

'Are you hungry, Amelia?' he asked, as he microwaved the milk. 'I thought we could order a Chinese for supper?'

But Amelia had no interest in food, because her instincts were telling her something about the picture in front of her was wrong, and adrenaline was surging throughout her body.

'No, I'm all right. You go ahead. I'll sort myself something out later,' she said, as she walked into the bedroom, shut the door behind her and collapsed onto the bed to think. Was he clinically depressed? Maybe bipolar? That might explain the change in mood. He'd gone through a bad patch after the break-up with Lesley, she knew that. Maybe there was much more to it, maybe he was afraid to admit that he had mental health difficulties. But then, what about those letters she'd seen him read and then fail to tell her about? Was there something there?

She thought about his closed study door and decided then and there that she was going to find a way to open it.

25

January 19th

Michelle

Five weeks until the final hearing

Michelle observed each familiar street, shop and pub from the car window as they drove from Malvern to Worcester. When they reached the outskirts of the town and drove into the greenbelt, she took a deep breath, keen to absorb as much of the country air as possible. She had always loved the rural areas around Malvern; when she'd run away from the children's home as a teen (running away was a bit of an exaggeration though, she thought – it was usually just for a day) she had often walked into the fields and commons and just sat there, inhaling the scent of fern, grass and gorse.

The fields she was looking at now were still in the depths of winter, but today was one of those days when the weak sun had managed to keep the clouds at bay, and its rays were greeting the ice-scorched earth with a meagre warmth. It hinted at spring, and that made her happy. She had always liked spring.

'So tell me again who this woman is?' asked Gillian.

'She's called Sally. She was the solicitor they gave me last time. I kept her card. Well, it was in a pile of stuff beside my bed in the flat, but I didn't throw it away…'

'But she didn't succeed last time, did she? Look, I know I've said this before, but… Mightn't it be better to get someone new? We have a friend who comes highly recommended.'

'No, I liked her,' said Michelle, her tone decisive. 'I mean, she tried. I felt like she cared. To be honest, I didn't help her much. She'd have done much better, probably, if I'd actually told her stuff.'

'Okay,' said Gillian.

She thinks I'm making the wrong choice, thought Michelle. Maybe I am? Perhaps I shouldn't follow my instincts? After all, I've been very wrong before.

'This seems to be it,' said Gillian, as they pulled up outside an ugly Sixties semi-detached house beside the busy ring-road. 'I think we can park here. It says it's for visitors.'

'That was lucky,' said Michelle, opening the door.

'Or worrying,' replied Gillian. 'They're obviously not very busy.'

Michelle decided not to answer her. Instead, she got out of the car, pulled her new red jumper, a present from Gillian, down over her hips, and walked towards the front door. There was a selection of bells beside the door. One of them had a handwritten note wedged into the transparent plastic slot next to it. It said, in swirly writing: 'S. Mucklow. Solicitor.' Michelle pressed it.

'Come in,' said a familiar voice, and a buzz signalled that they should enter. Michelle pushed the door open to be greeted by a dingy grey hallway, littered with flyers from fast food restaurants. Gillian gave Michelle a thoughtful look and they both walked over the threshold.

'I'm so sorry, I've been stuck in my office since breakfast and the cleaner hasn't been yet.'

It was 3 p.m.: that's a long stretch to go without even leaving a room, thought Michelle. Sally Mucklow was walking up the hallway towards them, leaning over every so often to pick up a stray piece of paper. She was wearing tight black trousers, a bright pink chiffon shirt, and flat pink shoes with pointed toes. 'I share this place with a couple of IT guys, but they're not the tidiest, unfortunately,' she said, holding her hand out. 'Apologies. I'm Sally. And Michelle… Wow, you look… great,' she said.

'Thanks,' replied Michelle, smoothing her hands down her jeans, which were also new. Gillian had told her that the social services money covered buying her new clothes, but she suspected that she might have been lying to make her feel better.

'Nice to meet you, Sally,' said Gillian, holding out her hand. 'I'm Michelle's…'

'… friend,' said Michelle, quickly. 'Or guardian angel, maybe? She's been helping me, anyway.'

Michelle looked at Gillian. She was sure she detected the hint of a blush in her well made-up cheeks.

'Right, well, that's great to hear,' said Sally. 'We all need one of those, and there definitely aren't enough to go round. Come with me, both of you. I'm at the back.'

Michelle followed Sally down the passageway and through a heavy white fire door at the end. They then emerged into a light, clean, bright room. It was painted brilliant white and furnished with a large white wooden desk, a white metal office chair, a grey sofa, two large grey armchairs and multiple splashes of colour everywhere Michelle looked. There were bright yellow cushions on the sofa, orange cushions on the chairs, and the telephone, in-tray and stapler on Sally's desk were all bright red. In the corner, a large potted palm tree shot up towards the ceiling, its fronds tumbling over themselves like a lithe gymnast.

'Welcome to my humble abode,' said Sally, sitting behind her desk and indicating that they should take a seat. 'I decided to make it feel a bit homely,' she said, smiling. 'Given that I spend more time here than at home.'

'It looks great,' said Michelle, sitting down opposite Sally.

'Really nice.' Gillian sat down next to her and took out a notebook from her handbag.

'I'll be taking notes on my laptop throughout our chat,' said Sally, noticing the notebook. 'I'm happy to share them with you both afterwards, if that would help?'

'That would be helpful, thank you,' replied Gillian. 'I always worry I'm going to forget details after important meetings.'

'Me too,' replied Sally, smiling. 'So it's lucky I can touch type. Now… Michelle. I am very glad that you agreed to meet with me today. I know that your attitude has changed a great deal since I met you last. I can see that with my own eyes. At the first hearing, you didn't want to tell me much about what had gone before. This time, I'm hoping things might be a bit different?'

'Yeah,' said Michelle. 'Sorry about that. I was so knackered after the birth, and after… the incident that put me in hospital, you know? And social services have treated me like shit since forever, so I didn't feel like doing what they wanted.'

'I understand that. Of course, it means we've lost a bit of time, and it was a great shame that you weren't able to be present at the case management hearing back in November. But no matter. Let's just focus on what's coming next. I was given some limited information from them about your past before the first hearing, but I'd much rather hear it from you. It would help me greatly, as we approach the resolution and final hearings. Do you think you could do that? Could you give me a potted history, as it were, of what has brought you here to me today?'

Michelle looked over at Gillian, who gave her an encouraging smile. What the hell, thought Michelle. I've already told her most of it. She knows the mistakes I've made, and she's still here, so… Why not.

'Well… How far back do you want me to go?'

'As far back as you feel comfortable.'

'Okay. Well, right, as you probably know, I was put in care when I was six. My parents, they were both addicts. My dad left us all when we were babies, and I have no idea where he is, and I don't want to know. And Mum, well, she wasn't capable. At all. She was wasted all of the time, both drink and drugs. So Nan – Mum's mum – and her second husband, they took us in, right? We lived with them for a couple of years and we were really happy. It felt like a proper family. And then one day, we were dropped off at a care home, and we never lived with family again.'

'You refer to "*us*",' said Sally. 'This would be you and your sister, Grace?'

Michelle felt a jolt of electricity pass through her when her sister's name was mentioned. She was so unused to anyone talking about her.

'Yeah. Me and Grace.'

'And she's three years younger than you?'

'Yeah. She was three when she… was taken away.'

'Social services took her away?'

'Yeah. She was adopted, they told me. They don't know where she is now, but they say they're looking. But I was too old for adoption. No one wanted me, you see. So we got separated.'

'You stayed in the care home?'

'Well, I was in and out of foster homes every so often, but yeah, I was mostly in care. The foster parents mostly didn't want to keep me with them, see. I used to run away, smoke in their houses, come home late stinking of weed and booze. I was really angry, you know? Like, *really* angry. Mostly at social services, but also at Nan. I thought she'd abandoned us.'

'But social services have told you more about why that happened now, I understand?'

Michelle took a deep breath. 'Yeah. She died. She didn't want to tell us she was dying. I sort of get it. She was trying to protect us. But… I'm still angry that social services didn't tell me. It meant I didn't get to say goodbye.'

No one spoke for a while. Sally kept typing for a few more

seconds, before looking up. 'God, sorry, I have just realised I should have offered you a drink. Do you want anything?' she said, looking at Gillian and Michelle.

'Nah, I'm okay,' said Michelle. 'Do you want anything, Gill?'

Michelle looked across at Gillian, and she saw that she had tears in her eyes. She shook her head.

'Anyway, yeah, so I was in a home until I was sixteen,' she continued. 'Then I left. Social services didn't want me to, they said they wanted to help me, but I dunno, they've told me so many lies over so many years... I didn't trust them. Still don't. So I left. I didn't have anywhere to go, like, but I didn't care. I just wanted out. I slept rough in the end, in Malvern and Worcester, wherever I could find other people like me. I tried to sleep out with other people – safety in numbers, like – but they were mostly blokes, and mostly they were off their tits on booze and drugs. One of them... tried to force me to have sex with him once. He was heavy, and strong...' – Michelle paused as a vivid memory of his hideous stench and his immense weight took hold of her – 'but Rob, my... ex, you know, he saw him doing it, and he dragged him off me. He properly walloped him, to be honest. Saved me, didn't he?'

'And Rob is baby Grace's father?'

'Yeah. Course he is. I haven't slept with no one else since I met him. I've been with Rob for three years now.'

Sally paused her typing and looked directly at Michelle.

'Social services say that he assaulted you just before the baby was born. And afterwards.'

Michelle clasped her hands on her lap and focused on the beauty spot just below her left index finger as she continued to tell her story.

'Yeah, he did.' There was a silence in the room as the other women waited for Michelle to continue. But she didn't, not immediately, because she was trying to think of a way to explain why she'd stayed, even though he'd hit her. 'He has

– had – a temper,' she said, eventually. 'But he's had all sorts of stuff happen to him, like me. His parents also abandoned him, see, and he was abused as a kid. So he can't control his anger sometimes. But he doesn't mean nothing by it.'

Sally looked hard at Michelle, her expression impassive.

'Why did he hit you?'

'He only did it when he was high, or when he was desperate for a hit. I don't think he knew what he was doing.'

'Was he angry that you were pregnant?' asked Sally.

'Nah, he wasn't. It was a mistake, though. We didn't plan it. And we both knew we couldn't keep her. Or, you know, that's what I thought for a long time… I've got a record, haven't I? Shoplifting, possession… And we don't have no money, neither. Not enough to look after a baby.'

'Why didn't you report any of the attacks to the police, Michelle?'

'Because like I said, he didn't know he was doing it. He was always really sorry afterwards. And because Rob is known to them, for drugs. They'd just think it was to do with that, a domestic, like, and ignore us. They don't take people like me seriously, they really don't. I don't trust the police.'

'I see. But social services offered you support, didn't they, so that you could keep her?'

'Yeah, they did. But they said I had to leave Rob for that, and… I know this is going to sound stupid now, but… Rob stuck by me, you know? He's the only person who ever stuck by me, really. I trust – trusted – him. I *needed* him. And I also thought… I really thought… I would be a shit mother. My mother's genes, you know? I have spent so long feeling like a waste of space, a waste of air… I thought she would be better off without me. Like my sister is.'

'But now…'

'Now, I feel like… like I can do it, you know? I can be a mother. I can be the mother Grace needs. I feel like, deep down, letting her go was the biggest mistake of my life. I know that it's going to be really hard, but I think keeping Grace with me, giving her the chance to grow up with her own flesh and blood, something I was denied... I think that's really worth it.'

'Thank you for being so frank with me, Michelle. I really appreciate it. I will make sure that everything you've said is communicated to the court. They need to understand why you didn't want to keep Grace initially – that will be one of our sticking points. They'll also need to be persuaded that you're in a good position now to take care of her. Have you thought about practical things? What plans have you got in place?'

'She's going to stay with us for a while,' said Gillian, suddenly. 'Sorry, Michelle, I know this is your meeting, but I wanted to make it clear that Mike and I are completely on board with this. We are happy for her and Grace to stay with us as long as it takes to get them both on their feet.'

'That's wonderful,' said Sally. 'And it will definitely help. But they will also need to be convinced that you're stable enough, Michelle, to cope – that you will not slide back to where you were before, during your darkest times.'

'I know that,' said Michelle. 'And I dunno. I feel so much better, but I don't know how to prove that. I mean, once a drug user, are you ever not a drug user? I promise though that I will do what social services want. And that's a big change for me. I never trust those bastards... Sorry for my language.'

'That's quite all right,' said Sally. 'We are all friends here. But best to not describe them like that in court.' Michelle smiled at her. I was right to trust her, she thought. She gets me. 'So what made you change your mind about co-operating with them, social services?' she asked.

'A few things, really. I reached rock bottom, didn't I? I tried to top myself. And then Rob disappeared. And that made me think again about some of the other decisions I've made, you know? And Gill and Mike… they've helped me see that there are people out there I can trust. They're like… amazing.'

'We just want to help,' said Gillian.

'… and I think because I feel safe with them, I've let down my guard a bit. I've always had it up before. And now I know that I really, really want Grace back. I've been trying to tell myself the opposite for months, but it was all a lie, wasn't it? It was a lie I told myself, that made me ill. The thing is, you see, I want her back more than anything.'

'Good to hear. Now, I have a copy of your parenting assessment and it looks fine, so that's good. But there's one other important thing to mention, before the resolution hearing takes place in a couple of weeks' time. Rob…'

'He's disappeared,' Michelle interrupted. 'He left the flat, and he's not replying to my texts…'

'I'm afraid I have some news for you that may be unwelcome, Michelle. I've had notification that Rob has appointed his own solicitor. He is also seeking custody of Grace.'

And just like that, the bottom dropped out of Michelle's world.

'He's done… what?!' she spluttered. 'But he doesn't even want her! He never…'

Michelle looked hard at Sally. She had stopped typing and was blinking furiously as she elaborated on this devastating piece of information.

'It seems that his family are paying for the head of a law firm in Birmingham to represent them. They're applying for custody as a family unit – his parents have offered to help him…'

'His parents? But he doesn't talk to his parents. They…' Everything Michelle had thought she'd known about her partner of three years suddenly started to dissolve. Hang on, she thought – he has a family? And they have… money?

'So he *has* parents, then?' she said. 'Parents with *money*?'

'It would seem so, yes. I have done a small amount of research into him, so that I'm prepared for court.' Sally pulled a piece of paper in front of her laptop and read from it. 'He attended a private school in Worcester until he was fifteen. Then he got involved in drugs, was expelled from there and then left home, from the sound of things. But he's recently been reunited with his family, I am told, and it seems that they're keen that he keeps contact with Grace.'

What a bastard, Michelle thought. He was fucking *playing* at being poor. All that shit about knowing how she felt, knowing how it was to have no family and no support, that had been a fucking *lie*. He'd had a safety net all of that time, all of that time they had been starving and stealing so that they could eat. Michelle wasn't angry anymore. No, she was *fucking furious*.

'Fucker,' she said, out loud. 'Sorry… I didn't mean…'

'Quite all right,' said Sally. 'Just don't say that in court.'

'So they're paying for it? They're not getting legal aid?' asked Gillian.

'That's right.'

'We could pay, too. Me and Mike,' Gillian said, looking across at Michelle.

'No…' said Michelle, an answer drawn from the dense, swirling mass of thoughts, hatred and lies that were now occupying her brain.

'I know I'm not the head of a top firm in Brum, but I promise you both that I'm more than capable of fighting this, even though I'm only on legal aid rates,' said Sally, sitting forward in her chair. 'I was there at the beginning, and I promise you, I'll be there until the end.'

'I am sure that's the case…' said Gillian.

'I really mean that,' said Sally. 'Honestly. I believe that we have a very strong case, particularly versus Rob, who has a history of violence and drug abuse. He has also only just begun to have an involvement with Grace at the contact centre…'

'So he's been to the contact centre?' said Michelle, unbelieving.

'Yes. I believe he started late last week,' she said.

Michelle felt sick. This was not the Rob she knew. That Rob would never have gone behind her back, and he definitely wouldn't have shown any interest in their child. He never had.

But what if she hadn't really known him at all? Had she *really* put all of her trust – all that was left of her trust, at any rate – in the hands of a man who wasn't even who he had said he was? He'd even gone to a private school. Jesus! He must have even faked that stupid accent of his, which had always been just a *touch* more 'local' than hers. Yep, he had betrayed her, the bastard. After everything. *How. Dare. He.*

She wondered when he'd been there, at the contact centre. Maybe he had left just as she'd arrived for her most recent visit? Had Grace's little fingers unwrapped themselves from Rob's hands just moments before they had grasped her own? And had his parents... She didn't even want to think about them. Who the hell were they, and why had Rob lied about them? She didn't want Rob anywhere near Grace. She had to stop him.

'Look, I know this is a huge amount to take on board,' said Sally. 'Why don't we call time for today, and I'll be in touch with any further questions I have before the resolution hearing. We still have two weeks before that happens, and then who knows, we might be able to make good progress then.'

'So is the adoption decision made then, at the resolution hearing?' asked Gillian.

'Oh, no, not usually. The resolution hearing is an opportunity for everyone to have their say. We're lucky that the judge delayed the need for the parenting assessment until the RH, and she will assess the social workers' assessments then, too. That means you have time to convince everyone – and I mean, everyone – that you are ready to parent Grace. The judge's final decision will be made two weeks after that, at the final hearing, after she's had time to read the guardian's final analysis – that's the report Marion Stone is writing. Sorry, that's a lot of "final".'

Michelle's stomach flipped, and she saw Gillian looking at her with concern in her eyes. Gillian reached for her handbag and stood up.

'Yes, I think that's a good idea if we go now,' said Gillian. 'Shall we head off, Michelle? I think you need a coffee and a cake. There's a nice cafe around the corner…'

Michelle felt as if she'd been kicked. All she wanted to do was to pull all of her extremities inwards, curl up into a ball and repel everyone. Every single person. The whole world. She was done with it all. Done. She could feel two pairs of eyes boring into her as she sat there with her eyes closed, fighting back the tears which she abhorred, but she didn't care what they thought of her. She had lost faith in everyone now.

'Why don't I go out and get us all a coffee from the cafe?' said Sally. 'I'll be about five minutes,' she said, walking swiftly to the door without waiting for a response.

Michelle opened her eyes when she heard the door click. Gillian was standing up next to her, with tears in her eyes, clasping her handbag to her stomach, as if it was a small child.

'Oh Michelle…' she said, tears rolling down her cheeks. 'I wish I could give you a hug…'

Michelle stood up before she could overthink it. She leaned into Gillian, who dropped her handbag immediately, and folded her arms around her.

As Michelle stood there – hugging only the fourth person she had ever hugged – she thought of her grandmother, her dead grandmother, the only other woman she'd ever previously trusted. She wondered what she would say now, if she could be there. How could she ever have thought that she'd have abandoned her without a fight?

'We will fight them for Grace,' said Gillian, into Michelle's left ear. 'We'll fight hard,' she said, rubbing her back. 'And we'll win. You'll see.'

A fight. *Yes*, Michelle thought, *that's what I'll do*. She could either roll over and let them all win, like she'd always done, or she could stand up to them. She might not have been old enough to fight for her sister when she'd been taken, but she was more than old enough to fight for her daughter. And this anger would give her all the energy she needed.

'Yeah,' she replied, finally. '*Yeah*. A fight. I'm ready for a fight.'

PART THREE

26

February 2nd

Judge Joshi

The resolution hearing

'All rise,' said the clerk, as Judge Prisha Joshi walked into the courtroom. 'Thank you,' said the judge, as she reached her desk. 'You may be seated.'

District Judge Joshi looked around her at the somewhat expanded crowd, compared to the previous hearing. She was particularly relieved to see that the baby's mother, Michelle, was present. She looks better, she thought. There's a bit more meat on those bones, and she's wearing a smart-looking pair of jeans and a shirt, rather than a stained hoodie and tracksuit bottoms. Someone, somewhere, is having a positive influence on her, she thought. Thank heavens for that. She no longer looks like she needs someone to chuck her a life buoy.

There were also several new additions sitting at two o'clock. One was a young man who looked to be in his twenties. He was flanked by a man and woman in their fifties, both wearing well-tailored, expensive-looking clothes. That young man must be Rob, Grace's father, she thought – but he was not at all who she had been expecting to see. This man had a sharp new haircut, a clean-shaven face, a well-ironed shirt and a smart tie. Everything she knew about Rob Allcott – his drug abuse, his alcoholism, his violent past – railed against the suave appearance of the man sitting in front of her. This should be interesting, she thought. What's going on here?

'Good morning,' she said, pulling her bifocals out of their case and placing them on her nose. 'As those of you present at the last hearing will recall, I decided to postpone the reading of the parenting assessment and the social workers' reports until this session. Are these now ready, Mr Shelley?'

The barrister for the local authority stood up. 'They are, madam. However, I need to make you aware of a significant change in regards to this case. The baby's father, Rob Allcott, has decided to contest the adoption. He is here in court, along with his parents, Mr and Mrs Allcott. They have appointed their own barrister, I believe.'

'I see,' said Judge Joshi. 'And where is this barrister?'

'He's stuck in traffic,' said Rob Allcott's father, in a broad Brummie accent. 'He's coming down from Birmingham, you see, and the traffic on the M5 is bad this morning.'

Judge Joshi could see Sally Mucklow smirking out of the corner of her eye. Fair enough, she thought; being late was hardly a good place to start.

'I see. Let's begin anyway,' she said. 'I have another case to fit in this afternoon. Mr Allcott – and by that, I mean, Mr Robert Allcott – could you please tell me what you are hoping to achieve, now that you are taking part in the proceedings?'

She watched as the young man stood up, smoothing a fly away strand of hair away from his face as he did so.

'I want custody of my daughter,' he said, quietly, in a cut-glass accent – a stark contrast to his father.

Judge Joshi heard a gasp coming from behind Sally Mucklow, and saw that Michelle Jenkins had a hand over her mouth. Was it that she hadn't expected him to say that, she wondered, or that she hadn't expected him to *sound* like that?

'You are aware, I hope, that entering proceedings at this stage does not give a very favourable impression?' she said, noting that Rob did not want to look directly at her.

Suddenly, there was a loud click, and the door to the courtroom swung open. A tall, overweight man in his early sixties walked in, and Judge Joshi sighed inwardly. It was Len Carraway. He was an utter, utter bastard; a very expensive bastard, for that matter. He was usually to be found defending high-profile murderers and rapists. This family clearly had *means*.

'This, I assume, is your counsel?' she said, not making any effort to hide her displeasure at his late arrival.

'Yes, madam, that's correct,' said Len, panting as he strode towards the front row of desks. 'Apologies. A lorry toppled over near Solihull. The roads were murder.'

Judge Joshi gave him her most fixed stare. She drove into Worcester from Solihull most days of the week and was usually generously early. It was all about allowing for contingency.

'Now that we're all assembled,' she said, after Len Carraway had sat down, his ample behind tumbling over the side of his chair. 'I want to recap and assess where we are. We now have a parenting assessment for Ms Jenkins, and two social worker reports – one for Ms Jenkins, and one for Grace, yes? And they have been circulated to all parties?' she said, looking around her, inviting responses.

'Yes, madam, but you don't have one for my client,' said Len.

'Indeed not, Mr Carraway,' she said. 'Because your client was not part of either of the previous two hearings.'

'My client, Rob Allcott, knows that his late arrival does not reflect well on him, madam. But that was because he was in rehab for his drug addiction. This was a success, I'm glad to say, and my client is now reconciled with his parents, who are fully supporting his application. They intend to support him both financially and practically, in parenting his child.'

'Your client, Mr Allcott, showed no interest in the baby when it was born, Mr Carraway,' she said. 'He didn't even visit her in hospital.'

'My client says that his partner, the baby's mother, did not want him there, madam. It was entirely Ms Jenkins' decision to put her up for adoption. Mr Allcott tells me he wasn't consulted. That being said, he has now begun visiting Grace at the contact centre, and you have his word that he will appear at each contact session from now on,' he said. Judge Joshi looked over at Rob Allcott, who seemed to be playing with his cufflinks, as if they were new toys.

She turned her attention to Sally Mucklow.

'Ms Mucklow, your client, Michelle Jenkins, wasn't here at the case management hearing. Furthermore, at the first hearing, we were told that she had expressed an intention to have Grace adopted. I understand that is no longer the case. Can you tell us what has changed, please?'

'Madam, thank you for taking the time to read my submission explaining Ms Jenkins' change of position,' said Sally Mucklow, standing up and picking up a large red lever-arch file. 'Yes, that's true; my client has now decided to contest the adoption. Madam, Ms Jenkins had just given birth at the first hearing, and any woman who's done similar will know that it's an incredibly confusing, hormonal time. It took some time for Ms Jenkins to reach an equilibrium, a place where she felt she could make the right decision. But she has made some very positive changes in her life since you last saw her – she has now left the home she shared with Mr Allcott, and is now living with two retired foster carers, Gillian and Mike Wade. They have provided her with a stable, safe, supportive home, and they have also offered to help look after baby Grace, should Michelle be granted custody.'

'Thank you, Ms Mucklow, for this information,' said Judge Joshi. 'You may sit down.' The judge took a deep breath and made an important decision as she did so.

'I am grateful that the three reports I asked for are ready,' she said. 'It is incredibly unfortunate however that the court did not have enough warning of Mr Allcott's decision to contest, to arrange for a parenting assessment to be carried out before this session. It is clear that such an assessment does need to be carried out, as a matter of urgency.'

Judge Joshi saw that Len Carraway was writing this down and underlining it. Good, she thought, you can earn your money. Make that happen.

'I am aware, however, that social services try to work to a maximum twenty-six-week target in foster to adopt cases, and I feel that it is in the child's best interests for us not to delay. I know this is unusual, but can I ask please that the parenting assessment for Mr Allcott is completed and sent to me well in advance of the final hearing in two weeks' time? In the meantime, I'd like to use our time in court today for cross-examination of the reports that we do have.'

'But madam...' said Len, who had stopped writing now. 'I urge you to delay so that we can ensure the assessment takes place in good time.'

'I understand your concern, Mr Carraway, but I will not allow latecomers to the proceedings to disrupt my timeline. Everyone's time here is precious, and I want to make sure that all parties are not kept in limbo for too long. I assure you that I will give Mr Allcott's parental assessment my full attention when it arrives.' Judge Joshi picked up her pen and turned to the children's guardian.

'Miss Stone. Can you tell me what your current position is in this case? It would seem that we now have two birth parents keen to retain custody.'

'Thank you, madam,' said Miss Stone as she got to her feet. 'I have now met with both the potential adoptive parents, and the birth mother on several occasions now, and I've written the lion's share of my report. I will however need to meet with Mr

Allcott at his earliest convenience, so that my final analysis can be as comprehensive as possible.'

'Thank you, Miss Stone. Well, it would seem that, in any case, we are not in any position to reach a resolution today,' she said, scanning the faces all around her. 'As you all know, the final hearing would normally be scheduled for a fortnight from now, but I'm going to allow an extra week,' – she noticed that Len Carraway was twitching in his seat – 'so that the parenting assessment for Mr Robert Allcott can take place. Once that and the guardian's Final Analysis is completed, we will circulate the reports amongst all of you, and then we will reconvene in three weeks' time – February twenty-third – for the final hearing. You may call witnesses for that if you wish, and you will also be able to cross-examine the other parties. Does anyone have any questions?'

Although Len Carraway looked like he might be about to speak for a moment, he seemed to think better of it and switched his attention to his notes. Judge Joshi was relieved that he wasn't going to make a fuss. Firstly, because she was aware that there was a child at the centre of this case, and she wanted to ensure that that child had a permanent home as soon as possible; and secondly, finishing this session earlier than planned meant that she might have enough time to nip out for a sandwich and a coffee before her second case of the day. Making judgements on only the contents of the court vending machine had a tendency to make her grumpy.

'All rise,' said the clerk after a second or two of silence had passed, and the assembled lawyers began to pack up their bags and engage in platitudinal chatter with their clients.

As Sally Mucklow stood up to talk to Michelle Jenkins, the judge looked in their direction. She could just make out a tear wending its way down the young mother's face, and an older woman sitting next to her tenderly wiping it away with a handkerchief. 'We'll fight them all,' the older woman said to Michelle. 'Don't you worry.'

Not for the first time, the judge wished that this most personal of human dramas did not have to inevitably descend into a bloody war.

27

February 10th

Michelle

Thirteen days until the final hearing

'Mind the sheep poo,' the woman said as they walked from the end of the drive, where Gillian had dropped her, into the big farmhouse. 'They graze all over the common here, and the number of times I've had to clean green muck off my stairs, you can't even imagine.'

Michelle didn't know what to say, so she kept her eyes on the ground, keen to avoid having to take her shoes off when she entered the house. Her socks had holes in.

'Right,' said the woman, rubbing her shoes vigorously on a brown wire mat by the door, 'welcome. Please follow me. By the way, you don't mind animals, do you? I have a whole menagerie, I'm afraid.'

'Nah, I love animals,' said Michelle, on comfortable ground. She preferred animals to humans most of the time.

'Great. Well, here you are. This is Amy, she's one of our sheepdogs. That' – she pointed to the corner of the stone-flagged kitchen to her left – 'is George the cockerel, and this' – she said, reaching down to stroke it – 'is Peppa, our… pig. Obviously. My daughter named her. It was kind of inevitable.'

Michelle looked down at the large black pig, its tough skin covered in wiry black hairs. It was looking at her quizzically. She reached down to pat it.

'Right, here we are. A haven of calm, sort of. Please do come in.'

Michelle followed the woman into a sort of parlour room, furnished with two large upright chairs and a small table. A dormer window looked out over a field, a large wooden dresser ran along one of the walls and a log fire was blazing in the grate.

'Ah, and it's nice and warm in here now, too. Lovely. I lit the fire a couple of hours ago. Please sit down,' said the woman.

Michelle took a seat in the chair that was nearest the window.

'I'll leave the door open a crack, so the animals can join us if they want to,' the woman said, as she took a seat opposite Michelle.

'Now, where were we? Yes. So, welcome. My name is Becky, and I'm a trained counsellor. As well as being a farmer, as you've seen. I've been offering counselling here for a decade now, and I want to start by saying that I'm completely unshockable. Completely bulletproof. And entirely discreet. You can say what you like in here, and it will only go as far as the animals. And only then, if they're within earshot.'

Michelle saw the door open a crack as Peppa the pig waddled into the room. The sight of her made her smile, and when Peppa made it to her chair, Michelle leaned over and stroked her, feeling her anxiety about the session dissipate as she did so.

'That's good,' she said, talking more to the pig than to Becky.

'So, do you want to tell me what you would like to start with?' Becky asked.

Michelle paused. She had never, ever had a therapy session before, and she felt awkward.

'My friends, Gillian and Mike, they thought it might help me, you know, to talk about the past. I had a shit time... Sorry for my swearing...'

'It's absolutely fine. Carry on.'

'I had a shit time as a kid. In and out of foster homes and that, then care homes. I got expelled from school. I lived on the streets for a bit.'

'I see. And does all of that affect the here and now? Does it… haunt you?'

'Yeah, I suppose. The thing is, I had a baby… I *have* a baby. Grace. And I have to go to court in a couple of weeks, to try to get her back. Social services thought she was safer away from me. And I have to try to change their minds. Or I'll never see her again.'

'Right. And this is part of that? Dealing with things that keep you up at night? Sometimes, you know, we are so hurt by things that happen to us, that we form a protective bubble around us. It gives us a sort of numbness, to try to protect ourselves. But it also means we can't move on.'

'Yeah, that sounds a bit like how it is.'

'Where do you want to start?'

Michelle moved her legs so that the pig could rest against her chair.

'I dunno. Maybe with the most recent bit. I had a boyfriend. Partner. The baby's dad. I trusted him, but… he turned out to be a shit. Like all of the other shits.'

'I see. How did he show his true colours?'

'I reckon he'd been showing them all along, but I didn't want to see them, you know? I thought he was protecting me, but in the end…' Michelle paused as she remembered the blows he'd rained down on her, the burns she'd tried to hide, '…to be honest, he was violent.' She waited for Becky to respond, but she didn't, and the silence seemed inviting, so she kept on talking. 'I always forgave him, believed him when he said it wouldn't happen again, because I needed to believe it. I thought I could trust him. But now… we had a court hearing to discuss stuff, he turned up and he was a completely different person.'

'In what way?'

'In *every way*. His accent, his clothes, the way he stood, the way he sat... It's like he lives in a different world to me, and he was playing at being poor, playing at being a drop-out. It's like he was enjoying watching me struggle, you know?' The pig nudged Michelle's hand, demanding attention. She responded with a tickle under her chin, and she looked up at her with an adoring stare. 'I feel like a total idiot,' she said, scratching between her ears. 'Like I should have seen it before. I can't believe he lied to me for so fucking long.'

'Being betrayed cuts deep,' said Becky. 'But just because he lied about where he came from, and he seems different now, it doesn't necessarily mean that everything you shared together was a lie.'

'I s'pose.'

'Definitely. He may have his reasons. Maybe he was lying to himself? I don't know. But what I do know is that you're not a fool. If anything, I'd say that this shows what a capacity you have for love and friendship. You gave him your trust and you stuck with it, and that's a great testament to who you are.'

Michelle looked up at Becky.

'Do you reckon?' she said, sitting back in her chair.

'Definitely. You have a big heart, I'd say. And trust me, that's not a bad thing in life.'

Michelle watched as the door opened even further and the cockerel came striding in.

'Now, let me get us some water,' said Becky. 'I should have done that before, I apologise. I'll just leave you with George. He loves a scratch. But I must warn you, he is prone to leaping onto laps with absolutely zero warning.'

'So was she nice?'

'She was really nice, yeah. I liked her.'

'Oh, I'm so glad. My friend Anne told me she was lovely. I was crossing my fingers for you. I know it's strange, telling a stranger how you feel.'

Michelle hauled a large box onto the trestle table, and began to unload it, placing the donated food – bags of pasta, flour, rice and cereal – out on display. It felt good, she thought, helping out here. It made her feel useful and it reminded her of her old job in the warehouse.

'She had loads of animals.'

Michelle saw Gillian smile as she sorted through the loaded supermarket bags which were lined up against the ancient church wall. 'Yes, I had heard that,' she said. *I bet you did*, thought Michelle. *She knew I'd love those animals. Gillian never misses a trick*. 'So will you be going back, do you think?' she asked, her head still deep in bags of tins and jars.

'Yeah, I think so,' said Michelle. 'It was good to talk about stuff. And I think it'll be good to have something to tell Marion, the guardian, when she visits tomorrow. Like I'm making progress, you know?'

'Agreed,' said Gillian, standing up and looking across the Priory, towards the main entrance. 'Now, I think we might have our first customer,' she said, noting a young man walking down the aisle pushing a buggy. 'Are you ready?'

'Yeah,' said Michelle, taking the last few items out of the box. 'Of course.'

'Oh, and can you put these out?' said Gillian, passing her a box of leaflets printed on bright yellow paper.

Michelle picked them out and held one in her hands. She read the first sentence several times, as she had recently learned to do, patiently waiting for the words to fall into the right order.

Mike was awesome, she had realised. He'd not only typed up her letters to Grace and to her old foster parents immediately, he'd also paid for someone to come to the house to help her with writing. And that person – a kindly bespectacled man called David – had diagnosed her with dyslexia. She had taken a while to believe him, but he'd assured her that her lifelong reading problems were due to the way her brain worked and not to do with her intellect, or, as she'd previously believed, her lack of it. He'd given her lots of exercises to do, and she was working through them, slowly. She was determined to try, at least, especially because Gillian and Mike really wanted her to. She cared more and more about what they thought.

'Hello,' said Gillian, greeting the man who'd just reached the food bank table. Michelle looked him up and down. He was dressed well, clean shaven and the baby in the buggy seemed well-fed and content. What had brought him here, she wondered. Why can't he afford to feed his family? There's got to be something wrong with the way the world works if people like him can't even make ends meet, she thought.

Michelle's attention was suddenly drawn to another parent and child. The woman – tall and thin, with a striking red bob – was walking down the central aisle pushing an expensive-looking buggy. Her eyes were unfocused, her stride wobbly. Poor woman, Michelle thought. She looks done in. Perhaps her baby doesn't sleep. The woman slowed down as she reached the part of the Priory where the choir sat. She was almost out of her field of vision now, but Michelle could just make out the profile of a man who'd walked out from where the organ was to come to talk to her.

Did they know each other? It seemed so. The man – skinny, a bit jumpy, with messy blond hair – was quite close to her now and his hand was on her arm, as if he was trying to calm her, or cheer her up. The woman, however, was not smiling. She looked haunted, Michelle thought. Or maybe angry? But not angry with the man, she decided. She seemed to be glad to see him, at least.

At that moment, Michelle's attention was taken by another visitor to the food bank. When she'd finished greeting them, selecting the goods and bagging them up to go, she looked over at the aisle once more to see if the woman and man were still there, having their emotional conversation in full public view.

But they were not. The aisle was empty once more and her visual sweep of the rest of the church only turned up two volunteer guides and Louis, who manned the till in the shop. Maybe I'll see her here again soon, she thought; I'll try to grab her and say hello next time. Now that Michelle was thinking more about her own problems, she realised that she was surrounded by people every day who were also fighting private battles. It helped her to know that she wasn't alone.

'You okay? Getting the hang of it?' asked Gillian, from the other end of the food bank tables.

'Great,' replied Michelle. 'Getting there.'

28

February 10th

Amelia

Thirteen days until the final hearing

'Come through,' said Mark. 'I apologise in advance for the mess.'

As Amelia pushed the buggy through the narrow front door of Mark's cottage, her first impression of the inside of his home was of darkness. It was a dingy February day outside, admittedly, but the front room, which you entered directly from the front door, was barely managing twilight; the solitary small window, low down, single-glazed and fringed with ivy, was hardly bringing in more light than a flickering candle.

'Hang on a sec,' he said, fiddling around behind a small blue sofa. 'There you go.' Amelia looked around her. The beamed ceiling was now emblazoned with fairy lights which had been strung backwards and forwards across its entire length, giving it the feel of a starry sky. 'These old buildings are dark, even in the summer,' said Mark, 'so I devised this so that I don't get down in the dumps.'

'It works,' said Amelia, meaning it. The hundreds of tiny lights reminded her of Christmas, joy and parties and they had made her feel better instantly.

'Would you like a drink?' said Mark. 'A cup of tea? Or something stronger?'

There was something about the safe space she was in, away from the contact centre, away from the apartment, that allowed Amelia to finally admit how broken she was feeling. Without warning, she began to cry.

'Oh, crikey,' said Mark, a look of fright and uncertainty on his face. 'Whisky, I think. It's good for upsets. I'll be back in just a tick.'

Amelia pulled a tissue out of her handbag, parked the buggy up beside the sofa and sat herself down. She was grateful that Grace was asleep.

'Here you go,' said Mark, holding out a small breakfast glass with half an inch of whisky inside. 'I don't have any ice, I'm afraid,' he said.

'That's fine,' said Amelia, taking the glass and then dabbing her nose with her tissue. 'It's lovely. Thank you.'

There was only one sofa in the room and no chairs, so Mark sat at the far end of the sofa, as far away from Amelia as he could possibly go. She wondered whether he was regretting inviting her back to his place.

'So, tell me,' he said, calmly. 'Starting from the beginning… what is it that's got you in this much of a state?'

Amelia took a mouthful of the liquid, swilled it around her mouth, swallowed, and felt it burn its way down her throat. But then it began to send warmth radiating out of her core, and she felt emboldened.

'Do you remember last time we met, I told you that Grace's birth mother was contesting the adoption?' she said.

'Yes, I remember.'

'Well, now the birth father is, too. Separately, but with his parents. And they're fairly wealthy, apparently. So likely to impress a judge.'

'Ah. I'm sorry.'

'Thank you. At the moment, it feels like, every day, I just about manage to get back on my feet, and then some huge battering ram comes along and knocks me back down again.' Amelia took a large gulp of whisky, hastening it down.

'That's so shit,' he said. 'So, so shit. What have the social workers said to you about it? Have they apologised?'

Amelia almost laughed at that.

'No, of course not,' she said. 'Piers wrote them a stinker of a letter telling them they'd taken advantage of us. I edited it to smooth some of its edges, but it was fair, I think. They just replied though with a long document citing every time they'd told us, in person or in writing, that foster to adopt wasn't a guaranteed process, that the baby could go back to the birth parents. They have told us that they didn't foresee either birth parent contesting and that was their reason for pursuing foster to adopt. But now that they are – it seems we are merely foster carers to them, nothing more special than that. We don't even get to be involved in the court process. We are... not relevant.'

'So no one cares how you feel?'

'Not particularly,' said Amelia, cradling her glass and raising an eyebrow. 'I mean, the court guardian – she's a senior social worker who speaks on Grace's behalf – she has visited us several times and her thoughts will feed into her final report. But really, we are irrelevant, I think.'

'So someone *has* witnessed how well you're caring for Grace, and what a wonderful home you are giving her?' said Mark.

'Yes, I suppose. Although I don't know about wonderful. Piers is... not great, at the moment. This has hit him hard. Even harder than I thought it would.'

'I can imagine.'

'He's such a coper, normally. Full of energy, ideas, confidence. But he has been... strange, since we got the news about the birth mother contesting. Restless. Not sleeping well.

Look – you won't tell anyone any of this, will you?' she asked, suddenly paranoid that Mark might tell other school staff about Piers' state of mind, and harm his chances of getting a promotion.

'Of course not,' he replied, noting that Amelia's glass was empty. 'Hang on a sec, I'll go and get the bottle.' Mark returned a few seconds later with a half-empty bottle of single malt, and poured Amelia another thumbful. 'So you were saying, about Piers?'

'Yes. He's been up and down, much more so than normal. Sometimes he's so prickly, so distant and I find I'm tiptoeing around him, and other times he's charming, full of energy, almost nicer than his normal self. But you know, maybe this is all in my head? I am thinking all sorts of ridiculous things, you know…'

'I think that's understandable. You're both going through a horrible time. What effect has the uncertainty had on you?'

'I feel… I feel –' said Amelia, staring into her glass at the amber liquid at the bottom, '– I feel exhausted. And defeated. Like I know we're going to lose her, and I just want to get it over with. No, hang on, I don't mean that…' she said, looking at Grace in the pram, her eyes brimming with tears, 'but I just can't cope with this pain for much longer.'

'When will you know?'

'In two weeks. That's when the final hearing is going to be held. We don't get to attend, of course, but we'll get a phone call when the decision has been made.'

'Oh, Amelia. You don't deserve any of this shit. You really don't. And look, for what it's worth, I think the judge would be insane to even think about letting anyone take Grace away from you. You are clearly an excellent mother.'

Amelia managed a smile.

'Was I really not rude to you, at school?' she asked. 'Since our last chat, I've been plagued by a fear that I was a selfish, bitchy teenage girl who was far too self-absorbed to notice everyone else around her, and how they might be feeling.'

'I've already told you – you were lovely,' he said. 'Friendly and caring. Honestly.'

'Phew,' said Amelia, taking another sip. 'That's something, at least.'

'Is there anything I can do to help at the moment?' asked Mark. 'I mean, babysit, or something?'

'That's sweet of you, very sweet, but we're okay. I just need to try to get Piers to open up, I think. Perhaps I need to get him to take time off work. He spends almost all of his time in his office when he's not at school. I barely see him. I just feel like he's internalising things.'

'He probably is,' said Mark. 'We men are rubbish at talking about how we feel. We're absolute masters at putting a face on things, even if it's not a very convincing one.'

Amelia nodded.

'You know, I've decided... you're going to think this is mad... that I should talk to his ex-wife,' she said.

'Piers has an ex-wife?'

'Yes. Lesley. They have a son together. I don't think he's told many people at school.'

'No, I had no idea. Wow. So you've never met her?'

'No. He hasn't ever encouraged me to, and you know, I've honestly never wanted to. Except now, because he's being so strange... Lesley must have got to know him well enough when they were together, surely, to be able to tell me what to do to help?'

Mark took a sip of his whisky.

'I imagine so. Will you tell Piers you're in touch?'

Amelia necked back the rest of the contents of her glass.

'I know I should,' she said, staring down at the empty glass, 'but you know, I don't think so. He'd be angry.'

They sat in silence for a moment.

'For what it's worth, I think you should try to make contact with her anyway,' said Mark, finally breaking the silence. 'Surely it would be a good thing if you got on? For his son?'

'You know, Mark, I think you're right,' said Amelia. She didn't know if it was the whisky or the company that was making a difference, but she was definitely feeling more confident about her plan. 'I should be heading back…' she said, aware that Grace would be waking soon. She would drop Lesley a line when she got back.

'Okay,' said Mark. 'But let me pour you one more thumbful before you wander home. It's good stuff, this.'

All the lights in the apartment were off when Amelia returned. She was surprised; it was 5 p.m., and Piers was usually home by now. She parked the buggy at the bottom of the stairs, removed Grace and carried her up to the living room. She put the still-sleeping Grace down in her bouncy chair and went into the kitchen to make her up a bottle. As she did so, she noticed that the door to Piers' study was slightly ajar. She had been trying to find an opportunity to look in there for ages, but Piers generally kept it locked, and he had the only key. Now was her time to strike.

Something was up with Piers, and she was certain that it was more than their uncertainty about Grace. He was just acting… weirdly. One minute he'd be sweetness and light, and the next, utterly furious, without any apparent reason for the change. She had no idea why, but she hoped that the study might give her a clue. After all, he spent so much time in there alone. She was sure that the mysterious letters he'd been receiving held at least part of the answer. Amelia left the microwave counting down and walked swiftly next door, knowing that Piers could return at any moment.

She flicked on the light. The room, which she'd often seen glimpses of when she'd been talking to him, was not how she'd seen it previously. It was tidy, for a start – books were stacked neatly, paper was separated into separate piles, all labelled with post-it notes or gathered with paper clips. It looked, frankly, like the study of an organised, dedicated teacher. Not at all like a mercurial man who'd just experienced a major emotional upheaval.

She lifted up a few of the pieces of paper on the desk. They were lesson plans, mostly, along with a copy of the application for a deputy head job at the college that he had filled in a few weeks previously. The previous incumbent had decided to move on, as Piers had suspected, and the vacancy was a huge opportunity for him. Michelle prayed his mental health would hold up for the interview.

She turned around and looked in the bin. It was empty; there was just a fine film of dust left in the bottom of it. Finally, she turned to the metal filing cabinet, which was in the corner of the room, all the while listening out for any sign of Piers arriving home. She pulled at the top drawer, but discovered it was locked. So – the key. Where would he have put the key? She looked on the windowsill, in the various mugs and bowls he used for stationery and pens, but could find no sign of it. Then she lifted up the rug under his chair – not there – and then peered behind his computer screen.

Bingo… there it was, attached to the back of the screen with blu tack. Why would he do that? It was properly odd. She removed the key and bent down in front of the cabinet. But as she did so, she heard a tell-tale click as Piers' key was inserted into the lock in their front door.

Shit, she thought. He mustn't find her in here. She bolted back upright, stuck the key back on the blu tack, checked she hadn't left anything out of place, flicked the light switch off and pulled the door closed.

She was in the kitchen retrieving the now sterilised bottle when Piers reached the top of the stairs. It was lucky it was so grim outside today, she thought; he must have spent a vital few seconds removing his coat and hanging it up on the rack before coming up to see her.

'Hello, darling,' he said, with a broad smile.

'Hello,' she said, smiling back and trying her best to breathe deeply, to calm down her rapid heartbeat. Piers leaned in for a kiss, and she held her breath, aware that she must smell of whisky.

'Had a good day?' Piers asked.

'Yes, lovely thanks,' she said, keeping her tone as light as possible. 'I took Grace for a walk into town. We popped into the Priory, and then went to see Dad. How was your day? Do you have an interview date yet? You're quite late back.'

'Yes! Heard today. It's a week on Wednesday, nine-thirty a.m. Just before the adoption hearing, but it can't be helped. I'm sorry I'm late, I got talking to Alec Stevens, you know, the head of sixth form? He's going for the job too. Don't think he's in with a chance, though, listening to him. Hasn't done much preparation. Where's Grace?'

'Oh, she's asleep in the lounge,' replied Amelia, relieved that he hadn't picked up on her unease.

'I'll go and see her and then I'll get some work done, I think, before dinner,' he said. 'What are we having?'

Amelia hadn't even thought about food.

'Oh, something Chinese,' she said, remembering that she had some hoisin chicken thighs in the freezer. That would do.

'Sounds great,' said Piers, coming back out of the lounge, and heading into the study. Amelia froze in the kitchen, anxious about what he would say when he found it was unlocked. But he said nothing. Not one word. He simply walked in, flicked the light on, and closed the door.

She stood in the kitchen, her heart still beating frantically, reflecting on what had just happened. She'd found nothing strange in his office, except for a locked filing cabinet and a hidden key. What should she make of that? Maybe his behaviour was normal, and it was her unease about the upcoming court case that was skewing her perception of him?

And yet she couldn't shake the feeling that she no longer knew or understood the man she'd married. Perhaps, she thought, this stressful period had simply shone a light in a dark part of their relationship, somewhere she hadn't really looked before. But if she was to stay married to him, she decided that she needed to understand what was driving him, and why he behaved the way he did. She needed to know where the anger and vitriol he only ever displayed towards her, behind closed doors, was actually coming from. And she knew who to ask about that. She got out her phone and sent her mother-in-law a text message.

> Hey Catherine, it's me. Do you happen to have Lesley's telephone number? I wanted to reach out to her to see if there's anything we can do to restore contact between Piers and Sebastian.

In the myriad dates that had followed their initial meeting in the wine bar over warm rosé on a sticky leather sofa, Piers had told Amelia that Lesley had been too controlling, too disorganised and too selfish to remain his wife. Amelia had not questioned this, because back then, in those heady days when he had been taking her out for expensive dinners, showering her with gifts and making her guest of honour at school events, she had been far too infatuated with him to do so.

So, she had accepted without question that Lesley had simply not hit the target he had set, while also understanding that *she* would be expected to hit it. As astonishing as it seemed to her now, she hadn't even minded that. It had been intensely flattering to be considered capable of meeting such a high bar. She had been so proud to be considered worthy. She hadn't ever anticipated that the bar would become something to batter her with.

Yes, she thought, *I need to speak to Lesley. There are things I simply have to know.*

29

February 23rd

Michelle

Final hearing, Day 1

Michelle stood in front of the mirror, frantically tugging her skirt down and removing imperceptible fluff from her jacket.

Gillian had taken her shopping to buy this outfit, but she still had her doubts about it. It reminded her of her school uniform, and that wasn't in any way a good thing. But she knew that bloody Rob and his stuck-up family would turn up dressed in Ralph Lauren or something, so she wanted to put up a decent fight.

And furthermore, she was different now, and she wanted to dress to reflect that. In her mind's eye, she placed the version of herself that had appeared at the first court hearing, back in October – just a day postpartum, wouldn't say boo to a goose, wearing the clothes she'd laboured in – next to this newer version.

She was still herself, definitely, but she was also a lot more confident, and that had a lot to do with the support Mike and Gillian had given her, and the sessions she'd been having with her counsellor, too. She had come to recognise that she had been self-harming with drugs and alcohol as a way of punishing herself both for her sister's removal and her own chequered history in care.

She was repeatedly being told now that neither of those things was her fault. And that was a huge ask, really. They were asking her to leave that long-held belief behind and to look at the world in a completely different way. She was struggling with it, but she had got to a point now where she could at least try to think that way, and that was a start.

And today – well, today was so important that she was mustering up all of the self-belief that she could manage.

Today, you see, was the first day of the final hearing. Sally had said that it would probably last a couple of days, so that meant that she might hear the judge's decision tomorrow, or if not, definitely the day after. It was hard to believe that she would know within three days whether she would have Grace with her for life, or whether she would never see her again.

Just the thought of the latter option made her want to vomit. On her most recent visit to the contact centre, she'd held on to Grace throughout the session, not wanting to share her with Gillian or the social workers, or to let her play with toys. She had literally clung on to her for every second she could, in case they were among their last together.

There was no way, absolutely no way that Rob and his parents, or those liars at social services (she had tried to drop the moniker, but she couldn't – the scarring was too deep) would take Grace away from her. When Grace had just been born, she could now see that she had been at her lowest ebb, and she hadn't been right in the head. She'd wanted to give her up because she had felt that she was incapable of *anything*. But now she knew differently.

The guy who had come to assess her for dyslexia had said something that had stuck with her. He'd quoted the actress Whoopi Goldberg – herself a dyslexic – saying that she saw her dyslexia as an advantage, because her brain saw information from a different perspective to everyone else. Michelle was starting to see that this was true. She might be different, but that different didn't have to mean bad. In fact, it could just mean special.

'You look lovely, Michelle,' said Gillian, coming out of one of the toilet stalls behind her and washing her hands at the adjacent sink.

'Are you sure?' she said. 'I feel like they'll all be looking at me thinking that I'm wearing a costume, or something.'

'Don't be silly. You are your own person, and that's nothing to do with what you're wearing. And anyway, everyone here is wearing a costume. Do you think that overpaid lawyer for the Allcotts wears a pinstripe suit at home? Do you think that judge wears a black bodycon dress when she's watching *Bake Off*? Nope and nope. We are all playing a part. All of us.'

'Okay,' said Michelle, still unable to shake the feeling that she was pretending to be someone she wasn't.

'Ready?' asked Gillian, drying her hands with a paper towel. 'Sally said she'd meet us at half past, to go through things before the hearing starts.'

Michelle nodded and followed Gillian out of the loos and into the court foyer, where Sally Mucklow was waiting. She was characteristically colourful – today's choice was a yellow shirt and a black skirt – and it looked like she'd recently had a new haircut. Her new look was sharp, bobbed, and it screamed 'don't mess with me', Michelle thought, which was just as well, because the Allcotts' barrister looked particularly keen for a fight.

'Hey, both of you,' Sally said. 'Shall we head over to the cafe over the road? We've got half an hour, and it might be nice to talk where we know nobody relevant is listening.'

Michelle and Gillian followed her to the crossing outside, across the busy ring-road and into a quirky cafe, which was furnished with mismatched furniture and junk-shop art, and which smelled of coffee and cinnamon buns. Frenetic jazz music was playing in the background and the customers already seated inside were making sufficient noise to mask the conversation of others. Michelle could see why Sally had brought them there.

'I always come over here with clients before cases,' she said, after she'd been up to the counter to order them their choice of hot drink. 'It's noisy but not too noisy, and more importantly, they make good coffee.' She smiled at Michelle then, and Michelle did her best to return the smile, although her stomach felt like it was being wrung through a mangle.

'So. Hopefully you have been able to read the reports that have been submitted to the judge?'

Michelle had read them, with Gillian's help. She'd had little sleep after she'd read the statement from the local authority, who were still adamant that their chosen route of foster to adopt was the best way forward, and she'd wanted to scream when she'd read Rob's statement, which was full of lies.

'I wanted to talk to you about them,' said Sally, noting Michelle's doubtful face. 'I know they don't seem overly hopeful. But the thing is, they are just a starting point. This hearing is our opportunity to point out the obvious holes in those reports and to put your point of view forward. And we will do that, okay?' Michelle nodded. 'And of course, we've submitted your own statement, which is very powerful. I am hopeful that it will make all of the difference.'

'But what about Rob's statement?'

'He hasn't got a shred of evidence for that. I'll challenge them heavily. Don't worry.'

Michelle was dubious. Given that he had been capable of convincing her that he was a total loser for several years, he was probably capable of convincing a judge that he was a total pussy cat.

'I do wish I could come in with you, Michelle,' said Gillian, rubbing Michelle's arm. 'But I'll be just outside, okay? We can have lunch together and talk things through.'

'Honestly, you don't have to wait. You'll be bored. And it's so uncomfortable out there,' said Michelle, knowing how bleak court waiting rooms always were.

'I don't care. I've brought a good book and a couple of magazines, and I'll have a walk around the block mid-morning. But I will never be far, okay? I'll be right there.'

'Thank you,' said Michelle. 'That means a lot to me.'

'No problem at all, lovely girl,' said Gillian. 'I'm doing this because you mean a lot to *me*.'

'Miss Jenkins? Ms Mucklow? It's time to go in now.'

Gillian squeezed Michelle's hand as the court clerk walked over to the Allcotts and their lawyer and gave them the same message. Michelle knew that her hands were sweaty, and she felt a bit self-conscious about that, but she also desperately needed the reassurance. Gillian let go a few moments later, so she stood up, wiped her hands on her skirt and pulled her jacket down, and walked towards the door to court five, following in her lawyer's wake.

She was all too familiar with this court now, with its harsh strip lights, two horseshoes of faux-beech tables, and the judge's desk on a raised platform at the front. Its only source of natural light was from long, thin rectangular windows near the ceiling on the right of the room. They were far too high to see what was going on in the world outside, and that contributed, Michelle thought, to the otherworldly, nightmarish feeling the room had. It felt to her like a sort of hell, where you had to convince others of your worth as a human being before you were allowed out again.

Sally led her to two chairs on the far right of the room and Michelle saw that Rob and his lawyer, Len Carraway, were sitting on the far left. His parents were waiting for him outside. She wondered whether they'd try to talk to Gillian. Probably not, she decided. They clearly thought that she was a violent psychopath, so would probably chalk Gillian up as being deranged by association, at the very least.

Several other people filed in behind them – Marion, the children's guardian; Philip Shelley, barrister for the local authority; Grace's social worker, Gloria; and, finally, her own social worker, Laura. Once Laura had entered, the door was closed, and seconds later, a door at the other end of the room opened and Judge Joshi walked in. Those who were already seated stood up for her arrival, before sitting back down when she gestured that they should do so.

'Good morning everyone,' said the judge, to a soundtrack of shuffling chairs and emptying briefcases. 'Thank you for arriving promptly. As you all know, we have a great deal to get through. So, just a few housekeeping notes before we get started.

'As this is a private hearing, it is against the law to record any part of it. Please make sure your mobile phones are off and put away. Time-wise, we are going to run through until about four p.m. today, with an hour off for lunch at one p.m. If, at any time, any of you need to take a break, for example, to go to the toilet, please let me or the court clerk know.'

Michelle wondered whether she'd ever feel brave enough to let this judge know she needed a wee. She was the very opposite of an approachable, nursery-teacher type, she thought. She was bristly and seemed hard as nails. I wonder if she has kids, she thought. That would change her views about this sort of thing, surely?

'Mr Shelley,' said the judge. 'As advocate for the local authority, I wonder whether you can begin for us? I think, given that this is the fourth hearing, we all know each other by now, so we can dispense with introductions.'

'Of course, madam,' he said, remaining seated, but turning

on his microphone so everyone in the room could hear him. 'Madam, you have a short case summary, a bundle of documents to do with this case, and position statements from both parents, all involved social workers and the children's guardian.

'It is still the local authority's view that Grace Jenkins, who is now twenty weeks old, should remain in the care of her foster parents, who would like to adopt her. The local authority pursued foster to adopt for very solid reasons, namely that they believed she was at risk of harm if left with her birth parents. Although some aspects of the case have changed, they still do not believe that either Miss Jenkins or Mr Allcott are emotionally or physically stable enough to provide the safe care that she needs and deserves.

'We are aware that Mr Allcott has put forward a proposal that he should share custody with his parents, and that Miss Jenkins proposes to live with two former foster parents, Gillian and Michael Wade, who have offered their support to help her care for the child. However, the local authority does not believe that either option will guarantee the child's safety, given the birth parents' shared history of drug abuse, criminal behaviour and violence.'

'Thank you for that summary, Mr Shelley,' said the judge. 'Who do you intend to call to give evidence?'

'Madam, I would like to call Gloria Reynolds, a social worker for Worcester County Council.'

Michelle watched Gloria, a woman she'd got to know well in the past month during the sessions at the contact centre, get out of her seat and head over to a small desk in front of the judge's bench. Michelle listened to her take the oath. Hearing Gloria's familiar voice saying something straight out of a TV drama felt incredibly odd. It added to her feeling of not belonging in that alien, frightening room.

Once she'd sworn on the Bible, Gloria sat down and poured herself a cup of water from the jug that was placed on the table next to her. She's deliberately avoiding looking at me, Michelle thought. *Of course* she is. I can just imagine what she's going to say. All of that pretending that she wanted to help me to sort my life out, and now she's going to stab me in the back.

'Mrs Reynolds, could you please confirm that you are Gloria Reynolds, a social worker working for Worcestershire County Council?' Philip Shelley asked.

'Yes, I am.'

'Thank you. Mrs Reynolds – how long have you been a social worker?'

'Twenty-five years.'

'How many child protection cases have you worked on in that time, would you say?'

'I don't know. Hundreds? Thousands?'

'Quite. Mrs Reynolds, can you please tell me why you and your team decided to pursue foster to adopt for Grace Jenkins?'

Gloria reached into her pocket for a tissue and blew her nose.

'We were very concerned for the safety of the child,' she said, replacing the tissue. 'Miss Jenkins and Mr Allcott have – *had* – a violent relationship, and their home is unsanitary, often devoid of food, and both of them are using – or at least, have traditionally used – drugs on a regular basis. We had tried and failed to get Miss Jenkins to accept our help to remove her from this situation many times. Also, Miss Jenkins originally seemed keen to have Grace adopted, and Mr Allcott showed no objection. Thus we were fairly confident that foster to adopt made sense. We don't go down that path unless we're ninety-nine per cent convinced it will work out. It's too hard for the potential adopters, otherwise.'

'I see. And what is your view now, given that Miss Jenkins and Mr Allcott are both hoping to gain custody of Grace?'

'I feel for Michelle, I really, really do,' she said, looking Michelle straight in the eye. 'She has come a long way in these past few months. But I'm afraid I still worry that she will return to Mr Allcott, as she has done before, and that she might slip back into old ways. It's hard to find a job and childcare and survive on a low income as a single mother. We know, on the other hand, that the baby will be safe and secure with her foster parents. So, reluctantly, I think foster to adopt is still the right thing for Grace.'

You're wrong, Michelle thought. *Very, very wrong. I am never, ever going back to that bastard.*

She so wanted to shout it out, to yell it at the top of her voice, but she didn't, for two reasons. One, because she was intimidated by the silence in the rest of the court, and two, because Sally was gripping her hand, a signal they had decided upon earlier. It meant 'stay quiet, you'll get your say later', and Michelle felt that she should at least try to adhere to that, out of loyalty to her lawyer.

'Madam, those are all the questions I have for Mrs Reynolds at this time,' the local authority's barrister said.

'Thank you, Mr Shelley,' said the judge. 'Now, Miss Stone,' she said, turning to the children's guardian, 'do you have any questions you'd like to ask Mrs Reynolds?'

'I do, madam,' she said, sweeping her hand across her mass of wiry grey hair. 'Mrs Reynolds – I am concerned that the local authority's plan to pursue foster to adopt, and their refusal to adapt their approach given recent developments, reflects blinkered thinking. Can you reassure me that you have properly reassessed your decision in this matter?'

Gloria looks a little flustered at that, thought Michelle. *Good.*

'I can assure you that we have regularly reviewed our decision,' said Gloria. 'Removing Grace from her birth parents was not taken lightly, and we have done all we can to help Miss Jenkins to get back on her feet. But we still feel that adoption is the best option for the safety of the child.'

'Thank you, madam, no further questions,' said Miss Stone.

'Ms Mucklow. Do you have questions for Mrs Reynolds?'

'I do, madam,' said Sally from her seat beside Michelle. 'My client has been in the care of social services since she was six, after she and her sister, also called Grace, were removed from the care of their maternal grandmother. Just a few weeks later, the pair were separated with no warning, when her sister was adopted. Is it any surprise that my client is distrustful of social workers, and the help they are offering?'

Michelle looked straight at Gloria, her eyes full of challenge.

'We are incredibly sorry for the wrongs committed by our department more than fifteen years ago,' she replied. 'We have apologised to Miss Jenkins. We have done our utmost in recent months to try to make up for those wrongs, including beginning efforts to trace Miss Jenkins' sister.'

'Were you working for the department when Michelle and Grace were taken into care?'

Gloria was now clasping her hands together and staring down at the desk.

'I began my career in social services in 2005. I believe the sisters were removed from their grandmother in 2007, so technically, yes, I was working in the department. But I was incredibly junior and I was not part of the team assigned to make decisions about the sisters.'

You *witch*, thought Michelle. You remember it all, don't you? And you are still trying to take my baby away from me.

'Oh, really?' said Sally. 'It's just that I requested access to Michelle's file, and your name comes up on several of the documents from that time.'

Gloria seemed to be sweating, Michelle thought. *Good for you, Sally – make her sweat buckets.*

'I may have written some reports,' she said, 'but I didn't make the decisions.'

'Do you think that it's acceptable that you should be a key decision maker on the future of Michelle's baby, when you were part of the team that separated her from her sibling – an incident that I believe was the catalyst for the downward spiral my client experienced for years afterwards?'

'I have many more years of experience now. And this case is being treated as something entirely separate...'

'Even so. Would it not have been professional courtesy to let Miss Jenkins know of your involvement?'

'Perhaps...'

'And, Mrs Reynolds, is it not also true that Miss Jenkins has shown an extraordinary fortitude in the past few months – leaving her abusive ex-partner, giving up drugs, and even volunteering at the food bank she used to use?'

'Yes, her progress has been pleasing and impressive,' said Gloria. 'But even so, she only began visiting Grace last month. Before that, we had only one visit at the contact centre soon after the interim care order was made. She ended that visit prematurely. It is our opinion that we have not seen enough of a sustained change to guarantee Grace's safety in the long term.'

'Madam, I object to Ms Mucklow's use of the term "abusive" in respect to my client,' said Len Carraway, piping up without warning. 'No charges have been filed against my client to that effect.'

'I understand your concern,' said Judge Joshi. 'However, social services have detailed significant injuries on Miss Jenkins on two separate occasions. I will allow it to stand, for now. You will have your chance to defend your client later on in this hearing.'

Len Carraway looks angry, but not as angry as I feel, Michelle thought. Are they really going to try to deny that Rob ever hit me? That's insane. She now regretted refusing, on each occasion, to press charges. She'd done that out of misplaced loyalty to Rob, and now she was going to be made to pay for that, clearly.

'Ms Mucklow,' said the judge, her tone signalling that she

was keen to get the hearing back on track. 'Do you have any more questions for Mrs Reynolds?'

'Yes, I do madam, thank you. One more, Mrs Reynolds. In the contact sessions in the last few weeks, you noted, in front of my client, that the baby seemed unusually attached to her. Isn't that right?'

'Yes, that's true. Grace seems very at ease with her. It has been wonderful to watch,' she said.

Do I detect a hint of regret in her voice, thought Michelle? Possibly. Just possibly.

'Thank you, madam. No further questions at this time.'

Judge Joshi flicked through her pile of papers and brought a different sheet to the top.

'I would like to call Laura King, Miss Jenkins' social worker.'

Michelle watched as Laura – just Laura (she'd dropped the 'lying' bit for her months ago) was sworn in.

After her affirmation was undertaken and her name and address recorded Laura sat back in her seat and clasped her hands on her lap. She looks nervous, Michelle thought.

'Mr Carraway, do you have any questions for Miss King?' asked the judge.

'I do, madam.'

'Miss King – how long have you been Miss Jenkins' social worker?' he asked Laura.

'Oh, not very long. I was put in post after Michelle – Miss Jenkins – was admitted to hospital last year, pregnant and with significant injuries. She'd voluntarily left the care of social services at sixteen and we'd lost track of her. But her injuries brought her back to our attention.'

'And was she co-operative, when you visited her in hospital?'

Michelle examined Laura's expression, aware that she'd behaved badly towards her social worker on numerous occasions. She was trying to smile at her, she thought, which was quite something. Michelle suddenly felt a surge of warmth towards the young woman who'd put up with so much abuse from her and yet kept coming back, regardless. She had underrated her, and she felt really bad about that.

'No, she wasn't. She didn't want me there. But...'

'I see. And after Grace was born, was she co-operative then?'

'Well, she told us that she wanted Grace to be adopted, but she resisted any other help from us. We tried to offer...'

'So you explained that if she made changes to her lifestyle, she could potentially keep her baby? But she didn't accept your help?' Len Carraway's pace and focus was relentless, Michelle thought.

'That's true,' replied Laura. 'But she has had such a hard time... really hard, and...'

'Miss King, can you tell me what explanation Miss Jenkins gave for the injuries she sustained on those two separate occasions?'

'She told me that she'd fallen.'

'I see. So she didn't tell you that Mr Allcott had hit her, at any stage?'

'Well no... but...'

'And how was she with you? Was she polite? Pleasant? Reasonable?'

'She was... angry and silent, mostly. But you see, her home life...'

'Yes, let's talk about her home life,' said Len, seizing on the topic like a dog with a bone. 'You say in your report that you believe her relationship with Mr Allcott was, I quote, "abusive". What evidence do you have for that?'

'Well, her injuries – she had bruising to her torso and cigarette burns on her body, too.'

'And these couldn't possibly have been inflicted by anyone else?'

'I'm sorry... I don't understand. Michelle and Rob spent almost all of their time together. She didn't go out much.'

'But other people came to the flat, did they not?'

'I suppose so,' answered Laura, her tone doubtful.

'Mr Allcott states that her injuries were inflicted by a drug dealer, a mutual friend of theirs, who was a frequent visitor to their home.'

'Michelle has never said anything about anybody else.'

'No, but then, you've only known her for about six months, isn't that correct?'

'Yes.'

'Mr Allcott claims that Miss Jenkins took to shoplifting to support her drug habit. Have you seen any evidence of this?'

'She has been arrested in the past for shoplifting, but it was always just food she stole, nothing worth much...'

'But has Mr Allcott been arrested for shoplifting also?'

'No, he has not, not that I'm aware of, anyway.'

'No further questions, madam,' said Len Carraway, sitting down with a flourish.

Michelle held her hands under the taps in the court toilets, scooped up a handful of cold water and swept it over her face, not caring if it hit her hair, or her clothes, or the wall.

'Michelle, lovely, it can't have been that bad.'

'It was horrible, Gillian. Like, really horrible. They made me sound like I don't give a shit about her. But I do, I love her, I love her so much, I just... I just can't...'

'Come on darling girl, it won't be as bad as all that. Anyway, the hearing is just getting started. There's lots of time yet. The guardian has to have her say...'

'She's a social worker, though. She'll side with *them*.'

'Maybe. Or maybe not. Look, let's see. And anyway, you said that Laura wasn't too bad?'

Michelle thought back to Laura's evidence, which had been drawn out and painful, both for Laura and herself. After

Len Carraway's questioning, Philip Shelley had taken a turn, pointing out social services' attempts to help Michelle on numerous occasions, which were all – unhelpfully, Michelle thought – documented and dated. When the record was read back to her, Michelle found she almost doubted herself.

Finally, Marion Stone had asked Laura for her view of Michelle's progress, and for her opinion of Michelle as a person and a mother. This question had resulted in one of the only positive things Michelle had heard said about her that day (or, in fact, ever). Laura had said that she was a 'resilient, brave, caring person'. She thought she'd heard Len Carraway cough when Laura had said that, but she wasn't going to let him steal away the warmth that phrase had given her.

'You absolutely can be – will be – an amazing mother, and they will see that,' said Gillian, drying her hands.

'But apart from what Laura said about me, and those lies about Rob's drug dealer being the one who hit me – *for fuck's sake*! Apart from that, everything else they both said was true, wasn't it? I mean, I did tell them I wanted her adopted, and I did break the law and nick stuff, and I did change my mind, and I did avoid the contact sessions for ages...'

'And then you turned everything around,' Gillian said, finding some hand towels and patting Michelle's face with them. 'And that's what the judge will see. I know she will.'

'Hmmm,' said Michelle, allowing Gillian to apply some of her face powder, which she'd retrieved from her handbag when she'd seen the state she was in.

'There you go. Much better. Now, shall we go and get some lunch?'

'I'm not hungry.'

'Don't be silly. You'll change your mind when you see a nice toasted sandwich on your plate. Come on, Sally is taking us back to the cafe. She's buying.'

***

'Mr Carraway, can you please set out the position of your client, Mr Robert Allcott?'

Back from lunch, stomachs full of substandard, expensive sandwiches and grab-bags of crisps, the hearing had got under way once more.

Sally had used the break to try to prepare Michelle – again – for what was about to come. It was like she'd spotted a tsunami on the horizon and she was frantically piling up sandbags to try to keep it at bay. Michelle had read the position statement they'd issued on Rob's behalf, with Gillian's help, and she had felt that that was bad enough. She'd almost thrown in the towel afterwards, overwhelmed by all of the bald-faced lies it contained. But Sally had been at pains to explain that because Rob's case was, in her opinion, 'weak', they were going to try to make Michelle look really, really bad in court to counter that. Michelle's instructions from Sally were, essentially, not to shout out, to swear, or ideally, to say anything at all today. She'd given her a mantra to help her along, which was: '*I will put it all right tomorrow*'. She'd written it on her hand in biro, to remind herself when it got really shitty.

Sally had told her, several times, that it was beneficial to give evidence on the second day, as her words would be fresher in the judge's mind. Michelle had the power to wipe all of Rob's lies away, she insisted. Michelle wasn't so sure, but she desperately wanted to believe it.

'Madam, my client, Robert Allcott, is applying for custody of his daughter, Grace,' said Len Carraway, again choosing to stand up, even though there was no requirement to do so. 'He is now living with his parents in a large house on the outskirts of Malvern, where there is ample room for Grace to live and grow. The family have considerable funds which they intend to use to educate Grace privately and provide for her every need.

My client has now finally escaped his relationship with Miss Jenkins, which he admits was unhealthy for both of them, and violent on her part. He tells me that he regularly had to restrain Miss Jenkins to prevent her from harming him.'

That *fucking bastard*, Michelle thought. She considered turning to look at him and raising her middle finger, but remembered her promise to Sally, and didn't do it.

'Is Mr Allcott giving evidence?'

'He is, madam.'

'Very well. Mr Allcott, could you please come forward?'

Michelle watched the only man she had ever loved get up from his institutional chair and walk over to the desk, his shoulders hunched, his face cast down. *He can't even look at me*, she thought. He was wearing the same new suit he'd worn to the third hearing, with a crisp white shirt and an innocuous blue tie. He was clean shaven, his nose ring was notably absent, and his hair was closely clipped. His mummy dresses him well, she thought.

'Mr Allcott, can you confirm your name and address, please?' said the judge.

'Yes, your honour,' he said, as if he was being tried for murder. 'My name is Rob... Robert Allcott, and I am living at...' there was a pause, while he cleared his throat, '... Meadowsmeet, Laburnum Road, Leigh Sinton, Worcestershire.'

Michelle heard Rob state his new address in an accent that was entirely alien to her and the bottom dropped out of her world. He absolutely had not been the man she thought he was, in any sense. There were only tiny echoes of the voice she'd grown to love – the occasional dropped H or T – but for the most part, he sounded like a posh twat now, she thought. Which he always had been, really, hadn't he?

'Thank you,' replied the judge. 'Would you like to swear on a holy book, or affirm?'

'Affirm, please,' said Rob. Good, at least he's not pretending to be a good Christian boy too, Michelle thought. That would really have stuck in his throat. She watched as he repeated the words of the affirmation, still staring straight ahead and refusing to look at her.

'Mr Carraway, do you want to start?' the judge said, addressing Rob's lawyer.

'Yes, thank you, madam. Mr Allcott – can you tell me why you have decided to seek custody of your daughter?'

Michelle watched Rob turn his head towards Len Carraway and lock his gaze.

'I realised I made a terrible mistake, not visiting her in hospital, and not going to see her in those first few weeks,' said Rob. This sounds like a speech he's had written for him, Michelle thought. He's word perfect. 'I was... doing what Michelle wanted. She told me not to go. She said it would be easier that way.'

'So it was her idea to have the baby adopted?'

'Yeah... Yes. It was her idea. I just went along with it.'

'So why have you now changed your mind about your daughter?'

'I won't pretend I was perfect before, and I'm not perfect now, but I have learned a lot about myself in the last few months, and leaving my... difficult relationship, and reconciling with my parents, has changed me a lot. I'm different now. I want to be a father. I don't want my daughter being brought up by strangers.'

'Mr Allcott. You say your relationship with Miss Jenkins was "difficult". Can you elaborate on that?'

'Yeah, uh...' said Rob, momentarily lapsing, Michelle noticed, into the voice she was more used to. 'I mean, yes, it was difficult. She was very unpredictable. I think she was so damaged by her shit... difficult childhood, so she had major hang-ups about things. And she would lash out sometimes. I had to hold her back.' His eyes darted towards where his parents were sitting.

Lash out? What a fucking liar, thought Michelle.

'Where was Michelle when you met?'

'She was homeless.'

'Was she using drugs then?'

'I think so.'

'And did you use drugs together, when you were sharing a flat?'

'Yes, we did. She moved in with me, and we egged each other on, I think.'

'And your dealer – he visited the apartment?'

'Yeah... yes.'

'And what was his relationship with Miss Jenkins?'

'They... fought. He tried it on with her. She refused him, and he hit her.'

But that was not how it had been at all and they both knew it, thought Michelle. After she'd thrown Rob's dealer off and kneed him in the balls, he'd screamed abuse at her and left the house, taking his drugs with him. Rob had been so enraged that his anticipated hit had been taken away that he had lunged at her like a madman, raining blows onto her stomach. After he'd beaten her, he'd gone out to find the dealer and got the drugs anyway. How, she didn't know, although she suspected he'd stolen something to pay for it.

'So it was this man whose blows landed her in hospital when she was pregnant?'

'Yes.'

Michelle watched Rob swallow hard. *You bastard*, she thought, remembering every time he'd hit her when he was high – or low. How could he even say those words, knowing it was all a lie?

I will put it all right tomorrow, Michelle started to chant in her head, over and over. *I will put it all right tomorrow. I will put it all right tomorrow.*

'Thank you, Mr Allcott. No further questions.'

I will put it all right tomorrow, she thought. I'll have to, or otherwise I'll never see Grace again.

30

February 22nd

Amelia

One day to final hearing

Amelia heard the door of the flat slam and winced. Partly because it was Grace's bedtime and she'd just put her down in her cot and any noise disturbed her, and partly because it was far, far too late for Piers to be coming home after an average day of teaching. He should have finished two hours ago.

He'd had the interview for the deputy headship that morning. Where had he been since the school day had finished? Why hadn't he messaged her to let her know he'd be late? Had he been celebrating, or… commiserating? She was desperate to know.

She took a breath and held it, waiting for him to walk up the stairs, take a right and come to find her in the nursery. Normally he'd land a kiss on her cheek before heading to the bedroom to take off his jacket and tie, undo his top button and then head into the kitchen for a cold beer. Tonight, however, he did not come to see her. Instead, she heard him head straight for the bathroom.

Curious and nervous, she tiptoed out of Grace's earshot and walked down the hall, pausing outside the bathroom door, which was shut.

'Are you okay, Piers?' she asked, whispering.

He didn't reply. Instead, she heard the tap being turned on, and the gush of water as the house's Victorian plumbing kicked itself into action.

'Piers?'

There was a squeak as the tap was turned off, a rustling sound and a loud exclamation as he apparently knocked into something – the sink, perhaps.

'Bugger,' he said, the first word he'd spoken out loud since he got home.

The door swung open and suddenly Amelia knew everything. The stench of alcohol coming from him, the fact his tie was askew, his unstable swagger.

'Oh Piers,' she said. 'I'm so sorry.'

'They gave it to that Stevens bloke,' he said, looking at the floor. 'He's got a degree from fucking Aberystwyth. Aberystwyth! And knows fucking nothing about leadership, *nothing*. They'll regret it.'

'Oh darling,' replied Amelia, unsure of how to respond, how to help. She was as shocked as he was, because he'd sounded so certain that the job was his. But the interview board had decided quickly – appointing the new deputy on the first day – so they must have been sure, mustn't they?

She wondered why. What had Piers said or done in the interview that they hadn't liked? She felt unsettled, because his charm and surety were like a comfort blanket for her, a reassurance that everything was going to be fine. And now, coming just ahead of a court case that was going to change their lives however it went, she needed that comfort more than ever.

'Come into the lounge, Piers, and I'll get you a drink of water,' she said, as if talking to a child. Piers followed her without question, landing heavily on the sofa cushions, his body appearing to crumple. She walked into the kitchen, got him a drink and returned to him, putting on the desk lamp and sitting in the armchair opposite.

'I'm sure he won't last long, if he's as you describe,' she said, watching him rubbing his eyes to wipe tears away before they became too obvious. 'They'll realise their mistake, I'm sure.'

'Yeah,' he said, his voice flat and small, as if it too was crumpling.

'Have you been in the pub?'

'Yeah.'

'Do you think… they didn't like something you said?'

Piers snapped his head up at her for the first time. His expression had changed. He was no longer diminished; he was angry.

'What do you mean?'

'I just meant… they must have had a reason. Something maybe they were looking for in particular? Something you can learn from?'

Amelia could already tell that this was a line of questioning he didn't like, but she wanted to understand, to know why. She had to know why her husband, who had always seemed to sail through everything, appeared to have scuttled himself.

'*For fuck's sake, Amelia.* No, I said everything they needed to hear, and much more besides. Why do you always have to bloody blame me for everything?'

She hadn't, though, Amelia thought. She had never blamed him, not even when his choice of job had landed them in this claustrophobic apartment, or when his sperm count had been found to be incredibly low, despite already fathering a son. *Not once.*

'I…' she started to reply but stopped when Piers threw himself upright and roared. She shrank back in her seat, petrified, as he launched himself at her. She thought for one moment that he was going to hit her, but he grabbed her by the shoulders instead.

'It's this bloody court case that'll be behind it,' he said, his face beetroot. 'You've been telling everyone that it's going to happen, and they will think it's because we're not good enough parents, won't they? That they are removing her because we're abusing her or something.' He was rocking her backwards and forwards now. She was too shocked to do anything about it. 'If only you'd kept your stupid mouth shut.'

He stopped shaking her for a brief moment, long enough for Amelia to seize the opportunity to stand up and run out of the room. She was actually afraid of Piers for the first time in her life, she realised.

'*Amelia! Come back! I'm sorry*,' he shouted, following her out of the lounge. She ran into the bathroom and locked the door behind her. 'I didn't mean it, Amelia. Please don't be like this. I need you. Come out here and give me a hug. I'm sorry.'

As she stood with her back to the bathroom door, her breathing hoarse and her heart thumping in her chest, she resolved to find out, once and for all, who Piers really was – because she was now certain that he was not at all who she had thought he was.

It was still dark when Amelia loaded Grace into the car, scraped the ice off the windscreen and set off for the south coast. She had spent most of the night fighting a flood of adrenaline, so had given up, got up early, eaten a cursory breakfast in the lounge, fed Grace her bottle and decided to get on the road before the rush hour took hold.

She had not told Piers where she was going. After last night, she didn't think he deserved an explanation. It was a hard enough day as it was, knowing that the final court hearing was happening, and that a huge decision was about to be made for them. She simply didn't have the energy to pander to Piers' crisis of confidence. She was beginning to feel that the school might have made the right choice appointing the other guy, after all.

She turned up the radio to try to drown the noise of her own heart. She was nervous about what lay ahead at the end of her journey, but there were two reasons why it was very necessary. Firstly, she just couldn't face the idea of spending the whole day at home, powerless, simply waiting for the axe to fall. And secondly, her anger at their treatment by social services was propelling her along, pushing her to take charge of the things in her life she *could* control. And one of those things, she now realised, was her marriage.

She had allowed Piers to steer her for years, but she hadn't allowed herself to see it. Now, her fury over the whole situation with Grace had made her want to grab the steering wheel, both literally and metaphorically, and control her own destiny, wherever that led. And let's face it, she thought, wherever that is has to be better than where I am now.

The sun, such as it was, was rising as she passed Fleet services on the M3, and by the time she had reached Lymington it was well established, emerging intermittently from behind a parade of small grey clouds, thawing frozen gutters, pavements and puddles. Three hours after she'd set off, Amelia threw open her car door and stood up and stretched, glad to be free of its confines. She was also grateful that Grace had slept most of the way, barring a small break to change her at the service station.

As she leaned down to retrieve her car seat, she couldn't stop an unwelcome thought coming into her mind, namely: what if this journey was the last she'd ever have with Grace? And – what if this was the last time she'd ever be alone with her?

Amelia had promised herself that she would try to live in the present today and would not think too hard about what was happening elsewhere. However, she was finding that this was impossible. Even when she made a huge effort to contain these thoughts safely behind a solid mental barrier, they kept ripping through, leaving her defences in tatters and detritus in their wake.

She took a deep breath to try to muster some energy, picked Grace's car seat up and walked down the small stone path which led to a solid oak, bright red front door. She pressed the doorbell and heard it ring inside the cottage, followed by the bark of a dog, a placating cry from a child, and footsteps coming towards the door.

'Oh, hello,' said the woman who answered the door. 'You're early. I'm sorry, I haven't got dressed yet. And you have... a baby? I didn't know. Wow.'

Amelia took Lesley in – her grey fluffy dressing gown, and matching grey slippers; straight, highlighted hair gathered into a messy top knot; a friendly, open face, devoid of any makeup.

'I know, I'm so sorry,' replied Amelia. 'It's just that I couldn't sleep, and... oh God, it's a long story.'

Lesley almost cracked a smile, Amelia thought, then thought better of it. 'That's okay. I was up, at least. The dog is getting old and incontinent, so I had to take her out for a wee an hour ago. Come on in.'

Amelia followed Lesley down a dark hallway into a small country-style kitchen which had beams crossing the ceiling and heat pumping out of an Aga at its heart.

'Coffee?' asked Lesley.

'Yes please.'

'Glad you said that,' she said. 'I am desperate for more caffeine.'

'Thank you so much for agreeing to see me,' said Amelia, as she watched Lesley prepare a cafetiere of ground coffee. 'I can imagine my phone call was a bit of a surprise.'

'No, not really,' replied Lesley, spooning coffee into the cafetiere. 'Although I was surprised that he decided to send you. He usually likes to take charge.'

Amelia got a sudden jolt.

'I'm sorry,' she said. 'I don't follow...'

'Piers didn't send you?'

'No. He doesn't know I'm here.'

'Ah,' said Lesley, turning around to face Amelia. 'Then why are you here? I assumed you wanted to see me about the letters, you see.'

'I... oh... God,' said Amelia, suddenly putting two and two together. 'Those letters were from you?'

Lesley's eyes opened wide.

'Yes. Right. Okay, I see we have a lot of catching up to do, not least, who this little girl is,' she said, looking at Grace, who was just starting to wake.

'Yes,' said Amelia, barely able to speak.

'I'll just put the lid on this, grab us some milk and some cups, and then we'll talk while we drink it, okay?'

Amelia nodded, and picked Grace up out of the chair, whilst Lesley finished making the coffee.

'So,' said Lesley, sitting down opposite Amelia at the oak kitchen table. 'Where shall we start?'

'The letters. I saw Piers reading a couple of letters, and I saw him rip one up and put it in the bin in his office. But I thought he was being threatened or something. I didn't know they were from you.'

'I see,' said Lesley. 'Well, it was sort of a threat. I've written to him twice, once a couple of months ago, and once more a few weeks ago now, a final demand, chasing maintenance payments for Seb. I'm going to have to seek legal help now, I think. He stopped paying them last year. I suppose the baby's arrival might explain why he now wants to rid himself of his previous responsibilities.'

'Oh my God. Did he? He didn't tell me.'

'Yes, I'm afraid so.'

Amelia sat there for a few seconds, thinking. Why would Piers not have told her about that?

'I'm so sorry. I had no idea,' she replied, finally. 'But I will do my best to get it sorted. I promise. Where is Sebastian?'

'Oh, in the other room, gaming,' Lesley replied. 'I can't get him off the bloody thing. But at least it's giving us time to talk in private. I don't want him knowing that his dad isn't paying for his upkeep anymore. Anyway,' she said, taking a sip of coffee, 'why did you want to talk to me, if it wasn't about those?'

'Piers has been acting... oddly,' she said, hugging the warm mug of coffee in front of her on the table. 'He's changed a lot in the past few months. I mean, it's been a difficult time. Grace – that's this little one – she's not mine – not ours, I mean – we are hoping to adopt her. But there's been a huge setback, and now it seems like she might be sent back to live with one or other of her birth parents.'

'Oh no,' said Lesley, with sincerity. 'How horrible for you.'

'Yes. It is horrible. It's shaken us both up. And then... yesterday. He went for a job, a promotion at the school, a deputy headship, and he didn't get it. When he got home last night he was furious. Raging. Distraught. Out of control. I've never seen him like that before.' Lesley nodded, as if she was far from surprised. 'But as I say, he's definitely been acting strangely for a while, and I thought you might know why. With all this shit we've been through, I've realised over the past few months how little I really know about what happened to him before. I was wondering if he has been drinking secretly, or something like that? Did he do that when he was with you?'

'Alcohol? God, no, not really. He only had the occasional heavy night. But if you were asking me about drugs, then I'd say a big fat yes,' said Lesley, deadpan.

'Drugs?'

'Yes. Cocaine, mostly.'

Amelia caught her breath.

'Really?' she asked.

'You didn't know? I'm surprised. He got terrible at hiding it when we were together. It was part of the reason I left him.'

'You... left *him*? Oh my God,' said Amelia, suddenly feeling vomit rise up her gullet.

'Are you okay?' asked Lesley.

'Could... you... take Grace for a few secs?' Amelia said, thrusting her into Lesley's arms. 'I think I need some fresh air.'

'Sure,' said Lesley, receiving the baby without question. 'I'll open up the French windows for you, you can go and have a wander in my wilderness of a garden.'

'Thank you,' said Amelia, bolting out of her chair at speed and taking deep breaths as Lesley found the key and unlocked the doors. Once she'd pushed them open, Amelia stepped outside and took a series of deep breaths, filling her lungs with frozen winter air. Then she bent over and allowed her body to sink down to the ground, as if she was recovering from a long run. Except she wasn't. Instead, she was feeling the aftershock after years of lies had exploded in front of her, without warning.

Piers takes drugs, she thought. *Piers is no longer paying maintenance for his son. Piers' first wife, Lesley, left him, rather than the other way around*. So much of her accepted reality had been shattered in the past few minutes and she needed time to process it.

She stood back up and looked around her. Lesley's cottage was on the outskirts of Lymington, within a mile of the sea. She could smell it. The air was different down here; it felt dense in her lungs, and damp. She was grateful for that, as it seemed to be soothing her, like a balm. She wrapped her arms around herself to ward off the cold and walked around the small cottage garden, which featured raised beds, a vegetable patch and a centrepiece of roses, which were all cut back brutally for the winter.

She heard knocking and looked up. Lesley was standing at the double doors cuddling Grace, who looked tearful. *Shit*, thought Amelia. I have to get myself together. I cannot behave like this. She waved acknowledgement and walked back and felt a wave of warm, coffee-scented air hit her when she opened the doors and stepped back into the kitchen.

'I'm so sorry,' she said. 'I don't know what came over me there.'

'That's fine,' said Lesley, holding Grace out for Amelia. 'Absolutely fine. Sit down. I'll get you some water.'

'Thank you,' said Amelia, sitting back down at the table, searching Grace's bag for the milk powder and a bottle so that she could give her a feed.

'Shall I make up a bottle for her?' asked Lesley, noticing what Amelia was doing. 'I think I remember how to... vaguely.'

'Thank you, that would be great,' said Amelia, incredibly relieved. She wasn't sure that she had the energy left to stand up again.

'No worries,' said Lesley, taking the powder and the bottle from her. 'So,' she said, putting the items down on the kitchen side. 'I'll pop some of the water from my kettle in here, and then put it in the freezer for a minute or so to cool it down, shall I?' Amelia nodded. 'Okay. So... I take it a lot of what I said earlier was news to you?'

'Yes,' said Amelia. 'All of it, frankly. Apart from that there had been letters. I knew about those.'

'Ah, yes. I sent two. The last one a few weeks ago.'

'Oh,' she said. 'Nothing more recent than that?' Amelia was thinking about the last letter she'd seen him with. It had to have been sent in the past two weeks.

'No, definitely not.'

Grace was crying now and Amelia felt like joining her. Who were the other letters from, and what else hadn't Piers told her about?

'I'm just going to put this in the freezer, okay? It should be cold enough in a few minutes.'

'Great,' said Amelia, rummaging around in the car seat for Grace's dummy. She found it, popped it in her mouth, and to her relief it soothed her, albeit temporarily.

'So tell me again, in more detail, about Piers and drugs,' she said, now that the crying had stopped and she was able to process her thoughts better.

'Are you sure?'

'Yes. Seriously, I've driven all of this way for answers. And I feel, frankly, like an idiot for not asking any of these questions before. It's like I've just woken up. Please, tell me. Everything.'

'Okay,' said Lesley, dropping two pieces of bread in the toaster. 'So, when I met Piers, he was clean. We had been at uni together, and aside from a bit of weed, he was straight as a die. He was really fit, really active, into mountaineering and expeditions. He had this big ambition to work in the Arctic. He was completely obsessed with it. He applied for various Masters courses and tried to get taken seriously as an academic, but he failed to get anywhere with it. Every door he tried to open just slammed shut. It hit him hard. Teaching was only meant to be a stopgap; he did it just because I was doing it, I think. We got married after our PGCE year, moved to London and he got a job at this huge comprehensive school in Wandsworth, with a super head, you know? It was very intense. He worked incredibly long days there, proving himself, I suppose, and there was a culture of drinking and partying afterwards. I think one of the other student teachers offered him some coke in the pub, and he accepted it. It gave him a huge buzz, he told me later; a whole load of energy. Then he accepted more, and met this guy's dealer, and then, I think, it became a habit. I didn't know anything about it at the time. I was pregnant with Seb, and naive. And you know how he is – he was so amazingly charming in the early days, I just couldn't believe he was anything but perfect.' Amelia nodded, her eyebrows raised. She knew exactly what Lesley meant. 'Anyway, to cut a long story short, I began to notice that he was acting oddly – he was suddenly sweating a lot at night and he was either bouncing off the walls, or almost comatose. And then, I noticed the money was going down. He hadn't wanted us to have a joint account, so I only noticed when we got red bills through the post,' said Lesley, taking the butter out of the fridge, the jam out of the cupboard and placing them on the table, along with two plates and two knives. 'He was spending so much money on drugs, he stopped paying for important things like rent. But I really hoped this was all ancient history. He promised me he'd kicked the habit after we separated.'

Amelia thought about Piers' odd behaviour in the past few months – his unexpected, unprompted warmth, his keenness for her to get out of the flat, the hours spent shut in his study.

'I wonder,' she said. 'I wonder.'

'I think the bottle will be cool enough by now,' Lesley said, retrieving it from the freezer, pouring the milk powder in, screwing on the lid and giving the bottle a shake. 'There you go, little Grace,' she said. 'For you.'

Amelia took the bottle gratefully, took out Grace's dummy, and inserted the bottle, which she began to suck greedily.

'Thank you for that,' she said. 'For the bottle, and for the truth.'

'It might not be the same in your case, though, remember that,' said Lesley, sitting down next to her, and pulling a plate of toast towards her. 'Do you want a piece? I made you one.'

Amelia decided that she needed something to line her stomach.

'Yes, please. That would be great.'

Both women spent a few seconds buttering the toast and spreading jam. When Lesley took her first mouthful, Amelia spat out the question she'd really come here to ask.

'Why did you break up? Was it the drugs?' she asked. 'I can imagine that put huge pressure on things.'

'You'd think so, wouldn't you?' she said, picking up the

cafetiere, pressing it down and pouring coffee out into two mugs. 'But it turns out I'm a complete fool. I thought we were so in love, we could cope with anything. I stayed with him, supported him while he went to Narcotics Anonymous, dealt with all of the stress when he went for promotions. As far as everyone outside our marriage was concerned, he was amazing. Charismatic. Charming.'

Amelia put her mug down.

'But not with you?'

'Not with me, no. He'd started out showering me with gifts and praise, but it didn't last long. Behind closed doors, he was… how should I put this… angry with me, very often. About everything I did. Looking back on it, it was truly hideous. I felt useless, utterly useless. I felt like I was going mad. I'd been on maternity leave with Seb, so out of the workplace, and that gave me low self-esteem anyway, so I didn't question it for a long time. But it was when he was at nursery, and I got back to teaching a few days a week, that I began to see it.'

Amelia sat back in her seat.

'Did you find yourself losing things a lot?' Amelia asked, as two well-trodden paths in her brain suddenly collided and her adrenaline surged.

'Yes. At first, I thought I was simply no longer capable. But later on, I began to believe he had been hiding them from me. Deliberately.'

'Oh my God,' said Amelia. 'Oh. My. God.'

'Does he try to control what clothes you wear?' Lesley asked.

'Yes.'

'And have you suddenly figured out that his generous gifts to you are in fact no replacement for a bank account?'

'Yes,' said Amelia, now almost unable to speak.

'Oh shit, now I feel really, really bad for not reporting him to the police.'

'The police? For the drugs?'

'No, I mean for coercive control. It became illegal in the UK in 2015, you know. I should have gone to the police about it, I know that now, but we had already separated and it seemed easier to let things lie. He was paying maintenance for Seb and I didn't want to rock the boat. But when I heard he'd got married again, I should have done something. I really should have. I'm sorry. I'm *so* sorry.'

Amelia sat in silence for a moment, listening to Grace drinking the final dregs of her bottle. Lesley was silent too, except for an occasional swallow as she made headway through her mug of coffee.

'*Fuck*. I feel like a total and utter fool,' Amelia said, finally, bringing her left hand up to her face, while her right hand continued to hold Grace, who seemed to be falling back to sleep.

A storyboard of memories from her relationship with Piers was running riot around her head: the glamorous man who'd wooed her in the wine bar; the expensive gifts he'd showered her with before they had become engaged; the showy wedding in the college chapel; the insistence that they should not share their infertility troubles with anyone else. He had been manipulating her all along, like a marionette, and she had willingly gone along for the ride. *What. A. Bloody. Idiot.*

Lesley got up from her seat, came around to Amelia's side of the table and placed her hands on Amelia's shoulders.

'Look. I know this is a lot to take on board, and I really, really shouldn't have left it this long. But it's not your fault. Seriously, it isn't.'

Amelia took a series of deep breaths, trying not to cry.

'At least you left him,' Amelia said. 'I've clung to him all of this time, like a complete idiot.'

'Oh, I took a lot of shit before I threw in the towel, don't get me wrong,' said Lesley, moving over to the kitchen cupboards and opening a door. 'A whole load of shit, trust me. It took him actually flirting with other women on WhatsApp, and various dating apps, before I finally saw the light. And that was probably just the tip of the iceberg.' Lesley walked back to the table and slapped a large pack of chocolate biscuits down on the surface. 'I think we need these,' she said. 'Chocolate helps most things, in my experience.'

Amelia looked across the table at Lesley. She was astounded by the other woman's honesty, her willingness to welcome her into her home, and the support she was offering her. And she was grateful that she'd been forewarned about this last element of Piers' behaviour – something which, she was fairly sure, he had yet to demonstrate to her, at least.

'Mum, can I have a snack?'

Amelia turned her head and saw that a boy had walked into the kitchen. He had closely clipped brown hair, pale skin, and looked tall for nine years old. She was transfixed; he was so much like his father.

'Yes, you can, but only after you tackle your homework,' Lesley replied. 'You have spellings to learn for Monday.'

'Seriously?' he said, his face a picture of injustice.

'*Yes, seriously*,' replied Lesley, smiling as Sebastian returned to the lounge, presumably, Amelia thought, to tackle his spellings. 'Boys. They are the worst,' she said.

'I can only imagine,' replied Amelia.

'Oh, sorry. I shouldn't be insensitive. I didn't think...'

'Oh, honestly, don't worry at all. But changing the subject... I should say thank you,' said Amelia, reaching out for a biscuit. 'Obviously for the chocolate, but also, thank you so much for everything you've said. I can't quite work out why you weren't more angry with me when I first arrived, given that Piers is trying to cut you off financially.'

'Oh, I know him well enough to know that he will still be totally in charge of his finances,' she said. 'He's obsessive about money. It's all about power.'

Amelia saw that Grace was coming round from her nap. She

lifted her up and placed her head over her shoulder, rubbing her back to help remove any wind she'd developed from her energetic feed.

'So, this little one,' said Lesley. 'You said you're hoping to adopt her...?'

'Yes, well, we were,' said Amelia. 'But I fear very much that we won't be able to. There's a court case going on in Worcester, right now, which will decide it all. That's why I came here today. I had to do *something*. Something I could control. Otherwise I'd feel completely powerless.'

'I get that,' said Lesley. 'But why do you think you won't get to adopt her? She seems so happy with you...'

'Believe it or not, the adoptive parents don't even get a look in during the trial,' she replied. 'We aren't relevant. This battle is between the birth parents, both of whom want her back, and social services, who want her to come to us.'

'Well, for your sake – and not for Piers' sake, let me make that clear – I do hope she comes to you. I can see how much you love her.'

'Yes, I do,' said Amelia, nuzzling Grace's downy head. 'I do. But sadly, I fear that love will not be enough.'

31

February 24th

Michelle

Final hearing, Day 2

'Miss Stone – can you please confirm your name and your role?'

'Yes, madam. I'm Marion Stone, the children's guardian appointed in this case. I work for Cafcass.'

'Thank you, Miss Stone,' said Judge Joshi, turning her attention once more to the wider group. 'Now, we have all read Miss Stone's final report into this matter. I'd like to ask Mr Shelley to begin questioning, please.'

'Certainly, madam,' he replied, picking up his copy of the report, which Michelle could see was full of pen markings and stickers highlighting sections he obviously wanted to raise. She knew that Sally's copy looked pretty similar. She'd read it out to her a few days previously and although it was long and confusing in parts, Michelle had found it surprisingly okay. It hadn't condemned her as a drug addict, or a thief, or as a waste of space. In fact, it had said pretty nice things about her. Which was a relief, given yesterday's car crash of a hearing. Today could only be better, she hoped. It definitely couldn't be worse.

'Miss Stone,' said the local authority's barrister. 'How many hearings of this type have you worked on in your career, would you say?'

'I can't give you an exact number, but I'd imagine well over fifty,' the guardian replied.

'And in how many of these cases did the child go back into the care of the birth parents?'

'Again, I can't give you an actual statistic,' she replied, 'but very few, I suppose. But they do, sometimes.'

'In your report, you lay out clearly how things stood at the time Grace was taken into local authority care. You appear to agree absolutely that this was the right decision?'

'Yes, I do. At that time, the birth mother was asking for adoption, the birth father wasn't expressing any interest in his child, and the couple's home life was chaotic.'

'But you think this has changed? The chaos is a thing of the past?'

'Yes, in the sense that the mother is now living with support in a stable environment and the father has taken a similar route, with the support of his parents.'

'However, the birth parents, previously in a long-term relationship, cohabiting, have split up. Do you feel that this provides a solid basis for the child's upbringing?'

'Given what they have each told me, I feel they are probably better apart than together,' Marion Stone replied, pulling herself up as she did so.

'And you were able to judge this, how? How many hours did you spend with them? Did you drop in on them unannounced?'

'No, I always arranged my visits.'

'Is it possible, therefore, that things might not be as settled as they seem?'

'That is always possible.'

'Quite. Miss Stone, moving on to the prospective adopters. They are a married couple, are they not?'

'Yes. They have been married for about six years, I believe.'

'And are they settled?'

'Yes, they share a home, have a stable income and have plenty of time to spend with the child.'

'And are they habitual drug users? Do they shoplift?'

Michelle saw Marion Stone give Philip Shelley a withering stare.

'Mr Shelley, you and I both know that we vet potential adopters very carefully. But that's not the point of this, is it?'

'Miss Stone – their suitability aside, it is to be assumed that they are caring well for Grace?'

'Yes. They have fully bonded with Grace, and her with them, I'd say.'

'What, in your opinion, would be the effect on Grace of removing her from their loving care, at this stage?'

Marion Stone poured herself a cup of water and took a sip before answering.

'Grace is now nearly five months old. She is capable of recognising familiar faces and will see her foster parents as primary caregivers – her mum and dad, essentially – at this stage. However, separation anxiety doesn't really kick in until eight months, so any transfer before that stage shouldn't upset her too much.'

'So, if care were to be handed over to either of the birth parents, you would effectively be separating baby Grace from the only people she really knows as her mother and father?'

'If you want to look at it that way – yes,' she replied, looking, Michelle thought, a little flustered.

'Thank you. No further questions, madam,' the lawyer said.

'Thank you, Mr Shelley. Mr Carraway? Do you have questions for Miss Stone?'

'I do, madam,' said Len Carraway, getting to his well-heeled feet. I bet those shoes cost more than my whole suit, Michelle thought. 'Miss Stone – I appreciated the time and obvious thought that you have put into your report. I see that you were impressed by the family unit my client, Robert Allcott, is now part of.'

'Yes, I felt that the support he is getting from his parents is most valuable. Their home is of course well set up, and they've given a lot of thought to how they will accommodate a new family member. I felt also that Mr Allcott seems determined to make positive changes in his life.'

'That's wonderful to hear, Miss Stone. Why, then, have you not recommended that Mr Allcott should have custody of his daughter, given your view on those subjects?'

'I had to take everybody's situation into consideration as a whole, Mr Carraway. I have to decide what is best for Grace in the long run – where she will be safest, and where she will be happiest. I have to consider the character of each adult in this case, their past behaviour and their current situation, and I also have to consider the possibility that they may fail in their effort to begin a new life and fall back into old ways.'

'What evidence do you have for that concern, Miss Stone?'

'It is always a risk, Mr Carraway.'

'And what evidence do you have for Mr Allcott's alleged drug use currently, or alleged abuse of his partner? My client says that he has put his drug use behind him. He recently took a drugs test, which he passed with flying colours.'

Pretty easy to do that when you're living with your mum and dad and it's been weeks since you last took anything, Michelle thought.

'No, Mr Carraway, but I trust the judgement of my fellow social workers,' replied Miss Stone.

'I see. No further questions.'

Len Carraway sat down, and Michelle thought, just for a second, that she saw the judge stifle a sigh.

'Right, Ms Mucklow. I assume you also have questions for Miss Stone?'

'I do, madam,' Sally replied. 'Thank you.'

Go on, Sally. Show them that I'm not a public liability, thought Michelle. Someone has to.

'Miss Stone, I was delighted to see that you were so positive about Miss Jenkins in your report,' Sally began. 'Indeed, in your conclusion, you said that you felt that Grace would be safe with her, and that returning her to her mother was a real option. Can you tell the court how you came to that conclusion?'

'Certainly, although of course I must point out that in my conclusion I also say that I feel she is also safe in her current setting. However, I wanted to give Miss Jenkins the benefit of the doubt and the opportunity to set out her stall here in court.'

'Yes, she will be giving evidence later on today,' Sally answered. 'However, in terms of your conclusions – can you tell me why you feel that Miss Jenkins would be a safe choice for Grace?'

'Michelle – Miss Jenkins – is, in my opinion, a very impressive young lady, who was given a terrible start in life,' she replied. 'I know that social services played its part in that, and I acknowledge that absolutely. At the time of Grace's birth, she was receiving no support from anyone, and I am not surprised that she considered surrendering her to be the best option. However, she has now found a very successful placement with experienced fosterers, and she has made great strides in her personal life. She has made it clear that her intention now, if the judge decides she should have custody, is to focus on Grace for the time being, with the support of the two other adults where she is living. I believe that this would be a safe way to begin her parenting journey, with ample support from social services. Should, as I say, the judge decide to pursue this path.'

'Thank you, Miss Stone. One more thing – you do not recommend in your report that Mr Allcott should be given sole custody of Grace, yet you are prepared to consider that option for Miss Jenkins. Why is that?'

'I did not feel that he was as dedicated in his intention to parent Grace as Miss Jenkins. When I spoke to him alone, he was somewhat lacklustre and unsure. I just didn't get the right message from him.'

'I see. Thank you, Miss Stone. No further questions.'

'Would you like a hot chocolate? I got one from the machine down the corridor earlier, and it wasn't too bad...'

'No,' Michelle replied.

'But some sugar will do you good, lovey,' said Gillian. 'Also, I've got some jelly babies in my bag.' Gillian reached into her large batik tote and pulled out a large, unopened bag of the sweets, tore off the corner, and held it out to Michelle. 'Go on. Have a few. You must be starving.'

'I'm not hungry.'

'I know you may not feel like you are, but trust me, you need something. Come on, lovey, take one, for me. I've been here all morning rooting for you, sending you positive vibes through the door, and the least you can do is eat one. Look, I'll let you have a blackcurrant one, okay?'

Michelle smiled briefly and took a sweet.

'Thanks. But honestly, I'm not hungry at all. It was still shit, Gill, even though the guardian had said nice things about me. I mean, she was nice, but she was hardly telling them to just hand Grace over, you know? She made it sound like I'm a kid, and that I need supervision. And I just know that this afternoon is going to be fucking awful.'

Gillian noticed that Michelle had finished the sweet, so held out the bag again. Michelle took another without a word.

'Giving evidence is your chance to set the record straight,' said Gillian. 'And Sally told us this morning that she had some new evidence, didn't she? Something that would make Rob look like the idiot he is? That's got to be worth watching, eh?' Gillian said, digging Michelle in the ribs. Michelle managed another brief smile.

'Yeah, I s'pose,' she said. 'But… I can't change the past, can I? I can't pretend that I refused to let them take her, or that I never took drugs, or that I never nicked stuff from shops… That bastard of a lawyer is going to shoot me down, isn't he? I can just see he's dying to do it. And the judge – she's got that report from Marion that makes me sound okay, you know, but she said in it she still had doubts about me. So all I need is Rob's fucking bulldog to throw shit at me that sticks, and I've had it. She's gone. I'll never see her again.'

'Where is Sally?' asked Gillian, clearly keen to change the subject. 'Has she gone to get lunch?'

'No, she said she had a meeting to go to,' Michelle replied. 'But I think she'll be back in a few minutes.'

'Okay,' said Gillian. 'In which case, I'll just go to find us a sandwich each, okay? I'll grab us a ready-made one from that newsagent down the road. I'll be back in five.'

'Sure,' said Michelle, glad to be given the chance to be alone with her thoughts. Gillian walked off at speed, keen, Michelle guessed, to be back to hear whatever Sally had to say. Michelle put her head in her hands and closed her eyes. She was interested in Sally's news too, of course, but doubted that anything could blow the 'new' Rob and his expensive brief out of the water now. They were going to try to sink her first; that she did know.

'Michelle?' a familiar voice said. Michelle sat back up and opened her eyes and looked at her social worker, Laura.

'Yeah?' she said, almost as a challenge.

'Can I sit down?'

'It's a free country,' she said. You're not getting a smile from me, she thought. No way. Not after your answers in court yesterday. *Call that trying to help me?*

'I'm so sorry that I didn't manage to pull things around for you yesterday,' Laura said, sitting down in the seat Gillian had just vacated. 'I did try, but I had to be honest, too, and the questions were quite skewed...'

'Yeah, whatever.'

'I mean it, Michelle. I am sorry. I want them to give you Grace.'

'Do you really?'

'Yes, I do. I really do.'

'Hmmm,' replied Michelle.

Then, Laura slid a letter across onto her lap.

'This is for you,' said Laura. 'It arrived at the office this morning.'

Michelle stared at the envelope, which was addressed to her, care of social services, with neat curly handwriting, an air mail sticker and stuck with unfamiliar stamps. The stamps said it had come from Australia. Michelle's stomach lurched.

'Is this what I think it is...?'

'I think so,' replied Laura. 'We didn't want to tell you we'd located her unless she was happy to get in touch. But this suggests that she's happy at least to write to you. I haven't read it, of course. Because it's for you.'

'Wow.'

'I know. Look, I won't stay, because you'll be wanting to read that ASAP. But I will be in court today, until the judgement.'

'Okay,' replied Michelle, although she was not really listening. She was fixated on the envelope, and the longed-for message that both terrified and excited her.

'Okay then. See you later,' said Laura, standing back up. 'Good luck.'

Michelle nodded but didn't shift her gaze from the envelope that she was grasping with both of her hands.

Part of her was afraid to open it.

What if it contained an angry note from her sister, telling her that she blamed her for everything, and never wanted to hear from her again? It was possible. But then, what if it contained something wonderful, like a story of a happy childhood and her adventures in Australia? Shit, Michelle thought. If it's the former, there's no way I'll be able to give evidence this afternoon. But if it's the second, I'll be dancing around the room. The only thing she had ever wanted to know was that her sister didn't blame her, and that she was content. That was all. To her, that was not a small thing; that was everything.

'I'm back! Amazing, I know. I used contactless and was on my way in a jiffy. Here you are – I got ham and cheese. Is that okay?' Gillian stood in front of Michelle for a brief moment before she realised why Michelle was not responding. 'Oh good lord – is that what I think it is?' she asked, sitting down next to Michelle. 'Is that a letter from Australia?'

'Yeah,' replied Michelle, her voice breaking. '*Yeah*.'

'Have you opened it yet?'

'Nope.'

'Why not?'

'Because it might have bad stuff in it. I should probably save it until later. Just in case.'

'Don't be silly. This is a letter from a sister you haven't seen since you were six years old. You need to open it now.'

'What if I can't read it? What if I can't make out the words?'

'Don't be daft,' said Gillian. 'Anyway, I'm here. I'll help.'

'Okay.'

Michelle's hands were shaking as she tore the top of the envelope. Inside was a folded sheet of lined paper. She reached inside and pulled it out, and as she did so, something slid onto her lap. Michelle reached out and picked it up. It was a passport sized photograph of a beautiful teenage girl; she had sleek brown hair, a long straight nose, dark brown eyes and a broad smile. Her skin was lightly tanned, and she was wearing a loose red vest and denim shorts.

'Oh my God,' said Michelle. 'She's… amazing.'

'She looks like you,' said Gillian. 'So much like you.'

Michelle unfolded the notepaper and began to read, with Gillian's help.

Dear Chelle (I still remember calling you that!)

It was amazing to receive your letter. My mum and dad, they're great (although a bit annoying!) but they have always tried to put me off tracing my birth family. I was always going to do it though, when I get to 18. I'm only two years off that now, so I was almost there, right? But now I don't have to wait.

I'm so glad you're okay, and how exciting that you have a baby! I can't wait to meet her. I'm good. I hate school but it's okay. I like science and cricket. I love the beach. I want to be a nurse.

Do you have an iphone? Can we facetime? I would love that.

Love,

Grace (your sister! Wow.)

By the time Michelle had finished reading the letter, there were blotches on the paper, making the blue ink run. Her heart was still racing and her hands were still shaking, but her grip on the letter was vice-like.

'How do you feel?' asked Gillian.

'She isn't angry with me,' said Michelle, ignoring the question. 'She isn't. She says she wants to talk to me. She's happy. Did you get that from the letter? I think she's happy.'

'Yes, I think she is,' replied Gillian. 'And she was never going to be angry with you, Michelle. You were six years old. You had no way of stopping her from being taken. You were not in control. As I keep telling you – *it was not your fault*.'

Suddenly, Michelle was back in that room with the Lego and the dolls, listening to her sister's cries of alarm as she was taken out of the house and bundled into a car. And then she remembered the locked door and the tall, strong woman holding her back, who didn't even try to comfort her when she cried.

'Yes,' she replied. 'Yes. I couldn't stop them.'

'No, you couldn't. Now, my lovely, eat your sandwich. You're going back inside in ten minutes.'

Michelle handed the letter to Gillian for safe keeping and opened the sandwich she'd bought her, which she now realised she was desperate to eat. She bit into it hungrily, the surge of adrenaline she'd just experienced creating what felt like a black hole in her stomach.

'Hello, both. Are you ready?' Michelle looked up from her food to see that Sally had returned. She looked slightly flustered, she thought, but she was smiling, so that was a positive sign, at least.

'Yep,' replied Michelle, meaning it. That letter from her sister had untapped a well of energy she had been unaware of. It was now coursing through her veins and she felt at that moment as if she could face anything that was thrown at her; absolutely bloody anything.

'Do you want to quickly go through all of the answers we discussed at our meeting last week, so that you feel prepared?'

'Nope, it's fine. I remember them. Let me finish my sarnie, and I'll be there,' said Michelle.

As Michelle threw the sandwich box in the bin, wiped her mouth with a tissue, took a swig of water from a bottle Gillian kept for her outside court and brushed down her suit, she thought: this is for you, Grace. *Both Graces*. This is for both of you.

'Thank you, everyone, for returning from lunch promptly. I understand from Ms Mucklow that we have a late witness to this hearing. I met with her over lunch and decided to allow her to give evidence, based on her important input in this case. I propose we hear what she has to say before calling Miss Jenkins to give evidence. Ms Mucklow, could you please explain to the court why you've called a new witness?'

'Yes, thank you, madam, for your consideration in this matter. I am calling Mrs Louise Wilcocks, who lives in the apartment above the unit where Mr Allcott lived with Miss Jenkins. Madam, she was the member of the public who called the police after the first significant assault and she heard the argument that preceded it.'

'Thank you for that explanation, Ms Mucklow. I'd like to ask the clerk to call in Mrs Wilcocks.'

Michelle watched as the clerk got up from his seat and went through the double doors back into the waiting room. As they waited for him to return, she found herself wringing her hands and crossing and uncrossing her legs, her agitation and disbelief making her limbs seem to take on a life of their own. Could this really be true, she thought? Could the old bat from upstairs really be about to come and take part in this hearing? If she didn't know better, she'd think she was dreaming. Michelle glanced over at Rob, who looked very uncomfortable, as if he had a really bad case of piles.

The door clicked and in walked the ancient woman from upstairs, propped up by a walking frame. How the hell does she get up those stairs by herself, Michelle wondered. And then the thought crossed her mind that she probably almost never got out of that flat, and Michelle suddenly felt ashamed. She'd lived there for two years and never seen that woman as anything other than a pain in the arse.

The clerk helped the old lady manoeuvre past the chairs and desks and lower herself into the chair in front of the bench. He then poured her a glass of water, which she sipped slowly. Michelle looked at her closely for the first time. She was a tiny woman, probably no more than five feet tall. She had dressed formally for the occasion – a brown jumper, a black calf-length skirt, tights and flat brown pull-on shoes. Her hair, which Michelle had often observed to be unkempt, was today pulled into a tight low bun. She looked neat and sensible and determined. She looked up then, directly at Michelle, and smiled. Michelle was taken by surprise, but she returned the smile instinctively. Wow, this is obviously a day for miracles, Michelle thought.

'Thank you for attending this hearing at short notice, Mrs Wilcocks. Can I ask you to confirm your name and address?'

'Yes, your honour. I am Louise Wilcocks, and I live at 5b, Symphony Road, on the Elgar Estate, Malvern.'

'Thank you. Do you want to affirm, or swear on a holy book?'

'I'd like to swear on the Bible, please, your honour.'

As the old lady repeated the now familiar words, Michelle found herself repeating her sister's words like a mantra. '*Grace, your sister. Wow! Grace, your sister. Wow!*'

'Ms Mucklow, as Mrs Wilcocks is your witness, would you like to begin the questioning?'

'Absolutely, madam,' Sally replied, looking directly at Michelle's former neighbour. 'Mrs Wilcocks – I don't want to keep you here longer than I need to, so let's get straight to the facts. Could you confirm what you heard on August the sixth last year, which I believe was the first time you called the police to attend Mr Allcott and Miss Jenkins' flat?'

'Yes, that's right,' replied Louise Wilcocks, her voice gentle, her accent a sing-song Brummie. 'It was terrible. I was frightened for her, I really was. She's such a slight girl, and I knew she was expecting, and he was really laying into her. He said all sorts of stuff which I don't want to repeat here…'

'He? Could you clarify who you mean, for the benefit of the court?'

'Yes. I mean Rob, her partner.'

'Thank you, Mrs Wilcocks. Could you try, for the record, to

repeat what you heard Robert Allcott say to Michelle Jenkins? It's important to get the facts out,' asked Sally.

Shit, she looks uncomfortable with this. Poor woman, Michelle thought.

'Yes, well, there was a lot of the "f" word, you know, and other swear words, but he was blaming her for not making any money that week. She'd been going out to work for a while – I saw her leave every morning – but I think she had to stop, for the babby. She was quite big by then and she looked knackered, you know. Anyway, then I heard her screaming, and there was a fight, a physical fight. I could hear things being thrown, and stuff being knocked over. That's when I called the police. I was worried about the babby, see.'

'I see. And how certain are you about what was said?'

'Those flats have paper-thin walls and floors,' she said. 'They were built on the cheap, that's what I always say. I can hear everything through them. I've hammered on the floor in the past to get them to turn the TV or the music down – my new hearing aid picks up everything. It's a curse a lot of the time, it really is.'

'I can imagine. Now, Mrs Wilcocks. What else did you hear in the months leading up to Mr Allcott and Miss Jenkins moving out?'

'In November, I think it was, there was another big fight. She was screaming, poor thing, really screaming. She'd only just had the babby and she must have been so tired.'

'Did you call the police on that occasion?'

'No, I didn't. I think I should have, really, but she went quiet quite quickly, and I lost my nerve.'

'Why did you lose your nerve, Mrs Wilcocks?'

'Because he – Mr Allcott, I mean – he'd come up and threatened me.'

'When did this happen?'

'After the first time. He came up and hammered on my door.'

'What exactly did he say?'

'I don't want to use the language. It's not right, it isn't. But basically, he told me not to get involved, and if I did it again, he'd see that I shut up. Words to that effect, you know.'

'Thank you, Mrs Wilcocks, for coming in to speak to us. No further questions, madam,' she said, turning towards the judge.

'Thank you, Ms Mucklow. Mr Carraway,' she said, turning to Rob's barrister, 'I presume you have questions for the witness?'

'Yes, I certainly do, madam,' he replied, shooting up out of his chair. Michelle examined his face. He had beads of sweat on his brow and just a hint of dampness under his armpits.

'Mrs Wilcocks – did you actually see any of these arguments?'

'No, your honour, but I heard them all. I have a good memory, you see, and my hearing aids...'

'So you don't actually know who was attacking whom, in these incidents?'

'No, but...'

'So it's possible, isn't it, that Miss Jenkins was the one attacking Mr Allcott?'

'I suppose. But I really don't think...'

'We are not interested in supposition here, Mrs Wilcocks. Only facts.'

The old woman looked chastened.

'I didn't see them fight, no. But I know who came to my door and threatened me. I do know that.'

'No further questions, madam,' said Len Carraway, sitting back down as quickly as he had risen to his feet.

Michelle pulled up her tights, pulled her skirt down towards her knees and said a silent, quick prayer of sorts, before she unlocked the toilet door and emerged back into public view. She'd asked for this break mostly so that she had a minute or so by herself, to unjumble all the thoughts in her brain, before she went back in to face the metaphorical firing squad. This was her one chance and she was determined not to waste it.

'Are you done?' asked Gillian, poking her head around the door. 'They're waiting for you.'

'Yeah, I am,' answered Michelle, giving her hands a quick wash and dry, and smoothing her hair, which she'd pulled back into a neat ponytail. 'Here we go. Ready or not.'

Gillian pulled her into a hug and gave her a kiss on the cheek. 'Go get 'em, girl,' she said, rubbing Michelle's back, like a mother would a child.

Michelle smiled and walked straight to the court doors. On the other side, an expectant crowd turned its collective head towards her as she walked towards the witness desk. She felt their eyes boring into her as she did so. Well, here goes nothing, she thought, as she sat down and pulled the chair into the desk so that she could rest her arms on it.

'Are you ready, Miss Jenkins?' asked the judge. Michelle wondered if she'd annoyed her by asking for a loo break.

'Yes, thank you,' she said, not wanting to say madam, because it sounded far too strange.

'Fine, then we will begin. Ms Mucklow, as Miss Jenkins' legal representative, would you like to start?'

'Thank you, madam, I will,' replied Sally. 'Miss Jenkins – I think it would be helpful if you could explain, in your own words, why you initially decided that Grace should be adopted.'

Michelle took a deep breath and began.

'I've been thinking about this a lot,' she said. 'The thing is, I was scared. Really scared of ending up on the streets again, and of letting Grace down, failing my daughter like I failed my sister, you know? I just couldn't trust myself. And Rob and I always had no food, or heating, or any money and I just knew we couldn't look after a baby. Not without a lot of help from social services, and given the shit I've taken from them in the past, I wasn't going to go there.'

'Rob Allcott says you persuaded him that the baby should be adopted.'

'Yeah, he does, doesn't he. But… He just went along with what I said. He never tried to persuade me otherwise. I got the feeling he just wasn't that bothered.'

'Why do you think he's now changed his mind, and decided he wants to keep the baby?'

'I dunno. I dunno whether he does, I mean, I wonder if it's just his parents who are interested, now they've found out about her. They've got all that money, and they've got their son back, and now maybe they want the set?'

Michelle could see, out of the corner of her eye, a furious-looking Len Carraway. Rob, on the other hand, looked impassive. He'd always been a good actor, she thought. After all, he'd convinced her that he was a working-class boy for years, hadn't he?

'Thank you, Miss Jenkins. Now, could you please tell the court what your situation is currently, and why you feel you are now the right person to be caring for Grace?'

Michelle nodded and recited the summary they'd written together.

'I'm living with an amazing couple called Gillian and Mike. They've fostered loads of kids of all ages, and now they are fostering me, sort of. They have a great house in Malvern, and they have offered to have me and Grace to live with them for as long as I need. I'm volunteering at the food bank at Malvern Priory twice a week, and I'm getting support for my dyslexia, which was diagnosed a few weeks ago. I'm going to go back to college and try to get my exams again, I think. And Grace – well, I love her, you know? I love her so much. The idea of not having her in my life, forever, it makes me break inside. I have a lot to make up for, I know that, but I want to be her mum. I *am* her mum.'

'Thank you, Miss Jenkins. No further questions,' said Sally, smiling at Michelle.

That part, Michelle knew, had been the easy bit. That had been the part she could easily prepare for.

'Miss Stone – does the children's guardian have questions for Miss Jenkins?' the judge asked.

'No questions, madam,' replied Miss Stone.

Relief flooded through Michelle. One less grilling, she thought. Only the local authority and Rob's lawyer left.

'Mr Shelley? Anything from the local authority?' Judge Joshi asked.

'Yes, your honour. Just one question from us. Miss Jenkins – you say that you will be able to stay with Gillian and Mike for a while. But have you given any thought to where you'll go afterwards? After all, you can't stay there forever.'

Shit, thought Michelle. No, I haven't, not really.

'Erm…' she said, picking her fingers, 'I think I'll have to talk to my social worker about that. She is nice, Laura. I didn't use to think so, but I do now. And she'll help me find somewhere. But I think Gillian and Mike will help me as long as I need, anyway.'

Was that enough, she thought, to convince a judge?

'Thank you, madam, no further questions.'

'Mr Carraway,' the judge said. 'I assume you have some questions for Miss Jenkins?'

'I certainly do, madam,' he replied, standing up for a final time.

'Miss Jenkins, your lawyer, Ms Mucklow, has made some serious accusations about my client in this hearing. Do you have evidence for these assertions?'

'No… it was just me and him, wasn't it? So I s'pose it's his word against mine. And Rob's dealer knows the truth, but I doubt he'll be coming to give evidence, will he?'

Calm, Michelle imagined Gillian whispering in her ear. *Calm*.

'So you could be making them up?'

'I could be, but...'

'Yes, indeed...'

'*I'm not finished*,' said Michelle, sitting back in her seat and glaring at him. 'I hadn't finished, had I? I said I *could* be, but I'm not. He hit me and he stubbed out his fags on my arms after he tried to pimp me out to his drug dealer in return for cocaine, and I refused. And the time before that, he hit me because I'd have to leave me job and he couldn't use my wages to fund his habit anymore.'

'*I never...*' shouted Rob suddenly, lapsing back into his old accent.

'Please remain quiet, Mr Allcott,' said Judge Joshi. 'You have already had your say.'

'Which bit didn't you do, Rob?' asked Michelle, looking directly at him. It was time, she felt, to cut any ties he felt still held. 'The pimping bit? The running away and leaving me for dead? The fag burns? Or the bruises?'

'Miss Jenkins, please restrict your conversation to your exchange with Mr Carraway,' said Judge Joshi, sounding, Michelle thought, a bit like one of her old schoolteachers.

'Okay,' she said, also sounding a bit, she suspected, like she had done during double Maths on a Friday afternoon.

'Miss Jenkins,' said Len Carraway, 'you seem determined to rubbish my client's personality, yet you chose to live with him for three years. You returned to him voluntarily after giving birth to Grace, even though social services offered to find you somewhere else to live. Are you really trying to tell us that he somehow made you stay?'

Michelle thought for a second, feeling the silence that fell as she did so. She knew that everyone gathered there was hanging on her every word.

'He made the *old me* stay, yes,' she said, aware for the first time that this was absolutely the truth. 'The *old me* believed he'd been born to a family like mine and so I never questioned that his accent sounded a bit off. The *old me* believed that he'd been abused as a child and so forgave him whenever he hit me. The *old me* believed him when he said I should go out and shoplift to get us food, because I'd get less punishment than him if I was caught. But the *new me* would never do any of those things. I'll never forgive him or believe him again. Never.'

'How long did she say she'd need?' asked Gillian, who was pacing the small distance between the two rows of seats outside the courtroom.

'She didn't really say,' Michelle replied. 'She just asked us to wait outside while she considered her decision.'

'Okay,' said Gillian, getting out her phone. 'I'll let Mike know. He's on tenterhooks at home.'

Michelle waited while she typed out the message – Gillian didn't know how to use predictive text, so messages always took her ages – and looked around her. Rob, his parents and his lawyer had disappeared to a different seating area. Laura and Gloria were standing up by the court doors, talking quietly, and Marion Stone was sitting in silence opposite her, tapping away on a laptop and working through notes. Sally, who was sitting beside Gillian, was also working, whether on her case or someone else's, she didn't know. Most likely, she thought, someone else's, as the final decision on this one was imminent.

'So how do you think it went this afternoon?' Gillian asked. 'How did your evidence giving go?'

Michelle thought about how feisty she'd been, how… rude she'd been. She cringed inside. What if the judge had her down as just a naughty school kid? She'd never let her have Grace, would she?

'It was hard,' she said. 'I lost my temper.'

'That's quite understandable,' said Gillian. 'There is a great deal at stake.'

'Yeah…'

'And you said Rob lost his temper too?'

'Yeah, he did.'

'Well, then.'

'But the judge could just decide to take her off both of us, couldn't she? And the guardian, she left it up to her. She said either option was acceptable. So… it's up to that judge, right? That old lady who's been looking down at me for months.'

'Don't be silly, Michelle. She sits higher up, doesn't she? She looks down at everyone.'

Michelle managed to raise a smile, largely to make Gillian feel better.

'Miss Jenkins, Mr Allcott? The judge has asked you all to return,' called the clerk from the court door.

'Well, it looks like I'm about to find out,' said Michelle, 'whether she likes me or not, right?'

'Good luck, lovely girl,' said Gillian, as Michelle got ready to return. 'I'll be right here for you afterwards; however it goes.'

32

February 24th

Amelia

Final hearing, Day 2

Despite the slippery, thawing surface under her feet, Amelia broke into a run. She was late for Julia's lesson. She hadn't meant to be out for so long, but her limbs and her brain had so enjoyed the feeling of her blood circulating, and her heart beating to its full potential, that she'd stayed out far longer than she'd intended. She had needed vigorous exercise, today of all days; the court judgement about Grace's future was due at some point today, and she desperately needed a distraction.

Grace's buggy was not equipped for running – Piers had never caved and bought her the right equipment – but Amelia had decided that a power walk up Malvern's considerable hills would be far better than nothing. As her heart pumped at double time and her calves flexed and stretched, Amelia had pushed a sleeping Grace past steaming coffee shops readying for the breakfast rush, pubs taking deliveries of kegs of beer, and old ladies giving their dogs their first walk of the day, clad in coats, hats and mittens. Amelia, on the other hand, was only wearing her running gear, because her body was currently its own furnace.

She had been walking down Church Street when she'd realised she only had twenty minutes before Julia's lesson was supposed to start. The revelations of the day before had been so disorientating, and the looming court judgement so frightening, that she had temporarily lost connection with her daily reality. She really had no idea what time it was, but thankfully her phone had alerted her, and so she had set off back down the hill at speed, Grace's buggy flying over bumps in the path and landing back down with a thump. Fortunately, Grace seemed to enjoy movement and she did not wake.

Amelia arrived back at the boarding house with only moments to spare. She unlocked the front door, lifted Grace out of her buggy and ran up the stairs to their apartment, keen to have time to get changed before Julia arrived. She had not seen her for several weeks – she had been off school poorly – so she was looking forward to catching up and finding out how her work was progressing.

But Julia did not arrive at her scheduled time. Initially relieved, as it gave Amelia time to wash her face and brush her hair, she grew frustrated as the clock ticked round – ten minutes late; now twenty – had she got the start time wrong? She checked her diary. No, she was correct. Getting angry now that she'd raced back for nothing, Amelia sent her a message. It was simply rude to waste her time like this, particularly today.

Amelia stood in the kitchen, listening to Grace gurgling next door. She'd finally taken a liking to the bouncy chair they'd bought her and it gave her at least a few minutes' grace, which she was using to make herself a cup of tea. The thought flashed into her mind that this might be the last day of use Grace would get out of that bouncer, but she thrust it aside. It did not do to dwell.

Instead, what she needed was action. She needed to do something to make today less achingly painful, and after her conversation with Lesley the day before, she knew what that should be. She needed to find out whether Piers was really on drugs. And for that, she needed to get back into the study.

Amelia left her tea stewing and ran down the stairs, left their door on the latch and popped her head into the matron's room, where Mrs Collins was sitting at her desk.

'Hello, Mrs C,' she said, sounding as chirpy as she could. 'I need to get something out of Piers' study in the flat, but he's at school all day, and he's got the keys with him. Do you have a spare set I could use?'

'Of course, Mrs H,' she replied, pulling open a large drawer and pulling out a set, labelled with a large yellow tag. 'Could you make sure you put them back when you're finished with them, though? I need to account for them all at the end of every day.'

'You star,' she said, trying to hide her surprise at how easy it was. 'Of course, no problem.'

Amelia ran back up the stairs, her adrenaline already pumping, despite knowing how ridiculous it was that she was excited about being given the keys to her own flat. She checked in on Grace, who was still content, staring at herself in a dangling mirror. Then she found the large Chubb key for Piers' study, turned the lock and walked inside.

It was like it was a completely different room to the study she had looked around a few weeks before. There were pieces of paper everywhere, some written on, some crumpled up, some marked with large, angry red crosses. In the corner, a shredder was vomiting strips of A4 out of its bin, down its sides and onto the floor. Amelia walked up to it and looked at the remnants. Some of it was definitely school correspondence, but there seemed to be bank statements and credit card bills there, too. Amelia moved over to the computer, found the key which had been blu-tacked to the back of the screen, removed it and put it in the filing cabinet lock.

Piers was not an ordered filer, it turned out. Some of the

files were so overstuffed that they had fallen off the rails, and many of them were unlabelled. Amelia decided to start at the front and work backwards methodically, looking for anything out of place. Ten minutes later, she was exasperated. There was nothing out of order there. She looked over at the computer, and decided that it was time to see what secrets it held. She turned it on, and it prompted her for a password. Shit, she thought, what the hell would that be? Just like the log-in for online banking, he'd never felt he needed to share it with her. She considered the options. First try: Grace. No joy. Second try: Amelia. No, of course not. Third try: Sebastian. Bingo! Amelia thanked the heavens that Piers wasn't too anal about computer security.

She examined his emails. These appeared normal; they were mostly either from his mother (many of them, she noticed, not replied to) or from school parents, asking about weekends away, homework requirements and reports of bullying. And then she examined his search history, which was full of school-related sites, some pages about foster to adopt guidelines, as well as a site offering help to fathers who are being pursued for child support.

Amelia raised an eyebrow at that, and then looked around her. Had he shredded all the letters he'd been getting? Had he successfully covered his tracks? And then she thought about Lesley's advice. Search the house, she'd said. He'll have hidden things somewhere you wouldn't think to look.

Amelia switched the computer off, closed the filing cabinet, put the key back where she'd found it, and locked the study. He'd never know she'd been in there, she thought, wondering now whether he'd left it open and tidy the previous time for her benefit, to try to put her off the scent.

She went into the bedroom and began searching his clothes drawers, under their mattress and behind the furniture. Nothing. Next, she looked in the lounge, where Grace was now asleep in the bouncer. She searched under the sofa cushions, behind books in the bookcase and underneath the rug. Still nothing. After that, she moved on to the kitchen, where she looked in all of the tins in the cupboard, and then into Grace's nursery, searching every single drawer, but drew a blank. Perhaps there's nothing to find after all, she thought.

There was only one place left. Amelia stared up at the loft hatch. Would he really put something up there? It would be a huge effort to get up there, but then, she'd never look in there, would she? Piers always put stuff away up there, not her.

There was only one way to find out whether she was right, she thought, going into their bedroom to find the pole that opened the hatch and pulled down the ladder. Piers had last been in there when they'd been putting away Christmas decorations. As far as she knew, no one had been up there since.

She climbed up the ladder and flicked on the light. It was fairly tidy and ordered; her paintings were stacked up on one side, covered with a dust sheet. On the other side was a pile of boxes, mostly of belongings they'd both brought into the relationship, which hadn't fitted in the apartment. They looked entirely undisturbed – they and the floor around them were coated in dust.

Then Amelia's eyes fell on the special box she'd given Piers to store up there, the one she had put Leila's dress in. It was stashed away neatly in the corner behind her, so she had to twist to see it. Its lid looked a little less dusty than the other boxes around it, and there were traces of footprints leading to it. She pulled herself up to standing and walked carefully over to the box – she was never sure whether to trust the boards in this loft – and lifted the lid.

When she saw what was inside, she felt bile rise up into her mouth. Sitting on top of the beautiful, delicate, tiny dress she'd folded so carefully were several small plastic bags with what looked like white powder inside.

That was bad enough.

But alongside these were two things she had long given up all hope of finding – her treasured Father Christmas ornament and her car keys.

She held each previously missing object in turn, absorbing as she did so the deliberate, cruel act that had brought them there. She couldn't believe it. Piers had actually stolen these things from her and put them here, with Leila's dress. Was he trying to convince her that she was mad? And why had he chosen this box, of all of the boxes in this loft? It was as if he had chosen the one place that would hurt her the most.

Next to the objects was a folded note.

She reached in and picked up the note and began to read.

Dear Mr Howard,

I am sorry about coming to see you today. I know what I did was wrong. But I can't keep away, I really can't. I think about you all of the time, and what we did... I think I am in love with you. Sorry if that is shocking. But I think you feel the same. Please email me and let me know you have read this, I can't live without you.

Love,

Julia.

Before coming up into the loft, Amelia had thought that she had found out so many hideous things about her husband in the past twenty-four hours that she was now numb to them all – but it turned out that she had been very, very wrong about that.

This extra piece of information was confirmation of a behaviour so monstrous that she was momentarily winded and unsteady on her feet. She grabbed the box and crawled slowly backwards down through the hatch and onto the floor downstairs, where she curled up into a foetal position, and howled. Like a baby, she was screaming to block out the rest of the world, yelling to anaesthetise her soul.

'Are you okay, Mrs Howard? I heard a terrible noise,' said Mrs Collins, calling up the stairs. Shit, thought Amelia – how could she explain this?

'I'm okay,' she replied, her voice breaking. 'I just fell down the loft ladder, that's all.'

'Oh, heavens,' said Mrs Collins, running up the stairs. 'Let me look at you. Is there anything broken?'

'I don't think so,' Amelia answered. 'I think I'm just shocked.'

'Let me help you to your feet. Can you get up?'

'Yes, I think so,' she said, wiping her eyes to try to hide the extent of her tears and then allowing herself to be helped up to a standing position. 'I think I'll just go and take a seat in the lounge with Grace,' she said. 'I just need a sit down, that's all.'

'Well, all right, my dear, but I'll go and get you a cup of tea, shall I, while you catch your breath?'

'Thank you, Mrs C,' replied Amelia.

She watched Mrs Collins walk down the stairs before heading into the bathroom. There, she opened the box, took out what she assumed was cocaine and thrust it into her pocket. Then she walked slowly to the lounge and sat down on the sofa. She looked over at Grace who was still, mercifully, asleep. She would need a feed soon, Amelia thought; even in the depths of despair, she couldn't forget the tiny human being who, at least for the time being, needed her. That thought helped her bring herself back to something approximating normality. She needed to get out of here, she thought. She needed to put some distance between herself and Piers while she decided what to do next.

'Here you go, Mrs Howard,' said the house matron, bringing her a cup of tea and a biscuit. 'Look, it's nearly lunchtime. I'll bring you up some lunch, shall I? And then shall I stay with you for a bit? Do you want some company?'

But Amelia knew exactly who she wanted to see. She wanted

to see someone who knew her a long time ago; someone who knew who she really was at her core, before all of the shit of the past decade had begun to send her mad.

'It's okay, Mrs Collins,' Amelia replied, her earlier resolve beginning to return. 'I'm going to give a friend a call.'

The sky was a steely grey when she parked the car outside the strip of Georgian workers' cottages. She wondered if it might snow. She also wondered, not for the first time in that short drive, whether this was a stupid thing to do. She hadn't called first. What if he was busy? After all, he taught, didn't he, and he had services to play at? But she told herself that if he wasn't there, she'd call Rachel instead. Both she and Jake would most likely be at work, she thought, but she reckoned they might come home an hour or two early for her, or give her a key so that she could wait in their house. She simply couldn't face going home, because when she did that, she'd have to address the long list of horrors in her marriage. Where on earth would she even start?

Amelia removed the car seat from the back seat of the car, picked up the changing bag and walked up to the front door, took a deep breath, and knocked. All fears that he might not be in were extinguished by footsteps in the hall, and the door swinging wide open within seconds.

'Amelia! How wonderful. What a nice surprise. Do come in,' said Mark.

'Thank you,' she said, picking up Grace and walking into the cottage. 'Thank you.'

'Now, to what do I owe this honour?' asked Mark, his face a broad smile. 'Are you okay? You look a bit… tired?' he said.

'Shocked,' she corrected him, sitting down on the sofa and placing Grace down on the floor next to her. 'I'm shocked. Very.'

'Oh, crap,' he said, loitering by the kitchen door. 'Have you had the court verdict?'

'No, not yet. That will happen later. It's not that.'

'Oh. Right. Then what is it? If you want to say… please don't feel you have to…'

Amelia decided she was simply tired of hiding things.

'It's Piers. I married the wrong man, you see,' she said, now laughing hysterically. 'Or rather, the man I thought I married doesn't exist.'

'Right, okay,' said Mark, still standing a significant distance away from her, Amelia noticed, as if she had something catching. 'I'm sorry to hear that.'

'Yes, I'm sorry to have to say it,' she replied. 'But there we are.'

There was a brief silence then, during which Mark disappeared into the kitchen, and reappeared with two open bottles of beer.

'I'm afraid we finished my whisky supplies last time,' he said. 'So I hope this will suffice?'

Amelia laughed again, loudly this time, and took a bottle from him. 'Yes, whatever,' she said. 'I'll take anything, frankly.'

'So tell me…' said Mark, sitting down at the other end of the sofa '… what on earth has been going on.'

'Piers is cheating on me,' she said, feeling her initial shock repeat on her as she said it out loud for the first time. 'With a teenager.'

'A… teenager? Are you sure?'

'Yes, I'm sure. The poor thing thinks they're in love,' she said, taking a large swig from the bottle.

'Ah.'

'But that's not all.'

'No?'

'He's taking drugs. Lots of drugs.'

'Shit. Are you sure? That's… I can't quite believe it…'

'No, neither can I. But he is. I found his stash.'

'Where?'

'In a box... A special box, in the loft. The bastard has been storing his secrets in the box I bought to store a dress I bought for our stillborn daughter.'

Amelia gulped down some beer to try to wash away the bitter taste in her mouth. She knew instinctively why he'd done it. It was a final act of control over her, to defile one of the only things she really cared about.

'What did you do, then? When you found the drugs?'

She reached into her pocket and pulled out the bags of powder and showed them to Mark.

'Are you going to tell anyone about it?' he said, his eyes bulging.

'I don't know.'

'*Fuck*,' said Mark, leaning towards her. He looked like he didn't know whether to offer her a handshake, or a stroke on her arm, or a peck on her cheek, but he definitely did look like he was trying to comfort her, she thought. She leaned forward and solved his dilemma by nestling her head into his neck. He didn't flinch when she did so, so she shuffled a little closer to him, so that their elbows were touching. It felt nice, she thought. Comforting. They stayed like that for some time, long enough for Amelia to finish her bottle of beer, before either of them spoke.

'I have wanted to do this with you for forever,' said Mark, suddenly and quietly.

'I'm *sorry*?' said Amelia, springing away from him. She was unsure if she'd misheard – the beer was beginning, she thought, to go to her head.

'I have always wanted to be close to you,' he said, a little louder this time.

'*Oh*.' Amelia suddenly felt incredibly awkward. She tried to move a little further away from him on the sofa.

'It's fine, I know I'm just a friend, and that's great, being friends with you is amazing. You're married, and I am... just a mate. But that's so much better than being someone you haven't even really noticed at school, so...'

'Oh Mark, I'm so sorry. I feel so bad about that. I wasn't really very confident myself at school, you see, so...'

'Sorry. Ignore me. Shall I get another beer?' he said, standing up and turning away from her, as if he was ashamed to exist. Amelia felt overwhelmingly guilty. She'd felt like that many times in her life, too.

'No, it's my fault, I shouldn't have... got so close to you. I was giving you the wrong idea,' she said.

'No, it's *my* fault...'

'Actually, come to think of it, yes, please do get me another beer,' Amelia said. Oh *fuck*, what do I say now, she thought. *I have enough problems, heaven knows...*

'Look, umm... so let's get back to what we were talking about before,' said Mark, and Amelia was pleased that he was changing the subject. 'Tell me more about Piers. When did you first notice things weren't right? You seemed so happy together.'

'Yes,' replied Amelia. 'We definitely looked that way. But I am getting the feeling that it's been wrong for a very long time, but I was too much of a twonk to see it.'

'I like that word, twonk,' said Mark.

'Me too,' said Amelia, laughing suddenly, and holding her bottle up, as if to say cheers. 'And thank you, for making me chuckle. I needed that today. You're a good friend, Mark.'

Mark smiled. She also saw a hint of disappointment in his face, too, but tried to ignore it. She couldn't process how she felt about Mark today. That would have to wait.

'But seriously... you're not to blame for any of Piers' behaviour, you know. He's an adult, in charge of his own actions. We all are. And for what it's worth, I have absolutely zero idea why he'd ever consider cheating on you.'

Amelia held his gaze for just a second too long, and then

pulled her focus away, determined not to allow the situation to escalate further. Instead, she looked at his slim torso, so different from Piers' muscular physique, and his face, which was sporting three-day-old, I-can't-quite-be-bothered-to-shave, stubble.

'Thank you,' she said, hugging her beer bottle to her chest. 'That's very kind of you, but you have no idea how I am at home. What do they say? You can't ever tell what's going on in a marriage unless you're actually in it.'

'No, that's true,' he replied. 'Now… shall we watch something ludicrously funny and totally inane for a bit? I have the boxset of *'Allo 'Allo*.'

'Perfect,' she said, relieved that this would mean the conversation was over.

'Another beer?' Mark asked, and she nodded.

It was dark when the phone rang. It took Amelia a while to register it, because she was laughing too hard at the troupe of talented actors squeezing every last innuendo out of a scene involving a sausage, a cow and a hearse.

'Is that your phone?' asked Mark, several bottles of beer down now, and very merry.

'Oh, shit, yes, it must be,' said Amelia, who was holding Grace with one arm, and drinking her third bottle of beer slowly with the other. She placed the bottle down on the floor and rummaged around in the changing bag, finally retrieving her phone from underneath a stash of nappies.

It was Piers. And just like that, that afternoon's mirage of warmth, friendship and fun disappeared in an instant. She had – for a very brief period – forgotten that her husband had actually violently shaken her, and the fact that they were expecting the court verdict that afternoon. But there was no running away from it, was there? She could ignore the call, but then another would come, and another, and eventually, eventually, the message would get through to her, wouldn't it? However much she ran?

Amelia took a deep breath and answered.

33

Michelle

Final hearing, Day 2: afternoon

'Thank you, all of you, for taking part in this very important hearing over the past two days, and for your patience and honesty,' said Judge Joshi, her bifocals pushed up her nose, her notes spread out on the desk in front of her.

'I have listened to everything you have all had to say, and I have read all of your written submissions in detail. I have now come to my decision, which I must add was a difficult one. I can see how much all of the adults in this case – the father, the mother, the social workers – believe strongly that their way is the right way.

'However, it is impossible to ignore the fact that at the centre of this case is a baby. She is entirely unaware of all of this, and that's probably for the best. My aim throughout this process is to reach a decision relatively quickly, so that Grace is able to be placed in her permanent home before she is old enough to be adversely affected by the change.

'I am also deeply aware of the feelings of the foster parents in this case, who set out on that fostering journey hoping to become Grace's parents. Although they have not been in court with us, they have also been in my thoughts, and their predicament also played a part in my decision.

'Ladies and gentlemen, it is my decision that Grace Jenkins should be returned to her birth mother, Michelle Jenkins.'

As the judge paused before explaining her reasoning, Michelle's heart began to beat so hard, she thought the entire room would be able to hear it. *Did she really say what I think she said*, she thought. A squeeze of her hand from Sally, gasps from the row behind, and a sigh of rage from the other end of the table suggested, however, that she had heard correctly.

Oh my *God*, she thought. *She's mine. Forever.*

'Why have I decided this?' the judge continued. 'Because, as I have said all along, this case is about Grace – her safety, first and foremost, but also her happiness. And as you know, the court always tries to keep families together if it can, and I am convinced that Miss Jenkins is in a good position now to bring up her daughter, and the support that she needs to do this is in place. I urge her to accept all help she is offered. I am also going to advise that contact with the birth father should be formalised, initially twice a week. In terms of returning Grace to her mother, social services will now need to inform the foster parents of the decision and plan a suitable phased handover.

'Thank you, ladies and gentlemen. That's all for today.'

Michelle watched the judge gather her things and head back out of the door from whence she had come the day before. When she had left the court and the door had shut behind her, the volume in the court shot up exponentially.

'*I knew we could do it, I knew we could*,' said Sally, jumping to her feet and pumping her fists in the air. 'Take that, Len Carraway,' she said, looking across at the barrister, who was in close conference with Rob.

Michelle wanted to stay and celebrate with Sally – after all, she'd made a huge difference to her case – but she had someone else she needed to see. She almost ran out of the court and into the lobby, and over to where Gillian was sitting, shouting '*We did it! Grace is coming home.*'

Gillian heard her words, leapt up from her seat and threw her arms around Michelle.

'*You clever girl,*' she said. 'I told you you could do it.'

Michelle turned around to see the court door open and Rob and his lawyer walked down the hallway to where his parents were waiting. They'd be disappointed, Michelle thought, not to have won themselves a shiny new trophy. But at least Rob could see Grace now, if he wanted to. It would be interesting, she thought, to see if he actually did.

Next out of the court was Marion Stone, who gave her a polite smile as she left at some speed, and after her, Gloria and Laura. Gloria looked slightly shocked, Michelle thought; she waved in Michelle's direction, said she'd be in touch very soon, and left, citing work reasons. Only Laura came over to speak to her.

'Well done,' said Laura, sounding, Michelle decided, quite genuine. 'I have wanted you to win for a long time.'

'But you went along with what the council wanted…'

'I had to do that, for my job. My boss said it was the right thing, and so, yes, that was our policy. But when I saw how you were with her, and how you'd changed so much of your life – I wanted it for you, I really did.'

'Thanks,' said Michelle. '*Thanks.*'

'And I was glad Mrs Wilcocks turned out for you,' said Laura. 'She took a bit of persuading.'

'Do you mean it was you who asked her to come?' said Michelle. 'I thought it was Sally…'

'It was me who tipped her off that she'd be a good witness,' said Laura, looking sheepish. 'I spoke to her first, too, to check she wouldn't mind me giving her number to your lawyer.'

'Well, thanks,' said Michelle. 'That was... really kind of you.'

'No problem. Any time,' she said. 'Oh, and I am meant to ask you – Rob has said he doesn't want to return to the council flat. It could be yours, if you want it? We could get it cleaned and decorated?'

Michelle thought back to the pain she'd endured in that flat.

'Nah, it's okay. I think I'll stay with Gillian and Mike for now, and then look for my own place in a bit. With your help, maybe?'

'That would be absolutely fine. Always happy to help,' replied Laura, smiling. 'In the meantime, we need to clear out the flat so that we can give it to another family. If you need things from it, I'd suggest you go in the next day or so.'

'I could take you now, if you like,' said Gillian, who had been gathering her things together, and was now standing next to Laura and Michelle. 'We could go on the way home?'

'Yeah, why not,' replied Michelle. 'I've got to get stuff ready for Grace now, haven't I? I've got loads to sort.'

'Yes, you do,' replied Laura. 'Gloria will call you, I think tomorrow, to arrange when Grace will be brought to you, and how. It's usually gradual, a few hours a day for a week, that sort of thing, before she's with you permanently. But she'll call you, as I say.'

'Okay, ta,' said Michelle. 'Shall we head off, Gill?'

'One more thing,' said Laura. 'Was the letter good news? The one I brought you?'

'It was ace,' replied Michelle. '*The best*. Thanks.'

'I'm delighted,' said Laura, the relief clear in her voice. 'Really, really delighted.'

Michelle watched as Laura turned away with a smile and headed for the exit.

'Chelle?' said a voice behind her. She swung around. Rob had broken off from the intense conversation he had been having with his parents, and had walked over to where Michelle was standing.

'I'm... sorry,' he said. His voice was more like the old Rob, now. Gone were the posh inflections – the Worcestershire lilt was back. You fake, *fake* man, she thought.

'For which bit?' she replied. 'For lying about who you are? For letting us practically starve and freeze to death when *Mummy and Daddy* could have bailed you out? For taking your anger and frustration out on me in bruises and mind games? Or for *leaving me for dead*?'

'All of it,' he said, looking down at the floor. 'I'm not proud of myself, Chelle.'

'No,' she replied, aware that Gill was standing by her side like a close protection officer, her stare boring virtual holes into Rob's skull.

'I do want to do right by you. By you and Grace. I'm going to get a job working for my dad, so...'

I should be *feeling* something, she thought to herself. I was with him for years. Why am I not sad? Regretful? Elated? Maybe, just maybe, she thought, I've experienced so much pain because of this man, I've reached my limit.

'Great. I guess the council will be in touch about child support,' she replied, genuinely pleased that he might be able to contribute to her weekly budget, which would certainly be tight for a bit.

'Okay...'

'And you'll be able to see Grace if you want. Social services will arrange it.'

'Yeah...'

He looked like he was moving towards her. For a hug, maybe? She wasn't going to stay around and risk it.

'I'm going to go now, all right? Are you ready, Gill?'

'Yes, ready,' said Gill, her chest puffed up so high, Michelle was surprised she could still see.

'Great. See you around, Rob,' said Michelle, walking away with Gill at her side. She did not look back. In fact, she found that she didn't even want to look back.

As they walked down the stairs towards the exit, Gill leaned over and gave her a squeeze.

'*Onwards*,' Gill said.

'Yes, onwards,' she replied, imagining the future laying itself out in front of her with each forward step.

'I think the power's off.'

'Yeah, I think the meter is empty. Rob didn't pay the bill.'

Michelle and Gillian were standing in the hallway of her old apartment. Gillian had just tried, and failed, to turn the lights on. It was now 5 p.m., and it was pitch black outside and close to freezing. It was also absolutely freezing inside the flat, and it stank of fags, and dust, and... God knows what, Michelle thought. But it was bad, really bad. How on earth could she have ever lived like this, she wondered?

'We could use the light on my phone to find stuff?' she suggested, keen at that moment to get out of the flat as quickly as possible.

'No, let's do this properly,' said Gillian. 'Is this a prepayment meter? Can't we just buy a top-up?'

'Yeah, you can get them from the shop around the corner,' replied Michelle.

'Fine, then, let's do that. Come on. We need heat and light for this, if we're going to do it properly.'

Michelle and Gillian walked around the corner of the building to the short strip of shops – a small pharmacy, a betting shop, and Mr Chaudhury's shop. As they walked, tiny flakes of snow began to fall. Michelle looked up at the dense, dark sky, pregnant with a million sister flakes, and instinctively poked her tongue out to taste one. Gillian looked over and saw her, laughed, and did the same. Seconds later, they were both running around in circles on the paved forecourt as the snow became heavier and heavier, settling on their arms and shoulders, forming a tiara of ephemeral diamonds on their heads.

Childish joy fully exercised, they arrived outside Chaudhury's with bright red cheeks, broad grins and clouds of vapour emitting with their every breath. Michelle pushed the door open to the familiar shop but paused when she saw who was behind the till. She had been hoping that it would be one of his sons, nieces or nephews, but no, it was Mr Chaudhury himself who was on shift that night. Shit, she thought – I feel far too guilty to look him in the eye.

Gillian pushed past her then and walked up to the till, unaware of how Michelle was feeling. 'Hello,' she said to Mr Chaudhury, 'we need a top-up, for the electricity, for my friend Michelle's flat. What's it called, Michelle – is it the key thingie?'

Mr Chaudhury looked over at Michelle and smiled. 'Miss Michelle, it's wonderful to see you back, and looking so well, too. How are you doing?'

'I'm a lot better, thank you, Mr Chaudhury,' she replied. 'I'm sorry for… you finding me there…'

'Oh, it was not a bother at all,' he said. 'I am glad I could help.'

'So you two know each other?' asked Gillian, with surprise.

'Yeah. Mr Chaudhury was there… when the ambulance came, you know? But I've been coming here for years,' Michelle said. 'I bought my first stuff here, food and that, when I first left care.'

'I remember it well,' said Mr Chaudhury. 'Very well. You were very polite, and very friendly. Yes, I have always remembered that.'

Suddenly, the guilt overwhelmed Michelle. She had stolen from this man, and here he was being friendly, and kind.

'Mr Chaudhury, I wanted to say,' she said, aware that Gillian was there, and that what she was about to say might alter how she viewed her, 'I haven't always paid for everything I've taken from this shop. I...'

'Oh, my dear, I know.'

Michelle was dumbstruck.

'You... know?'

'Yes, I know. But I could also see that you were struggling, you know, and you were not taking expensive things, anyway. So I didn't say anything.'

'I'll pay you back. I will, honestly, when I get a job.'

'Yes, yes. That's fine. Whenever you are ready. Honestly,' he said. 'I am just, as I say, happy to help.'

Michelle was close to tears. Gillian noticed, and stepped in. 'You're a good man,' said Gillian. 'Thank you so much for looking after my Michelle, when she really needed it.'

'Not at all, madam,' he said. 'Not at all. Are you, may I ask, a family member of Michelle's?'

'Oh no, not really,' she replied. 'I'm a foster...'

'She's my... foster mum,' replied Michelle, with confidence. 'Yes. *This is Gillian, my foster mum.*'

Gillian swept Michelle in her arms after she'd said that, and they both stood there for five wonderful seconds, hugging in the middle of Chaudhury's megamarket, next to the tins of beans, the stack of loo rolls and the ice cream freezer.

'Great, well, that's lovely,' said Mr Chaudhury, in his most business-like voice. 'May I ask would you like a ten-pound or a twenty-pound top-up? With twenty, you get a free bag of pork scratchings this week. It's on special.'

34

Amelia

Grace was stirring. From her position in the hard, upright chair in the corner – usually used as a dumping ground for clean clothes – Amelia had been watching her sleeping soundly for hours. Grace's breaths had been shallow and rhythmic, barely discernible beneath the thick sleeping bag she had tenderly placed her in the night before, her eyes awash with tears. Now, however, Grace was growing restless, wriggling within the bag's confines, stretching her arms above her head as if surrendering to the day.

Amelia stood up and walked over to the window. It was 7 a.m. and still dark outside, but the thick layer of snow that was now lining the streets and gardens outside gave the orange streetlights a brighter glow. Round about now, the boys would be waking up in their dormitories, spying the snow and racing each other to get dressed and out of the house, desperate to be the first to land a snowball.

Amelia had watched the snow fall all night. She had tried to sleep at first but had eventually realised that it was destined to evade her. Too much had happened in one day for her brain to relinquish control; it was still full of Piers' betrayal, of course, but mostly, Grace's impending removal.

Gloria had phoned Piers with the news at 5 p.m. the previous day, and he had duly phoned Amelia. She'd been several beers down at Mark's house, of course, and Piers had been furious about that, especially because he'd had to pay for a taxi to bring them both home. Mostly, though, he had been furious that Grace was going to be taken away from them, and in that, she was with him, at least.

She could barely believe it, even though it was exactly what she had been fearing since Grace had been brought into their lives. The news just seemed too shocking, too monstrous to be real. And yet it clearly was, because they'd had an email confirming it, too, and she was expecting another call from Gloria in an hour or two, to explain how they wanted to arrange the 'handover'. But then, she had other ideas about that.

Grace was awake now, but not yet crying. Amelia leaned over the crib, picked her up gently and carried her into the kitchen, to make up her morning bottle. On the way, she looked in on Piers, who was fast asleep. He'd been a cat on hot bricks for most of the previous evening; she was amazed he'd managed to drop off at all.

It had been a frosty night, both outside and inside. They had barely spoken. She'd reheated some leftovers and served them up for dinner – but neither of them had eaten much – and then he had spent most of the evening locked in his study, which had been something of a relief to her. She had nothing to say to him at this point. Given the ton of bricks that had just landed upon them both, she decided she'd have to wait before tackling the problems in their marriage. Grace had to leave them first.

Amelia screwed the top on Grace's bottle – she'd learned now to do everything one-handed – and walked into the lounge and sat down on the sofa. She'd been there for a few minutes, Grace's swallowing the only noise in the room, when their bed creaked, footsteps padded their way around the room, and their bedroom door opened.

'Amelia?' he said, looking in the lounge. 'Oh, there you are. I wondered.'

'I couldn't sleep,' she said. 'You know…'

'Yeah, I know,' he said, coming into the room and joining her on the sofa. He leaned across to kiss her on the cheek and she flinched.

He didn't notice. He wasn't really there in the present either, she realised. Neither of them was.

'I can't face having to say goodbye to her every day for a week, or two weeks, Piers,' said Amelia.

'What do you mean?'

'I can't face the idea of a phased handover. It would be like having somebody rip off a sticking plaster a millimetre at a time every day, over an open wound. It will hurt more if we do it that way. I'm sure of it.'

'So what are you saying?'

'She should go today,' said Amelia, feeling an acute sense of loss the very minute she'd said it. But she still knew it was the right thing to do.

'But we haven't spoken to a lawyer. We could maybe appeal?'

'The decision is final, Piers. You and I both know that. We've lost. She isn't ours anymore. She never was.'

'No,' he said, sweeping his hand over his hair, which was uncharacteristically messy. Then she saw that there were tears in his eyes. After years of playing the bullish alpha male, he now appeared to actually be imploding. But instead of comforting him, she remained where she was, feeding Grace. There was no way in hell she was getting any closer than this to him again, ever, she thought. A few minutes later, Piers got up and left the room.

'Are you absolutely certain about this?' Gloria asked. She was standing in the front hall, surrounded by bags of clothes, a baby bouncer and a huge box of toys. 'We can do this gradually, you know. It might be easier that way?'

'No,' said Amelia, her voice flat. This was an evil she had to banish quickly. Postponing the inevitable would not make it go away. 'Take her now.'

She had dressed Grace with elaborate care, rubbing cream into every crease in her legs, kissing her tummy as she did up her snap vest, rolled up her striped tights and smoothed her knitted dress down over her podgy arms and body. She had stared at her then, a long intense stare, trying to capture every detail of her so that she could recall her whenever she needed. Then she leaned down and inhaled her smell, which was a combination of baby bath, nappy cream, washing powder and milk. Then finally she sat back and watched Grace wave her feet in the air and catch them with her hands – a trick she had only recently mastered.

The doorbell had rung shortly afterwards. Amelia had gone to answer it. Piers was nowhere to be seen, although he knew that Grace was leaving. He had gone in to see her in the nursery before he'd left for work, as if it was a completely normal day, and had left without saying a word to Amelia. It was as if, now they were no longer parents, they had nothing in common anymore. Or perhaps, thought Amelia, simply that he was in so much pain, he couldn't bring himself to speak.

And so it was that she was alone when Gloria arrived to collect Grace. Amelia had packed up as many clothes as she could, along with a few of her toys and accessories, like her bottles and bouncer. As she had stripped the cot bed, her gaze lingered over a small reindeer soft toy, Rudolph, they had bought Grace for Christmas. He had become a favourite, something for Grace to wrap her fingers around when she was trying to go to sleep. She'd often walk in to check on her and find the reindeer's antlers thrust up against Grace's nose or mouth, like comforting hands. Amelia had picked it up, thrust it in her back pocket and kept on clearing. Rudolph was destined to be the last toy standing.

'Take her. *Now*,' she repeated.

Gloria stepped forward. Amelia took a deep breath, gave Grace a lingering kiss on her forehead and then handed her cherished little body over to the social worker. Gloria took her, turned around swiftly, picked the car seat up from the floor by her feet, and carried them both out to her car. Amelia brushed aside the first tear – destined, she knew, to be one of many – and wrapped her cardigan more tightly around her waist.

It was freezing outside, but Amelia wanted to stay until she was out of sight. So she stood there in the doorway of the house watching Gloria load the bags and boxes into the car, rushing to get inside before the snow – which had recently begun falling again after a brief respite – made their driveway too difficult to navigate. The car was loaded within minutes, and, satisfied that Grace was safely loaded, Gloria looked back at the door of the house and gave Amelia a wave.

'I'll be in touch,' she shouted, 'to let you know how she gets on.'

Amelia nodded in response, afraid that if she tried to speak, she'd yell for her to *stop*, and *not to take her*. Every cell in her body wanted to run after that car and seize her, but she knew that that was madness. She had to accept what the judge had decided, and, like Leila's stillbirth, this was yet another pain that she was just going to have to confront and live with.

Amelia watched as the social worker's car made its way slowly to the gate, its tyres making tracks in the snow. As it turned left and headed up into town, she noticed that the snowfall was intensifying. By the time she'd shut the door and headed back to their dark, empty flat, the car's tracks had vanished.

* * *

Three hours later, Amelia was standing in the hallway of their apartment, surrounded by bags and boxes filled with her own belongings. She simply could not face another night near Piers, and this seemed to her now to be the only sensible option. Separating her stuff out from his, and deciding what to take, had felt like a sort of cleansing and it had also distracted her from the hideous pain she felt every time she remembered Grace being taken away, and that was far more vital.

She had decided to send Piers a text message telling him she'd left him a note in the flat. It would be several more hours before he arrived back home and read her lengthy letter, in which she laid out what she'd discovered about his activities, and what she had decided to do.

But now, however, she needed somewhere to go. She grabbed her thickest coat, boots, hat and scarf and began the short walk across town to her father's flat.

'Dad?' she called out as she opened his front door.

'In the lounge,' he said, replying instantly. Amelia said a silent prayer of thanks for whoever convinced him to finally use his hearing aids. She needed him to hear her, today of all days.

Her father was sitting looking out of the window at the snow. 'It's beautiful, isn't it?' he said when he saw her approaching. 'Do you remember when it snowed so heavily, they had to close the school early for Christmas? You and your mum built a huge snowman and dressed it in school uniform. Do you remember?'

Amelia didn't reply. Instead, she sat on the floor by her father's feet, and let out the tears and howls she'd been suppressing since she'd watched Grace being driven out of her life, forever.

'Darling, *darling*. What's wrong?' he said, patting her on the head.

Amelia didn't know how to respond, or even if she was capable of it. Her father had never been very good at emotional conversations; the best he'd managed on her wedding day had been a pat on the back, and a 'you look lovely, darling'. But he was all she had left of family, and right now, the only person she wanted to see.

'She's gone, Dad. Grace has gone,' she said, quietly. 'The judge said she could go back to live with her birth mother.'

'Oh darling. I'm so sorry,' he said. 'She was a lovely little girl.'

'Yes,' she said, reaching into her pocket for a tissue.

'And I know how happy she made you. And that was so lovely, because I always want to see you happy.'

'Yes. She did.'

'Do you think you and Piers will try to adopt again? Or is it too soon for that?'

Amelia stared out of the window at the falling snow, trying to think of the right words to explain the car crash that was now her marriage.

'I don't think so, no. I'm not sure we would cope with that,' she said.

'Oh? Are there problems at home, Amelia?'

'I think there might be, Dad. I think there might be.'

They both sat there in silence for a few moments, watching an enterprising robin trying to crack the ice in the water dish on the bird table.

'Do you think it's going to brighten up in the next day or so?' her father asked, without a hint of irony, or acknowledgement of the importance of what she'd just said.

Amelia laughed, despite the angst she was feeling. In a way, she was relieved, for this was how her father had always been, and this was how he always would be. Here, at least, there was consistency and normality. She had no desire to talk to him about her marital problems. It was simply enough that he knew things were not great.

'I think it might stop snowing this evening,' she said, still looking out of the window, before adding – 'Can I come and stay here for a bit, Dad?'

'Of course, darling,' he said. 'Is it that bad?'

'Yes,' she replied, still deliberately not looking at him. She couldn't shake the shame that her marriage had failed, even now.

'Then, of course,' he replied, sounding as if she'd just asked him to put the kettle on, or whether he fancied a custard cream. 'Although I won't be here for much longer, I think.'

Amelia turned around and looked at her father. 'What do you mean? You're not dying, Dad, are you?'

Her father chuckled.

'We're all dying, my dear,' he replied. 'But no. At least, not yet. No, I meant to tell you – I've applied for a space in those new assisted living flats they're building up near Link Top. I quite fancy the view there, and it will be nice to know there's someone on hand all of the time, just in case. It will also mean you don't have to come and check on your old dad too often. I'm sure you have many more interesting things to do.'

'But I love you, Dad…'

'I know you do, darling. But you have your own life to lead. And so do I. As I say, I'm not dead yet.'

'No. Of course not.'

'Well, then.'

'So can I bring my stuff around and stay tonight?'

'You can stay as many nights as you like, darling, until I move.'

'Thank you.'

'Don't be silly.'

Amelia gave herself a mental and physical brush down, and stood up, wiping her eyes with her sleeves.

'I'll see you later, then?' she said.

'Yes.'

She walked out of the room and into the entrance hall.

'Amelia?' her father called out.

'Yes?' she replied.

'Could you bring some milk, when you come? I think we've only got a pint.'

Amelia smiled and closed the door behind her.

Amelia could see the grey, acrid smoke billowing up into the early afternoon sky before she'd even turned into the drive of the boarding house. It was not at all the weather for a garden fire, she thought, beginning to panic. Was the house on fire? She broke out into a run, fearing the worst.

It was only when she'd got closer to the building that it became obvious that the house was not the source of the flames. Instead, she could see that a small bonfire had been lit in the back garden. She ran around the side of the house and saw that Piers was out there, feeding it.

He was wearing jeans and a thin cotton shirt, with his sleeves rolled up. His face was lit up by the flames; the flickering orange light rendering his eyes hollow and his mouth a black hole. From her position at least ten metres away, Amelia could see that he had a pile of objects behind him and he was methodically picking them up, one by one, and placing them on top of the fire. As she got closer, she could see that they were her belongings.

'You absolute bastard,' she screamed, running up to him. '*You absolute fucking bastard*.' She reached out and grabbed a bag he was just about to put on the fire and tussled with him for it. He was too strong, however – he wrenched it out of her hands and threw it on the fire, and she watched, devastated, as the nylon bag began to melt and its contents, some of her clothes, became consumed by flames and smoke.

'I didn't think you'd want any of this shit,' he said, looking straight at her with a look that frightened her. 'Anyway, I bought it all for you, so I can do what I like with it. And you never looked good in it anyway.'

Amelia realised that Piers had bought her those clothes – every single one of them. He had been dressing her in clothes even *he* didn't like. Clothes that made her look like a dull, strait-laced headmaster's wife, perhaps?

'Did you marry me just because of Dad?' she asked, suddenly realising.

'What?'

'Did you marry me because you thought it would make it easier for you to get promoted?'

'Seriously? You reckon you have that much influence on anything? You're pathetic,' he said, throwing another bag in.

Amelia looked towards the house, where she could just make out the faces of some of the boarders, who were no doubt enjoying this unscheduled horror show. She suddenly thought about her art collection, which was, she hoped, still in the loft.

'Oh, don't worry about your paintings. I left them there,' he said, reading her mind. 'They don't deserve to be seen by anyone anyway. I might slash them to pieces later.' Piers laughed, a sound that seemed to fill the darkness.

'I know about the drugs, Piers.'

Amelia saw a flicker of fear in Piers' eyes.

'Bully for you. Loads of people take cocaine, Amelia. We're not all trussed up, frigid people like you.'

Amelia thought back to the nights she'd submitted to sex with him, even when she'd been grieving or exhausted, and the rage inside her grew.

'*And* I know that you're refusing to pay for Sebastian. Lesley told me.'

'That bitch is a liar.'

'Is Julia lying, too?'

Piers stopped what he was doing – reaching into the pile behind him for a box of her books – and stood stock still, staring at her.

'Oh, she's been making stuff up, has she? She's a sad little girl, fantasising about an older man. It happens all the time. No one will believe her.'

'I *saw* the message she wrote to you, Piers.'

Piers laughed.

'Oh, did you like my joke, by the way? Putting Julia's little declaration of love in that box containing all of your failed hopes and dreams? It felt poetic. Anyway, you left it behind in the box, didn't you? I've destroyed it now. No one will believe it existed.'

So he's been in the loft, she thought. *He went looking for his drugs and he knows I've taken them. And he knows that I've seen the things he stole from me, too.*

'Why did you take those things from me, Piers? The ornament? My keys?'

Piers didn't answer, but she understood in an instant why he had. She realised that he'd known he'd been losing control, and taking those things, things that meant something to her, things that she was very attached to or actually needed for her freedom, had made him feel powerful.

And then she understood why naive, sweet Julia had been so appealing to him. He'd lost control of the woman he'd married, hadn't he, so he needed to replace her with someone he *could* control. Who better than a shy, vulnerable teenager?

'I've still got your drugs, Piers,' she said. 'Your fingerprints will be all over them. And I doubt you'll pass a drugs test today, will you?'

Amelia looked at her husband across the fire. The flames were higher now, and the heat haze was making his features seem to melt. His grimace looked like a clown's frown. Piers turned around then and picked up something else from his pile. It was the box she'd used to store the dress she'd bought for Leila; the one he'd used as a hiding place for his ugliness.

He is not going to take that dress from me, she thought. *He can destroy all of my other belongings, but he will never take that.*

As he moved to throw it in the fire, she launched herself at him with all of the power she could muster. They both fell over in the snow, a cloud of powder exploding around them as they tumbled to the ground. Piers landed first; Amelia landed on top of him, winding him. And as she emitted a huge roar of hatred, of triumph and of freedom, she grabbed the box from his grasp and pulled away, sprang upright and began running down the pathway at speed.

She was fit and she knew he would be unable to catch her. She turned around when she reached the gate and saw that he hadn't even tried. He was just standing there on the lawn in the fading light, glaring at her.

'*I'm calling the headmaster now*,' she yelled. 'So you had better pack *your* bags, too.'

Amelia rang the doorbell, panting, the icy air turning her breath into microscopic crystals. She'd run the whole way.

'Melia?' said Rachel as she answered the door.

'*She's gone*,' said Amelia, still clutching the box to her chest.

'Oh, lovey,' said Rachel. 'I did wonder, when I didn't hear back after I texted you yesterday. I'm so, so sorry.'

'Thank you,' replied Amelia, taking several deep breaths to try to calm herself down. 'It was my decision that Grace went today. They wanted to do it gradually, but I wanted to get the horror over with. And Piers… well, the thing is… Can we chat?'

'Of course,' replied Rachel. 'Come on in, it's freezing out here.'

Amelia followed Rachel down the corridor into the kitchen, where she hit the button on the kettle and pulled two mugs out of the cupboard. The house was warm and smelled of washing powder and toast. Amelia began to relax.

'I'm assuming you'll want tea,' said Rachel, pulling two teabags out of the cupboard. 'Now, tell me everything. If you want to.'

Amelia nodded and put the box down on the kitchen table, before putting her hands on the worktop behind her, leaning back.

'There is just so much to say…'

'Okay, look, let me take these teabags out…' said Rachel, 'and then let's head into the lounge to sit down.'

Amelia watched her as she spooned them out and dumped them in the bin, before picking up the box and following her friend into the living room. They sat down opposite each other on the chairs they'd all sat on just before Christmas, when Grace was sleeping in the car seat, and Piers had got angry when Rachel had asked why Amelia didn't have a job.

'So…' said Rachel, handing Amelia a steaming mug of muddy-brown tea.

Amelia took a deep breath and told her friend everything – about her decision to let Grace go that morning; about Piers not getting the job; about his drug habit and his relationship with Julia.

'Oh shit. I just can't take this in, Amelia. I can't even imagine how you must be feeling. You must be in *shock*, no?'

Amelia thought about that. She felt utterly exhausted by what she'd gone through in the past couple of days, there was no doubt about that. And she *was* shocked, definitely, although not, when she really thought about it, about losing Grace. She had known deep down that that was how that particular story would end.

'I knew Grace would go, I just *knew* it,' she said. 'I've known ever since they told us her mother was contesting – and even before that, to be honest.'

'Oh, lovey,' said Rachel, giving her a hug.

'Thank you,' she said, absorbing the much-needed embrace.

'Honestly, as horrendous as it is – I'm in so much pain, I can't even begin to explain how it feels – I think I've known for a while that my marriage wasn't good enough for Grace. If that judge *had* decided to let her stay with us, what would I be doing now? Could I have kept her, now that I'm leaving Piers? It had to end this way, didn't it? I couldn't have given her the home she deserved.'

'You seem remarkably calm about it all,' said Rachel, releasing her from the hug.

'Do I? I'm not really. I'm definitely shocked, the shock of grief, I think. I feel numb. I mean, how much loss can one person take? I guess I'll have a major fall in the coming days – but for now at least, I think I need to keep going.'

'Where *are* you going? Where will you stay?'

'Oh, back to Dad's for a short while, I think. He says I can. And then I need to figure out what next. I have a lot of figuring out to do.'

'If there's anything I can do to help, just let me know. I really do want to help.'

Amelia thought for a moment. 'I could really do with your help moving what's left of my stuff – whatever Piers didn't manage to burn – to Dad's, actually. But only if you have time?'

'Sure. You know what, I'll text Jake,' she said, pulling out her phone. 'He can leave his assistant managing the shop for a bit and go and get your things. Piers won't dare mess with him. And he's got a work van, so he can fit everything in, including your paintings. Give me your dad's address. Consider it done.'

'Thank you *so* much,' said Amelia, relief flooding through her, knowing that she wouldn't have to see Piers again today. Or, hopefully, ever.

'Don't be silly. It's only a small thing.'

'You're amazing, Rach. A wonderful friend.'

'You daft thing,' said Rachel, patting Amelia's arm. 'I'm only doing it so I can blackmail you into giving me some of your art for my walls.'

Amelia smiled, despite her sorrow and her shock.

'So do you want to stay here this afternoon, while Jake moves your things? Maybe have a nap, if you can? I can change our bed sheets for you…'

'No,' said Amelia, knowing instinctively where she needed to go next; knowing instinctively who else she needed to hold close. 'There's someone else I need to see,' she said, mentally picturing the route to Mark's door.

Epilogue

April

Michelle

As Michelle pushed the buggy through the churchyard, she looked around at the carpet of daffodils beneath the trees and in between the gravestones. She'd got so used to walking through here in winter; it was so lovely to see some colour in here, after all that darkness and cold, she thought.

She exited the church grounds at the Church Street gate, crossed over the road and squeezed through the door of Gemma's, a recently-opened independent coffee shop. She spotted two comfy armchairs free in the corner and made her way over there, parking Grace's buggy facing the wall. Satisfied that her sleeping daughter was both comfortable and secure, she took her coat off, sat down in one of the chairs and waited.

Minutes later, the door opened and in walked a tall, slim woman with bright red hair cut into a sleek bob, wearing skinny jeans and a bright green woollen wrap coat. Amelia had texted her description so that she knew who to look out for, but she certainly hadn't told her how striking she was. She looked… awesome, Michelle thought. And she felt like she'd seen her before, but she just couldn't place her. She raised a hand to wave, and Amelia smiled, and returned it. She walked over to the chair and held out her hand.

'Hello,' she said. 'I'm Amelia. And you must be… Michelle,' she said, her voice quivering. 'I'm sorry,' she said, putting both hands on the back of one of the chairs, as if she was steadying herself. 'I think I need to sit down. I can't quite believe this is happening.'

'Ha, I know,' said Michelle. 'Come on, sit down. I think they'll come over to take our order. That's what happened when I was last here, anyway.'

'Good,' replied Amelia. 'I'm sorry, for being such a flake. I…'

'No worries, honestly,' said Michelle. 'I think this is strange, for you *and* me.'

'Yes.'

Amelia looked longingly then at the parked buggy.

'Oh go on, have a look,' said Michelle, realising what Amelia wanted. 'She's sleeping at the moment, but we can get her out later, when she wakes up.'

Amelia stood up immediately and peered into the buggy, staring silently at Grace. Michelle watched the other woman looking at her daughter with love and affection, and instead of the jealousy she thought she might feel, she felt nothing but thankfulness.

'You were amazing with her, they said,' Michelle said. 'And I'm so grateful.' Amelia looked at her, and Michelle could see that there were tears in her eyes. 'Oh I'm sorry, I didn't mean to make you cry,' she said, trying to make light of it. 'Come on, let's order something to drink, and then we can catch up and make it less weird. What do you want? They do a nice hot chocolate. And cake.'

Gillian had brought them here to celebrate Grace's return in late February, and Michelle could still taste the rich carrot cake she'd eaten that day. It had been their first trip out together in the real world and it had certainly been a day to savour.

Amelia sat back down and scanned the drinks menu and Michelle motioned for the waitress to come over. After they'd both chosen their drinks and the waitress had left to prepare them, Michelle retrieved the card she'd brought with her out of her bag.

'This is for you,' she said, holding it out. 'From Grace and me.'

She watched Amelia open it and take in the words which she had written, slowly and painstakingly, that morning. Her lessons with her tutor were helping, but she still took forever to write things.

'Thank you so much,' said Amelia, her eyes still threatening tears. 'You didn't have to do this...'

'Yeah, I did,' said Michelle. 'I mean, the social workers told me I didn't have to, but it made sense to me, for you to keep in touch with Grace. After all, you were there for her in the first few months, when I wasn't, and when she came back to me, I just kept thinking about you, and how sad you must be feeling. So...'

'Well, I'm very grateful,' Amelia said. 'I never thought I'd see her again.'

'I remember how that feels,' said Michelle, her mind taking her to dark places she didn't want to revisit. 'And I wouldn't wish that feeling on anyone.'

The two women exchanged a look of mutual understanding.

'So how about your husband? Didn't he want to see her too?' Michelle asked.

'Oh – didn't social services say? We've split up,' said Amelia.

Michelle was startled; this was news she hadn't been expecting. Social services had always given the impression that the family Grace had been placed with were really solid, really safe.

'I'm really sorry. Was it because of Grace coming back to me...?'

'No. It was about a lot more than that,' replied Amelia, who, Michelle noticed, was wringing her hands underneath the table.

'We had big problems. More than I really realised. The foster to adopt nightmare just made them more obvious, that's all. In the end, you know… I realised our whole marriage was just this huge lie.'

'Oh my God,' said Michelle. 'You have had the shittest time… I'm sorry.'

Amelia looked straight at her and her hands were still.

'You have nothing to be sorry for,' she replied. 'You're the one whose baby was taken away. I can't even begin to imagine what you've been through. I'm surprised you don't hate me, for having her for all that time.'

'Don't be stupid.' Michelle had no idea what else to say. She'd never really thought much about the couple who had been looking after Grace. It had been too painful. But now, faced with this real woman, this emotional, raw, human woman, she felt unexpectedly tender towards her. 'Did he hit you?'

'No,' replied Amelia, her eyes wide. 'Not… that, not… really. But other stuff… he… controlled me. Or at least tried to. And drugs…'

'Yeah, I know all about that crap,' replied Michelle. 'Been there, done that, got the sorry t-shirt.'

The two women sat in silence for a second or two.

You can never tell, can you, thought Michelle. *People can look really rich, really sorted, but you can never tell what's going on underneath, ever. It doesn't matter how much money you have; money isn't a magic shield against pain.*

'How about you and… Grace's dad?' asked Amelia after the pause.

'Oh, yeah, we went the same way, in the end. He showed his true colours, didn't he, and I'm better off out of it. He was a prick. End of. He didn't even turn up for most of the contact sessions.'

'Fair enough,' replied Amelia, smiling at the waitress who'd brought over their drinks. 'Where are you living now, then?'

'I'm staying with this couple, Gill and Mike,' Michelle replied, sipping her hot chocolate. 'They used to foster a lot, and they're sort of fostering both of us at the moment, until I get back on my feet. And I'm getting there now, definitely. I'm enrolling in a care worker course at college in Worcester which starts in September, and I'm going to try to re-take some of my GCSEs. Gill and Mike say we can stay with them long term, but I'm thinking of asking social services to help me find a flat there. It'll be nice to live somewhere other than Malvern, finally, and to have somewhere of my own. And I can put Grace in the college nursery while I study.'

'Sounds fantastic,' replied Amelia, cradling her mug.

'How about you? How are you –' Michelle looked down at her lap as she tried to formulate the words '– doing, without Grace, I mean? Will you try to adopt another baby?'

Amelia put her mug down.

'I don't know. I had a baby once, a stillborn baby…' *Oh Jesus, this poor woman*, thought Michelle. 'It was a lot to get over. I don't think I *am* over it, to be honest. And I'm getting on a bit, both to try to get pregnant again, or to adopt, so… Who knows? Maybe, in the future. But not now. I need to focus on me for a bit, I think.'

'Are you thinking about getting out of Malvern, too?'

'Ah, no,' replied Amelia, blowing on the froth on the top of her coffee. 'Maybe, for a few holidays, you know, there's lots of the world I want to visit, but oddly enough, since leaving Piers, I've realised how much I love this place. It's my home, and I won't let him ruin it for me. He's buggered off anyway, now he's lost his job.'

'Oh, has he? Is that weird, being on your own?'

'I feel bad about saying this, but no. I keep busy. I run a lot on the hills, and I'm an artist, and there's so much here to be inspired by. And I have great friends. So no, I think I'm staying. And also…'

'You're an artist? That's cool,' said Michelle. 'Do you sell your stuff?'

'I'm starting to, a bit,' Amelia replied, taking a sip of her drink. 'My friend's husband has a music shop here and he's started hanging my work on the walls, and people sometimes like it and buy it. Which is nice. But mostly I'm teaching art now at the adult education college. It's great fun teaching adults how to draw, and how to make collages and how to paint. I love it.'

'Have you got your own place now, then? Now that you're single?'

'Well, yes and no,' she replied. 'I'm still staying with my elderly father in his flat, but we rub each other up the wrong way, frankly, and he's about to sell it and move into sheltered housing anyway. But I think I'll soon be...'

Amelia's explanation was interrupted by Grace's cries.

'Ah, so her nap is over,' said Michelle, leaning into the buggy and unclipping Grace. 'Gracey, guess who I have here,' she said, picking her up. 'It's *Amelia*. You might recognise her, I think,' she said, holding her up so she could look around, 'she's the very nice lady who looked after you when you were tiny.'

'May I?' said Amelia, holding out her arms and smiling through her tears.

'Of course,' said Michelle. 'Be my guest.' She watched as Amelia took her daughter in her arms and tenderly stroked each limb, before planting a kiss on her forehead. Grace looked very relaxed with her, she thought. Which was amazing, because she was usually very nervous of strangers. But of course she wasn't a stranger, was she?

'I'm happy to meet up whenever you like,' said Michelle. 'Even when I move to Worcester, it's only just down the road.'

'I'd like that very much,' said Amelia, who appeared to be mesmerised by Grace's smile. 'Very much.'

***

It was dark outside by the time Amelia and Michelle had finished talking. It had been really easy to pass the time, Michelle thought, which was amazing, given how much older Amelia was and how posh she sounded. But she had seemed nice, really nice, and she was so pleased she'd decided to do this. She felt so much better for it.

'I had better go,' said Amelia. 'But it has been wonderful. Amazing. Brilliant. All of those sorts of words!' she smiled. 'I can't thank you enough.'

'Oh, don't be daft,' Michelle replied. 'I'm just grateful you've offered to babysit.'

Amelia grinned and reached round for her coat. 'Are you walking back?' she asked, looking at the darkness outside.

'Oh, no,' replied Michelle. 'Mike said he'd come and get me at five. I'll just walk up to the pharmacy and buy some more nappy cream and he'll be here to get me.'

'That's great,' said Amelia, as Michelle stood up, put her own coat on and unlocked the buggy's brakes.

'Lead the way,' said Michelle, following Amelia through the assault course of tables and chairs to the cafe door. Out on the street, Michelle gave Amelia a brief hug, waved goodbye to her, and began to walk up the hill. When she had walked a few steps, she turned around, realising that she hadn't asked her new friend how she was going to get home.

She was just in time to see Amelia leaning in to kiss a tall, thin man who'd just emerged from the Priory gates. He was carrying a leather bag in his hand and his blond hair was dishevelled. Michelle thought she recognised him from her food bank sessions.

And then she suddenly remembered where she'd seen Amelia before. She had been the woman she'd seen in the Priory, she thought. The angry woman, being soothed by… this man. Yes!

It was the same man. He definitely wasn't Amelia's ex-husband then, she thought. Which was, from what she had told her, a very good thing.

As soon as she'd watched Amelia take that man's hand and walk out of sight down the hill, Michelle began her ascent of Church Street once more. She smiled down at Grace in the buggy.

'Come on then, little love,' she said, admiring the Worcestershire Beacon above them, which was just visible in the dim evening light. 'Let's go.'

Author's Note

This novel was inspired by two wonderful women.

Firstly, my friend Lisa, who fell in love with a baby who had been placed with her using the foster to adopt scheme, only for him to be removed and placed back in the care of his family. It was her experience and her grief that inspired the character of Amelia.

As I watched Lisa's situation play out and offered what support I could, I was struck by the vulnerability of all parties involved in the case, their fates entirely in the hands of the courts. I could see that both the prospective adopters and the baby's birth family were going through hell, and it was this agonising reality that inspired my story.

Secondly, I was inspired by the excellent journalist Louise Tickle (www.louisetickle.co.uk) whose work fighting for access to report on the family courts has shone a vital light on the way they operate and raised important questions about the way vulnerable parents are treated by the system. Her advice, contacts and expertise helped me greatly as I planned *Grace*.

Finally, a note about the book's setting. I grew up in Malvern. It is very much a real place (and well worth a visit) and Malvern Priory is a real church. However, the characters I've created within them are fictional, and Langland College and the Elgar Estate are both figments of my imagination.

Book Club Questions

- The way that Michelle was treated as a child has significant implications for the way she behaves as an adult. Can you say the same about Amelia?
- Although Amelia did not give birth to Grace, she takes on a maternal role. What, in your opinion, makes a mother?
- Amelia and Piers appear to be a 'perfect couple' when you first meet them. When did you start to feel that something wasn't quite right?
- Why do you think Rob decided to return to his parents after Michelle's overdose?
- Currently, prospective adopters have no role to play in court cases like the one portrayed in *Grace*. Do you think this is fair?
- Amelia and Michelle come from completely different backgrounds, and yet it could be argued that they have very similar personalities. Do you agree?
- How do you feel about the decision Michelle's grandmother made to put her grandchildren back into care and not tell them about her illness?
- Who did you want Grace to stay with, and why? Did that change as you read the book?

Acknowledgements

I did a lot of reading before I wrote this book, but it was the people I interviewed as part of my research who really helped me put the flesh on the bones of my story. These include a senior family court judge (who asked to remain anonymous), adoptive parent Lisa, social care practitioner Sarah Hosford and the journalist Louise Tickle, who reports on the family courts. It was so important to me that I portrayed things as accurately as I could, with the usual caveats, of course, that this is a work of pure fiction. Any errors or omissions are my own.

Thanks, too, to my editors at Head of Zeus – Thorne Ryan and Hannah Smith – whose input always made everything better.

Next, thanks to my awesome agent Hannah Weatherill at Northbank Talent for her industry knowledge, guidance and friendship, and also to my trusted group of early readers – Teil Scott, Theresa Ricketts, Catherine Ramsden and Vicki Shenkin-Kerr, who all give really useful, honest feedback, which is so important.

Finally, I'd like to give as many hugs as I am able to my husband Teil and children Raphie and Ella, who continue to fill my heart with joy and provide me with a wonderful reason to keep on dreaming (and writing) every day.

About the Author

VICTORIA SCOTT has been a journalist for two decades, working for outlets including the BBC, Al Jazeera, *Time Out* and the *Telegraph*. She lives on a Thames island with her husband, two children and a cat called Alice, and when she's not writing she works as a university lecturer and copywriter. She has a degree in English from King's College London and a Postgraduate Diploma in Broadcast Journalism from City University, London. Victoria's debut novel, *Patience*, was a Booksellers' Association Book of the Month.